Lynne Graham was born in Northern Ireland and has been a keen romance reader since her teens. She is very happily married, to an understanding husband who has learned to cook since she started to write! Her five children keep her on her toes. She has a very large dog, who knocks everything over, a very small terrier, who barks a lot, and two cats. When time allows, Lynne is a keen gardener.

Louise Fuller was once a tomboy who hated pink and always wanted to be the Prince—not the Princess! Now she enjoys creating heroines who aren't pretty push-overs but strong, believable women. Before writing for Mills & Boon she studied literature and philosophy at university, and then worked as a reporter on her local newspaper. She lives in Tunbridge Wells with her impossibly handsome husband Patrick and their six children.

INDIAN PRINCE'S HIDDEN SON

LYNNE GRAHAM

CRAVING HIS FORBIDDEN INNOCENT

LOUISE FULLER

MILLS & BOON

First Published in Great Britain 2020
by Mills & Boon, an imprint of HarperCollins*Publishers*
1 London Bridge Street, London, SE1 9GF

Indian Prince's Hidden Son © 2020 by Lynne Graham

Craving His Forbidden Innocent © 2020 by Louise Fuller

ISBN: 978-0-263-27801-9

MIX
Paper from
responsible sources
FSC® C007454

Printed and bound in Spain
by CPI, Barcelona

INDIAN PRINCE'S
HIDDEN SON

LYNNE GRAHAM

CHAPTER ONE

IT WAS A dull winter day with laden grey clouds overhead. Fine for a funeral as long as the rain held off, Jai conceded grimly.

In his opinion, English rain differed from Indian rain. The monsoon season in Chandrapur brought relief from the often unbearable heat of summer, washing away the dust and the grime and regenerating the soil so that flowers sprang up everywhere. It was a cool, uplifting time of renewal and rebirth.

His bodyguards fanned out to check the immediate area before he was signalled forward to board his limousine. That further loss of time, slight though it was, irritated him because, much as he knew he needed to take security precautions, he was also uneasily aware that he would be a late arrival at the funeral. Unfortunately, it was only that morning that he had flown in from New York to find the message from Brian Allerton's daughter awaiting him, none of his staff having appreciated that that message should have been treated as urgent.

Brian Allerton had been a Classics teacher and

house master at the exclusive English boarding school that Jai had attended as a boy. For over two hundred years, Jai's Rajput ancestors had been sending their children to England to be educated, but Jai had been horribly homesick from the moment he'd arrived in London. Brian Allerton had been kind and supportive, encouraging the young prince to play sport and focus on his studies. A friendship had been born that had crossed both age barriers and distance and had lasted even after Jai went to university and moved on to become an international businessman.

Brian's witty letters had entertained Jai's father, Rehan as well. A shadow crossed Jai's lean, darkly handsome face, his ice-blue eyes, so extraordinarily noticeable against his olive skin, darkening. Because his own father had died the year before and Jai's life had changed radically as a result, with any hope of escaping the sheer weight of his royal heritage gone.

On his father's death he had become the Maharaja of Chandrapur, and being a hugely successful technology billionaire had had to take a back seat while he took control of one of the biggest charitable foundations in the world to continue his father's sterling work in the same field. Jai often thought that time needed to stretch for his benefit because, even working night and day, he struggled to keep up with all his responsibilities. Suppressing that futile thought, he checked his watch and gritted his teeth because the traffic was heavy and moving slowly.

Brian's only child, Willow, would be hit very hard by the older man's passing, Jai reflected ruefully, for, like Jai, Willow had grown up in a single-parent family, her mother having died when she was young. Jai's mother, however, had walked out on Jai's father when Jai was a baby, angrily, bitterly convinced that her cross-cultural marriage and mixed-race son were adversely affecting her social standing. Jai had only seen her once after that and only for long enough to register that he was pretty much an embarrassing little secret in his mother's life, and not one she wanted to acknowledge in public after remarrying and having another family.

It was ironic that Jai had come perilously close to repeating his father's mistake. At twenty-one he had become engaged to an English socialite. He had been hopelessly in love with Cecilia and had lived to regret his susceptibility when she'd ditched him almost at the altar. In the eight years since then, Jai had toughened up. He was no longer naive or romantic. He didn't do love any more. He didn't do serious relationships. There were countless beautiful women willing to share his bed without any promise of a tomorrow and no woman ever left his bed unsatisfied. Casual, free and essentially *forgettable*, he had learned, met his needs best.

As the limousine drew up outside the cemetery, Jai idly wondered what Willow looked like now. Sadly, it was three years since he had last seen her father, who had turned into a recluse after his terminal illness was diagnosed. She had been away from home studying on his last visit, he recalled with an effort. He had not regretted her absence because as a teenager she had had a huge crush on him and the amount of attention she had given him had made him uncomfortable back then. She had been a tiny little thing though, with that hair of a shade that was neither blond nor red, and the languid green eyes of a cat, startling against her pale skin.

Willow stood at the graveside beside her friend, Shelley, listening to the vicar's booming voice as he addressed the tiny group of mourners at her father's graveside. Brian Allerton had had no relatives and, by the time of his passing, even fewer friends because as his illness had progressed he had refused all social invitations. Only a couple of old drinking mates, one of whom was a neighbour, had continued to call in to ply him with his favourite whiskey and talk endlessly about football.

A slight stir on the road beyond the low cemetery wall momentarily captured Willow's attention and her breath locked in her throat when she realised that a limousine had drawn up. Several men talking into headsets entered the graveyard first, bodyguards spreading out in a classic formation to scan their surroundings before Jai's tall, powerful figure, sheathed in a dark suit, appeared. Her heart clenched hard because she hadn't been expecting him, having assumed that the message she had left at his London home would arrive too late to be of any use.

'Who on earth is *that*?' Shelley stage-whispered in her ear, earning a glance of reproof from the vicar.

But no, contrary to Willow's expectations, Jai, technology billionaire and media darling, had contrived to attend and, even though he had missed the church service, she was impressed, hopelessly impressed, that he had actually made the effort. After all, her father had, during his illness, stopped responding to Jai's letters and had turned down his invitations, proudly spurning every approach.

'Wow…he's absolutely spectacular.' Shelley sighed, impervious to hints.

'Talk about him later,' Willow muttered out of the corner of her mouth, keen to silence her friend. Shelley was wonderfully kind and generous but she wasn't discreet and she always said exactly what she was thinking.

'He's really hot,' Shelley gushed in her ear. 'And he's so tall and *built*, isn't he?'

Jai had been hugely popular at school when Willow was growing up in the little courtyard house that had gone with her father's live-in employment. The last in a long distinguished line of Rajput rulers and warriors, Prince Jai Singh had been an outstanding sportsman and an equally brilliant scholar and Willow had often suspected that Jai had been the son her father would've loved to have had in place of the daughter who had, sadly, failed to live up to his exacting academic standards.

And even though it had been three years since Willow had seen Jai she still only allowed herself a fleeting glance in his direction and swiftly suppressed the shiver of awareness that gripped her with mortifying immediacy. After all, a single glance was all it took to confirm that nothing essential had changed. Jai, the son of an Indian Maharaja and an English duke's daughter, was drop-dead gorgeous from the crown of his luxuriant blue-black hair to the toes of his very probably hand-stitched shoes. Even at a distance she had caught the glimmer of his extraordinarily light eyes against his golden skin. His eyes were the palest wolf-blue in that lean, darkly handsome face of his, a perfect complement to his superb bone structure, classic nose and perfectly sculpted mouth.

Jai, her first crush, her only infatuation, she conceded in exasperation, her flawless skin heating with the never-to-be-forgotten intense embarrassment of her teenaged years as the mourners came, one by one, to greet her and she invited them back to the house for an alcoholic drink as specified by her late parent, who had ruled against her providing traditional tea and sandwiches for the occasion. Even so, she would have to make exceptions for the vicar and for Jai.

As Jai strode towards the small group, his keen gaze widened infinitesimally, and his steps faltered as soon as he recognised Willow, a tiny fragile figure dressed in black, with an eye-catching waterfall of strawberry-blond waves tumbling round her shoulders that highlighted bright green eyes and a lush pink mouth set in a heart-shaped face. The shy, skinny and awkward teenager, he registered in surprise, had turned into a ravishing beauty. His teeth clenched as he moved forward, inwardly censuring that last observation as inappropriate in the circumstances.

A lean hand closed over hers. 'I apologise for my

late arrival. My deepest condolences for your loss,' Jai murmured softly.

'Hi… I'm Shelley,' her friend interrupted with a huge smile.

'Jai…this is my friend, Shelley,' Willow introduced hastily.

Jai grasped Shelley's hand and murmured something polite.

'Come back to the house with us,' Willow urged him stiffly. 'My father would've liked that.'

'I don't wish to intrude,' Jai told her.

'Dad wouldn't see anyone while he was ill… It wasn't personal,' Willow told him chokily. 'He was a very private man.'

'Your dad was right eccentric,' Shelley chimed in.

'His desire for privacy must've made his illness harder for you to deal with,' Jai remarked shrewdly. 'No support. I know you have no family.'

'But Willow does have friends,' Shelley cut in warmly. 'Like me.'

'And I am sure she is very grateful for your support at such a difficult time,' Jai responded smoothly.

That reminder of her isolation hit Willow hard. Losing her father, who had been her only parent since her mother had died when she was six, was already proving even tougher than she had envisaged. Worse still, the reality that they were stony broke, for those last months had broken her father's heart and hastened his end. Evidently fantasising about leaving his daughter much better off than they had been, her father had, as his life had drawn to a close, begun using his pension

fund to play with stocks and shares without seeming
to grasp the risk that he was taking.

Convinced that he was onto a winning strategy,
Brian Allerton had been devastated when he'd lost all
his savings. He had spent his last months grieving for
the mistake he had made and the truth that he was
leaving his daughter virtually penniless. They were
fortunate indeed that her father had arranged and settled the expenses of his own funeral as soon as he had
appreciated that his condition was incurable. But only
their landlord's forbearance had kept a roof over their
heads as they had inevitably fallen behind with the
rent, and that was a debt that Willow was determined
to somehow settle.

'I'll get by,' she parried with a stiff little smile. 'Dad
and I were always alone.'

'Let me give you a lift,' Jai urged smoothly.

'No, thank you. Our neighbour, Charlie, is waiting
outside for us,' she responded with a rueful smile that
threatened to turn into a grimace.

Shelley, proclaiming that *she* would've enjoyed the
opportunity to travel in a limousine, hurried after Willow in dismay as she turned on her heel to head out
to the ancient car awaiting them beyond the cemetery
wall. Willow, not having noticed her friend's disappointment, was all of a silly flutter, and furious with
herself, butterflies darting and dancing in her tummy
and leaving her breathless as a schoolgirl simply because she had been talking to Jai. Any normal woman
would have grown out of such immature behaviour by
now, she told herself in mortification. Unfortunately,

through living with and caring for her father and lack of opportunity, Willow hadn't yet managed to gain much real-world experience of the opposite sex.

Aside of a couple of summer residential stays, she had always lived at home, having studied garden design both online and through classes at the nearest college. Add in the work experience she had had to complete with a local landscape firm, the need to earn some money simply to eat while they had steadily fallen behind with the rent, the demands of her father's illness and his many medical appointments, and there hadn't been enough hours in the day for Willow to enjoy a social life with her friends as well. Gradually most of her friends had dropped away, but Shelley had been in her life since primary school and had continued to visit, oblivious to Brian Allerton's cool, snobbish attitude to her.

Willow arrived back at the tiny terraced house and she put on the kettle while Shelley set out the drinks and a solitary tray of shortbread. Just as Jai arrived, the vicar anxiously asked Willow where she was planning to move to.

'My sofa!' Shelley revealed with a chuckle. 'I wouldn't leave her stuck.'

'Yes, I'll be fine with Shelley until I can organise something more permanent. I have to move out of here tomorrow. The landlord has been wonderfully understanding but it would be selfish of me to stay here one day longer than necessary,' Willow explained, thinking that, tough though the last weeks had been, she *had* met with kindness in unexpected places.

* * *

A *sofa*? Willow was homeless? Expected to pack up and move in with a friend the same week that she had buried her father? Jai was appalled at that news. Honour demanded that he intervene but Willow had been raised to be proud and independent like her father and Jai would have to be sensitive in his approach. He was convinced that out of principle Willow would refuse his financial assistance.

'Coffee, Jai?' Willow prompted as she handed the vicar a cup of tea.

'Thank you,' he murmured, following her into the small kitchen to say, 'Was your father at home at the end, or had he been moved to a hospice?'

'It was to happen next week,' Willow conceded tightly, throwing his tall dark figure a rueful appraisal, her heart giving a sudden thud as she collided involuntarily with ice-blue eyes enhanced by wondrously dense black lashes. 'But he didn't make it. His heart gave out.'

In an abrupt movement, she stepped back from him, disturbingly conscious of his height and the proximity of more masculinity than she felt able to bear. The very faint scent of some designer cologne drifted into her nostrils and she sucked in a sudden steadying breath, her level of awareness heightening exponentially to add to her discomfiture. She could feel her face heating, her knees wobbling as her tension rose even higher.

'What are you planning to do next?' Jai enquired, shifting his attention hurriedly from her lush pink lips and the X-rated images bombarding him while he questioned his behaviour.

Yes, she was indisputably beautiful, but he was neither a hormonal schoolboy, nor a sex-starved one, and he was challenged to explain his lack of self-discipline in her radius. She did, however, possess a quality that was exclusively her own, he acknowledged grudgingly, a slow-burning sensual appeal that tugged hard at his senses. It was there in the flicker of her languorous emerald eyes, the slight curve of her generous lower lip, the upward angle of challenge in her chin as she tilted her head back, strawberry-blond hair falling in waves tumbling across her slim shoulders like a swathe of rumpled silk.

'I'll be fine as soon as I find full-time work. These last weeks, I was only able to work part-time hours. Once I've saved up some money, I'll move on and leave Shelley in peace.' She opened the fridge to extract milk and Jai noticed its empty interior.

'You have no food,' he remarked grimly.

'I genuinely haven't had much of an appetite recently,' she confided truthfully. 'And Dad ate next to nothing, so I haven't been cooking.'

She had removed her coat and the simple grey dress she wore hung loose on her slender body. Her cheekbones were sharp, her eyes hollow and his misgivings increased because she looked haunted and frail. Of course, common sense warned him that nursing her father would have sapped her energy and left her at a low ebb. Certainly, she was vulnerable, but she was a young and healthy woman and she would probably be fine. But *probably* wasn't quite good enough to satisfy Jai. He would make his own checks and in the short term he would do what he could to make her future less insecure.

Willow watched Jai leave, a sinking tightening sensation inside her chest as it occurred to her that she would probably never see him again now that her father was gone. Why would she want to see him again anyway? she asked herself irritably. They were only casual acquaintances and calling him a friend would have been pushing that slight bond to the limits.

Shelley departed only under protest.

'Are you sure you're going to be OK alone here tonight?' the brunette pressed, unconvinced. 'I don't feel right leaving you on your own.'

'I'm going to have a bath and go to bed early. I'm exhausted,' Willow told her ruefully. 'But thanks for caring.'

The two women hugged on the doorstep and Shelley went on her way. Willow cleared away the glasses and left the kitchen immaculate before heading upstairs for her bath. First thing in the morning a local dealer was coming to clear the house contents and sell them. There wasn't much left because almost everything that could be sold had been sold off weeks earlier. Even so, her father's beloved books might be worth something, she thought hopefully, her teeth worrying at her lower lip as she anxiously recalled the rent still owing. It would be a weight off her mind if she could clear that debt because their landlord belonged to her church and she suspected that he had felt that he'd had no choice but to allow them to remain as tenants even though the rent was in arrears. The sooner he was reimbursed for his kindness, the happier she would be.

The bell shrilled while she was putting on her pyjamas and she groaned, snatching her robe off the back of the bathroom door to hurry barefoot down the steep stairs and answer the door.

When she saw Jai outside, she froze in disconcertion.

'I brought dinner,' Jai informed her as she hovered, her grip on the robe she was holding closed loosening to reveal the shorts and T-shirt she wore beneath and her long, shapely legs. He drew in a stark little breath as she stepped back and the robe shifted again to expose the tilted peaks of her small breasts. In a split second he was hard as a rock, his body impervious to his belief that he preferred curvier women.

'D-dinner?' she stammered in wonderment as Jai stepped back and two men with a trolley moved out from behind him and, with some difficulty, trundled the unwieldy item through the tiny hall into the cramped living room with its small table and two chairs.

Those wolf-blue eyes of his held her fast, all breathing in suspension.

'My hotel was able to provide us with an evening meal,' he clarified smoothly.

No takeaways for Jai, Willow registered without surprise while she wondered what on earth such an extravagant gesture could have cost him. Of course, he didn't have to count costs, did he? It probably hadn't even occurred to him that requesting a meal for two people that could be transported out of the hotel and served by hotel staff was an extraordinary request. Jai was simply accustomed to asking and always receiving, regardless of expense.

'I'm not dressed,' she said awkwardly, tightening the tie on her robe in an apologetic gesture.

'It doesn't bother me. We should eat now while it's still warm,' Jai responded as the plates were brought to the table, and she settled down opposite him, stiff with unease.

A bottle of wine was uncorked, glasses produced and set by their places.

'I thought you didn't drink,' she commented in surprise as the waiters went back outside again, presumably to wait for them to finish.

'I take wine with my meals,' he explained. 'It's rare for me to drink at any other time.'

His eyes had a ring of stormy grey around the pupils, she noted absently, her throat tightening as her gaze dropped to the fullness of his sensual lower lip and she found herself wondering for the first time ever what Jai would be like in bed. She had been too shy and immature for such thoughts when she was an infatuated teenager and, now that she was an adult, her mental audacity brought a flood of mortified colour to her pale cheeks. Would he be gentle or rough? Fiery or smoothly precise? Her thoughts refused to quit.

'Why did you feel that you had to feed me?' she

asked abruptly in an effort to deflect his attention from her hot cheeks.

'You had no food in the kitchen. You've just lost your father,' Jai parried calmly as he began to eat. 'I didn't like to think of you alone here.'

He had felt sorry for her. She busied herself eating the delicious food, striving not to squirm with mortification that she had impressed him as an object of pity. After all, Jai had been raised by his benevolent father to constantly consider those less fortunate and now ran a huge international charity devoted to good causes. Whether she appreciated the reality or not, looking out for the needs of the vulnerable had to come as naturally to Jai as breathing.

'Why are you moving out of here tomorrow?' he pressed quietly.

Willow snatched in a long steadying breath and then surrendered to the inevitable, reasoning that her father could no longer be humiliated by the truth. She explained about Brian Allerton's unsuccessful stock-market dealing and the impoverishment that had followed. 'I mean no disrespect,' she completed ruefully, 'but my father was irresponsible with money. He never saved anything—he only had his pension. All his working life he lived in accommodation provided by his employers and most of his meals and bills were also covered and it didn't prepare him very well for retirement living in the normal world.'

'That didn't occur to me, but it should've done,' Jai conceded. 'He was an unworldly man.'

'He was so ashamed of his financial losses,' she

whispered unhappily. 'It made him feel like a failure and that's one of the reasons he wouldn't see people any more.'

'I wish he had found it possible to reach out to me for assistance,' Jai framed heavily, his lean, strong face clenched hard. 'So, you are being forced to sell everything? I will buy his book collection.'

Willow stared across the table at him in shock. *'Seriously?'*

'He was a lifelong book collector, as am I,' Jai pointed out. 'I would purchase his books because I want them and for no other reason. We will agree that tonight and hopefully that will take care of your rent arrears.'

Willow nodded slowly and then frowned. 'Are you sure you want them?'

'I have a library in every one of my homes. Of course, I want them.'

Willow swallowed hard. 'How many homes do you have?' she whispered helplessly.

'More than I want in Chandrapur but it is my duty, as it was my father's, to preserve our heritage properties for future generations,' he countered levelly. 'Now let us move on to other, more important matters. Your father was too proud to ask for my help. I hope you are a little more sensible.'

Reckoning that he was about to embarrass her by offering her further financial help, Willow pushed back her plate and stood up to forestall him. 'I'm going upstairs to get dressed first,' she said tightly.

Jai sipped his wine and signalled the staff to remove the dishes and the trolley. He pictured Willow sliding out of the robe, letting it fall sinuously to her feet before she took off the top and removed the shorts. His imagination went wild while he did so, his body surging with fierce hunger, and he gritted his teeth angrily, struggling to get his thoughts back in his control.

Upstairs, Willow stood immobile, reckoning that Jai taking her father's books could well settle the rent arrears. Did he really want those books? Or was that just a ploy to give her money? And when someone was as poor as she was, could she really afford to worry about what might lie behind his generosity?

Her attention fell on a sapphire ring that lay on the tray on the dressing table. It was her grandmother's engagement ring and it would have to be sold too, even though it was unlikely to be worth very much. Her father had refused to let her sell it while he was still alive, but it had to go now, along with everything else. She could not live with Shelley without paying her way. She would not take advantage of her friend's kindness like that.

She spread a glance round the room, her eyes lingering on the precious childhood items that would also have to be disposed of, things like her worn teddy bear and the silver frame housing a photo of the mother she barely remembered. She couldn't lug boxes of stuff with her to clutter up Shelley's small studio apartment. Be practical, Willow, she scolded herself even as a sob of pain convulsed her throat.

She felt as though her whole life had tumbled into

broken pieces at her feet. Her father was gone. Every-thing familiar was fading. And at the heart of her grief lay the inescapable truth that she had *always* been a serious disappointment to the father she loved. No mat-ter how hard she had tried, no matter how many tutors her father had engaged to coach her, she had continu-ally failed to reach the academic heights he'd craved for his only child. She wasn't stupid, she was merely average, and to a man as clever as her father had been, a man with a string of Oxford degrees in excellence, that had been a cruel punishment…

Downstairs, enjoying a second glass of wine, Jai heard her choked sob. He squared his shoulders and breathed in deep, deeming it only natural that at some point on such a day Willow's control would weaken and she would break down. There had been no visible tears at the funeral, no emotional conversations afterwards that he had heard. Throughout, Willow had been polite and pleasant and more considerate of other people's feelings than her own. She had attempted to bring an upbeat note to a depressing situation, had behaved as though she had already completely accepted the changes that her father's death would inflict on her.

When the sounds of her distress became more than he could withstand, Jai abandoned his careful scrutiny of her father's books—several first editions, he noted with satisfaction, worthy of the fine price he would pay for them. He drained his glass and forced himself to mount the stairs to offer what comfort he could. All too well did he remember that he himself had had little support after his father's sudden death from a massive stroke. Thousands had been devastated by the passing of so well-loved a figure and hundreds of concerned relatives had converged on Jai to share his sorrow, but Jai hadn't been close enough to any of those individuals to find solace in their memories. In reality only *he* had known his father on a very personal, private level and only *he* could know the extent of the loss he had sustained.

Willow was lying sobbing on the bed and Jai didn't hesitate. He sat down beside her and lifted her into his arms, reckoning that she weighed barely more than a child and instinctively treating her as such as he patted her slender spine soothingly and struggled to think of what it was best to say. 'Remember the good times with your father,' he urged softly.

'There really *weren't* any…' Willow muttered chokily into his shoulder, startled to find herself in his arms but revelling in that sudden comforting closeness of another human being and no longer feeling alone and adrift. 'I was always a serious disappointment to him.'

With a frown of disbelief, Jai held her back from him to look down into her tear-stained face. The tip of her nose was red, which was surprisingly cute. Her wide green eyes were still welling with tears and oddly defiant, as if daring him to disagree. 'How could that possibly be true?' he challenged.

'I didn't do well enough at school, didn't get into the *right* schools either,' Willow confided shakily, looking into his lean, strong face and those commanding ice-blue eyes that had once haunted her dreams. 'Once I heard him lying to make excuses for me. He told one of his colleagues that I'd been ill when I sat my exams and it *was* a lie... Dad wanted a child he could brag about, an intellectual child, who passed every exam with flying colours. I had tutors in every subject and I *still* couldn't do well enough to please him!'

Jai was sharply disconcerted by that emotional admission, which revealed a far less agreeable side to a man he had both liked and respected. 'I'm sure he didn't mean to make you feel that way,' he began tentatively.

Willow's fingers clenched for support into a broad shoulder that felt reassuringly solid and strong and she sucked in a shuddering breath. It was a kind lie, she conceded, liking him all the more for his compassion. Even so, she was still keen to say what she had never had the nerve to say before, because only then, in getting it off her chest, might she start to heal from the low self-esteem she had long suffered from. 'Yes, Dad did mean it. He honestly believed that the harder he pushed me, the more chance he had of getting me to excel! He didn't even care about which subject it might be in, he just wanted me to be especially talented at *something*!'

'I'm sorry,' Jai breathed, mesmerised by the glistening depth of her green eyes and the sheer passion with which she spoke, not to mention the unexpected pleasure of the slight trusting weight of her lying across his thighs and the evocative coconut scent of her hair. The untimely throb of arousal at his groin infuriated him and he fought it to the last ditch.

'Dad wasn't remotely impressed by my studying

garden history and landscaping. And that's why I'm crying, because I'm sorry too that it's too late to change anything for the better. I had my chance with him, and I blew it!' Willow muttered guiltily, marvelling that she was confiding in Jai, of all people. Jai, who was the cleverest of the clever. It didn't feel real; it felt much more like something she would imagine to comfort herself and, as such, reassuringly unreal and harmless. 'I never once managed to do anything that made Dad proud of me. My small successes were never enough to please him.'

And the sheer honesty of that confession struck Jai on a much deeper level because he wasn't used to a woman who told it as it was and didn't wrap up the ugly truth in a flattering guise. Yet Willow looked back at him, fearless and frank and so, *so* sad, and his hands slid from her back up to her face to cup her cheek-bones, framing those dreamy green eyes that had so much depth and eloquence in her heart-shaped face. She looked impossibly beautiful.

He didn't know what to say to that. He did not want to criticise her father, he did not want to hurt her more, and so he kissed her…didn't even know he was going to do it, didn't even have to think about it because it seemed the utterly, absolutely natural next step in their new understanding.

CHAPTER TWO

THE TASTE OF JAI, of fine wine and a faint minty after-flavour, threw Willow even deeper into the realms of fantasy.

Because fantasy was what it felt like, totally un-threatening fantasy in which Prince Jai Hari Singh, Maharaja of Chandrapur, kissed *her*, Willow Aller-ton, currently unemployed and soon to be homeless into the bargain. Being in his arms didn't feel real but, goodness, it felt *good*, the delve of his tongue into the moist aperture of her mouth sending a shower of fire-works flying through her tummy, awakening a heat that surged enthusiastically into all the cold places in-side her, both comforting and exhilarating all at once.

It was everything she had dreamt she might find in a man's arms and it felt right as well as good, glo-riously right as if she had been waiting her whole life for that moment and was being richly rewarded for her patience. In the dim light from the bedside lamp, Jai's eyes glittered with the pale ice of polar stars, but the ice that powered him burned through her like a rejuve-nating drug, banishing the grief and the guilt and the sadness that had filled her to overflowing. Her fingers drifted up to curve to his strong jawline.

'I like this,' she whispered helplessly.

'I like it too much,' Jai conceded in a driven undertone, lifting her off his lap to lay her down on the bed where her strawberry-blond hair shone in the lamplight, leaning over her to cover her lush mouth with his again.

'How...*too much*?' she pressed.

'I was trying to comfort you, not—'

Featherlight fingers brushed his lips before he could complete that speech. 'Kiss me again,' she urged feverishly. 'It drives everything else out of my head.'

She wanted forgetfulness, not the down-to-earth reminder that such intimacy was untimely. Jai's stern cautious side warred with his libido, his body teeming with pent-up desire. They were alone and free-to-consent adults, not irresponsible teenagers. He gazed down at her and then wrenched at the constriction of his tie with an impatient hand, suddenly giving way to the passionate nature that he usually controlled to what he deemed an acceptable level. The allure of her pink ripe lips was more than he could withstand.

That next explosive kiss sealed Willow's fate, for she could no more have denied the hunger coursing through her than she could have denied her own name. There was also a strong element of wonder in discovering Jai's desire for her. That was thrillingly unexpected and wonderfully heartening, that she could have it within her to mysteriously attract a man well known for his preference for gorgeous models and Bollywood actresses, a gorgeous, incredibly sexy man, who could have had virtually any woman he wanted. It changed her view of herself as the girl next door, low on sex appeal.

'I want you,' Jai ground out against her reddened mouth as he shed his jacket with a lithe twist of his broad shoulders.

Only for a split second did she marvel at that and then all her insecurities surged to the fore because she was skinny and lacked the curves that were so often seen as essential to make a woman appealing to a man. But an internal voice reminded her that Jai wanted her, and she opened her mouth beneath the onslaught of his, let her tongue dart and tangle with his, feeling free, feeling daring for the first time ever.

There was intoxication in the demanding pressure of his mouth on hers and the long fingers sliding below her top to cup a small pouting breast while he toyed with the tender peak. Her body arched without her volition as that sensual caress grew more intense, tiny little arrows of heat darting down into her pelvis to make her extraordinarily aware of that area. Her hips shifted as he pulled her top off, exposing the bare swell of her breasts, bending over her to use his mouth on the plump pink nipples commanding his attention. She tingled all over, goose bumps rising on her arms as he suckled on the distended buds. Between her thighs she felt hot and damp and surprisingly impatient for what came next.

And she knew what came next, of course she did, but her friends' bluntness on the topic had warned her not to expect triumphant bursts of classical music and glimpses of heaven in the final stages. It would be her first time and she was aware that her lack of experience would not affect his enjoyment but that it might well detract from hers. All a matter of luck, a friend had told her sagely.

Dainty fingers spearing through Jai's silky black hair, Willow was revelling in the intimacy of being able to touch him while still marvelling over how fast things could change between two people. Yet she had no doubts and was convinced she would have no regrets either because she had already reached the conclusion that she would rather have Jai as her first lover than anyone else.

Jai dragged off his shirt, returned to kiss her again, his wide, powerful torso hard and muscular against hers. She made a little sound of appreciation deep in her throat even as her hands skated up the hot, smooth skin of his ribcage to discover the muscles that flexed with his every movement. She couldn't think any more beyond that moment because the craving he had unleashed grew stronger with every demanding kiss and utterly controlled her, dulling her brain with an adrenalin boost that was wholly physical.

She writhed under his weight as he traced the hot, swollen centre of her, touching her where she desperately needed to be touched so that her body arched up to him, her heartbeat thundering, her entire being quivering with feverish need. A finger penetrated her slick depths and she gasped, all arousal and captive energy, wanting, *wanting*…

'Is it safe?' Jai husked, wrenching at his trousers to get them out of his path and so overexcited he barely recognised himself in his eagerness but her response, the passage of her tiny hands smoothing over his over-heated body, had pushed him to the biting edge of a hunger greater than anything he had ever known be-fore.

Safe? *Safe?* What was he talking about? She wasn't expecting any more visitors; they were alone. Of course, they were safe from interruption or the poten-tial embarrassment of discovery.

'Of course, it is,' Willow muttered.

Jai came down to her with a wolfish smile of relief. 'How very fortunate… I don't think I could stop un-less you ordered me to.'

'Not going to,' Willow mumbled, entranced by the fierce black-fringed eyes above hers into absolute still-ness.

Jai tipped her legs back and slid sinuously between them, shifting forward in a forceful surge to plunge into her. Eyes closing, Willow felt the burn of his in-vasion as her untried body stretched to accommodate him and then a sharp stab of pain that jolted her even as he groaned with satisfaction.

'You're so tight,' he breathed appreciatively.

The pain faded and, as it had been less than she had feared, her stress level dropped, and her body re-laxed to rise up against his as he withdrew and forged back into her again. Little tendrils of warming sensa-tion gathered in her pelvis and the excitement flooded back, kicking up her heartrate simultaneously so that even breathing became a challenge. She moved against him, hot, damp with perspiration, losing control because the insidious tightening at her core stoked her hunger for him. His fluid insistent rhythm increased, and she felt frantic, pitched to an edge of need that felt unbearable. She lifted to meet his every thrust, need driving her to hasten to the finish line and then, with a swoosh of drowning sensation, the tightness transformed into an explosion of sheer pleasure unlike any she had ever envisaged and she fell back against the pillows, winded and drained, utterly incapable of even twitching a limb.

'That was incredible,' Jai purred like a well-fed jungle cat in her ear, long fingers tracing the relaxed pout of her mouth and trailing down to her shoulder to smooth the skin before he pressed his mouth hungrily to the slope of her neck. 'All I really want now is to do it all over again.'

The tension of discomfiture, of not knowing how to behave, beginning to rise in Willow ebbed. He was happy, *she* was happy, there was nothing to fret about. *Again*, though? She had assumed that men were once-only creatures in need of recovery time, but Jai was already shifting sensually against her again, his renewed arousal brushing her stomach. That he could still want her that much gratified her and she smiled up at him.

That smile full of sunshine disconcerted Jai. His conscience twinged and it took him a moment to recognise the unfamiliar prompting because it was rare for him to do anything that awakened such a reaction. 'You do realise that this…*us*, isn't likely to go anywhere?' he murmured.

'How could it? I'm not an idiot,' Willow parried in

surprise and embarrassment that he felt the need to tell her that they had no future as a couple.

'I didn't want you to get the wrong impression,' Jai told her levelly. 'I only do casual with women and I never raise expectations I have no plans to fulfil.'

'Neither do I,' Willow assured him cheerfully, secure in her conviction that he had not guessed that she was inexperienced and relieved because pride demanded that he believe that he was no big deal in her life. 'I wouldn't want you getting the wrong idea about me either.'

Faint colour edged Jai's high sculpted cheekbones because no woman had ever dared to tell *him* that he was just a casual encounter. 'Of course not.'

'Then we're both content,' Willow concluded, refusing to recognise the little pang of hurt buried deep within her...hurt that she wasn't a little different from other women in his eyes, more special than they were, somehow less of a casual event in his life. He was telling it as it was and she should be grateful for that. This way she knew exactly where she stood and she wouldn't be weaving fantasies around phone calls that would never come or surprise visits. After all, he didn't have her phone number and even she didn't know where she'd eventually be living. She and Jai really *were* ships that passed in the night.

'I want to kiss you again,' Jai breathed with a raw edge to his dark deep voice.

He had only one night with her, and he wanted to make the very most of the best sex he had ever had. He would move on; she would move on. That was the

way of the world, yet a stray shard of guilt and regret still pierced him because she was so open with
him, so impervious to his wealth and status. He would
check that she was all right from a safe distance, stay
uninvolved, he promised himself. He supposed there
were ties between them that he was refusing to acknowledge lest they make him uncomfortable. He had
vague memories of her as a child, could remember her
shouting his name in excitement at sports events and
could recall the way her eyes had once clung to him as
though magnetised. But she had grown out of all that.
Of course, she had.

'I'm cold,' Willow admitted, snaking back from him
to tug the edge of the duvet up and scramble under it
with a convulsive shiver.

Jai peeled off his trousers, shaken that in his haste
to possess her he had not even fully undressed. Nothing cool or sophisticated about that approach, he told
himself ruefully, wondering what it was about her that
had made him so downright desperate to have her. For
the first time with a woman sexual hunger had overwhelmed him and crowded every other consideration
out. It was something more than looks, maybe that
unspoiled natural quality of hers, not to mention her
disconcerting honesty in assuring him that he was just
a one-night stand and that she had no desire to attach
strings to him. Jai didn't think he had ever been with
a woman who *didn't* want those strings, no matter how
coolly she was trying to play the game. He was too rich
and too powerful not to inspire women with ambitious
hopes and plans.

'Let me warm you,' Jai urged, hauling her into contact with his hot, muscular length, driving out the shivers that had been assailing her.

And it all began again and this time she was wholly free of tension and insecurity and the excitement rose even faster for her. The pleasure stole her mind from her body and left her exhausted. She dropped into sleep, still melded to Jai and still amazed by what had happened between them. At some stage of the night he kissed her awake and made love to her again, slow and sure this time, and achingly sexy. It occurred to her that Jai had made her initiation into sex wondrously sensual but, even then, she knew she ached in bone and muscle and would be wrecked the next morning.

In the dull light of dawn, she was surprised when Jai shook her awake. Dressed in his dark suit and unshaven, he stood over her, studying her with wolf pale blue eyes that burned. He yanked back the duvet, rudely exposing her, and said roughly, 'There's blood all over the sheet! Did I hurt you?'

Willow wanted to die of humiliation where she sat and she snatched at the duvet in desperation and covered up the offending stain, her face burning as hot as a furnace. 'Of course, you didn't. I didn't realise I would bleed the first time,' she whispered shakily. 'I know some women do but somehow I assumed I wouldn't...'

Slow, painful comprehension gripped Jai and rocked him to the depths of his being. He stared down at her in dawning disbelief. 'Are you saying that you were a virgin?'

'Well, it's not something I can lie about now, is it?'

Willow muttered in embarrassment, her chin coming up at a defiant tilt. 'But I don't know why you would think that you have a right to make a production out of something that is my business and nothing to do with you.'

'I would not have chosen to sleep with you had I known I would be your first,' Jai framed fiercely.

'Well, if that was a personal concern of yours, you should've asked in advance,' Willow countered mutinously. 'It's not as if I dragged you into bed!'

'How the hell could I have guessed that you were still a virgin at your age?' Jai demanded.

'I'm only twenty-one. Twenty-two in a few months,' she added stiffly. 'I'm sure I'm not that unusual.'

Jai was not appeased. She was years younger than the women he usually took as lovers, but he hadn't registered that fact the night before, had been too turned on and in too much of a hurry to register anything important, he conceded, angry at his own recklessness.

'Perhaps not, but I assumed you were experienced,' he admitted flatly.

'Well, now you know different. Can we drop this discussion? I want to get washed and dressed,' Willow told him without any expression at all, her small, slight body rigid with wounded pride and resentment in the bed as she continued to hug the duvet to her. 'You know last night was lovely…but now you've ruined it.'

'I'll see you downstairs,' Jai countered grimly.

Willow scrambled out of bed as soon as the door closed behind him and then winced, her body letting her know that such sudden energetic movements would be punished. Just at that moment she did not want that reminder of the intimacy they had shared when Jai, so obviously, regretted it. She pulled out fresh clothing and trekked across to the small shower room. A damp towel lay on the floor and she bent to scoop it up and lift it to her nose. It smelled ever so faintly of Jai while her body smelled even more strongly of him. Shame engulfed her in a drowning flood of regret. Evidently in sleeping with him she had made the wrong decision, but surely it had been *her* decision to make?

Of course, there had been men who'd shown an interest in her in recent years, but none had attracted her enough for her to take matters any further. She had never been much of a fan of crowded clubs or parties and her father's demand that she come home at a reasonable hour had proved to be a restriction that had turned her into a deadbeat companion for a night out. She had taken the easy way out when faced with her father's domineering personality and she had spent her free evenings at home watching television and catching up with Shelley, none of which had given her any experience of how to handle Jai in a temper. But never again would she lie down to be walked over by an angry male, she told herself urgently. From now on she would stand her ground and hold her head high, even if she did have misgivings about her own behaviour.

Jai paced the small living room, feeling the claustrophobic proportions of its confines in growing frustration. Willow was twenty-one years old. Far too young for an experienced man of twenty-nine. Why hadn't he remembered how young she was? What had he been thinking of? The answer was that he *hadn't* been thinking, hadn't stopped to think *once*. Everything that had happened with Willow had happened so fast and had seemed so deceptively natural that he had questioned nothing and now it was too late to change anything.

'Last night was lovely...but now you've ruined it.'

That complaint, towering in its naivety, echoed in his ears and made him flinch. As a rule, he avoided starry-eyed girls and she was one he should definitely have avoided getting more deeply involved with. A woman who'd had a massive crush on him as a teenager? How much had that influenced her willingness to give him her body? He emitted a harsh groan of guilt and self-loathing.

A decent man didn't take advantage of a vulnerable woman! And what had he done?

Within hours of her father's funeral, when she was grieving and distressed, he had pounced like some sort of self-serving seducer. She had deserved more care and consideration than he had given her. Yet he had started out simply trying to offer both care and consideration and could not for the life of him explain how trying to comfort her had ended up with them having sex. She hadn't flirted with him. She hadn't encouraged him but she hadn't said no either. Was that what he was blaming her for? No, he was blaming her for not telling him that she was a virgin, for not giving him that choice...

'I'll have to nip out to get something for breakfast,' Willow told him from the doorway.

Jai swung round, his eyes a pale glittering brilliance in his lean, darkly handsome face. 'I'll eat back at the hotel,' he told her drily. 'Why didn't you tell me that I would be the first? I wouldn't have continued if I'd known. I feel as though I took advantage of your inexperience.'

'It didn't occur to me that I should tell you. I wasn't really thinking. I don't think either of us were. Everything happened so fast,' Willow murmured defensively, wishing he would have given her the time to provide breakfast and sort matters out in a more civilised manner. But Jai, she was beginning to recognise, was much more volatile in nature than she had ever appreciated. Without skipping a beat, he had taken the dialogue they had abandoned in the bedroom straight back up again, which suggested that while she'd showered and dressed, he had merely continued to silently brood and seethe.

'There's nothing we can do about it now,' she pointed out thinly.

Jai looked back at her, scanning her small, slight figure in jeans and a top. Even with the shadows etched below her eyes, she was still lovely, eminently touchable, he reflected as he tensed. Daylight and cold reason had not made her any less appealing. 'No, but it was *wrong*.'

'You don't get the unilateral right to say that to me,' Willow snapped back at him. 'It was *not* wrong for me!'

'You had a crush on me for years,' Jai countered levelly. 'Is that why it wasn't wrong for you?'

Willow's soft mouth opened and closed again as she

gazed back at him in horror, hot, painful colour slowly washing up her cheeks. 'I can't believe you are throwing that in my face.'

'It's relevant to this situation,' Jai breathed sardonically.

'The only person making a situation out of this is you!' Willow condemned, fighting her mortification with all her might. 'Yes, I may have had a crush on you when I was a schoolgirl, but I grew out of that nonsense years ago!'

'I'm not sure I can believe that some sentimental memory didn't influence you.'

'It didn't. Whether you believe that or not is up to you,' Willow replied curtly. 'I'm all grown up now. I don't have any romantic notions about you…and if I had, you'd have killed them stone dead.'

Her continuing refusal to be influenced by his attitude surprised Jai. He was accustomed to those he dealt with coming round to his view and supporting his opinion, but Willow was stubborn enough and independent enough not to budge an inch. Meanwhile those bright green eyes, reminiscent of fresh ferns in the shade, damned him to hell and back.

'Then let's get down to business,' Jai suggested, disconcerting her when she was bracing herself for another round of the same conversation. 'I want to buy your father's books.'

Willow regrouped and contrived to nod. 'I'm content with that.'

'Is the dealer you mentioned last night a book dealer?'

'Nothing so fancy...why?'

'At least two of the books are quite valuable first editions and you could do better auctioning them,' Jai warned.

'I haven't time for that. I didn't know any of them would be worth anything,' she completed stiffly.

'I will buy them at a fair price but you may wish to take further advice.'

Willow groaned out loud. 'Oh, Jai... I don't think you're likely to cheat me!'

'Very well. The books will be packed for you and collected later this morning and I will pay you in cash as that may be more convenient for you right now,' Jai murmured levelly. 'Will you allow me to pay for you to stay in a hotel until you get on your feet again?'

'Would you be offering me that option if you hadn't slept with me last night?' Willow asked suspiciously.

His eyes clashed with her sceptical appraisal. 'Yes.'

'No. Thanks, but no,' Willow told him without hesitation. 'I don't mind staying with Shelley for a while.'

'Will you accept any further assistance from me?' Jai enquired.

'I'd prefer not to,' Willow responded truthfully.

'Life isn't always that straightforward,' Jai replied wryly as he settled his business card on the table. 'If at any time you need help, you can depend on me to deliver it, no strings attached. Phone me if you are in need.'

'And why would you make me an offer like that?' Willow demanded shortly.

'I wish you well,' Jai admitted levelly.

Willow spun around in a rather ungainly circle and went to open the front door. 'I'll get by fine without you,' she told him with a defiantly bright smile. 'But thanks for caring.'

And on that hollow note, Jai departed. As soon as he was gone, Willow felt empty, exhausted and horribly hurt. She would never see him again except in newspapers or magazines at some glamorous or important event, but that was for the best because Jai had rejected her on every level. He had switched back to treating her like a distant acquaintance, whom he was willing to help in times of trouble, smoothly distancing himself from their brief intimacy.

He not only regretted sleeping with her, but also suspected that she had slept with him because she had once been infatuated with him. He had made mincemeat out of her pride and humiliated her.

Goodbye, Jai, she thought numbly. *Goodbye and good riddance!*

CHAPTER THREE

WILLOW SAT ON the side of the bath and waited for the wand to give her a result while Shelley sidled round the door, too impatient to wait outside. 'Well?' she pressed excitedly.

'Another thirty seconds,' Willow muttered wearily.

'I love babies.' Shelley sighed dreamily.

'So do I… I just thought it would be years before I had one. And maybe it will be,' Willow contended, trying not to be too pessimistic.

After all, skipping a period wasn't always a sign of pregnancy even in a woman with a regular cycle. But then there was also the soreness of her breasts, the occasional light-headed sensation and her sudden sensitivity to smells and tastes that had never bothered her before. Yet Willow still couldn't credit that an unplanned pregnancy could happen to her. Surely Jai had used condoms? She hadn't thought to check or ask him, had simply not even considered the danger of conception, which had been exceedingly foolish when it was she who would fall pregnant if anything went amiss. Maybe a condom had failed, maybe during the night he had forgotten to use one, maybe she was just one of the unfortunate few who conceived regardless of the contraception used.

'Congratulations!' Shelley carolled irrepressibly and grabbed her into an enthusiastic hug. 'You're pregnant.'

Willow paled. 'Are you sure?' she gasped, peering down at the wand for herself, and there it was: the line for a positive result.

'You'll have to go to the doctor ASAP,' Shelley warned her. 'I mean…you must be at least eight weeks along now and you should be taking vitamins and stuff.'

In no hurry to approach a doctor for confirmation, Willow wandered back out to the very comfortable sofa she slept on and sank heavily down. *Pregnant!* Just when her life was slowly beginning to settle again into a new routine, fate had thrown her onto a roller coaster of a ride that would destroy all her self-improvement plans. Of course, there were options other than keeping the baby to raise, she reminded herself doggedly, even while she knew that neither termination nor adoption had any appeal for her.

But how on earth would she manage? Currently she was waitressing in the bar that Shelley managed. The tips were good, particularly at weekends, and in another couple of months she would have saved up enough for a deposit for a little place of her own. After making that move, she had planned to polish up her CV and start trying to find work in the landscaping field that would pay enough for her to live on. She had her qualification now and even the most junior position would be a good start to a decent career and perhaps, ultimately, her own business. Throw a baby into the midst of those plans, however, and it blew them all to smithereens!

And yet the prospect of having Jai's baby was already beginning to warm her at some deep level, although she felt guilty about feeling that way. He mightn't have wanted her, but he couldn't prevent her from having his child and she did love babies, and the thought of one of her own pleased and frightened her in equal parts. She didn't have a single relative left alive, but her baby could be the foundation of a new family, she reflected lovingly.

She had lain awake on the sofa many nights reliving that night with Jai, wishing she didn't feel like such an immature idiot for having slept with him in the first place and wishing that she didn't miss him now that he was gone again. She wasn't kidding herself that she was in love with him or anything like that, but she could not deny that Jai, the Maharaja of Chandrapur, had always fascinated her and that he had attracted her more powerfully than anyone else ever had. Those were the facts and she tried not to dress them up. She felt that she should've called a halt to their intimacy, but she hadn't and the coolness of his departure had been her punishment. He had hurt her, but she tried not to dwell on those wounded feelings because what would be the point in indulging herself in such sad thoughts?

'I'll help you every step of the way,' Shelley told her, sitting down beside her to grip her hand comfortingly. 'We'll get through it together…and at least you won't have to worry about money, not with the father being rich.'

'I'm *not* going to tell Jai!' Willow exclaimed in dismay. 'He didn't want me so he's even less likely to want a baby with me!'

'It takes two to tango.'

'And one to have common sense, and neither of us had any that night.' Willow sighed and then groaned out loud. 'Why should I make him suffer too? It would be so humiliating as well. I can't face that on top of everything else.'

Shelley's freckled face and bright blue eyes were troubled below her mop of brown curls. 'Well, then, what are you planning to do?'

'I don't want to tell Jai… To be frank, I don't want anything more to do with him,' Willow admitted unhappily. 'I'll work this out without bothering him for help. Somehow I'll work it out even if it means living on welfare benefits to survive.'

Two weeks later, while Willow was at work, Shelley had to deal with the surprise of Jai himself turning up on the doorstep asking after Willow because he hadn't heard from her. Aware that her friend wanted no further contact with him, Shelley lied and said that Willow had moved out and hadn't yet sent her a forwarding address. Jai left his mobile number with her.

Thirteen months later, the private investigation agency Jai had hired to find Willow finally tracked her down and, in the midst of his working day in his London office, Jai immediately settled down with a sense of urgency to flick open the ominously slim file.

The first fact he learned was that the investigation team had only contrived to find Willow by covertly watching and following her friend, Shelley. Jai was disconcerted to learn that Willow's friend had lied to him when he had only had Willow's best interests in mind. He would have been satisfied with the assurance that she was safe and well. He assumed that Willow had confided in her friend and it was conceivable that that night he had spent with her had muddied the water in her friend's eyes and made his motivations seem more questionable, he conceded grudgingly.

After all, what could Willow possibly have to hide from him? Why would she get lost and neglect to get in touch with him when he had been so specific on that point? Had he offended her to such an extent?

He knew he had not been tactful. He had been too outspoken. He had embarrassed her, hurt her, he recalled unhappily. But he had been very shocked to realise that he had taken advantage of her innocence and his self-loathing on that score had still to fade, as had his recollections of that night. It seemed even worse to him that the memories of her still remained so fresh. Averse as he now was to any kind of casual encounter, he had not been with a woman since then. He had broken his own code of honour unforgettably with Willow and had buried himself in work while struggling to come to terms with that depressing truth.

Her disappearance and continuing silence had seriously worried him and had only made him even more determined to locate her.

The bald facts of what came next in the file shook Jai to his essentially conservative core and he was instantly grateful that he had refused to give up on his search for her because she was in trouble. Willow had had a child and was now living in a hostel for the homeless, waiting for the local council to find her more suitable accommodation. A *child*? How was that possible in so short a time frame? Had she turned to some other man for comfort after he had left her? He focussed back on the printed page and his blood ran cold in his veins when he saw the birthdate of the child and then, startlingly, his own middle *name*... Hari.

Far across London, Willow knelt on the floorboards while Hari sat on his little blanket and mouthed the plastic ball he was playing with. Everything went into his mouth and she had to watch him like a hawk. He was almost seven months old and, although he couldn't yet crawl, he had discovered that he could get around very nicely just by rolling over and over so that he could get his little chubby hands on anything that attracted his attention. And *everything* attracted Hari's attention, which meant that she needed eyes in the back of her head to keep him safe.

She had not known that it was possible to love anyone as much as she loved Hari. Her love for the father she had continually failed to please paled in comparison. From the moment Hari had arrived he had become her world and she was painfully conscious that as a mother she had nothing to offer in material terms. Sadly, moving into the hostel had been a necessity to get on the housing list. Shelley hadn't wanted them to move out of her apartment but staying any longer hadn't been an option in the chaos that she and Hari had brought to her friend's life. So she might be, for the moment, a less than stellar mother to her son, but in time she would get better and provide him with a decent home where their life would improve.

The knock that sounded on the door made her jump and she peered through the peephole to identify another resident, the woman from the room next to hers, before she undid the lock.

'Reception asked me to tell you that you have a visitor waiting down in the basement,' the woman told her.

Willow suppressed a sigh and bundled Hari, his blanket and a couple of toys up into her arms. Visitors weren't allowed to enter the rooms in the hostel, but the basement was available for necessary meetings with housing officials, social workers and counsellors. Willow hadn't been expecting anyone, but the number of people now involved in checking up on her and Hari and asking her to fill in forms seemed never-ending.

My goodness, maybe somewhere had finally been found for her and Hari to live, she thought optimistically as she walked down the steps to the basement to enter a large grey-painted room furnished mainly with small tables and chairs, few of which were occupied. She hovered in the doorway and then froze when she saw Jai standing by the barred window that overlooked a dark alleyway.

Jai looked so incredibly out of place against such a backdrop that she could not quite believe her eyes and she blinked rapidly. Clad in a black pinstriped suit teamed with a white shirt and gold tie, he looked incredibly intimidating. But he also looked impossibly exclusive and gorgeous with that suit sharply tailored to a perfect fit over his tall, powerful frame. The stark lighting above, which flattered no one, somehow still contrived to flatter Jai, enhancing the golden glow of his skin and the blue-black luxuriance of his hair and accentuating the proud sculpted lines and hollows of his superb bone structure. He was stunning as he stood there, absolutely stunning, his light eyes glittering in his lean, strong face, and she swallowed convulsively, wondering how he had found her, what he wanted with her and how on earth she could possibly hide Hari from him when she was holding him in her arms.

Jai noticed Willow at almost the same moment, lodged across the room, a tiny frail figure dressed in jeans and an oversized sweater, against which she held a child. And he stared at the child in her arms with helpless intensity and, even at that distance, he recognised his son in the baby's olive-toned skin and black hair. His *son*… Jai could not work out how that was possible unless Willow had lied to him about it being safe for them to make love without him taking additional precautions. But just at that moment the *how* seemed less significant than the overpowering and breathtaking sense of recognition that gripped him when he glimpsed his infant son for the first time.

Willow walked towards him and he strode forward to greet her, noticing that she was struggling to carry the child along with the other things she held. Without hesitation, Jai extended his hands and lifted the baby right out of her arms.

Hari chortled and smiled up at him. Evidently, he was a happy baby, who delighted in new faces. Jai looked into eyes as pale a blue as his own, his sole inheritance from his British mother, and knew then without a shadow of doubt that, hard as he found it to credit, this child *had* to be *his* son, *his* child, *his* responsibility. He moved away again, and Willow hovered, feeling entirely surplus to requirements, until one of the four bodyguards seated at a nearby table surged forward to pull out chairs at another table and Jai took a seat with Hari carefully cradled in his arms.

Willow dropped into the seat beside Jai's and Hari grinned at her while he tugged at Jai's tie. 'How did you find me?' she whispered.

'A private detective agency. They've been trying to trace you for months,' Jai imparted, his wide, sensual mouth compressing at that unfortunate fact. 'I only wish I'd found you sooner.'

'I can't imagine why you've been trying to find me,' she confided.

'But isn't it fortunate that I did?' Jai traded smoothly as he stroked a gentle finger through the spill of Hari's black hair. 'You must realise that you cannot stay in such a place with my son.'

Paper pale at that quiet declaration, Willow gazed

back at him. '*Your...son?*' she almost whispered, shaken by the certainty with which he made that claim.

'He is my image. Who else's son could he be?' Jai parried very drily as if daring her to disagree or throw doubt on the question of his child's parentage. 'And as this is not somewhere that we can talk freely, I would like you to go back to your room right now and pack up all your belongings to leave.'

'I can't do that. I'm here waiting to get a place on a council housing list and if I leave, I'll lose my place in the queue,' she protested in a low intent voice.

Jai settled Hari more securely on his lap. 'Either you do as I ask...*or* I will seek an emergency court order to take immediate custody of Hari as he is at risk in such an environment. That is unacceptable. Be warned that I hold diplomatic status in the UK and the authorities will act quickly on my behalf if I lodge a complaint on behalf of my heir. The usual laws do not apply to diplomats.'

In sheer shock at that menacing information, Willow went rigid, her blood chilling in her veins. 'You're threatening me with...legal action?' she gasped in astonishment, barely able to believe her ears. '*Already?*'

Jai sent her an inhumanly cool and calm appraisal, the dark strength of his resolve palpable. 'I will do what I must to put right what you have got wrong...'

Stabbed to the heart by that spontaneously offered opinion, Willow bent her head. *No judgement here*, she thought sarcastically, but she was so deep in shock that Jai would actually threaten her with losing custody of her child that she didn't even know what to say back to him. She didn't want to take the risk of being too frank, didn't want to row in public, didn't want to make a bad situation worse by speaking without careful forethought. She sensed that the Jai she had thought she knew to some degree was not the Jai she was currently dealing with. This was Jai being ruthless and calculating and brutally confrontational, which, logic warned her, had to be qualities he had acquired to rise so high and so fast in the business world. Unluckily for her, it was not a side of him she had seen before or had had to deal with.

'We will not argue here in a public place,' Jai informed her in the same very polite tone. 'We will both ensure that the needs of our child remain our first consideration.'

'Of course, but—'

'No, there will be no qualification of that statement,' Jai interposed levelly. 'Now, please pack so that we can leave this place behind us.'

Willow leapt upright and reached down for Hari.

'I will look after him while you pack,' Jai spelt out as he too stood up, towering over her in her flat heels with Hari still clasped in his arms.

'You could walk away with him while I'm upstairs,' Willow pointed out shakily, not an ounce of colour in her taut face as she looked up at him fearfully.

'I give you my word of honour that I will not do that. You are his mother and my son needs his mother,' Jai murmured soft and low, the hardness of his expression softening a little. 'Although I grew up without mine, it would never be my choice to put my son in the same position.'

Willow backed off a step, still uncertain of what she should do. 'If I pack, where are you taking us to? A hotel?'

'Of course not. To my home here in London,' Jai proffered as Hari tugged cheerfully at his hair. 'I have already had rooms prepared for your arrival.'

'You took a lot for granted,' Willow remarked help-lessly.

'In this situation, I can afford to do so,' Jai told her without remorse.

And with that ringing indictment of her ability to raise their child alone, Willow headed upstairs. There wasn't much for her to pack. She gathered up Hari's bottles and solid food and put them into the baby bag Shelley had bought her. She settled the bin bags filled with their clothing and Hari's toys into the battered stroller, donned her duffle coat and wheeled the stroller to the top of the stairs before stooping to lift it and battle to carry it downstairs. Halfway down the second flight one of Jai's bodyguards met her and lifted it out of her arms.

'Is that the lot?' Jai asked, turning from the reception desk, Hari tucked comfortably under one arm.

'Yes. I left stuff with Shelley.'

'There's a form for you to fill in. I put in the for-warding address,' Jai advanced.

Willow was surprised that there was only one form because before she had even moved into the hostel, she'd had to fill out a thirty-page document. She signed her name at the foot, briefly scanning the address Jai had filled in, raising a brow at the exclusivity of the area. Mayfair, no less. Five minutes later, she was climbing into a limousine for the first time in her life, breathless at the unknown ahead of her.

Jai strapped Hari into the car seat awaiting him.

'When did you learn to be so comfortable around babies?' Willow asked tautly.

'There are many children in my extended family. High days and holidays, they visit,' Jai told her. 'I was a lonely only child. Hari will never suffer from a lack of company.'

On her smoothly upholstered leather seat, Willow tensed, registering that Jai was already talking about her son visiting India. She supposed that was natural, and an expectation he would obviously have. Even so the prospect of her baby boy being so far away from her totally unnerved her, and she couldn't help feeling overwhelmed, most especially when Jai had already threatened her with legal action.

'Now for the question that taxes my patience the most,' Jai breathed, his nostrils flaring with annoyance, his light eyes throwing a laser-bright challenge. 'Why would you move into a homeless shelter rather than ask me for help?'

Willow froze. 'There's nothing wrong with living in a homeless shelter. They're there for when people are desperate.'

'But you weren't desperate, not really. You could've turned to me at any time. And don't try to misinterpret my question. I probably know a great deal more than you about the individuals who use such shelters. Some are those who have fallen on hard times through no fault of their own, others have mental health issues or are drug addicts or ex-cons. None of those elements make a homeless shelter safe or acceptable for a child,' Jai completed harshly.

'Nonetheless there are quite a few children living in them!' Willow shot back at him stubbornly.

'Why didn't you contact me?' Jai demanded, out of all patience with her reluctance to answer his original question. He had been denied all knowledge of his son for more than six months and that enraged him, but he was grimly aware that this was not the right time to reveal his deep anger, particularly not if he wanted her to tell him the truth.

Willow swallowed convulsively. 'I didn't think you'd want to know. It was my problem. He's my child.' She hesitated. 'When I was pregnant, I was afraid that you would want me to have a termination and I didn't want to be put in that position. I didn't want to feel guilty for wanting to have my own child. It was easier to get on with it on my own and I managed fine while I was pregnant and still able to work.'

'I would never have asked you to have a termination. Hari is my child too,' Jai retorted crisply. 'I would have ensured that you had somewhere decent to live and I would have supported you.'

Willow sighed. 'Well, it's too late now to be arguing about it.'

Jai's eyes flashed at that assurance and he struggled to repress his anger, because her misplaced pride and lack of faith in him had ensured that his son had endured living conditions that were far less than his due.

'So, how *did* you manage to conceive when you told me it would be safe for us to have sex?' he asked next, battening down his volatile responses to concentrate on the basic facts.

Willow could feel her whole face heating up and she glanced across at Jai with noticeable reluctance. *Safe* to have sex? That was what he had meant that night? She shook her head slowly as clarity spilled through her brain and she squirmed in retrospect over her own stupidity. 'I misunderstood. When you asked if it was safe, I assumed that you were asking if we would be interrupted…if I was expecting anyone,' she admitted stiffly, her cheeks only burning more fierily at the look of incredulity that flared in his ice-blue eyes. 'I'm sorry. I wasn't thinking about contraception. That danger honestly didn't cross my mind.'

And the whole mystery of how she had become pregnant was clarified there and then, Jai conceded in a kind of wonderment. She had misunderstood him, and he had been too hot for her to reflect on the risk that he had never taken with any other woman. They had had unprotected sex several times because the young woman he had slept with had still had the mentality of a guilty, self-conscious teenager, determined to hide her sex life from the critical grown-ups. He supposed then that he had got exactly what he deserved for not considering questioning the level of her sexual experience.

Or was he being very naive in accepting that explanation? Was it, indeed, possible that Willow had *wanted* to become pregnant by a rich man? A rich man and a baby by him could secure a woman's comfort for a comfortable twenty years. In one calculating move, such a pregnancy would have solved all Willow's financial problems. And not contacting him and keeping him out of the picture until the child was safely born could well have been part of the same gold-digging scheme to set him up and profit from her fertility in the future.

Jai frowned, ice-blue eyes, enhanced by velvety black lashes, turning glacier cool as he surveyed her. She looked tired and tense and hadn't made any effort to do herself up for his benefit, but then, why would she bother when she was now the mother of his son and already in an unassailable position in his life?

At the same time, he had made the first move that night after the funeral, at least, he *thought* he had. In truth, all he recalled was the heady taste of her lips, not *how* he had arrived at that point. The pulse at his groin kicked up a storm at that recollection, reminding him that he was still hungry for her. His jaw clenched. He would soon find out if she was mercenary and, really, it didn't matter a damn, did it? After all, whatever she was, whoever she turned out to be, he *had* to marry her for his son's sake…

CHAPTER FOUR

WILLOW WALKED INTO the Mayfair town house and was plunged straight into palatial contemporary décor that was breathtakingly large and impressive.

'Come this way,' Jai instructed, heading straight for the elegant staircase with Hari still clasped to his powerful chest. 'My former *ayah*, Shanaya, arrived this morning. She has a full complement of staff with her and they will look after Hari while we talk.'

'Ayah?' Willow questioned with frowning eyes.

'She was my nursemaid...nanny—whatever you want to call it,' Jai explained. 'She is a kind and gentle woman. You need have no fear for our son's welfare while he is with her.'

Willow didn't want to hand over care of Hari to anyone, no matter who they were, particularly when she could not imagine that she and Jai had much to discuss. He had threatened her to make her vacate the homeless shelter and he doubtless planned to press his advantage by making her accept his financial support. Using the threat of legal action straight away had warned her that he would not listen to her protests. His bottom line, his closing argument would always zero in on what was best for Hari. And how could she argue with that sterling rule when she wanted the same thing?

Therefore, bearing in mind that she did not expect to be spending very long in Jai's luxurious town house, she pinned a pleasant smile to her face to greet the grey-haired older woman awaiting her in a room already furnished as a nursery. She had three smiling younger women by her side, all of them dressed in brightly coloured saris, and they welcomed Hari with a sort of awed reverence that disconcerted Willow. Hari, however, did love to be admired and he beamed at all of them.

'His Royal Highness is very confident,' Shanaya remarked approvingly in hesitant English.

'His Royal Highness?' Willow hissed in disbelief as Jai whisked her back out of the room again.

'Hari is my official heir, known as the Yuvaraja in our language. He is a very important child to my family and to our staff,' Jai explained, ushering her downstairs and into a very traditional library lined with books and pictures and what looked like a wall of official awards. 'This was my father's room and, although I have certainly not kept it like a shrine, I did not have it updated after his death like the rest of the house. I still like to remember him seated here at his desk or drowsing by the fireside with his nose in a book.'

Willow had faded memories of the older man on his visits to the boarding school, which he had once attended himself. She also recalled him taking tea once in their small home with her father, the correctness of his spoken English, the warmth of his smile and the tiny brocade box filled with sweets that he had dug out of his pocket for her.

'It means a great deal to me that you named our son after me,' Jai admitted.

Willow went pink. 'I wanted to acknowledge his background.'

'Hari has been a family name for generations. My father would have rejoiced in our son's existence.'

'In these circumstances?' Willow said uncomfortably. 'I hardly think so.'

'I assume you are referring to Hari's illegitimate birth,' Jai breathed in a raw undertone. 'That problem will vanish as soon as we marry.'

Willow's knees shook under her and she had to straighten her back to stay upright. Her incredulous gaze locked to his lean, dark features and the flaring brilliance of his pale gaze. 'I beg your pardon?' she murmured with a frown. 'As soon as we…*marry*?'

'Hari's birth will be legitimised by our marriage. He cannot take his place as my heir *without* us getting married,' Jai countered levelly. 'I want us to get married as quickly as it can be arranged.'

Willow gave up the battle with her wobbly knees and dropped heavily into a comfortable armchair beside the Georgian fireplace. Slowly she shook her head. 'Jai…men and women don't get married any more simply because a child has been born.'

'Perhaps not, but Hari can only claim his legal right to follow me if we are man and wife. It may seem old-fashioned to you, but it is the law and it is unlikely to be changed. My inheritance, which will one day become his, is safeguarded by strict rules. My business interests I can leave to anyone I want, but my heritage, the properties and land involved and the charitable foundation started up by my grandfather can only be bestowed on the firstborn child, whose parents must be married for him to inherit,' Jai outlined grimly.

Disconcerted by that information, Willow snatched in a deep jagged breath. 'But you can't *want* to marry me?'

'I don't want to marry anyone right now,' Jai admitted wryly.

Willow stiffened, reckoning that she had just received her answer about how best to treat his proposition. His suggestion that they should marry was sheer madness, she reasoned in astonishment. Her entire attention was now welded to him. A blue-black shadow of stubble was beginning to accentuate his wide mobile mouth and a tiny little shiver ran through her, her breasts tightening and peaking below her sweater, those little sensations arrowing down into her pelvis to awaken a hot, tense, damp feeling between her thighs. She thrust her spine rigidly into the embrace of the chair back, furious with herself but breathless and unable to drag her attention from the wild dark beauty of Jai as he paced over to the desk, his stunning eyes glittering over her with an intensity she could *feel* and which mesmerised her.

'Obviously you don't *want* to marry me,' she remarked in a brittle undertone.

'Aside of my little flirtation with the idea of marriage when I was twenty-one, I have always hoped to retain my freedom for as long as possible,' Jai confessed with a twist of his shapely mouth as he studied her, appreciating the elegant delicacy of her tiny figure in the overly large chair, but not appreciating the way his attention instinctively lingered on the swell of her breasts below the sweater and the slender stretch of her denim-clad thighs. 'I planned to marry in my forties, while my father was even older when he took the plunge. Hari's birth, however, has changed everything. I cannot deny Hari his right to enjoy the same history and privileges that I had.'

'I understand that, *but—*' she began emotively.

'No matter what you say, it will still come down to the same conclusion. Our son *needs* his parents to be married,' Jai delivered with biting finality. 'Only imagine his angry bitterness if some day he has to watch another man inherit what should have been his…because *if* you refuse to marry me, I will inevitably marry another woman and have children with her. It is my duty to carry on our family name and a second son born from that marriage will become my heir instead.'

The content of that last little speech shook Willow rigid because she realised that she didn't want to imagine *any* of those events taking place…*not* Jai marrying someone else and fathering children by her and certainly *not* her son hurt by being nudged out of what could have been his rightful place. It was a distressing picture, but Jai was being realistic when he forced her to look at it. Sooner or later, it seemed, he had to marry and have a child and why shouldn't his firstborn son benefit from their marriage?

'You're ready to bite the bullet because Hari and I would be the practical option?' Willow suggested tightly.

'Those are not the words I would have used,' Jai chided. 'This may not be what I once innocently planned, but Hari is here now and, as his parents, shouldn't we do what we can to make amends for his current status?'

Willow stared stonily at the rug on the floor, because it was an unanswerable question. Of course, Hari should be put first, not left to reap the disadvantages his careless parents had left him facing. Would her son even want to follow in his father's footsteps to eventually become the Maharaja of Chandrapur? She reckoned that, as an adult, her son would want that choice and wouldn't wish to be denied it over something as arbitrary as the accident of his birth. She swallowed hard. 'Right, so if I agree to marry you, what sort of marriage would it be?'

'A normal one,' Jai murmured, soft and low, a little of his tension dissipating as he grasped that she was willing to proceed. 'Of course, if we are unhappy together we can separate and divorce but we will both make a big effort for Hari's sake because two parents raising him together must surely be better than only one.'

Of course, neither of them knew what it would be like to grow up with two parents, Willow conceded. But she had seen that dynamic in the homes of her friends, parents pulling and working together to look after their families. She had also visited the homes of single-parent families and had only noted there that the parent carried a much heavier burden in doing it all alone. Would she and Jai be able to provide Hari with a secure and happy home? Jai didn't love her, while she was still insanely attracted to him, she acknowledged uneasily, lifting her head to collide with the frosty glitter of his eyes, feeling the almost painful clench of internal muscles deep down inside.

'Do you think we could do it?' she whispered.

'I think we *must* for his benefit,' Jai countered levelly. 'And as soon as possible. Are we agreed?'

Almost mesmerised by the blaze of his full attention, Willow nodded very slowly. 'Yes.'

She was going to marry Jai and the concept was surreal: Jai the playboy with his polo ponies and trophies, his heritage palaces, his long backstory of glamorous and impossibly beautiful former lovers. Yet she was so ordinary, so unexciting in comparison, she thought in dismay. Even worse, he didn't want to marry *her* and he had admitted it.

But that honesty of his was good, she told herself fiercely. Should she be ashamed of the reality that the very idea of being freed from all her financial worries was a relief? Did that mean that she was greedy? Or simply that she was tired of feeling like an inadequate mother? Without Jai, she had found it impossible to give Hari the comfort and security he deserved. With Jai, everything would be different. In addition, she would have far more rights over her own son if she married Jai. In terms of custody they would be equal partners then, she reasoned, and no matter what happened between her and Jai she would have very little reason to fear losing access to her little boy.

What would it be like, though, being married to a man who didn't love or really want her? Jai hadn't even wanted her enough to ask to *see* her again, she reminded herself doggedly, reeling from the toxic bite of that fact. Yes, sure, he had tried to check up on her a couple of months afterwards, she conceded grudgingly, but by that stage only an ingrained sense of responsibility towards Brian Allerton's daughter had been driving him, nothing more personal.

Of course, she didn't love him either, she reminded herself doggedly. All the same, she couldn't take her eyes off Jai when he was in the same room and her heart hammered and her mouth ran dry every time he looked at her. If she was honest with herself, she was sort of fascinated by Jai, always hungry to know more about him and work out what made him tick. He had accepted Hari without question and moved them straight into his home.

Yes, he had threatened her with legal action but only on Hari's behalf, not to take her son away from her, indeed only, it seemed, to pressure her into leaving the hostel and agreeing to marry him. With shocking shrewdness, he had accomplished that objective within hours, she registered in belated dismay. Yet he had done it even though at heart he didn't *want* to marry her! But that was the mystery that was Jai. He was volatile and emotional and very hot-blooded, yet he was still apparently willing to settle for a practical marriage...

* * *

Jai watched Willow walk away from him to return to their son. Evidently, he was about to acquire a wife. He gritted his teeth, for being forced to marry to bring Hari officially into the family was even less attractive than increasing age prompting him to the challenge. Marriage was difficult, as his parents' failure to surmount their differences proved. But he knew in his heart that he *owed* Willow a wedding ring. It *was* that simple, because what he had done with her broke every principle he had been raised to respect: he had greedily and irresponsibly taken an innocent woman and slept with her when she was vulnerable, and even in the act he had not protected her as he should've done.

He found it hard, though, to forgive her for hiding Hari from him and denying him precious moments of his son's babyhood that would never be repeated. But he had to set that anger aside, he reminded himself fiercely, shelve the pointless regrets that he could have been such an idiot and concentrate instead on the present. He should be relieved that she still attracted him, even if he resented the constant disturbing pull of her understated sensuality. He didn't know how she still had that effect on him, and he wasn't planning to explore it again, not until they were safely, decently married.

'You look a treat,' Shelley said, patting Willow's hand as they travelled in a limousine to the civil ceremony at the register office.

Willow shivered, scolding herself for having picked

a wedding dress unsuited to autumn, but then she had been living on a dizzy merry-go-round of change and struggling to adapt throughout the past week in Jai's London home. Agreeing to marry Jai had been like jumping on an express train that hurtled along at break-neck speed. He had pointed out that getting married in Chandrapur would entail a solid week of festivities while getting married *discreetly* in London would only require an hour and a couple of witnesses.

She had spent most of the week with Hari because Jai had been busy working. She had, however, seen Jai at mealtimes and had tripped over him in the nursery more than once. Surrounded by a bevy of admiring nursemaids, Jai was attempting to get to know his son and Hari was thriving on the amount of attention he was receiving. Willow could already see that the biggest problem of her son's new lifestyle would be ensuring that Hari did not grow up into an over-indulged young man, unacquainted with the word 'no.'

Her wedding gown left her arms and throat bare. With cap sleeves, a crystal-beaded corset top and a sparkly tulle skirt, it was a fairy-tale dress and very bridal. In retrospect, Willow was embarrassed about the choice she had made and worried that it was too excessive for the occasion. But who knew if she would ever get married again? And when she was faced with choosing her one and possibly *only* wedding dress, she had gone with her heart.

Luckily, she had had Shelley's support when a stylist had arrived at the house and informed her that she had been instructed to provide Willow with a whole new wardrobe. A huge wardrobe of clothes tailored to fit Willow had been delivered within forty-eight hours, outfits chosen to shine at any possible occasion and many of the options decidedly grand. Hari now also rejoiced in many changes of exclusive baby clothing. Jai, Willow reckoned ruefully, was rewriting their history and redesigning his bride into a far more fashionable and exclusive version of herself. Did he appreciate that that determination to improve her appearance only revealed that he had previously found her unpolished and gauche?

She walked into the anteroom with Shelley by her side. Jai approached her with his best friend, Sher, and performed an introduction. Sher was the Nizam of Tharistan and he and Jai had been childhood playmates. Sher was tall, black-haired and as sleekly handsome as a Bollywood movie star. Beside her, she felt Shelley breathe in deep and slow as though she was bracing herself and she almost laughed at her friend's susceptibility to a good-looking man until it occurred to her that she was even more susceptible to Jai.

'You chose a beautiful dress,' Jai murmured. 'It will look most appropriate in the photographs.'

'What photographs?' she asked with a frown.

'I have organised a photographer to record the occasion. Brides and grooms always want to capture such precious memories on film, I believe,' he advanced calmly. 'A photo will be released to the local media in Chandrapur and some day Hari may wish to look at them.'

Willow grasped that he had wanted her to look suitably bridal in the photographs and understood that there was nothing personal in the compliment. He was simply keen for her to visibly fit the bridal role so that the haste that had prompted their marriage was less obvious.

They entered the room where the ceremony was to take place. Willow focussed on a rather tired-looking display of flowers in a cheap vase and tensed as Jai threaded the wedding ring onto her finger. She turned in the circle of his arms, thinking numbly, *I am married to Jai now*, but it didn't feel remotely real. It felt like a fevered dream, much as that night in his arms had felt.

It felt a little more real when she shivered on the steps outside and posed for the photographer that awaited them. Jai smiled down at her, that killer smile of his that made her stupid heart flutter like a trapped bird inside her chest, and she remembered him smiling down at her that night in the aftermath of satisfaction. And, of course, Jai was pleased, she told herself ruefully—he had accomplished exactly what he wanted for Hari.

They returned to the house for a light lunch. Hari was brought down to meet Sher and then Sher offered to give Shelley a lift home.

'Does he have a limousine?' Willow asked with amusement in her clear eyes after she had hugged her scatty friend and promised to invite her out to Chandrapur for her annual holiday.

'I should think so. Sher made his fortune in the film

world before he went into business,' Jai told her. 'And we need to make tracks now for the airport.'

'I'll get changed.' But, still immobile, Willow hovered in the hall as Jai closed the distance between them and reached for her, his eyes as bright as a silvery blue polar flame.

'It is a shame that you have to take off that dress without me to do the honours,' Jai husked soft and low, his fiery attention locking so intently to the luscious pout of her pink lips that a convulsive shiver rippled through her slender frame. 'But if I joined you now, if I even dared to *touch* you, we would never make the flight this side of tomorrow.'

Her breath feathered dangerously in her throat, her entire body quickening and pulsing in response to that heated appraisal and the smooth eroticism of those words while he kept his lean, powerful frame carefully separate from hers. Her five senses were screaming with a hunger that hurt, the achingly familiar scent of him, which only made her want to be closer to taste him, the tingling in her fingertips at the prospect of touching him, the rasp of his dark deep voice in her ears throwing up the recollection of his ecstatic groan in the darkness of the night. It was an overwhelmingly potent combination.

'Go upstairs, *soniyaa*,' Jai urged thickly.

On trembling legs, Willow spun away, only to get a few steps and halt again to turn back to him. 'What does that mean?'

'In Hindi? Beautiful one,' he translated.

Shaken, Willow climbed the stairs, breathless from

the spell he had cast over her, the sheer shocking effect of that high-voltage sexuality focussed on her again. And yet he had not touched her once since she had moved into his house, had left her alone in her bed, maintaining a polite and pleasant attitude without a hint of intimacy when they met at occasional meal-times. Why was that? Why had he kept his distance even after she had agreed to marry him?

It had made Willow feel that his former attraction to her had been a short-lived thing, a flash in the pan, one of those weird, almost inexplicable incidents that struck only in a moment of temptation. Now it seemed that Jai was much more drawn to her than he had been willing to reveal but, while he had maintained his reserve, he had damaged her self-esteem because the awareness that she still craved him when he did not seem to return that compliment or share that weakness had felt humiliating.

After checking on Hari, who was enjoying a comfortable nap after his midday feed, Willow changed into one of her new outfits, an elegant fitted sheath dress and slender high heels teamed with a jacket for the cooler temperatures of London.

She had never travelled in a private jet before and Jai's was spectacularly well-appointed in terms of comfort and space. She sat down beside Hari's crib in the sleeping compartment and fell deeply, dreamlessly asleep. Jai glanced in at the two of them and when he saw her curled up on the bed next to his son's crib, his chest tightened, and he breathed in deep and slow. They were his wife and child, his family now, and, in spite of what he had expected, he didn't feel trapped. No, so intense was his hunger for her that he couldn't think further than the night ahead when that raw hunger would finally be sated.

Willow's strawberry-blond waves tumbled across the pristine pillow, her soft mouth tranquil, her heart-shaped face relaxed in slumber. She was a beauty and his tribe of relatives would greet her like manna from heaven for they had long awaited his marriage. Hari would simply be the cherry on the top of an award-winning cake.

Willow wakened to the news that they were landing at Chandrapur in half an hour and with the time difference it was almost lunchtime. Hari occupied the first fifteen minutes until Shanaya took over and the remainder of the time Willow hurtled around showering and changing.

Jai's bodyguards moved round them as their party emerged from the VIP channel and a roar of sound met her ears. Dozens of photographers were leaning over the barriers with cameras and shouting questions. The flashes blinded her. Until that unsettling moment she had forgotten how famous Jai was in his birth country. Single as well as very good-looking and immensely successful, he was highly photogenic and a media dream. His sports exploits on the polo field, his business achievements and the gloss of his playboy lifestyle provided plenty of useful gossip-column fodder.

'Sorry about that. I should've timed the announcement of our marriage better,' Jai breathed above her head as he steered her down a quiet corridor and back out to the sunlit tarmac. The heat of midday was more than she had expected as she scanned the clear blue sky above them and she was relieved to climb into the waiting vehicle that, Jai assured her, would quickly whisk them to journey's end.

'Where's Hari?' she gasped worriedly.

'In the car behind us. I often make this transfer by helicopter but Shanaya doesn't trust a helicopter with a child as precious as Hari.' Jai chuckled.

Precious, Willow savoured, enjoying that word being linked to her son. A crush of noisy traffic surrounded them, and she peered out of the windows. There were a lot of trucks and cars, colourful tuk-tuks painted with bright advertisements and many motorbikes with women in bright saris riding side-saddle behind the driver in what looked like a very precarious position. Horns blared, vehicles moved off and then ground to a sudden halt again to allow a herd of sacred bulls to wander placidly through the traffic. Bursts of loud music filtered into the car as they drove along beside a lake. By the side of the dusty road she saw dancers gyrating.

'It's a festival day and the streets are crammed. Luckily our palace isn't far,' Jai remarked.

Our palace.

Willow almost smiled at the designation, for she had never dreamt that those two words used together would ever feature in her future. 'So, you're taking me to where your family's story began—'

'No. My family's story began at the fortress in the

fourteenth century. Look out of the window,' Jai urged. 'See the fort on the crags above the city…'

Willow looked up in wonder at the vast red sandstone fortress sprawling across the cliffs above the city. 'My ancestor first invaded Chandrapur in the thirteenth century. It took his family a hundred and forty years of assaults and sieges but eventually they conquered the fort. We will visit it next week,' he promised. 'At present it's full of tourists…we would have no privacy.'

'Then, where are we going now?'

'The Lake Palace,' Jai told her lazily. 'It's surrounded by water and a private wildlife reserve and immensely private. It is where I make my home.'

'So you like…have a *choice* of palaces to use?' Willow was gobsmacked by the concept of having a selection.

'The third one is half palace, half hotel, built by my great-grandfather in high deco style in the twenties. We will visit there too,' Jai assured her calmly.

'*Three?* And that's it…here?' Willow checked.

'There is also the Monsoon Palace. A very much loved and spoilt wife in the sixteenth century accounts for that one,' Jai proffered almost apologetically. 'I leave it to the tourists.'

'You own an awful lot of property,' Willow remarked numbly.

'And now you own it too…as Sher reminded me, I didn't ask you to sign a pre-nuptial agreement,' Jai parried, shocking and startling her with that comment.

'We did get married in a hurry,' Willow conceded ruefully.

'Let us hope that neither of us live to regret that omission,' Jai murmured without expression.

'I'm not greedy. If we ever split up,' Willow told him in a rush, rising above the sinking sensation in her stomach at that concept, 'I won't *ever* try to take what's not mine. I'm very conscious that I entered this marriage with nothing and all I would ask for is enough to keep Hari and I somewhere secure and comfortable.'

'My biggest fear would be losing daily access to my son,' Jai confided with a harsh edge to his dark, deep voice.

Willow suppressed a shiver. 'Let's not even talk about it,' she muttered, turning to look at a quartet of women, their beautiful veils floating in the breeze as they carried giant metal water containers on their heads.

On both sides of the road stretched the desert, where only groves of acacia bushes, milk thistle and spiky grass grew in the sand. It was a hard, unforgiving land where water was of vital importance and only a couple of miles further on, where irrigation had been made possible, lay an oasis of small fields of crops and greenery, which utterly transformed the landscape.

His hand covered her tense fingers. 'We won't let anything split us up,' Jai told her. 'Hari's happiness depends on us staying together.'

'Did you miss your mother so much?' Willow heard herself ask without even thinking.

'I was a baby when she deserted my father and I have no memory of her,' Jai admitted flatly as he removed his hand from hers. 'I met her only once as an adult. I don't talk about my mother...*ever.*'

Willow swallowed painfully hard as her cheeks burned in receipt of that snub and she knew that she wouldn't be raising that thorny topic again.

CHAPTER FIVE

THEY DROVE ALONG a heavily wooded and fenced road and over a very decorative bridge on which a cluster of pale grey monkeys was perched. A tall archway ushered the car into a large central courtyard, ringed by a vast two-storey white building, picturesquely ornamented with domed roofs and a pillared frontage. Only then did Willow appreciate that they had arrived at the Lake Palace.

As she climbed out of the car, she was surprised to see a group of colourfully clad musicians drumming and playing with enthusiasm to greet their arrival. A trio of maids hurried down the steps fronting the long pillared façade of the building, bearing cool drinks, hot cloths for freshening up and garlands of marigolds. Behind them, from every corner of the complex poured more staff.

'It's traditional,' Jai dismissed when she gaped and commented.

'But why on earth do you employ so many people?'

Jai frowned. 'My father raised me to believe that our role in society is to provide employment wherever we can. Yes, I appreciate that we don't *need* the five-star triumphal welcome that my ancestors all enjoyed, but you must also appreciate that those who serve us rely on their employment here. One person may be responsible for keeping an entire tribe of relatives. Never seek to cut household costs unless you see evidence of dishonesty,' he warned her.

'I wasn't criticising,' Willow backtracked uncomfortably, self-consciously skimming her gaze across the lush garden fronting the palace instead. Glorious shrubs were in full bloom all around them. She couldn't immediately identify even one of the shrubs and was immediately keen to explore a new world of tropical plants. She turned as the other cars drew up behind them and immediately moved forward to reclaim Hari from Shanaya, her heart lifting as her son greeted her with a huge smile.

'I keep up the traditions as my father did,' Jai murmured softly by her side, lifting his son from her as the baby stretched out a hand to touch him and screwed up his face at his failure to make contact with his father. 'I employ as many people as possible. When I was younger, I was less far-seeing. When a household custom seemed outdated, I banned it, but it wasn't always possible for those involved to find another position on my staff. Modernising is to be welcomed but not if it means I'm putting people on the breadline to achieve it.'

'I understand,' Willow murmured, aware of the stares from the assembled staff, whom Jai invited closer to see their son. The level of their appreciation for the little boy in Jai's arms warmed her from inside out.

One of the gardeners approached her with a beautiful pink and yellow flower and extended it to her before bowing very low.

'He is proud to be the first to welcome the new Maharani to her home and he swears that even the frangipani blossom is not your equal,' Jai translated with an amused grin.

They walked into a huge circular hall fashioned entirely of marble and supported on carved pillars while Jai directed her towards the curving staircase and up to the landing. He walked down an imposing corridor lined with portraits of the former Maharajas of Chandrapur and showed her into a room already set up as a nursery for Hari.

Willow reclaimed her son and sat down with him.

'When you're free I'll join you for a late lunch. I have some work matters to take care of,' Jai told her before leaving again.

Hari needed to be changed and fed and there were innumerable staff hovering, eager to take care of his needs for her, but Willow didn't want to lose her position of being first and foremost in her baby's life, nor did she want him exposed to too many new faces and different childcare practices at once. Overpowered by the grandeur of Jai's home, she also needed a moment or two of doing ordinary things to feel comfortable again. Thanking everyone cheerfully for the help she wouldn't accept, she saw to Hari herself before finally laying him down for his nap.

When she emerged from the nursery again, a mous-tachioed man in a bright red turban and traditional attire spread open an inlaid brass door on the other side of the landing and bowed his head in a deferential invitation. Willow passed by him into the most breathtaking interior and her steps slowed as she paused to admire the intricate glass mosaic tiles set into the walls to make superb pictures of a bygone age. Depicted on the walls were hunting scenes with elephants and tigers and grand and very vivid ceremonial processions. Talking on his phone, Jai was striding across the shaded terrace beyond the room that overlooked the lake. In that airy space a table and chairs were arranged.

Willow watched him move, absorbing the elegant grace of his lean, powerful figure as he moved and talked, spreading expressive fingers, shifting his hands this way and that in fluid stress or dismissal of a point. A thrill of desire pierced her soft and deep, making her breath catch in her throat. He was so extremely good-looking and she was married to him now, which still didn't seem real to her. His head turned as he noticed her hovering for the first time and the heat of his stare sent the blood drumming up beneath her skin.

Willow sank down into a dining chair. A napkin was laid over her lap with a flourish by a bearded middle-aged man.

'This is Ranjit,' Jai explained, dropping his phone down on the tabletop and settling down opposite her. 'He speaks excellent English and oversees our household. Anything you need, you ask him, and he will provide it. After we've eaten, I'll show you around.'

'It's a fascinating building and the surroundings only make it more exotic,' she commented, watching a crocodile slide off a mudflat into the lake, his two beady eyes creepy bumps above the surface as he swam. 'But I shouldn't like to meet that gator on a dark night.'

'For safety we only ever leave this building in vehicles. I'll take you on a mini safari some afternoon, although it's amazing how many of the animals you can view from up here. Sooner or later, they all visit the water. He's not a gator, by the way, he's a marsh crocodile.'

'I don't know much about wild animals,' she confided. 'Only what I've learned from watching documentaries. Tell me, why so many palaces?'

'Every generation wanted to be current. Centuries ago this palace and the land around it was for the royal family to hunt.' Jai grimaced. 'And now it's a wildlife reserve. The original fortress above the city is magnificent but could not possibly be adapted to modern life and my grandfather's deco palace is more of a showpiece than a home. Approximately two thirds of that building is now an award-winning hotel and the remaining wing remains ours. We will entertain my relatives and friends there at a party to be held in a few weeks to celebrate our marriage. Is there anyone you wish to invite on your own behalf?'

'No relatives left alive,' she reminded him. 'And no friends who could afford to fly out to India just for a party.'

'I would cover the expense for any of your guests. Shelley?'

Willow winced and coloured. 'She has no holiday leave left. She had to take time off to help me with Hari after he was born.'

His ebony brows furrowed. 'Why? Was he very challenging?'

'No, I was the problem,' Willow confessed. 'I had to have an emergency Caesarean and it was a couple of weeks before I was fit enough to look after him on my own. They don't keep you in hospital after surgery for long these days.'

Jai compressed his lips. 'And yet you *still* didn't think of contacting me for help?'

'We got through it,' Willow muttered with a troubled shrug.

'Why…an emergency?' he pressed. 'What happened?'

'I'd been in labour for hours and it wasn't progressing as it should've done. Hari was a big baby and they had to operate for his sake.' Willow relaxed a little as the food arrived and relaxed even more when she registered that it was entirely a British chicken meal without even a hint of spice.

Jai's high cheekbones were prominent beneath his bronzed skin. He could have lost his son without ever knowing he existed. He could have lost Willow as well. The acknowledgement shook him and her lack of guilt on that score annoyed him, no matter how hard he worked at suppressing such negative reactions. Jai was accustomed to being in charge, used to women who were eager to please him, certainly not a woman who shunned his support and thrust her independence unapologetically in his face. Or perhaps it was the fact that she *still* refused to admit that she had made a mistake in not telling him that she was pregnant. Had behaved as though he could have no possible importance as a father in his son's life.

Or, more probably, had she thought of her own father's cruel indifference to her feelings when she'd failed to meet his exacting academic standards? Possibly she had decided that a father figure was not so necessary. Jai, however, had enjoyed a father who was caring and supportive and it was a role he took very seriously. Suddenly impatient, he thrust his plate away and stood up.

'Let me show you the palace,' he urged, watching as she rose to her feet, her jewelled eyes bright in her heart-shaped face, her lush mouth pink and succulent. Even as he dragged his attention from her mouth, he was hard and full and throbbing. The result of more than a year's celibacy, he told himself in exasperation. In those circumstances, it was natural, even normal, for him to be almost embarrassingly wound up. He had not gone that long without sex since he became an adult. There was no reason whatsoever for him to get worked up about the prospect of having sex with his wife when it was a purely practical element of a marriage undertaken simply to confirm his son's status.

He escorted her downstairs to the two-storey library that had been his father's pride and joy. Sheltered beneath one of the domes, it rejoiced in a twisting narrow marble staircase to the upper floor.

Willow stopped dead to look around herself in amazement at the towering columns of bookcases. In several places there were alcoves backed by stained-glass window embrasures and upholstered with comfortable cushions, little reading nooks, she registered in fascination, never having entered so inviting a library space. 'It's absolutely gorgeous,' she murmured appreciatively. 'I may not be academic but I love to read, so it's ironic that all the books here will mostly be in another language.'

'No. There are many English books in this library.' Jai watched her sink down into one of the reading nooks. A tiny delicate figure in a pale blue dress that somehow brought out the peach glints in her hair and the perfect clarity of her porcelain skin, against which her green eyes gleamed like emeralds.

Willow inched back on her elbows until she was fully reclined, her head resting back against a soft cushion, and grinned. 'I can tell you now... I'll be spending time in here.'

Jai studied her with helpless intensity. She was entirely unaware of her own appeal, entirely divorced from the reality that her hem had ridden up and a deeply erotic view of the space between her slender thighs was open to him. Without even being aware of it, prompted more by his senses than by anything else, Jai moved closer. 'You're the most beautiful thing in here,' he said in a driven undertone.

'Less of the sauce, Jai...as Shelley would say,' Willow teased, coming up on her elbows again and preparing to get up. 'I'm not and have never been a beauty. You don't need to say that sort of stuff to me just because we're married. I don't expect it.'

Jai moved so fast she was startled when he came down over her, caging her in the nook with his lean, powerful body. 'I very rarely say anything I don't mean,' he rasped, coming down to her to claim her mouth with a hungry brevity that only made her crave him more. 'It is for me to tell you that you are beautiful, not for you to disagree, because what would *you* know about it?'

Willow blinked, disconcerted by that sudden kiss. 'Well…er…'

'Because you haven't got a clue!' Jai growled in reproof, pushing down on her with his lean hips and shifting with sinuous grace against her pelvis to acquaint her with his arousal.

It was the most primal thing he had ever done to her and it set Willow on fire, inside and out. It was as though he'd lit a pulse in the most sensitive area of her body, a part of herself she had more or less forgotten existed after the discovery that she was pregnant. There had been no more lying awake restless in the night hours, shifting in frustration while she wantonly recalled the heated expertise of his body on hers. No, she had shut that sensual side down, recognising that that was what had got her into trouble in the first instance and that, with a child on the way, she had more important stuff to focus on. But in that moment, there was *nothing* more important than the powerful allure of Jai's hot-blooded invitation and the wanting took her by storm. Her arms reached up of their own seeming volition and snaked round his neck to pull him down to her.

'No, *not* here…perhaps some other day but not on

what is virtually our wedding night,' Jai specified authoritatively.

Willow pushed him back from her, the taste of humiliation burning in her cheeks and souring in her mouth, which had so readily, so eagerly opened for his. She came upright, smoothing down her rucked-up frock like a bristling kitten. He was always so much in control that it infuriated her at that moment. One minute he was luring her in, the next pushing her away! It bore too many reminders of how much he had craved her that first night in contrast with his cold withdrawal the next morning.

'One of the servants is sweeping rugs on the upper level,' Jai added in an undertone. 'I could order him to leave but it seems unnecessary when we have a bedroom.'

'I suppose by the time you get to your age you get settled in your ways!' Willow snapped back at him tartly, because she was mortified and not really listening, had been so far gone to common sense indeed for several seconds as she reached for him that she wouldn't have noticed if a trumpet band had marched past her. 'I'm more of an al fresco kind of girl!' she added, even though she wasn't quite sure that those two words matched what she had intended to convey: an image of her being more sexually brave and adventurous than he was, which was of course ridiculous when he was the only man she had ever been with and his experience was presumably much greater than hers.

'No. I know that my bride deserves a level of care and esteem from me that she did not receive on the last occasion we were together,' Jai countered flatly, wondering what other sexual expectations she had of him, coming to grips with that apparent challenge with a shot of adrenalin charging through his veins.

In reality, Jai had never been challenged or questioned in the bedroom. Women invariably reacted as though everything he did there was incredible and told him so repeatedly. For the first time he wondered if it was a fact that he *was* too conservative, raised as he had been by a rather elderly parent from a different generation from those of his peers, a father with a distinctly Victorian take on the opposite sex.

Willow rolled her eyes at him, eyes that turned a darker catlike green in temper, he noted, marvelling that he had gone twenty-nine years on Planet Earth without ever before meeting a woman prepared to disagree with him. On the surface she seemed so mild in temperament and shy, although she was a wild woman in bed, Jai acknowledged, reaching for her hand, finding she snatched her fingers back, smiling because he was genuinely amused.

And that sunlit smile of Jai's steamrollered the temper out of Willow as though he had thrown a bucket of water over her because, deep down inside, she *knew* she was being childish, bitter and insecure and that he hadn't earned that response. She looked up at him and those eyes of his were bright between lush black curling lashes and her heart literally went ka-boom inside her and clenched. She slid her hand back into his and in silence they left the library.

'I'll show you the rest of the place some other time,'

Jai told her, walking her along the corridor to the double doors at the other end of the landing. A servant somehow contrived to snake at phenomenal speed round from the other side of the landing and throw the doors open for them and quietly shut them again in their wake.

The main bedroom was another awe-inspiring room, all of a glitter, with flowers and foliage hand-painted in shades of cream and gold with tiny inset mirrors everywhere on the walls, reflecting light into an interior that could otherwise have seemed dark because there were no windows. Instead there were densely carved stone screens open to the elements to filter in fresh air.

'It was remodelled a century ago. It used to be part of the *zenana* where the royal women lived in *purdah*, only allowed to be seen by male family members. My father could still remember elderly relatives who grew up in that lifestyle, men and women living separately,' Jai told her softly as she fingered the screen to look out through the tiny holes to the courtyard below, trying to imagine what it would have been like to only have a view of a life one was not allowed to actively share.

'It must've been horrible,' she whispered, her tiny nose wrinkling up expressively.

'Perhaps not if it was all a woman knew. Going back only a handful of generations, we are talking mainly about women who couldn't read or write or really do anything without a host of servants. Of course, there were exceptions, the educated daughters of more enlightened men, who were able to establish more equal relationships with their husbands. Women prepared to shout back…like you.'

Willow whirled round. 'Like *me*?' she gasped. 'Jai, I'm one of the most easy-going women you'll ever meet!'

Ice-blue eyes gleamed, sentencing her to stillness. 'Not in my experience…and I like it,' he completed almost as an afterthought.

Was your mother like that and was that why your parents divorced? she suddenly wanted to ask, and her teeth worried at her lower lip before she could make that mistake. 'You…do?'

'If I have expectations of you, naturally you must have expectations of me,' Jai traded, settling his hands to her slender hips in the smouldering silence that seemed to be filtering through the room.

Her heart was banging so hard inside her chest that even catching her breath was a challenge. She gazed up into those extraordinary pale blue eyes welded to her and her heart hammered even faster while a clenching sensation assailed her between her thighs. Sometimes he struck her as so beautiful, he left her breathless. No points for that inane thought, she tried to scold herself, but her body wasn't listening when right at that moment she craved Jai's mouth more than she had ever craved anything. And he gave it to her, hot and hard, exactly what she wanted and needed, the urgency of his lips on hers, the tangling of their tongues, the sudden tightening of his strong arms around her quivering form. She was only dimly aware of her feet leaving the floor and being brought down on the wide low bed.

With an effort, Jai restrained himself from tearing off her clothes like a barbarian because he was burning up for her. It would be different between them this time, the way it *should* have been the night of Hari's conception, he assured himself, snatching in a sustaining breath as he raised her up from the pillows to run down the zip on her dress with the finesse he had somehow forgotten that first time. Stray half-formed thoughts were running through his brain, his father confiding that love in combination with unalloyed lust was a trap of the cruellest order, a trap that had almost destroyed the older man. Jai had always known that he didn't have to worry about such a weakness because he was controlled, cautious, far less naive and trusting than his unfortunate parent had been when he had fallen like a ton of bricks for Jai's mother. Cecilia, the apparent love of his life when he had been twenty-one, Jai conceded cynically, had done that much for him, at least.

Jai lifted the dress over her head and the instant he glimpsed the pouting perfection of her tiny breasts cupped in something white and intrinsically feminine, the blood ran roaring through his veins. He gritted his teeth, briefly marvelling at the fierce possessiveness shock-waving through him. Willow was his wife, the mother of his son, and it was perfectly natural for him to experience such responses, but it was something new, which had to be why alarm bells were shrieking inside his head.

'What's wrong?' Willow asked abruptly.

'Nothing whatsoever, *soniyaa*,' Jai declared, crushing her mouth under his in a surge of denial at those alarm bells.

Willow's hands crept up to his shoulders, her anxious gaze pinned to his lean, darkly handsome face. 'Take your shirt off,' she almost whispered.

Jai laughed at her sudden boldness, watching the colour build in her cheeks as he leant back and loosed the buttons before peeling it off, enjoying the way in which her eyes stayed glued to him, recognising with satisfaction that his bride wanted him as much as he wanted her. He slid off the bed and began to strip, deliberately taking his time, reacting to the synergy between them.

Willow rested back against the pillows, entranced by the display because she hadn't seen Jai naked on the night of the funeral, had only caught little glimpses of him in the dim light filtering into her bedroom from the landing. And the more he took off clothes-wise, the harder it got for her to breathe through her constricted lungs, because he was a masculine work of art, dark-hair-dusted, lean muscles flexing with his every movement, that long, powerful body of his making her fingers tingle and her breasts swell and tighten inside her bra. She had not known that it was even possible for such a response to assail her and it shook her and then he was coming back to her on the bed, a symphony of lean bronzed masculinity, boldly aroused, and she acknowledged the surge of dampness at the heart of her with burning cheeks.

'What are you blushing about?' Jai husked, sliding a hand to her slender spine to release her bra.

'I liked watching you undress,' she said, as if that was some kind of revelation.

'Let me tell you a secret,' Jai rasped, long fingers curling round a straining nipple. 'I would like watching you undress just as much. I want you as much as you want me…'

'Honestly?' Willow exclaimed as she quivered all over, not quite believing that statement of his.

Jai watched her soft pink mouth open and suddenly he knew he was done with talking, the raw hunger he was struggling to keep within acceptable boundaries overpowering him. He pressed her back against the pillows with the force of his mouth on hers, all the keyed-up ferocious urgency of his need released in that kiss.

Willow squirmed beneath his weight, her hands lifting to clutch at the smooth skin of his strong shoulders, the sheer heat of him an education, a memory, another burning coal to add to the bonfire in her pelvis and the hot, sweet ache stirring there. 'Oh, Jai…' she muttered, pulling her lips free to get some oxygen back into her starved body. 'I don't know what it is that you do to me but it's almost scary.'

That admission so exactly matched Jai's thought about her effect on him that it spooked him, and he buried it fast, too full of need to concentrate on anything else…

CHAPTER SIX

WILLOW QUIVERED AND shook as Jai worked his sensual path down over her squirming body.

She was back in that sensual world where her heart hammered and her body burned with hunger. Her nipples were stiff little points begging for his attention and he dallied there a long time, driving her insane with frustration as her hips rocked on the mattress because she wanted more, *needed* more. 'Jai, *please*...' she gasped, the burning ache throbbing between her thighs more than she could bear.

'This time, we're going to do this *right*,' he ground out, his bright gaze glittering with resolve.

'But there is no right or wrong here...only what we want,' Willow protested, running an exploring hand down over a long, lean expanse of his torso and delving lower, finding him, stroking him, revelling in the satin-smooth hardness of his thrusting manhood, which every cell in her body craved.

Above her, Jai groaned, pushed her hand away, determined not to be deflected by his hunger. But her fingers slid up into his hair to drag him down to her so that she could have his mouth, the deep delve of his tongue, the awesome nip of his teeth along her sensitive lower lip until she was panting for breath and straining up to him, slender thighs wrapping round his narrow hips to hold him there.

Anticipation was licking through Willow in a raging storm of electrifying impulses as she tangled with his tongue, arched her back so that the hard wall of his chest abraded the straining tips of her breasts and ran her hands down his long, lean flanks. Her hunger was racing out of control, the way it always seemed to be with Jai, and she knew she would be mortified later, but just then she couldn't prevent herself from urging him on by every means within her power.

And with a raw expletive, Jai suddenly surrendered without warning. He reached for a condom, dealing with it fast before pushing her back and plunging into her so hard and deep that her neck extended, and her head fell back. Her hair tumbled like rumpled silk across the pillows as she cried out at the raw sweet force of that invasion. He rode her like a runaway horse and she angled up to him in feverish yearning, the wild excitement he fired in her shock-waving through her in a storm of response. It was everything she remembered from that first night, the naked, burning, demanding heat of the violent passion that had brought her alive. There was nothing cool about it, nothing scheduled or controlled. It took over, wiped everything else from her brain and it was, she dimly registered, incredibly addictive.

All the lean power that was Jai drove her to an explosive orgasm that went splintering through her and lit up every nerve ending in her trembling body. In the aftermath of what had felt like a hurricane striking and devastating every sense, she was weak.

'Epic,' Jai breathed with driven honesty, yet still furious with himself for having failed to meet his own standards yet again and for having fallen on her like an animal. Once again he questioned what it was about her that made everything go wrong when it should have been going right *this* time around, and that only put him in mind of something else he was keen to discuss. No time like the present, he decided, tugging her into the shelter of his arms and dropping a kiss on her smooth brow.

'I wish I'd been around when you were carrying Hari,' he admitted.

Surprise winged through Willow and she was so taken aback she sat up to look down at him while simultaneously thinking how very beautiful he was in the sunlight filtering in through the screen. A five o'clock shadow accentuating his superb bone structure, his extraordinarily light black-fringed eyes intent on her. She swallowed hard. 'Yes, well, it's not something we can do much about now.'

'No?' Jai pressed. 'But surely you regret the decisions you made back then.'

Willow stiffened. 'I'm not sure that I do. I did the best I could at the time, and I believed I was doing what was best for both of us.'

Jai sat up with a jerk, his lean, powerful bronzed body tense. 'But you were wrong and *I* missed out on you being pregnant and on Hari's arrival, not to mention every little change in him during the first seven months of his life!' he shot back at her with unexpected ire.

Willow breathed in deep. 'Well, I'm sorry about that,' she muttered uncomfortably, wondering why on earth he was in such a dark mood.

Jai sprang out of bed. 'I don't think you're one bit sorry for having denied me knowledge of my own child!' he fired back at her accusingly.

'Obviously I'm sorry that it upset you but be fair,' Willow urged, disconcerted by that sudden anger of his. 'I honestly didn't realise how much Hari would mean to you or that you would feel so committed to our child once you found out about him.'

'Had it been left to you I would *never* have found out about him!' Jai intoned grimly. 'And I still don't understand what I did or said to deserve that treatment.'

Hugging the sheet round her, Willow had turned very pale, registering that she was finally catching a glimpse of the kind of feelings that Jai had, for whatever reason, concealed from her. He was still furious that she had not told him that she was pregnant. 'It was the way you treated me the morning after that night we spent together,' she told him honestly, for that was the truth of how she had felt at the time.

'Nothing I said justifies your silence when you were carrying my child and in need of my support!' Jai launched back at her without hesitation.

'I managed perfectly well without your support,'

Willow snapped back defensively. 'But that morning you condemned me for not telling you that I was a virgin, insisting that you would never have touched me had you known.'

'That was the truth!' Jai sliced in ruthlessly.

'You also said that what we had done was *wrong*,' she reminded him stubbornly. 'And you accused me of still having a teenaged crush on you. I don't know many women who would've wanted to contact a bloke who said stuff like that afterwards.'

'It was your duty to contact me!' Jai interposed icily.

But Willow was only warming up, a keen memory of her feelings back then awakened by his censure. In a sudden movement she bodily yanked the sheet from the bed and left it, but only after wrapping it securely round her, and her colour was high. 'Oh, forget your stupid duty, Jai…it was how you made me *feel* that ruled how I behaved!' she slammed back at him. 'You made it sound like sleeping with me was the biggest *mistake* you had ever made.'

Jai flung his proud dark head back, his sensual mouth flattening into a thin hard line. 'It *was*…'

'Well then, don't be surprised that I didn't get in touch because if that night was such a mistake for you, I was in no mood to tell you that, to add to that mistake, I had also conceived a child that you obviously would not want.'

'Those are two separate issues,' Jai objected. 'My night with you was ill-advised but my child could *never* be a mistake.'

'You see how you're simply changing your wording to make yourself sound better?' Willow condemned angrily and, although she was always slow to anger, she was very, very angry just at that moment because, once again, Jai was making her feel bad. 'Why is it so hard for you to accept that you are not the only one of us to have pride? And you humiliated me that morning and made me feel *awful*. You spent more time talking about my father's books than you did on what had happened between us!'

'That is untrue.'

'No, it is true!' Willow hissed back at him, green eyes blazing. 'I disagreed with what you said about that night and, because I dared to disagree, that was the end of the discussion. You didn't *care* about how you were making me feel.'

Jai registered that a huge argument had blossomed and decided to walk away rather than continue it, continuing it being beneath his dignity in his own mind. He flung open the concealed door in the panelling to the en suite bathroom and closed it firmly behind him, shaken by the fire in his bride and forced to consider her explanation by the essential streak of fairness that he had been raised to respect.

He had *not* humiliated her, he told himself fiercely as he stepped into his luxury rainforest shower, and then he recalled an image of her standing, small and pale and stiff, that morning. Well, *if* he had humiliated her, he had certainly not intended to do so. All he had done was express his feelings concerning their sexual encounter. But he had done so to a former virgin, who

could understandably have felt very rejected by such a
negative attitude, his conscience slung in with unwelcome timing. He had consciously been trying to distance himself from a chain of events that shamed him,
he acknowledged grimly. And she had vehemently disagreed with him and he hadn't known how to handle
that, he conceded in grudging addition.

The door of the en suite bathroom opened, Willow
finally having realised that the panelling effectively
concealed doors into dressing rooms and other facili-
ties only obvious to someone who actually saw a door
being used.

'And now you're doing it to me again!' Willow
declared angrily from the doorway, incensed by his
departure. 'Walking away because I disagree with
you!'

In the spacious shower cubicle Jai grimaced. 'I'll
join you in a few minutes and we'll talk.'

'Oh, don't bother on my account!' his bride said
sharply. 'It's probably jet lag but I'm exhausted and
I'm going back to bed for a nap!'

Tears lashing her hurt eyes and angrily blinked
back, Willow clambered back into the comfortable bed
and curled up into a brooding ball of resentment. Some
people didn't like conflict and maybe he was one of
them. Obviously, she needed to brush up on her com-
munication skills and stop her temper jumping in first
because she was willing to admit that nobody had *ever*
made her as angry as Jai could. He was the very first
person she had ever shouted at and in retrospect she
was full of chagrin and regret because even she knew

that that was not the way to persuade anyone round to a new point of view.

But she just felt so wounded by his outlook because those months pregnant and alone but for Shelley had been very tough. And she truly hadn't appreciated that Jai was still so bone-deep outraged at her failure to tell him that she had conceived. No, he had managed to hide that reaction very effectively until he'd got her to the altar, she reflected bitterly, and only now was she seeing that, for all his appearance of frankness, Jai was much more complex below that surface façade of cool than he seemed and quite capable of nourishing reactions that she'd not even begun to detect.

But then, shouldn't she have expected a few surprises when they were only really getting to know each other now? When it was only a practical marriage rather than one based on love and caring? Well, he definitely had all the caring genes when it came to their son, Willow conceded reluctantly, he just didn't have them for *her*. She felt hollow inside, as if she had been gutted, and a quiver of self-loathing ran through her that she could still be so sensitive to Jai's opinions.

He thought she had let Hari *and* him down by not informing him that she was pregnant. He would hold it against her to the grave, she thought morosely, suspecting that Jai was as proverbially unforgiving and hard as that vast sandstone fortress above Chandrapur. He expected, he wanted perfection and she had a whole pile of flaws. Jai had flaws too but, unlike her, seemed supremely unaware of them. Of course, she rather suspected that his father had been of a very dif-

ferent nature from hers, not the type to linger on his
child's every failing. On that deflating note, Willow
fell asleep.

A smiling, dark-skinned face above hers wakened
her with a gentle touch on her shoulder.

'I am your maid, Alisha,' the young woman informed her, bobbing her head. 'His Royal Highness
the Maharaja will be dining in an hour.'

Dimly, Willow registered that daylight had gone
and wondered in dismay how long she had slept, before glancing at her watch and discovering that she had
slept for far longer than she had planned.

'I have run a bath for you…but there is a shower…
it is your choice,' Alisha added with yet another huge
good-natured smile. 'I have also laid out clothes for
you.'

Willow was bemused by being awarded that amount
of personal attention until it occurred to her that she
was receiving it purely as a mark of respect towards
Jai's wife, a sort of reflected glory she felt ill-prepared
to handle. But she would have to *learn* to handle it, she
told herself urgently, because she was living in a formal
household crammed with servants and she was always
going to be the Maharani of Chandrapur within these
walls even if she didn't feel as though she had any true
right to such high status and esteem.

'A bath would be great,' she agreed, since it had
already been run for her, and she sat up to slide her
arms into the silky robe being extended for her use,
thinking that Shelley would adore hearing about such
luxuries because that kind of personal attention was

non-existent in the world in which she and her friend had grown up in. Not so much a world, she ruminated wryly, as the school of hard knocks, which had formed them both from childhood.

Her bathroom was separate from Jai's, Willow realised with a guilty grimace as she sat in her bath surrounded by floating rose petals and some sort of scented oil. No wonder he had seemed startled by her following him in there to confront him yet again, she conceded, heat flushing her cheeks in sudden mortification. No, arguments when she was overtired and cross were not to be recommended, she conceded ruefully, although she had said nothing that even now, calmer and cooler, she would have been willing to retract.

Her maid had laid out a long dress for her and Willow winced, getting a hint of what her life was expected to be like in the Lake Palace. She was supposed to dress up simply to dine with her bridegroom. Had she been a more conventional new bride, she would've been doing that automatically though, she reflected ironically, an arrow of remorse piercing her that that was not the case between her and Jai. On the surface their marriage might seem normal but underneath it was a sham, bereft of the understanding, love and knowledge that what he had termed 'a normal marriage' would need to thrive.

Alisha directed her downstairs, where Ranjit guided her across the echoing main hallway into yet another splendid room furnished with a formal dining table and chairs. Coloured glass panels portraying a fanciful forest full of fantasy animals decorated the walls and it was wonderfully cool and air-conditioned.

'So, some of this place is air-conditioned,' Willow remarked as Jai strode in, and in stark comparison to her moreover, barefoot and clad with almost laughable informality in an open-necked red shirt and well-fitted designer jeans that outlined his lean hips and long, powerful thighs. As always, he looked amazing and her breath shortened in her throat as involuntarily she relived the feel of his hot skin below her stroking fingers, the springy softness of his black hair and, ultimately, the crashing intoxicating surge of his mouth on hers.

Burning up with chagrin inside her own skin, Willow dropped hastily into a chair.

'Yes, those rooms where it was possible without seriously damaging the décor. If you find our bedroom too warm, just tell me. I will make it possible there too, but I do not expect us to spend much time here during the hottest months of the year,' he imparted smoothly, his dark low-pitched voice, richer than velvet, brushing against skin suddenly pebbling with goose bumps. 'The summer heat can be unbearable.'

Willow nodded as a wide selection of little bites was brought in to serve as a first course and Ranjit carefully indicated the spicy items lest they not be to her taste, while Jai talked about the local sights he intended to show her. She tried a sample of flavours while wondering if Jai intended merely to act as though that argument had not taken place, but, once the staff had melted away with delivery of their main course, Jai fell suddenly silent and she glanced up from her plate anxiously to find those wolfish ice-blue eyes locked hard to her.

'There is something I must say,' he began, uncharacteristically hesitant in tone. 'There are times when we will perceive events in a dissimilar light because of the different cultures in which we grew up...'

'Obviously,' Willow breathed tightly.

'The morning after we spent that first night together is one of those events. For me, it *was* inexcusably wrong to take a woman's virginity when I was not in a serious relationship with her. I could not treat that as though it was something of no consequence, but I was equally guilty of having made the assumption that you would *not* be so innocent, living in your more liberal society,' he completed levelly.

'Jai, I—' Willow began awkwardly, not having foreseen quite how much of an issue that had genuinely been for him.

'Let me finish,' he urged, topping up her wine glass with a lithe and elegant hand. 'I felt very guilty that day. I was deeply ashamed of my behaviour. I took advantage of you when you were grieving and alone and in need of support.'

'It didn't feel that way to me,' Willow protested, breaking in.

'We are talking about how it felt to be *me* that morning,' Jai reminded her drily. 'I felt like a total bastard, who had seduced an innocent young woman, and clearly how I felt fed into making you feel rejected and insulted...but that result was *not* intentional. I remained sincerely concerned for your well-being, which is why

I attempted to see you again a couple of months later, by which time you must've known you were pregnant.'

At the reminder, Willow flushed a discomfited brick red. 'And Shelley lied for me and said she didn't know where I was because she *knew* I didn't want to see you again,' she filled in for him uneasily. 'I'm sorry but that was just how I felt back then. I was a bit naive. I was feeling well and I thought I would manage fine without you. Before I forget, can I ask you something off-topic?'

His winged ebony brows drew together in a frown at that query. 'You can ask me anything although I cannot always guarantee an answer.'

'Why did I have to get all dressed up in a long fancy gown when you're wearing jeans and no shoes?'

And the tension still thick round the table just evaporated then and there as Jai flung his handsome dark head back and laughed with disconcerting appreciation of that simple question. Raking a long-fingered brown hand through his silky black hair, he surveyed her with amusement still glittering like stardust in his bright black-lashed eyes. 'I can only assume that it was my mother's practice or my grandmother's practice to get "all dressed up" for dinner because that is how long it has been since this palace had a mistress. Your maid will have been given advice on what you would want to wear for such an occasion and, since you are English, it may well date back to the years of the British Raj,' he warned her with a wide smile. 'And be generations out of date. You don't need to dress up for dinner for my benefit. You can wear whatever you like, *soniyaa.*'

That smile of his and the endearment on top of the explanation he had carefully outlined melted that hard little knot that had formed in Willow's chest earlier that day. Jai was trying and she recognised that, respected him for it, *liked* him for it. But at the other end of the scale she was wondering what other misunderstandings would crop up when there were such basic differences between their outlooks on life. Even so, stifling that anxious thought, she smiled back at him, shaken to discover how fast she wanted him again, as if that afternoon of passion had only been a dream.

'This evening I will show you around what remains of your new home and tomorrow we will go out and explore,' Jai promised her lazily.

And the week that followed was full of enjoyment, occasional challenges and surprises and the beginning of a fascination with her surroundings that rooted deep. There was the ancient old gardener who brought her flowers every day, and the cook who had a burning desire to know what her favourite foods were, and the sharing of playtimes with Hari and his father, so that a lifestyle that at first had seemed strange became her new normal. Hari was always surrounded by loving carers and it was not unusual to hear his chuckles as he was rocked in a solid-silver nursery swing that had rocked his ancestors for generations and which really should have been in a museum.

Willow visited the Hindu temple and the white marble park of elaborate ancestral tombs that overlooked the holy lake. She accepted garlands and blessings and small gifts for Hari as well as her share of the awe that

Jai's mere presence inspired amongst the locals. She posed for photos for the local journalists, who were much more respectful than those they had encountered at the airport.

She learned that English was widely spoken and became less intimidated by strangers, her confidence growing at the warm welcome she received everywhere. She explored the massive old fortress on the cliffs above the city, bowled over by its magnificent décor and huge rooms, with Jai by her side sharing funny stories about his heritage, which no guide could ever have equalled. And she saw a tiger in the wild for the first time, ironically not on the mini safari in an open-topped SUV that Jai had taken her on, but from the shaded dining terrace she watched the animal slink in his glorious orange and black striped coat out of the jungle to pad down at his leisure to drink at the edge of the lake.

By day they explored the sights but by night, mostly, they explored each other, she reflected with a wanton and slightly self-conscious little wriggle of recollection. She couldn't keep her hands off Jai, and it seemed to be a case of a mutual chemical reaction. Jai electrified her every time he touched her, but when he had pressed her down in one of those reading nooks in the library that day, and possessed her with uninhibited passion in one of their most exciting encounters to date, she had realised afterwards, by his faint but perceptible discomfiture, that Jai wasn't in control either.

Jai was pondering that problem for himself in his office. He had been spending too much time with his wife and not enough time working, he censured himself, well aware that he was sidestepping the real issue nagging at him. He had married her for his son's sake, he reminded himself impatiently. He had planned on a perfectly civilised but essentially detached and sophisticated partnership in marriage, in which both of them nourished their own interests and friendships. He had never planned on hot, sweaty, wildly exciting naked encounters in every secluded corner of his home. He had never planned to keep her awake half the night in the marital bed to the extent that she regularly fell asleep in the afternoon heat, exhausted by his demands. Nobody needed to warn Jai that he was already in the grip of the overpowering lust that he had been warned against many times.

And that acknowledgement disturbed Jai on every level. He didn't do love; he flatly refused to do love. He was a great believer in moderation in all things. He had, after all, grown up with the tragic evidence of what love could do to a man, not to mention his own disillusionment at the hands of his former fiancée, Cecilia. Love, however, had totally broken his father, a strong man, a good man, an intelligent man, yet none of those strengths had saved him from the consequences of losing the wife he had adored. His father's depressions, loneliness, bitterness, his inability to replace that lost wife with even a female friend, had taught Jai how dangerously harmful those softer emotions could be for a man when it came to a woman.

He didn't want the stress of that complication with Willow: he was determined not to *need* her, to look for her when she wasn't there or to allow her to sink so deeply into the fabric of his everyday life that she became more important than she should be. Liking, kindness and respect were absolutely all that were required from him as a husband and anything beyond that would be madness…a madness that he wouldn't touch.

CHAPTER SEVEN

A WEEK AFTER Jai reached that decision, and unhappily warding off her low spirits as a result of that decision, Willow was dealing with the post her social secretary had gathered for her to peruse.

Yes, she was tickled pink by the idea that she could possibly require a social secretary. Only after she had seen the pile of invitations, congratulatory letters and wedding gifts in Samaira's small office had she realised that she had been ridiculously naive not to appreciate that Jai's position with an international charity foundation, his local role as a former ruler and his recent marriage would not also make demands on *her*.

'And there was *this*,' the tiny, beautiful Samaira finally declared, sliding a sheet of paper across the desk and rising at the same time to leave the library. 'It's an email that arrived on the Maharaja's historical website and I was given it by his PA, Mitul. He took the liberty of printing it out, which I hope was correct,' she added hopefully. 'We felt that the enquiry was for you and best given to you.'

Surprised by that seemingly unnecessarily detailed explanation, Willow frowned and glanced down at the paper, looking first at the signature. Milly St John, a name that meant nothing whatsoever to her. She studied the couple of lines in the message before comprehension gripped her with sudden dismay.

As you have recently married my son and are the mother of my grandson, I would be very grateful if you would agree to meet with me alone and in private at my hotel in Chandrapur on the seventeenth.'

Willow paled, because it was an extraordinary request from a woman that Jai would not even discuss. It was also a hot potato that had passed quickly from hand to hand, the staff probably striving to work out the best way to deal with it since Jai's aversion to anything relating to his mother was clearly well known. And Samaira was right, it *was* an invitation for Willow but undoubtedly not one of which Jai would approve.

'Thank you,' Willow said quietly, keen not to embellish the staff grapevine by commenting on an email that had very probably already caused a wave of gossip and speculation.

And while she was pondering that problem and what to do about it, she too left the library and wandered down to the far end of the palace in the direction of the suite of offices that had been neatly tailored from what had once been staff quarters. There she hesitated, uncertain that she even wanted to raise such a prickly topic, for in recent days Jai had become progressively more elusive. Yes, she had accepted that he would have to return to work, but she had not appreciated quite how much business would occupy his time. He usually joined her for dinner but rarely for breakfast or lunch, invariably rising before her and retiring after she had. She was relieved, however, that in spite of that relentless schedule he had still made time for their son, even if any notion of making time for *her* seemed to have died a total death after that first glorious week together.

Willow understood, however, that he was very busy, and she wasn't the clingy type. She didn't need him to fill the daylight hours when she had Hari to occupy her, a beautiful garden and an entire library of books, but she couldn't help thinking that Jai was treating her rather like a new and shiny novelty whose initial lustre had quickly worn off and ended up boring him instead. On that note, she turned her steps in another direction and decided to ask him what she felt she needed to ask him over dinner instead.

Later, Jai strolled out to the big domed terrace that was shaded throughout the day and cool. Willow sipped her wine and savoured his long-legged grace and sheer bronzed beauty with his black-lashed arctic-blue eyes glittering. A little quiver ran through her slender length, her breasts peaking almost painfully below the bodice of the sundress she wore, a clenching sensation tightening deep in her pelvis so that colour flared up in her cheeks. 'Hello, stranger,' she heard herself say even though she had not intended to make any comment on his recent inaccessibility.

Jai lifted a black brow in query, as if that greeting had totally taken him aback.

'I haven't seen you since I woke to see you walking out of our bedroom yesterday morning,' Willow pointed out, watching the faint rise of colour that scored his exotic cheekbones with curiosity. 'Hey, I'm not complaining. I'm just pointing it out.'

Disconcerted by that statement, Jai breathed. 'Has it really been that long? I'm sorry but I had to attend a board meeting for the foundation last night. It ran late and I didn't want to disturb you, so I used another room.'

'I think you need to learn to delegate more,' Willow responded with determined lightness. 'It's not healthy for anyone to be working twenty-four-seven.'

Jai gritted his teeth, belatedly recognising in that moment that he had gone to quite absurd lengths to avoid his wife for the sin of attracting him too strongly. He dimly wondered if there was a streak of insanity somewhere in his family genes. What had seemed like such a good idea a week earlier had now blurred and become questionable. In the midst of scanning her tiny slender figure in a sunflower-yellow dress, which accentuated the strawberry-blond waves curling round her piquant face and framed her catlike green eyes, he reckoned that no normal man would have behaved as he had done: resisting his beautiful wife's allure as though she were both toxic and dangerous.

He could only assume that the literal act of getting married had afflicted him with some very weird and deferred form of cold feet. All to prove some kind of point to himself? That he was in control? And able to *wreck* his marriage before it even got off the ground? He breathed in deeply, recognising in bewilderment that his usual rational outlook inexplicably seemed to always send him in the wrong direction with Willow.

'Even with the party scheduled, next week won't be half as frantic for me,' Jai assured her hurriedly as Ranjit poured the wine and retreated.

'Good,' Willow replied with a smile that lit up her face like sunshine. 'But the party event has also given me some questions I feel I *have* to ask you about your background.'

Jai tensed. 'My…background?'

'I feel awkward about asking but I feel I should know the basic facts, because I will be mixing with your relatives, who presumably already know those facts, and I don't want to trip up in my ignorance and say anything that sounds stupid,' Willow outlined, trotting out the excuse she had prepared and reddening hotly because simply telling him the truth would have come much more naturally to her.

Yet in her heart of hearts she had already guessed that Jai would absolutely forbid her to have anything to do with his mother, but Lady Milly was *her* mother-in-law and Hari's grandmother and, although she was a stranger, Willow still felt that she surely ought to have the right to form her own opinion.

'Facts about what?' Jai prompted.

'About why your parents broke up, about why your mother left you behind,' she murmured tightly, guilt still jolting through her in waves.

'My mother is the daughter of an English duke, which is still virtually all I know about her. The marriage didn't last long and ended in divorce…' Jai compressed his sensual mouth into a flat bitter line '… *because* apparently she believed that her alliance with an Indian and the birth of a mixed-race child were adversely affecting her social status.'

'That's weird… I mean, if she believed that why would she have married your father in the first place?' Willow pressed with a furrowed brow.

'I have never had a conversation with her, consequently I don't know,' Jai admitted flatly.

'You've never even *met* her?' Willow exclaimed in disbelief.

'I don't think you could call it a meeting… I did run into her once quite unexpectedly at a public event and she pretty much cut me dead. Her second husband and children were with her,' Jai explained, and his strong bone structure might have been formed with steel beneath his olive skin, his forbidding cast of features as revealing of his feelings on that occasion as the ice in his gaze.

'That was unforgivable,' Willow conceded, shocked and unhappy on his behalf.

Jai frowned. 'Of course, she did attempt to come back from that very low point. Shortly afterwards, she came to my London home in an attempt to see me, but I had her turned away. In fact, there were several attempts, but I have no desire to either see or speak to her. She sent letters as well, which I returned unopened.

At this stage in my life and with my father dead, I see no reason to waste time on her.'

Willow, however, saw with great clarity that Jai had been cruelly hurt by his mother's twin rejections and that, no matter what he said in that measured and cool voice of his, he was still scarred by the damage his mother's abandonment had inflicted. And so stubborn too, so set in his views that he had completely rejected the olive branch and the explanations that the woman had tried to offer. Of course, in such circumstances that was his right, she accepted ruefully, resolving in that moment not to interfere on behalf of a woman who, it seemed, was a most undeserving cause. She herself would sooner have cut off her arm than walk away from Hari.

'I'm sorry I asked,' she told him truthfully. 'I can't blame you for feeling the way you do about her.'

And she decided not to mention the personal approach that had been made to her by his mother, which would undoubtedly only annoy Jai and where was the point in that? It would be yet another wounding reminder of the wretched woman that he didn't need. No, she would stay safely uninvolved in a matter that was none of her business and ignore that email.

Jai strolled round the courtyard garden with her after dinner, but Willow was quiet and withdrawn in receipt of that unexpected attention. After all, she really didn't know where she stood with Jai any more. Her first week with him had been magical and then he had virtually vanished, and with that vanishing act all her insecurities had been revived. Why would he want to spend time with her when he had never really wanted to marry her in the first place? How could she feel neglected when she had known beforehand that she was entering a marriage without love? How could she even complain?

'I screwed up this week,' Jai declared, in a driven undertone.

In silence, Willow shrugged a stiff shoulder and hovered below the ancient banyan tree in the centre of the garden, which sheltered a sacred shrine much revered by the staff. '*I* didn't complain about anything,' she reminded him with pride, studying him with clear green eyes.

Her problem, though, was that Jai was gorgeous, in whatever light and in whatever clothing. Nothing detracted from his sheer magnificence: the luxuriant black hair, the chiselled cheekbones and flawless skin, the stunning ice-blue eyes and the dramatic lashes that surrounded them, and he had an equally beautiful body, she allowed, her face warming at that unarguable acknowledgement. Unfortunately for her, on every physical plane, Jai drew her like a magnet. One certain look, one smile and she was all over him like a stupid rash and that both infuriated her and made her feel weak and foolish. After the week she had endured of being ignored in *and* out of bed, she knew that in reality she meant very little to Jai and it felt degrading to still be attracted to a man who could simply switch off and forget her very existence.

The real source of Willow's frustration, however, was, undeniably, that she had no idea what was going on inside his head. She was beginning to wonder if it was possible that, aside of sex, Jai hadn't a clue how to behave in the sort of relationship that a marriage required. The first week with him had been heavenly and she had been so happy with him that she had practically floated, but the past week of being ignored had been a sobering wake-up call that hurt her self-esteem. One minute she had seemed as necessary to him as the air he needed to breathe, the next she had become the invisible woman.

'I will spend more time with you from now on,' Jai intoned with deadly seriousness.

Willow paled and walked on down the path. 'Don't push yourself,' she heard herself say curtly, the colour of embarrassment stinging her cheeks.

'It's not like that,' Jai assured her levelly, lifting a long-fingered brown hand to rest on her shoulder with an intimacy she resented because it reminded her too much of those carnal, expert hands sliding over her body.

'Well, going by the past week, it *is* like that,' Willow replied, squaring her slight shoulders and stepping away to break that physical connection. 'You don't know what you want from me…apart from the obvious…*sex*,' she condemned between gritted teeth. 'And this past week, not even that. You married me and I don't think you know what to do with me now that you've got what you *said* you wanted!'

Evidently stunned by that disconcerting burst of frankness, Jai briefly froze, his darkly handsome features taut.

'Goodnight, Jai,' Willow murmured quietly and walked back indoors, for once proud of herself for not succumbing to the sexual infatuation that had entrapped her into something that felt disturbingly like an obsession.

Why was she feeling like that? Even not seeing Jai hurt, never mind not being touched by him or talking to him. Somehow, he had sparked off a hunger inside her that tugged at her through every hour of the day and she resented him for reducing her to that needy level. He should've started their marriage on cooler, more detached terms if that was how he intended it to be. Instead he had given her deceptive false messages and had shaken her up from the inside out.

Well, she was not some pushover for him to lift and literally *lay* whenever he fancied, she was strong, independent and nobody's fool, she reminded herself doggedly. She might not have been her father or Jai's intellectual equal, but had always been shrewd when it came to people and the often confusing difference between what they said and what they actually did. She knew how to look after herself even if she had once been foolish enough to succumb to a one-night stand with Jai.

Tense from that encounter in the garden, she went upstairs to look in on Hari as he slept, safe and smiling in the baby equivalent of the Land of Nod, probably dreaming of being rocked in a silver swing by devoted handmaidens while being fed ambrosia. If only life were so simple for her, she thought wryly. Lifting her head high, she scolded herself for that downbeat thought. She had Hari and life was very good for him. She had health and security too. There *was* no excuse for feeling that her life lacked anything. In that mood, she scooped up silk pyjamas from her cavernous collection of lingerie and went for a bath.

She was lying back on her padded bath pillow engaged in aggressively counting the many blessings she had to be grateful for when, with a slight knock and only a momentary hesitation, the door opened to frame Jai on the threshold, tall and lean, dark and hazardous, pale eyes glittering like stars framed by black velvet. Willow jerked up in surprise and hugged her knees with defensive hands, feeling invaded. 'I didn't ask you to come in.'

Jai tilted his dark head back, a dangerous glint in his bright gaze. 'What makes you think I need permission to speak to my wife?'

Willow lifted a pale brow. 'Courtesy?'

Jai closed the door and sank down on the edge of the bath, deliberately entering her safe space. 'Courtesy won't get us anywhere we want to travel right now.'

Willow lifted her chin. 'Then get out of here...*now*!' she challenged.

Disturbingly, Jai laughed and trailed a forefinger through the rose petals swirling round her knees. 'I don't think so. I am where I *want* to be. If you can be direct, so can I. I want you.'

At the sound of that declaration the blood drummed up through Willow's body like an adrenalin boost. 'Since...*when*?' she mocked.

'I can't switch it off. With you, it's a primal and

very basic urge and it hurts to deny it.' Jai's fingertip glided up out of the water to slowly stroke the soft underside of her full lower lip and her heart hammered at an insane rate.

'So, why did you?' she whispered unevenly.

'I thought I should. I don't know why. I don't like feeling out of control,' Jai admitted thickly, his mesmeric gaze holding hers with sheer force of will. 'And you often make me feel out of control…'

And a huge wave of heat that had nothing to do with the temperature of the water shot up through Willow. Her brain was blurring as though it had been enveloped in fog. She could feel her own heart thrumming inside her chest, the tautness of her pointed nipples, the pool of liquefying warmth at her core, but she couldn't think straight and when he angled his mouth down to hers, her mouth opened, only anticipation guiding her. His mouth on hers was like paraffin thrown on a bonfire, shooting multicoloured sparks of heat through every fibre, and only a slight gasp escaped her throat when he lifted her, dripping, out of the water and melded his lips to hers again with all the urgency she had dreamt of.

'I'm soaking wet! This wasn't supposed to happ—' she began, common sense struggling to get a look-in as he laid her down on the bed and arranged her like some ancient sacrifice on an altar.

'Shush, *soniyaa*,' Jai breathed hungrily against her mouth and she was vaguely aware of him peeling off his clothes in the midst of kissing her, but she was too connected to the sheer power surge of his urgency to make even the smallest complaint.

He ran his palms slowly down over her smooth body as if reacquainting himself with her slender contours and she shivered, every skin cell primed for more, her breath trapped in her throat as if breathing might prevent the excitement already licking through her. He slid down the length of her, all lithe bronzed grace and tenacity, his skin hot where it brushed hers, his bold arousal brushing her stomach, filling her with heat and the kind of wanting that burned. He tipped her thighs back, settled his lips to the most sensitive part of her quivering body and slowly, surely, with his mouth and his wickedly knowing fingers, proceeded to drive her out of her mind with throbbing waves of pleasure. She squirmed and then she writhed, unable to stay in control and flying involuntarily into an intense climax, with his name breaking from her tongue and then the taste of herself on her lips as he kissed her with ferocious demand and settled over her.

From that shattering point on, it was as it always was between them: wild. He plunged into her with a growl of satisfaction and she gasped in delight from the first thrust, the delicious stretching of her tingling body, the sleek hardness of his body driving over and in hers and the raw sexual connection that destroyed her every inhibition. He flipped her over onto her hands and knees, pressing her down, entering her powerfully and deeply again, making every sense sing in high-voltage response. Sobs of excitement were wrenched from her convulsing throat as another climax seized hold of her and shock-waved through her with an intensity that wiped her out. She flopped flat on the bed like a puppet who'd had her strings cut, smiling dizzily into the silk bed cover at his shout of completion, knowing that never in her life before had she dreamt of that much excitement and that much drowning pleasure.

'No more starting work at dawn, no more late nights,' Jai breathed with ragged resolution as he turned her limp length over and back into contact with the hot, damp heat of his body, sealing her there with both arms, his hands smoothing her slender back in a soothing motion.

'You're going to delegate?' she whispered with effort because it was a challenge to kick her brain into gear again.

'With the foundation, yes. My life has changed now that I have you and Hari and I need to adapt,' he murmured, setting the edge of his teeth into the exact spot on the slope of her neck that drove her crazy and making her jerk against him. 'In many ways.'

And Willow was satisfied by those assurances. He was making a major effort. He hadn't approached her simply for sex. No, he had recognised that change would be required from both of them if their marriage was to survive and that was good, wasn't it? She shouldn't *still* want more, should she? She couldn't understand the lingering hollow sensation in her chest, particularly when her body was already warming up again to the stimulation of his.

Of course, he wasn't going to start talking about emotions—that was a female thing, wasn't it? Concentrate on the positives, she told herself sternly. Both of them were finding their way in a new and very different situation as parents and partners. Of course, there would be misunderstandings and clashes along the way. All that should really matter was that Jai cared enough to put in the work to keep their relationship ticking over.

Obviously, he was unlikely to ever give her the kind of rapturous reception he gave Hari every time he lifted his son into his arms. She had seen that look, that intense emotion he hid around her and, if she was honest, had envied her son, who had inspired love in his father practically at first sight. But she was only human and it was normal to make comparisons, even if they were unwise comparisons, because love and devotion had featured nowhere in their agreement. Even worse, logic warned her that Jai, a tough businessman to his fingertips, would stick exactly to the deal he had made with her.

She didn't have what it took to inspire Jai with romantic feelings. That had been made clear to her the morning after their first night together. Yes, he had visited to check on her a couple of months later but that had only been a knee-jerk sense of responsibility she owed to his friendship with her late father. It had not related to her *personally*. Her main attraction for Jai was self-evidently the passion that virtually set fire to their bedsheets and she was beginning to recognise that she ought not to be turning her nose up at that rather lowering truth when it might well prove to be the glue that kept their marriage afloat in the future.

Or would familiarity breed contempt? She shivered,

wondering why her thoughts continually took a negative direction around Jai. What was the matter with
her? Why couldn't she simply be content with what
they had? Why was she always seeking...*more*?

CHAPTER EIGHT

JAI LOOKED MAGNIFICENT.

Indeed, Willow was flooded by distinctly sensual and, admittedly, superficial impressions of Jai garbed in traditional Maharaja dress in readiness for the party that would introduce her as his wife to his family and friends. In the black and silver frogged silk tunic and pants, he took her breath away. In fact, virtually everything about the pomp and ceremony of the occasion and their surroundings was having the same effect on her. His grandfather's art deco palace was a sumptuous building with soaring marble columns and ceilings, glittering Venetian glass chandeliers and intricately designed marble floors and even the furniture and the grounds around the building matched that splendid classic elegance, but Jai had been quite correct: it was too grand a place for mere comfort.

As soon as they had arrived in their finery and in advance of the party, official photographs had been taken in the Greek-style marble temple in the centre of the lawns. They had leant against pillars, posed on the layers of steps, looked pensively into each other's eyes until she'd succumbed to an uncontrollable bout of giggles and then she had twirled in her gown for the photographer to show off the full skirt of her gorgeous dress.

She had felt remarkably like a Bollywood movie actress and Jai had told her that all photos taken for special occasions had a dash of that spirit in India. When she had asked Jai if she should don a sari to blend in better at the party, Jai had only laughed before informing her that many of their guests would be European and that some of his countrywomen would dress traditionally while others would wear the latest Western fashion, that, in actuality, however she chose to dress would be acceptable.

Willow had picked a spectacular ball gown out of her crammed wardrobe, a brilliant cerise-pink shade much favoured by Rajasthani women. The finest lace covered her shoulders and upper arms, the style closely tailored to her slender figure down to the hip and then flaring out in volume into the beaded silk skirt. It was one of those ridiculously beautiful fairy-tale dresses that made a woman feel like a million dollars and to complement it she had worn very high heels. In addition, Jai had brought her a glorious emerald and diamond necklace and earrings, which had belonged to his grandmother, as well as having gifted her a diamond bracelet and a gold and diamond watch that very same week. It was little wonder that she kept on wanting to pinch herself to see if she was still living in the real world because, only weeks earlier, she could never have dreamt that such incredible luxury would ever feature in her life.

In the echoing marble hall, there was a huge display of wedding gifts and they wandered around examining them. Willow was disconcerted by the large amount of jewellery she had been given, gleaming gold necklaces and armbands and earrings, and there were even some pieces for Jai, which he assured her with a groan that he would never wear. She strolled up to him when he was holding something in his hand and signalling his hovering PA, Mitul, to ask him a question.

With an exclamation in his own language he set the ornate little box down again in haste, his sensual mouth compressing. Curious, Willow scooped it up. 'What is it?' she asked.

'An eighteenth-century *inro*—an ornamental box in which Japanese men used to carry seals or medicine. I collect them,' he told her in a curt undertone.

'A very good friend must've given it,' Willow assumed, because everything on the tables struck her as valuable. 'But why are you annoyed? Was it an unsuitable gift from the friend concerned?'

'In my opinion, yes,' Jai conceded crisply. 'The giver is my ex-fiancée, Cecilia.'

'The one that ditched you?' Willow gasped in surprise.

All of a sudden, Jai grinned, the tension in his lean, handsome features evaporating again. 'You're no diplomat, are you, *jaani*?'

Willow reddened because she knew that she hadn't

been tactful. 'I know nothing about her...but what up-
sets you about the present?'

'That I have only just learned that she and her husband have been invited to the party. Odds are that
she won't come. But if she does, it's entirely *my* fault
that she received an invite,' he acknowledged in exasperation. 'I told Mitul to use the same guest list for
my friends that was used ten years ago at a party I
held here. But he didn't work for me back then and
he wouldn't have recognised the significance of her
name. Of course, I should've checked the list myself.'

'It's a very big party,' she reminded him. 'Will it
really matter if she turns up?'

Jai shrugged, a brooding expression etched to his
flawless features, his wolf eyes veiled by his lashes.
'Her presence would be inappropriate at a reception
being staged for my bride's introduction.'

'Well, if she turns up, *I'm* not bothered,' Willow
confided, reckoning that she only had curiosity to be
satisfied in such a scenario. 'It must be almost ten years
since you were with her. I have the vaguest memory
of Dad mentioning your wedding being cancelled and
I was so young back then that it feels like a very, *very*
long time ago.'

'You have a wonderfully welcome ability to ignore
developments or mistakes that would enrage and distress other women I have known,' Jai remarked, his
pale glittering gaze fully focussed on her as he smiled
down at her appreciatively.

Her heartbeat sped up so much she almost clamped
her hand to her chest, and she swallowed back the dry-

ness in her throat. 'But that doesn't mean that I'm not
nosy,' she told him playfully, fighting her susceptibility to that smile with all her might, for he might have
the power of command over her every sense but she
didn't want him influencing her brain into the bargain.
'Tell me about her…'

'Some other time,' Jai parried, closing down that in-
formational avenue without hesitation, the hand he had
braced lightly against her spine urging her forward to
greet the couple who had entered. 'Our first arrivals…
congratulations, Jivika! How did you get your husband
out the door this early?' he asked with a grin, clearly
on warm, relaxed terms with the older couple.

'I thought your bride might enjoy some support at
a family event like this and, like most men, I doubt it
even occurred to you that this *is* a rather intimidating event for a newcomer,' the older woman said drily
to Jai as she walked towards Willow and extended
her hand. 'I'm Jai's aunt, Jivika, his father's sister. I'll
give you the lowdown on the family members to avoid
and those you can afford to encourage,' she promised
with a surprisingly warm smile lighting up her rather
stern features.

'Jivika!' her husband scolded.

Jai just laughed. 'I could put my wife in no safer
hands. Willow, be warned… Jivika was a leading barrister in London and retirement is challenging for her.'

'Only during Indian winters,' his aunt corrected.
'The rest of the year we live in London.'

Willow was grateful for the older woman's assistance as a slow steady flood of guests flowed through

the giant doors and drinks were served in the vast drawing room. 'Grandad was *so* pretentious,' Jivika said of her surroundings.

And her commentaries on various relatives were equally entertaining. Willow got used to asking Jai's aunt to identify guests and when she saw her husband deeply engaged in conversation with a tall, shapely blonde, beautiful enough to pass as a supermodel, she couldn't resist asking who she was.

'Cecilia Montmorency. What's she doing here?' Jivika asked bluntly in turn.

Jolted by that name, Willow explained the mistake on the guest list while becoming disconcerted that Cecilia was constantly touching Jai's arm and laughing up into his face in a very intimate manner. She registered that she was not quite as safe from jealous possessiveness as she had cheerfully assumed. But then how could she be? Jai must have *loved* Cecilia to want to marry at the age of twenty-one, and love was a binding emotion that people didn't tend to forget, not to mention a deeper layer of commitment that Willow had lacked in her marriage from the outset.

'You're seeing a not-so-merry divorcee on the prowl for her next meal ticket,' Jivika commented. 'It must be galling to know that she once dumped one of the richest men in the world.'

It was Willow's turn to stare and exclaim, *'Jai's...?'*

His aunt smiled. 'I like that you didn't know but you can bet your favourite shoes that Cecilia knows what he's worth down to the last decimal point.'

Willow guiltily cherished the older woman's take on

Jai's ex as a gold-digger and, relaxing more and more in her company, she became more daring and asked about Jai's mother, asking what sort of woman she had been that she could walk away from her child.

'Been listening to Jai's version of reality, I assume?' Jivika shot her a wry glance. 'Jai was indoctrinated by my brother from an early age. Milly *didn't* walk away from her son by choice. My brother, Rehan, fought her through the courts for years and succeeded in denying her access to her son, even in the UK while Jai was at school there. In the end she gave up—the woman really didn't have much choice after the legal system in both countries had repeatedly failed her.'

Stunned by that very different version of events, Willow studied the other woman in disbelief. 'Why didn't you tell Jai?'

Jivika spread her hands and sighed, 'At first, loyalty to my much-loved but misguided brother and, since his death, no desire to raise sleeping dogs and upset Jai. He's astute. He's capable of making his own decisions. It's not my place to interfere and he could hate me for it.'

Willow swallowed hard, thinking of the judgements she had made about Jai's mother simply by listening to *his* opinion of his mother's behaviour. That he might not know the truth had not once occurred to her. Now she was barely able to imagine what it would be like for him to learn that the father he had loved and respected had lied to him for years on the same subject and she fully understood his aunt's unwillingness to intervene.

Jai deserved to know the truth and yet who would want to be the one to *tell* him? she thought ruefully.

Sher joined them and was about to move on when a question from Jivika revealed that Willow had trained as a garden designer. His handsome features sparked with sudden interest and he turned back to say, 'I'll call over in a few days and put a project in front of you...*if* you're interested? I have a garden to restore.'

'I'd be happy to offer advice but I haven't had a huge amount of working experience,' Willow admitted ruefully, because Hari's impending birth and her need to earn money had forced her to put her potential career on a back burner.

'Good enough for me,' Sher told her reassuringly. 'What counts is not the number of projects you have completed but whether or not you have the eye and the skill and can interpret my preferences.'

'I'll let you decide that,' Willow said, colouring a little with relief, encountering Jai's bright shrewd gaze as he joined them and swept her onto the dance floor with the quite unnecessary explanation that it was expected of them.

'You seem to have managed beautifully without me by your side,' Jai observed.

Willow looked up at him, wondering why she couldn't decide whether that statement was supposed to be a positive or negative comment. Her nose wrinkled and she smiled. 'Having your aunt by my side was like having an entire army backing me,' she confided with helpless honesty.

Jai laughed out loud. 'I'm very fond of Jivika,' he admitted. 'She was particularly stellar when I was home-sick in London as a child. Of course, she and my father were very close.'

Not quite as close as they could've been, Willow reflected, thinking of that exchange relating to Jai's mother, before conceding that the Singh family dy-namic was vastly different from anything she had ever seen before, because even his family treated Jai with the reverence his status as Maharaja commanded, a bred-in-the-bone awe that his father must have enjoyed as well. Such men might not have the right to rule any longer in a republic, but the people still viewed them as being very special and unquestionably royal. Every month Jai held an audience at which any of his father's former subjects could approach him for advice or as-sistance of any kind and he still saw it as his duty to give that attention to those in need.

'So, my family and friends haven't been as intim-idating for you as Jivika feared?' Ice-blue eyes in-spected her face with unmistakeable concern.

Touched by that consideration, Willow shifted a lit-tle closer to him and his arms tightened round her be-fore his hands smoothed down to the gentle curve of her hips. 'No, everyone's been wonderfully welcom-ing. How was Cecilia?' she dared.

The faintest colour fired the exotic slant of Jai's hard cheekbones. 'Unchanged. She has one of those amaz-ingly bubbly personalities that always charms, even though she's been through what sounds like a pretty brutal divorce. I was surprised that her arrival and her approach didn't annoy me more…but then we broke up a long time ago and, looking back, I'm prepared to admit that at that age I was more of a boy than a man. It's time to forgive and forget.'

Willow hadn't been prepared to detect quite that much enthusiasm on the topic of the ex who had jilted him. Dimly, she supposed it was healthier that Jai wasn't bitter and had clearly long since moved on from that period of his life.

'She'll probably visit us. She's gasping to meet Hari,' Jai added lightly.

'Why on earth would *she* want to meet Hari?' Willow demanded with an astonishment she wasn't quick enough to hide.

'Because he's my son and possibly because she can't have children of her own,' Jai proffered, his intonation cool and on the edge of critical, his far too clever ice-blue eyes locking to her flushed face, his lean, strong length stiffening a little against her as he moved her expertly around the floor. 'That's why her husband divorced her. Apparently, he's desperate for a son and heir.'

Willow's brain kicked into gear again. 'How very sad,' she remarked, literally stooping to the level of *forcing* fake sympathy into her voice. 'But I thought she had come only for the wedding.'

'No, seems she's doing a tour of Rajasthan while she's here,' Jai interposed, the tension in his lean, powerful frame dissipating again. 'I said I'd draw up a list of sites she shouldn't miss…'

As if there weren't at least a thousand tour guides for hire in Chandrapur alone, Willow thought sourly, because tourism was a huge source of income in the Golden Triangle, as the area was often described.

'I'm sure she would find that very helpful,' Willow commented blithely, annoyance with him, even greater annoyance with Cecilia and a tumble of confusing emotions raining down on her from all sides. Jai was teaching her to lie like a trooper, as the saying went, she conceded guiltily, but nowhere in their relationship was there any given right for her to make a fuss on such a score as a too-friendly ex-girlfriend. They had a marriage of convenience, not a love match, such as he had once almost achieved with Cecilia.

There was no avoiding the obvious: she was jealous and possessive of the man she had married. Disquiet gripped her. When had that happened? How had she failed to notice such responses creeping up on her? In the midst of her turmoil, Jai kissed her, one hand on her shoulder, one framing her face, and she fell into that kiss like a drowning swimmer plunged fathoms deep without warning. Her body lit up like a firework display, nipples tightening, pelvis clenching as if he had done something much more intimate than press his sensual mouth to hers. But then Jai had a way with a kiss that could burn through her like a flame. Like honey being heated, she was warming, melting, pressing closer to the allure of his hard, muscular physique, no detail of him concealed by the fine silk he wore. An arrow of satisfaction pierced Willow then, for Jai might have talked fondly about his ex but it was still *his wife* who turned him on.

'We'll have to stay on the floor,' Jai growled in her ear. 'I'm not presentable right now.'

Willow chuckled, her cheeks colouring, for over the past week she had learned that she and Jai always seemed to scorch each other when they touched. She wanted to reach up and kiss him again, more deeply and for longer, but she resisted the urge, reminding herself that they were surrounded by people.

Later, Jivika and her husband were leaving when the older woman signalled her, and Willow walked over to her with a wide smile. 'It occurs to me that a wife who is loved could tackle that difficult subject we discussed earlier,' she murmured sibilantly. 'If you break the ice, I will be happy to share all that I know with my nephew.'

Willow maintained her smile with difficulty, but she could feel the blood draining from her face because she was *not* a loved wife, not even close to it, she acknowledged painfully, utterly convinced that her strongest bond with Jai was sexual rather than emotional. And that awareness stabbed through her in an almost physical pain, she registered then in dismay. Of course, she had kind of known from the start that she wanted more than sex from Jai, but somehow it hadn't crossed her mind that she was *already* much more deeply involved in their relationship than he was.

There was no denying it: she had fallen hopelessly in love with the man who had married her only to legitimise his son's birth. It had started way back that first night when she had fallen into bed with him and Hari had been conceived in the flare-up of passion between them…and if she was honest with herself, even though she didn't feel she could be *that* honest with Jai, it was an attraction that Jai had *always* held for her.

That long-ago adolescent crush had only been the first indication that she was intensely susceptible to Jai and exposed to him as an adult, the remnants of that crush had simply morphed that first week they were married into something much more powerful. She loved him. That was why she was constantly insecure and prickly and, now, possessive of him. If she hadn't been in love with him, she would have been much less anxious and hurt when he'd chosen to step back from her during the second week they had been together.

And nothing was likely to change, she reflected, deciding to tuck away all her anxiety and bury it, because there was nothing she could do to change either Jai's feelings or her own. It was what it was, and she had to live with it. Certainly, interfering on his mother's behalf, as even his aunt had feared to do, was out of the question.

Even so, she *did* feel that she should meet Lady Milly discreetly and discover the facts for some future date when hopefully she and Jai would have been married long enough for her to trust that they had a stable relationship. After all, it seemed wrong that she, as Jai's wife, should also stand back and do nothing while the poor woman suffered for sins she hadn't committed. It might not be her business in many ways, but Willow had a strong sense of justice. It would do no harm for her to at least listen to the woman while simultaneously introducing her to her grandson, she told herself squarely.

Furthermore, Jai still had the time to mend his relationship with his mother, who clearly loved him. His mother had to love him, for why else would she have fought for years to see him again? Her persistence was self-explanatory. What was more, Milly was family and surely everyone was willing to go that extra mile for a family member? Jai now had a chance that Willow had never had with her own father. She had failed to win her father's love time and time again because really the only thing he had appreciated in a child was the ability to achieve top academic results. But Jai's mother was offering love even after multiple rejections. Unfortunately past hurt and pride would prevent Jai from giving his mother the chance to redeem herself, but what if Willow could take that chance for him and use it?

Cecilia arrived at the Lake Palace for a visit the following afternoon and caught Willow unprepared. She was down on her knees playing with Hari in the nursery with tumbled hair and not a scrap of make-up on when Jai strolled in with Cecilia in tow and not the smallest warning. In that moment, Willow genuinely wanted to kill Jai. She sat up with a feverishly flushed face and struggled to smile politely as Cecilia dropped gracefully down beside her and exclaimed over the resemblance between Hari and Jai.

'He's got your eyes, Jai!' Cecilia crooned in delight, smoothing a hand over Hari's curls. 'He is adorable.'

'Yes, he is,' Willow conceded fondly, stifling her irritation with difficulty.

'Do you remember your father taking us on a tour of the desert that first summer?' Cecilia asked Jai.

And that was the start of the 'do you remember?' game that stretched throughout coffee downstairs as Cecilia encouraged Jai to reminisce about friends from their university days and brought him up to speed on the activities of those he had lost touch with. Willow might as well have been a painting on the wall for all the share she got of the conversation, while Cecilia became more and more animated at the attention she was receiving. It was a total surprise to Willow when Jai smoothly mentioned that they were going out to lunch, an arrangement that was news to her, and moments later Cecilia began making visibly reluctant departure moves.

'So, when was this lunch with Sher arranged?' Willow enquired curiously on the steps of the palace as the blonde was driven off by her driver in an SUV.

'Oh, that's tomorrow,' Jai admitted with a tiny smile of superiority as he absorbed her surprise. 'It was time for Cecilia to leave.'

Disconcerted, Willow turned back to him. 'You mean—?'

'I lied? *Yes*,' Jai interposed with dancing eyes of amusement at her astonishment. 'I will always be polite to Cecilia but I have no wish to socialise with her. Yesterday I was curious, today I was bored with her.'

Relief sank through Willow in a blinding wave. 'But I thought—'

'That I am still naive enough to be duped by a woman who chose to welcome a richer man into her bed?' Jai said, sliding an arm round her slender spine. 'No, I'm not.'

'A richer man?' Willow queried, recalling his aunt's opinion of the beautiful blonde.

'Within a month of breaking off our engagement, Cecilia was married to the owner of a private bank. Her affair with him began while she was *still* with me,' Jai breathed with sardonic bite. 'Shortly before her change of heart, she had learned that my sole wealth at that point was based on my share of the family trust, and at the time my business was only in its infancy. She went for a more promising option—a much older man with a pile of capital.'

Still frowning, Willow glanced up at him. 'But when it happened you must have been devastated.'

'Not so devastated that I didn't eventually recognise that I'd had a narrow escape,' Jai quipped with raw-edged amusement. 'Her marriage to a man old enough to be her father was the first evidence of her true nature. My mother made the same move,' he extended in a rare casual reference to his parents' marriage. 'Money must've been her main objective too. I can't believe she ever loved my father.'

Willow set her teeth together and said nothing, thinking that his father really had done a number on him, leaving him not one shred of faith in the woman who had brought him into the world and, by achieving that, had ensured that Jai never became curious enough to meet the woman and decide for himself.

Jai came to bed late that night because he had been working. He was a tall sliver of lean, supple beauty in the moonlight, sliding in beside her and reaching for her in almost the same movement.

'You can't,' she told him, feeling awkward because it was that time of the month.

'You mean—?'

'Yes,' she confirmed drowsily.

'Doesn't mean I can't hold you, doesn't mean I can't kiss you,' Jai teased, folding her into his arms regardless. 'This is the very first time I've met with that restriction since my engagement.'

Thinking of all the years he had been free and single, Willow said, 'How can it be?'

'After Cecilia the longest I stayed with a woman was a weekend. It was a practical choice for me, selfish too, I'll admit, but I didn't want anything deeper or more lasting.'

'Oh, dear, and here I am planning to last and last and *last*,' she whispered playfully. 'Maybe you'll eventually love me too because you're stuck with me.'

His lean, strong physique tensed. 'No, the love trail isn't for me. That would be excess, and we don't need it to be happy or raise Hari together. Be practical, *soniyaa*. What we've got is much more realistic.'

A hollow sensation spread inside Willow's chest along with a very strong urge to kick the love of her life out of bed. It was early days, though, she reminded herself, and she was being greedy and impatient. In a year's time she might have grown on him to such an extent that he did love her. Or was that simply a fantasy? If he hadn't been bowled over by her from the outset, she was unlikely ever to become the sole and most important focus of his wants, logic warned her. Unfortunately for her, her heart didn't jump at the words, 'practical' or 'realistic.'

CHAPTER NINE

THEY LUNCHED WITH Sher the following day at his family home, which his late father had allowed to fall into rack and ruin.

Only a small part of the ancient Nizam of Tharistan's palace had so far been made liveable, and they dined in that wing on a shaded terrace overlooking a vast stretch of uncultivated land, which Sher admitted had once been the gardens. At Willow's request he had gathered old records, paintings and photographs from Victorian times in an effort to provide some evidence of what the gardens had once looked like, for what remained was simply undergrowth with the occasional hint of the shape of a path or flowerbed.

'It'll be a massive project,' she warned him. 'And hugely expensive.'

'Not a problem for Sher.' Jai laughed.

'Would it be possible for me to take these records and old photos home with me?' Willow pressed the other man. 'What you really need is an archaeological garden survey done.'

'No, I'll be content with something in the spirit of

the original gardens, rather than requiring an exact replica,' Sher admitted. 'I'll bring the old maps over to you tomorrow. I keep them in a climate-controlled environment but as long as you wear gloves handling them, they'll be fine.'

'I can't wait to see them,' Willow confided, excitement brimming in her sparkling green eyes, all her attention on Sher. 'Of course, I'll wear gloves.'

Lunch with two highly creative people was not to be recommended, Jai decided at that point, unless you were of a similar ilk. And Jai *wasn't*. A garden was only a green space to him that complemented a building. Books, technology and business alone held his interest.

When they had climbed back into the limo, Jai thought he should warn his wife of the possible pitfalls of what she was planning. 'As you said, it will be a huge project,' he reminded her smoothly. 'Do you really know what you're taking on?'

Willow straightened her shoulders and turned to him with an eager smile. 'I can't wait!'

'But it will demand a lot of your time.'

'What else do I have to focus on?' Willow prompted.

Myself and my son, Jai reckoned. But he was too clever to say it out loud, admitting that it sounded like something his elderly father would have said and inwardly wincing at the comparison. 'I had been hoping that you would take on some duties with the foundation when you have the time to decide which of our charitable groups would most interest you,' he commented, and it wasn't a lie, he reasoned, even if that possibility had only just occurred to him. 'It would get you out and about more and give you a role of your own.'

'That's a wonderful suggestion,' Willow said warmly. 'But maybe best saved for when I've fully found my feet here.'

'I thought you already had…found your feet,' he admitted.

'Different country, different culture, different languages, different *everything*,' she enumerated with quiet emphasis. 'I love my life here but right now I'm still acclimatising to the changes. I don't think I'm quite ready yet to step out in a social setting as your Maharani, particularly when everyone will be expecting someone like you, experienced at making speeches and knowledgeable about community work.'

That explanation silenced Jai because he immediately grasped that he had not even considered the changes that her move to India on his behalf had made to her life. Rare discomfiture afflicted him. Had he always been so self-absorbed that he only saw in terms of what best suited him? That disposed to be selfish and arrogant? He gritted his teeth at the suspicion and said no more, quite forgetting the irritation that his best friend had inexplicably evoked in him.

The next morning, Sher brought the maps over and, together, he and Willow pored over the old parchments in the library, Jai soon taking his leave. Searching for evidence of former paths, banks, sunken areas and even small garden buildings, they discovered a wealth of useful facts. Thoroughly enjoying herself, Willow did sketches and made copious notes while Sher talked at length about what he liked to see in a garden. When Jai walked in again, they were trading jokes about what they suspected was the marking for an ancient surprise fountain that had been designed to startle the ladies as they walked past by drenching them.

For a split second, Jai froze on the threshold. Willow and Sher were on a rug on the floor laughing uproari-ously, one of his friend's hands on her slim shoulder to steady her as she almost overbalanced in her mirth into the welter of papers that surrounded them.

'Lunch,' Jai announced coolly.

'Oh, my goodness, is it *that* time already?' Willow carolled in astonishment, almost as if she hadn't been camping out in the library for a solid four hours with his best friend, Jai thought in disbelief. Evidently when in Sher's company time had wings for his wife.

Sher's entire attention was pinned to Willow's face. His friend was attracted to her. Jai had already guessed that, for Willow was a classic beauty, but then Sher was attracted to a lot of women and, as a former Bollywood star, he flirted with *all* of them, be they grandmoth-ers or teenagers, because he was accustomed to play-ing to admiring crowds. Even so, Jai trusted Sher with his wife, *totally* trusted him. He was fully aware that his friend would never *ever* cross a line with a mar-ried woman because that same scenario had destroyed Sher's parents' marriage.

No, Jai didn't blame Sher for the intimate scene he had interrupted, he blamed Willow for getting too friendly, for curling up on the floor and making herself recklessly, dangerously approachable, *his* Maharani, acting like a giggly, frisky schoolgirl, he thought furiously. A man less sophisticated than Sher might have read her signals wrong and taken advantage, might have *made a move* on her, the concept of which sent such a current of lancing rage shooting through Jai that he clenched his lean hands into angry fists of restraint by his sides.

He wouldn't lose his temper when he spoke to Willow later, but he would give her useful advice on how to keep other men at a safe distance, advice she certainly needed if what he was seeing was likely to be typical of her behaviour in male company.

'You've been very quiet,' Willow commented over dinner, hours after Sher had departed, leaving her free to spend a contented afternoon pondering the old photos while trying to visualise the lush and colourful garden that Sher would most enjoy.

That was the moment that Jai became aware that what he had *planned* to say to his wife didn't sound quite the same as when he had first thought the matter over. He breathed in deep and decided that tact was all very well, but it might not get across the exact message he wanted to impart and that message was too important to hold back.

'You flirt with Sher and I dislike it,' Jai delivered bluntly, pushing back his chair and rising from his seat with his wine glass elegantly cupped in one lean brown hand.

For the count of ten seconds, Willow simply gaped at him in disbelief. *He did not just say that, he could not have accused me of* that, she was thinking, and then she looked at him, really looked at his lean, darkly handsome face, and realised by the glitter of his ice-blue eyes and the taut line of his sensual mouth that, no, sadly, he hadn't been joking. She was stunned, incredulous that he could have misunderstood her banter with Sher to that extent, and then just as quickly angry at the speed with which he had misjudged her. In turn, she too rose from her chair and left the table.

'For goodness' sake, I don't flirt with Sher,' she said defensively. 'It's only a friendly thing, nothing the slightest bit suspect about it. I don't know how you could possibly think otherwise.'

Jai's cool appraisal didn't waver. 'But I do. You need to learn how to keep a certain distance in your manner with other men.'

'And you need to learn how not to be irrationally jealous!' Willow slammed back at him without warning, her patience tested beyond its limits and flaming into throbbing resentment.

Those two words, 'irrational' and 'jealous,' struck Jai like bricks. He didn't do either emotion. Unfortunately, those same words also hooked into a phrase his aunt had, many years earlier, once used to describe his father. Later, when challenged by Jai, Jivika had withdrawn the comment and, unfortunately, Willow's use of those offensive words sent a wave of antipathy travelling through him. 'I'm not jealous, Willow. I'm merely asking you to monitor your behaviour in male company.'

'But you'd really prefer me *not* to have male friends?' Willow darted back at him.

Disconcerted by that surprising question, Jai frowned. 'Well, yes, that may be the wisest approach.'

'So, quite obviously, you *are* the jealous, possessive, irrational type you think you aren't…or possibly a throwback to the dinosaurs when men and women didn't make friends with the opposite sex?' Willow shot back at him wrathfully. 'Obviously you have about as much self-awareness as a stone in the wall! Sher's like the brother I never had!'

'You don't have a brother!' Jai fired back at her.

'Didn't I just say that?' Willow exclaimed furiously. 'There was no flirting between us, nothing anyone could criticise. I like him and that's *it*! I certainly don't fancy him.'

Marginally mollified by that admission and aware that Ranjit was loitering in the dining room beyond the doors opening out onto the terrace, Jai murmured in an effort to lower the volume of their dispute, 'I'm not even saying that you knew that you were flirting. It may have been quite unconscious on your part.'

'Well, it must have been unconscious because I don't think I even know *how* to flirt, with my lack of experience in that field!' Willow slung back at him even louder. 'Whatever you think you *saw* between Sher and me, you got it wrong, Jai.'

The doors eased shut with diplomatic quietness and colour edged Jai's spectacular cheekbones. She was being unreasonable, and he didn't know how what he had said had escalated into a full-blown acrimonious scene. He was not the jealous type and he was never, ever irrational and, had he been possessive, he would have stopped Sher from offering her the project in the first instance. And now, he wished he *had* done that, he conceded grimly.

'I didn't get it wrong,' he insisted, refusing to yield an inch.

Willow lifted her chin, outraged green eyes locking to his. 'You got it wrong in every way possible,' she told him succinctly. 'There was no flirting but if you can't even admit that you're jealous, how is anyone to persuade you that you're wrong? All right, I'll even make it easier for you. I'll admit that initially I was jealous of Cecilia.'

'Why on earth would you be jealous of *her*?' Jai demanded in astonishment.

'Because she was all over you like a rash at the party and at no time did I see *you* pushing her away and respecting the sort of boundaries you're accusing me of breaking with Sher!' Willow accused.

'That was a different situation,' Jai argued. 'She was a friend long before I became more deeply involved with her.'

'Oh, have it your own way!' Willow snapped back in frustration, wishing she could get inside his head to rearrange his brain into a pattern she could recognise. 'I'm done here. I've got nothing more to say to you until you admit that you're a jealous, possessive toad, and then I *might* forgive you for insulting me!'

Beneath Jai's speechless gaze, Willow rammed open the door and vanished back into the palace without another word. He refilled his wine glass and stood looking out over the lake, watching a sloth bear slurp a noisy drink at the edge of the lake while the chitter chatter of monkeys at dusk filled the air. Slowly he breathed in deeply, telling himself he had been foolish to assume that marriage would be an easy ride.

And yet it generally *was* with Willow, he conceded grudgingly. She had slotted into his life as though she had always been there, and he shared more with her than he had ever shared with a woman. At the outset, he had assumed that their marriage would be all about Hari, only it wasn't. Their son was a point of connection, but it was Willow's unspoilt, gentle nature, her lack of feminine guile and her interest in learning about everything that was new to her that continued to intrigue Jai. The flirting, most probably, had been unconscious, he decided, and possibly he should have kept his reservations about the degree of friendliness between his wife and his best friend to himself.

After all, he fully trusted Sher, so why hadn't he had the same amount of faith in Willow? Hadn't he once even cherished the insane suspicion that Willow might have been a fortune hunter? Was he so truly a prisoner of his father's unhappy past and Cecilia's mercenary betrayal that he could not trust a woman? That idea shook him and put him into a brooding mood before he went back to his office to work, as was his wont, to escape his uneasy thoughts.

Several hours later, he entered their bedroom quietly and discovered the ultimate bed-blocker blinking up at him in the moonlight: his son, snuggled up next to his mother. Hari closed his eyes again and Jai went off to find another bed.

Willow woke early the next morning with Hari tugging at her hair, and looked down at her son in surprise because she hadn't intended him to spend the night with her, had simply fallen asleep while cuddling him for comfort. *It's not safe to sleep with him,* her conscience reproached her, and she freshened up and returned Hari to the nursery staff, who greeted him as though he had been absent a week. She breakfasted alone, assuming Jai was already in his office because he was fond of dawn starts. Her annoyance with him was still intense, but she was troubled by the stand-off she had initiated the night before because Jai could be as stubborn and unyielding as the rock she had compared him to.

Willow sighed. She had had to confront him. He had not given her a choice and how could she compromise? The answer was that on such a dangerous point of contention, she *couldn't* compromise, not if she wanted their relationship to have a future. That truth acknowledged, she frowned as she realised that this was also the morning Jai's mother had invited her to meet her. She hadn't had time to dwell on that thorny issue in recent days but now it was first and foremost in her mind.

Did she ignore that invitation as Jai would unquestionably expect her to do, or did she meet Lady Milly because she now knew, thanks to Jivika, that Jai's mother had been cruelly misjudged?

Surely she had a right to discover the facts of the situation for herself? Or, even as Jai's wife, was that background none of her business? Sadly, Jai was too

loyal to his father's memory to take advantage of the
same opportunity, she reflected, and that was tragic.
Maybe she could be a peacemaker, a go-between, she
thought optimistically. If the meeting went the right
way, it could bring Jai a great deal of happiness, she
reasoned, her heart lifting at that optimistic prospect.
Even Jai's aunt, however, had been unwilling to run
the risk of getting involved and yet Jivika was neither
a weak nor timid personality. Willow's teeth worried
anxiously at her lower lip as she weighed the odds and
then a rueful smile slowly crept across her lips because
when it got down to basics, it was a simple decision.

Jai had been badly damaged and hurt by his conviction that his mother had abandoned him as a baby.
Willow loved him, even when she was angry with him.
If there was anything she could do to ease that pain
that Jai fought to hide from the world, she *would* do
it. And if he rediscovered a lost mother from the exercise, it would be well worth the risk she took and far
more than she had ever managed to achieve with her
own father, she conceded sadly.

A couple of hours later, Willow walked into the Royal
Chandrapur, an exclusive boutique establishment on
the other side of the city. From reception, she wheeled
Hari's buggy into the tiny lift and breathed in deep.

The first surprise was that the small blond woman
who opened the door to her appeared to be much
younger than she had expected. Well-preserved, she
assumed, meeting eyes of the same startling pale blue

as her husband's and taking in the huge smile on the other woman's face.

'I didn't think you'd come,' she said frankly.

Willow winced. 'I almost didn't. Jai doesn't know I'm here,' she admitted guiltily.

'And this is…little Hari?'

As the door closed behind them, Jai's mother knelt down by the side of the buggy and studied Willow's son in fascination. 'He is spookily like Jai was at the same age,' she whispered appreciatively. 'Just a little older than Jai was when I left India.'

Willow breathed in deep and settled into the seat the other woman indicated with a casual hand. 'What I don't understand is, if you wanted contact with Jai why did you virtually cut him dead when you did finally meet him as an adult?'

'Let me start at the beginning and then perhaps you'll understand better. If you don't, that's fine too. I'm grateful you came here. First of all, I am Milly… and you are… Willow, I gather?'

Willow harnessed the very rude impatience tugging at her and nodded with a smile.

'Would you like tea?'

'No, thanks. Being here with you makes me a little nervous. Let's talk about whatever we have to talk about,' Willow urged.

'A little background first, then,' Milly decided, seemingly magnetised by the tiny fingers Hari was stretching out to her. 'May I lift him?' she asked hopefully.

Leaning down, Willow detached the harness and

watched her son being scooped gently into his grand-mother's arms.

'Where do I start?' Milly sighed then. 'I was twenty and Jai's father was fifty when we married. My family were against it from the start because of the age gap but I was madly in love and I thought I knew it all.'

'I didn't know that there was such a big age gap be-tween you,' Willow admitted.

'The marriage didn't work from the start. Rehan wanted a quiet little wife, who stayed at home, and I was very independent. He was insanely jealous and controlling but the assaults didn't begin until after Jai was born,' Milly murmured flatly.

Willow's clear gaze widened in dismay. 'He *hit* you?' she exclaimed.

Milly nodded. 'We had terrible rows and he couldn't control his temper. But I'm talking about slaps and kicks, not severe beatings.'

'Abuse is abuse,' Willow opined.

'When my mother was dying, I had to return to Eng-land to be with her and, before I left, I made the mistake of telling Rehan that I believed we should separate. My biggest mistake, though, was agreeing to leave Jai be-hind until I came back. I was only away for two weeks,' Milly proffered. 'Rehan attended my mother's funeral and brought what he said were divorce papers for me to sign but they were all in Hindi. I was so relieved that he was willing to let me go without a fuss that I signed… I hadn't the smallest suspicion that I was surrendering my right to have custody of my son or access to him and by the time I realised that it was too late.'

'Jai's father tricked you?' Willow was appalled.

Milly lifted a thick file on the small table between them and extended it. 'If you can do nothing else, give this to Jai. It's the proof of all the years I fought through the courts to try and regain access to him. I failed.'

'But why, if you *wanted* to see him, did you deny him or whatever it was you did when you *did* see him?' Willow demanded bluntly.

'My husband and stepchildren didn't know Jai existed at that stage,' Milly volunteered shamefacedly. 'Steven, my second husband, knew about my marriage to Rehan but I didn't tell him that I'd had a child. My battle to see Jai consumed a decade and a half of my life and I got nowhere in all that time. I needed to move on to retain my sanity and make a fresh start. But I *will* admit that I was fearful of telling Steven that I had been deprived of my right to see my own child because, with three kids of his own, it might have made him doubt the wisdom of marrying me.'

The picture Willow was forming became a little clearer in receipt of that frank admission. 'Steven had three children? They're not yours?' she prompted.

'He was a widower with a young family when we met. I did hope to have another child, but I was almost forty by the time we married and it didn't happen. It was only a few months afterwards that I ran into Jai in the flesh,' his mother confided with tears in her eyes. 'Someone actually introduced me to him… I was floored—there he was in front of me with his face stiffening as he realised who I was and I had been too scared to tell Steven about him! I walked away because I didn't know what else to do with other people all around us. I wasn't prepared.'

'And then you tried to see Jai afterwards to explain,' Willow filled in with a grimace. 'And it was too late. The damage was done.'

Milly's regret was palpable as she rocked Hari, who was curled up in her arms, perfectly content. 'If only people stayed this innocent.' She sighed. 'I left a baby behind and now he's a man and they're much more complicated.'

Tell me about it, Willow ruminated uneasily, wondering whether she should go straight back to the Lake Palace and tell Jai who she had been with, or whether to go shopping instead in an effort to make her cover-up lie the truth, which would give her time to choose the optimum moment for such a revelation. But would there ever be a right moment to tackle so very personal and controversial a subject?

Deepening the deception she was already engaged in, however, felt even more wrong to her. Indeed, even being with Milly without her son's knowledge felt wrong to Willow at that moment. But good intentions had to count for something, didn't they? She argued with herself as she lifted the file and told Milly that she needed to get home but hoped to see her again. The older woman's answering smile was sad, as if she seriously doubted the likelihood of them ever having a second meeting, and she thanked Willow heartily again for being willing to see her and giving her the chance to meet her grandson. When Willow mentioned Jivika's input, Milly simply rolled her eyes, unimpressed.

'Jivika is sincere,' Willow insisted defensively.

'But nothing's changed. My ex-husband and, by the sound of it, now Jai as well have too much influence, too much status to be treated like ordinary people.' Milly studied her with embittered eyes. 'They may not rule any more but they're still royal in the eyes of thousands. That's why I never had a hope of fighting Rehan and winning. It was never an equal playing field. There were witnesses, who could've supported me but who were unwilling to expose their Maharaja for the man he really was.'

'I'm truly sorry,' Willow muttered uncomfortably. 'I can't promise anything, but I will *try* to talk to Jai some time soon.'

Even if it cost her *her* marriage? she asked herself worriedly as the limo drove back to the palace with Hari dozing contentedly in his child seat. Or was that an exaggerated fear? Who could tell how badly Jai would react? No, it wasn't her place to act as a persuader, she reasoned uneasily. She would admit to meeting up with his mother and give him the file and leave it at that. She had interfered enough. He would make up his own mind about what, if anything, he wanted to do with what he learned.

When Jai went in search of Willow mid-morning he assumed she had gone to see Sher until he recalled that his friend had mentioned a trip to Mumbai that day, and he phoned her driver instead to discover where she had gone. A hotel? A moment later he rang the hotel and without hesitation requested a list of the British guests staying there. Only a few minutes beyond that he knew the only possible reason for his wife's visit to the Royal Chandrapur and he could not credit that, after what he had told her, she could have gone to meet his mother. It outraged him and it didn't make sense to him. Even so, by the time acceptance of that unwelcome fact had set in, his outrage had settled into a far more dangerous sense of betrayal.

When Willow climbed out of the limo carrying her sleeping son, eager hands were extended to take him back to the nursery and his lunch. Straightening, she headed up the shallow marble steps and saw Jai poised in the empty hall. One glance at the narrowed chilling glitter of his eyes and the forbidding coolness of his lean, strong features and her stomach dropped as though the ground beneath her feet had suddenly vanished. Her mouth ran dry and she swallowed painfully.

CHAPTER TEN

'YOU KNOW WHERE I've been,' Willow guessed, her fingers biting into the heavy file she clasped in one hand. 'Let me explain.'

'Let me make it clear from the start—there *is* no acceptable explanation,' Jai asserted, his shadowed, well-defined jaw line clenching hard as he strode into the library.

He leant back against the desk in the centre of the room, tall and lean and bronzed and beautiful, and her heart clenched because there was a look in his eyes that she had never seen before and it frightened her. He looked detached, wholly in control and calm but utterly distant, as if she were a stranger.

'How did my mother contact you?' Jai shot the question at her.

'By email. One of your staff gave it to me.' Willow shrugged awkwardly. 'I suppose they didn't want to give it to you. I wasn't even going to mention it to you after what you'd told me about her, but then I had a conversation with…er…someone at the party that made me realise that there are two sides to every story.'

Jai elevated an eloquent black brow. *'Someone?'*

Stiff as a board, Willow angled an uneasy hand in dismissal. 'I'm not going to name names. I don't want you dragging anyone else into this mess. I don't want you to be angry with anyone but me.'

'I'm not angry. I am stunned by your intrusion into a matter that is confidential. But I am repelled by what can only be your insatiable curiosity and your complete lack of sensitivity!' Jai enumerated in a voice that shook slightly, belying his contention that he was not angry.

Willow's tummy turned over sickly and her natural colour ebbed. 'I intended to tell you.'

'But you still went to see her,' Jai condemned harshly. 'You knew how I would feel about that and yet *still* you went to see her—to do *what*? To discuss long-past events that are none of your business? To listen to her lies?'

'It's not rational for you to place a complete block on her side of the story or to assume that she's lying without hearing the facts,' Willow dared, but then fear of the trouble she had already caused between them punctured her bravado. 'But I *am* very sorry that I've upset you.'

Jai raked long brown fingers through his luxuriant black hair. 'You let me down. You deceived me.'

'I didn't deceive you!' she gasped in dismay.

'Not telling me that you were planning to meet her was a deception, an unforgivable deception!' Jai ground out in a raw undertone. 'You quite deliberately went behind my back to do something which you knew went against my principles.'

'But I had good intentions,' Willow muttered frantically, her chest tightening at the bite of that threatening word, 'unforgivable,' being attached to anything she had done. 'Feelings always win out over principles with me.'

'I trusted you.'

'No, you've never trusted me. You don't even trust me with your best friend,' Willow reminded him helplessly.

A tinge of dark colour edged Jai's high cheekbones and he studied her grimly. 'I got over that. I worked it out for myself. I *was* jealous of the bond you seem to have forged with Sher and it unsettled me,' he admitted flatly. 'I wasn't thinking logically when I spoke to you yesterday and the issue would've been cleared up last night had you not taken Hari to bed with you. I didn't want to disturb you.'

'You mean…you came to see me later on?' Willow prompted in surprise.

Jai jerked his arrogant dark head in confirmation.

'Thank you for that,' Willow acknowledged tautly, conceding that at least that issue now seemed to have been laid to rest, but not comforted by that knowledge when a bigger abyss seemed to have opened up between them. A gulf she was wholly responsible for creating, she conceded wretchedly.

And she wasn't surprised by that, not now, when she could see the very real damage that she had done with her foolish attempt at undercover sleuthing on his behalf. Jai still emanated tension and the raw glitter of his pale eyes and the compression of his lips remained unchanged. He was convinced that she had betrayed his trust. She had hurt him, and she hadn't meant to, but that wasn't much consolation for her at that moment. Hurting Jai when she had intended only to help him was a real slap in the face.

But then what had she thought she could possibly accomplish when the subject of his estranged mother was still so raw with him that he didn't even like to discuss it? Trying to play God usually got people into trouble, she reflected unhappily. Her handling of the issue had been downright clumsy and poorly thought through. Her hand ached with the tight grip she still had on the file in her hand and she settled it down heavily on the desk.

'Your mother gave this to me.'

'I don't want it…whatever it is,' Jai bit out.

'It's a record of all the legal action she took while you were still a child when she was fighting to gain access to you. Solicitor's letters, family court decisions. It's all there in black and white. I can explain why she couldn't face speaking to you in public as well.'

'I'm not interested.'

'Well, that's your decision,' Willow agreed tightly. 'But if you want my opinion—'

'I *don't*,' Jai sliced in curtly as he swept up the file in one powerful hand. 'I will ensure that this is returned to her.'

'All right.' Willow raised her hands in a semi-soothing gesture as she stepped back from the desk.

'I won't say any more. I may have blundered in where angels fear to tread but I didn't mean to cause this much trouble or harm anyone.'

Jai stared at her with unnerving intensity. 'Why *did* you do it?'

Willow could feel the blood in her face draining away with the stress of that simple acerbic question. 'I thought I could help. I suppose that was pretty naive of me.'

'*Who* did you wish to help?' Jai demanded in a savage undertone of condemnation. 'I'm a grown man, Willow. My father is dead, and I grew up without a mother. I didn't miss my mother because I never knew her. I am more concerned by the damage you have done to us.'

'Us?' she repeated uncertainly.

His lean, darkly handsome features hardened, his eyes chilling to polar ice. 'How do you think that we— our marriage—can possibly come back from this betrayal?' he slung at her rawly.

Willow stared back at him in shock at that stinging question. Was he saying that he truly could not forgive her for what she had done? Perspiration broke out on her brow. Suddenly she felt sick, shaky with fear.

Jai paced angrily away from her as though he could not bear to be too close to her. 'You keep secrets from me,' he condemned harshly, his distaste unhidden. 'You kept your pregnancy and the birth of my son a secret. You kept my mother's email a secret and you intended to keep your visit to her a secret as well for who knows how long!'

'Only because I wanted to meet her and give her a chance!' Willow argued in desperation.

'You said I lacked trust and understanding but have you considered your own flaws?' Jai asked with cruel clarity. 'What do I care about a woman who walked away from me thirty years ago? You and Hari are supposed to be my family now *and* the only family I need. But when I look at the deceit and disloyalty you are capable of, I feel like a fool and I cannot see a future for us!'

Frozen to the beautiful Persian rug, Willow watched Jai walk back out of the library again while her heart plummeted to basement level. Shattered, she just stood there. If he couldn't see a future for them, where did that leave her? Did that mean he was thinking about a divorce? *Truly?* Was their marriage over now because she had angered and disappointed him? But Jai believed that she had betrayed him and that went *deep*.

When she walked through the hall, Ranjit reminded her that lunch was ready. Although she had absolutely no appetite, she struggled to behave normally, to behave as though her life hadn't just fallen apart in front of her, and she headed out to the coolness of the terrace with a heavy heart, praying that Jai would join her and give her the chance to reason with him.

There, however, she sat in solitary splendour, striving to act as though nothing had happened while pushing food round her plate. She had messed up. Correction, she had messed up spectacularly. Jai had moved on from his dysfunctional beginnings. He might still be sensitive about his mother's apparent desertion, but he had learned to live with it, and he hadn't needed her stirring up those muddy waters again.

More tellingly, Jai was much more disturbed by the truth that she had kept secrets from him and acted without his knowledge. Her heart sank because she *was* guilty of making those mistakes and had little defence to offer on that score.

She hadn't known Jai when she'd conceived a child with him. She hadn't known how straight and blunt and honest he was or how much he valued those traits. Loving him, however, she had blundered in, convinced she could act as a peacemaker between him and his estranged mother. How on earth had she been so stupid that she had gone digging into his past, believing that she could somehow heal old wounds and make him happy? Nothing was ever that simple and adults were much more multifaceted than children. As he had reminded her, he was an adult now with a different outlook and values and he was infinitely more disturbed by the reality that the wife he had just begun to trust had let him down than by old history.

Jai had looked at her and found her wanting, Willow registered sickly. Her own father had always looked at her in that light, as his disappointing daughter, who had failed to live up to his fond hopes for her. Being a disappointment was nothing new to Willow but, when the judge was Jai, her failure to reach his standards cut through every layer of skin and hurt as fiercely as an acid burn. Distressed, she left the table to go and find Jai again and attempt to explain the motivation behind her interference.

He wasn't in his office and she wandered through the beautiful rooms until she found him in the relatively small room that his father had used as a study. Above the desk hung a handsome portrait of his late father, Rehan, in a traditional Rajput warrior pose. Jai was in an armchair, his lean, lithe body sleek and taut in an innately graceful sprawl. He had a whiskey glass in his hand and a reckless glitter lit up his bright gaze. Willow's eyes zoomed straight to the file that lay open on the desktop.

'I need to explain things,' she murmured tautly. 'You have to understand why I did what I did…'

'What's to explain?' Jai asked flatly, his wide sensual mouth settling into a grim line. 'There is no arguing with what's contained in that file. Obviously, the father I idolised lied to me all my life and behind those lies there *must* be even worse revelations. People with nothing to hide don't lie.'

'Jai… I—'

'The someone who tipped you off could only have been my aunt, Jivika,' Jai guessed, rising abruptly from his seat. 'Jivika will know everything and that's who I need to speak to now and finish this.'

Willow froze on the threshold of the room, recognising the pain darkening his eyes and shrinking from it in the knowledge that she had inflicted it on him by forcing him to deal with painful truths. 'Let the dust settle first. Mull it over. And don't forget,' she muttered ruefully, 'we all have a good side and a bad side. No matter what you find out one fact doesn't change—you still had a wonderful father who loved you.'

'Who told me that my mother was the love of his life…and yet, according to those documents, he abused her,' Jai breathed with a shudder of revulsion, his shame at such a revelation palpable. 'He lied on so many different levels that are unpardonable. Jivika, however, will know everything and she's family. It will be confidential. I have to know it *all* now.'

For the first time, Willow understood why Jai's aunt had resisted the temptation to interfere, because the ugly truth about his parents' marriage had devastated Jai, rolling a wrecking ball through his every conviction and fond memory. 'I was so naive about this situation,' she confided with heartfelt regret. 'I thought I could fix things but all I've done is cause more damage.'

'No,' Jai contradicted squarely, springing upright and towering over her. 'Even the toughest truths shouldn't be concealed from those concerned.'

'Even when you consider what it's done to our relationship?' she pressed unhappily.

'You were trying to right an injustice. I can respect that,' Jai told her tightly. 'But I don't know if I can accept it and still live with you.'

His savage honesty crushed her. It contained none of the emotion she had longed to see coming in her direction. As Jai left the palace to visit his aunt, her tummy gave a nauseous flip and she turned away again, reckoning that whatever he learned would only cause him more distress. Ultimately, Jai *could* forgive her because she had exposed a truth that should never have been hidden from him, but it didn't mean he would like her for it or that he would want to continue their marriage with a woman he didn't feel he could trust. Nor was he likely to love her for shining a bright light over his father's deceit and his mother's victimhood. And love was what she was always seeking from Jai and least likely to receive, because love had much more humble beginnings.

Sometimes she thought that she had fallen in love with Jai the first time he smiled at her. Or had it happened when he wrapped an arm round her and offered her comfort, showing her a level of tenderness and understanding that she had never experienced before? Yet, it had been his raw, uninhibited passion that had exploded her out of the almost dreamlike state in which she had then lived her life, humbly accepting her limitations while doggedly following her own path and striving to rise above her father's dissatisfaction with her. In matters of the heart, however, she had been naive until Jai came back into her life. Back then she had kept safe within narrow guidelines, never taking a risk, never allowing herself to want anything that seemed as if it might be out of reach. Jai, however, had been a huge risk, and marrying a man so far removed from her in terms of looks, status and wealth had been a challenge because right from the start she had felt out of her depth.

And now she was drowning in a deep sense of loss because she knew that Jai would never look at her in the same way again. Whatever she had achieved, whatever wrong she had tried to put right, she had been disloyal to him and once again she had acted behind his back, employing the secrecy that he abhorred. A prey to her tumultuous emotions, Willow found it impossible to settle to any task while Jai was still out.

Mid-afternoon, she heard the musicians strike up and watched Ranjit make a beeline for the entrance before forcing herself to walk upstairs and take refuge in their bedroom. If he wanted to discuss anything with her, he could come and find her. In the short-term it would be tactless of her to intrude when he probably still needed time and space to absorb what he had learned. Fed up with the warring thoughts assailing her and the almost overwhelming desire to run to his side and offer comfort, she kicked off her shoes and lay down on the bed, fighting her own inclinations to leave him alone rather than crowd him. After all, if she crowded him, she might only encourage him to dwell on the negative feelings he had been having about their marriage before his departure.

When Jai strode through the bedroom door and gave her a brilliant shimmering smile, it utterly disconcerted her. In consternation, Willow sat up and stared at him.

'After what I said to you in my state of shock, I'm surprised that you're still here,' Jai admitted tautly, 'and not on the first flight back to London.'

'Some of what you said was fair. I *did* keep secrets, but only because I didn't want to upset you. I honestly believed that telling you I was pregnant would be the worst news you'd ever heard,' Willow confided ruefully. 'And I couldn't face it.'

'After you, Hari's the best thing that ever happened

to me,' Jai murmured in confident rebuttal. 'I didn't appreciate that when I first found out about him. But he gave us the chance to be together in a way that I could cope with.'

Her smooth brow furrowed because she didn't understand. She had expected Jai to return angry or despondent, but he was demonstrating neither reaction. 'Cope with?' she queried.

'I've never been into relationships. I've avoided normal relationships as if they were toxic,' he reminded her uncomfortably. 'My father never recovered from losing my mother and I was always very aware of that. It made me very reluctant to get in too deep with a woman and, when I did break that rule, I ended up with Cecilia and that was a hard lesson too. I didn't have another relationship until I met you and that's why it's been rocky between us and I've been...' his shrug was uneasy '...all over the place with you.'

'All over the place?' she repeated uncertainly.

'When I married you I assumed we would have a detached marriage where after a while we each operated separately, but it didn't turn out like that and I found the closeness that seemed so natural between us...well, for me it was primarily unnerving. I hadn't bargained on feeling that way and I backed off fast,' he extended ruefully.

Recalling the second week of their marriage, Willow released a sigh. 'That hurt me.'

A wry smile slashed the tension from Jai's beautifully modelled mouth. 'And you called me on it, which was typical of you. I wasn't used to that either. Women have always treated me as though everything I do is right and amazing...and then *you* came along.'

Willow winced. 'Yes, and then I came along,' she echoed unhappily.

'And you challenged me every step of the way. You insisted that I treated you with respect. You had your opinions and your own way of looking at things and, while you were happy to listen to my viewpoint, you were independent, and I've never met with that before in a woman. You disagree with me. You were different and I liked that,' he admitted tautly. 'It's a remarkably attractive talent, frustrating too, but I've discovered that I find it much more stimulating than having my ego stroked.'

Willow breathed in deep, wondering where the conversation was heading. 'Really? Well, that's fortunate because I think you have a very healthy ego as it is. You'd become unbearable if I agreed with everything you said.'

Jai laughed softly. 'Probably, but not while you're around,' he acknowledged. 'I haven't been a mega success at being a husband, have I?' He shifted an expressive brown hand and groaned. 'You get to me on levels I never expected to visit with a woman. It throws me off balance and then I get all worked up and I overreact like I did last night when I accused you of flirting with Sher...and as I did today.'

Willow nodded slowly. 'I hope you now realise that's there's nothing—'

'I was jealous,' Jai framed with grim finality. 'Jealous for the first time ever, so *that* meant the fault had to be yours, not mine. I didn't want to *talk* about it last night. I wanted to slide into bed with you and whisper, "I'm a jealous toad," and drown my hurt pride in sex, but you had Hari with you and I didn't want to disturb the two of you. I bet Hari would have started crying if you tried to return him to his lonely cot.'

Her natural smile drove what remained of her tension from her heart-shaped face. 'Oh, dear…' she whispered, and she extended a forgiving hand to him. 'You should've woken me. I wouldn't have minded. I didn't mean to fall asleep with Hari. I was sort of using him like a teddy bear for comfort.'

'I'd much rather you used me for comfort,' Jai confided, closing his hand over hers and using that connection to tug her off the side of the bed and into his arms. He covered her mouth slowly and urgently with his and kissed her breathless. She leant against him for support, letting the remainder of her tension drain away.

'I went to see your mother because—' she began awkwardly.

'No, not now,' Jai interrupted, pressing a fingertip against her parted lips. 'Let tonight be for us. Anyway, I'm reasonably intelligent. I've already worked out *why* you did it.'

'Have you really?' she asked.

'Yes,' Jai assured her with satisfaction. 'I'm getting better at understanding how your mind works. Jivika dropped you in it. Her knowledge has been burning a hole in her brain for years and she jumped at the chance to share. And, you being you, you couldn't resist the urge to try and create a happy ending for everyone involved.'

'Principally you,' Willow whispered. 'It was arrogant of me to think I knew best.'

'And even more arrogant of me to start ranting about disloyalty and deception because the woman I know and love isn't capable of that kind of betrayal,' he concluded.

Willow froze. 'Know…and *love*?'

'Passionately love,' Jai qualified levelly. 'I love you in a way I have never loved any woman and I didn't even realise it was love. I told myself all sorts of face-saving lies when I stopped having sex with other women after that night I spent with you.'

Her gaze flew up to his in shock. 'Are you saying that you weren't with anyone else after me…all those months?' she prompted in disbelief.

'Yes. I persuaded myself that my celibacy was down to guilt at having taken advantage of you. I even assumed that I'd somehow gone off sex. When I tried repeatedly to check up on you afterwards, I told myself it was because I felt responsible for your well-being. In fact, what I was feeling was really quite simple, I just wanted to *see* you again, but I wasn't ready to admit that to myself.'

Willow, however, was still in shock and concentrating on only one startling fact at a time. 'You mean all that time while I was pregnant and raising Hari you didn't—'

'I haven't been with anyone else since our first night,' Jai confirmed. 'I didn't *want* anyone else. What

I found with you was so good that every other experience paled in comparison. So, yes, I was in love with you from way back then and, no, I didn't understand that.'

Willow's eyes rounded in wonder and she looked up into those gorgeous arctic-blue eyes and suddenly she was smiling. 'I love you too,' she told him quietly and without fanfare.

'I was hoping so,' Jai admitted, smiling down at her with love and tenderness gleaming in his intent gaze. 'I mean, you had the bravery to confront me with something everyone else ran scared from, and I very much hoped that love gave you the strength to go against my wishes in the belief that what you found out might make me happier.'

'You understand,' she breathed in relief.

'Of course I do. In the equivalent position I would have done the same thing for you. I very much regret that I wasn't around when your father was doing a number on your self-confidence,' he confessed. 'It also made me appreciate that he had a side to his character that I never saw, a less presentable side.'

'I'm sorry about what you've had to hear about your father.'

'Later, not now,' he insisted again, brushing her hair back from her cheeks and reaching behind her to run the zip down on her dress. 'Tonight is all about us and I'm determined that nothing will come between us.'

'*Literally!*' She gasped as her dress pooled round her feet and he dispensed with her bra even faster.

Jai skimmed off her panties and lifted her back onto

the bed, standing back from her to strip off his clothes with near indecent haste. 'I'm burning for you,' he groaned.

He came down to her, his skin on hers feverishly hot and his sensual mouth hungry and urgent, both hands holding hers to the mattress until they fought free to sink into his luxuriant hair. In the space of minutes her life had been transformed by the simple truth that the man she loved not only understood her, but also loved her back with all the fierce emotion she had long craved. Happiness flooded her like a rejuvenating force, every insecurity forced out and forgotten because what she had most wanted in the world had suddenly become hers.

'I'm crazy about you,' Jai husked in the aftermath of their unashamed passion. 'I couldn't wait to get back here to be with you because I so much regretted what I'd said to you and nothing else mattered. The past is the past and I don't want to revisit it, now that the truth is out.'

'Meaning?' she prompted.

'There will be no recriminations. Not on my part. We all get a clean sheet. My father's behaviour almost destroyed my mother and the guilt of knowing that and remaining silent tormented Jivika for years. We'll leave all that behind us now and my mother will be part of our lives,' he outlined.

'You've *seen* your mother? You've spoken to her?'

'Yes, but only very briefly,' Jai told her with a rueful smile as he looked down at her, his lean, darkly handsome face pensive. 'Unfortunately, she's flying back to London tomorrow and it's her stepdaughter's wedding in a couple of days, so she couldn't delay her flight. But she's planning to come back for a visit in a few weeks and spend time with us.'

'She must've been shocked when you showed up at the hotel,' Willow remarked.

'Shocked, delighted, tearful. We have a lot to catch up on, but we'll take our time,' Jai murmured, curving an arm round Willow to press her closer. 'And if it wasn't for you I wouldn't even have had the opportunity to meet her and give her that chance. For that I owe you a debt I can never repay.'

'Oh, I'll take it out of your hide somehow,' Willow teased, running an appreciative hand down over a long, lean, hair-dusted thigh. 'Don't you worry about that. You'll be paying it off for a very long time and, I promise you now, it's likely to use up every ounce of your surplus energy.'

Jai burst out laughing and crushed her lips under his. 'I love you so much, *balmaa*.'

Willow succumbed to a shameless little wriggle of encouragement and pressed her mouth tenderly to a bare brown shoulder. 'I love you too and I'm going to have to learn Hindi to know what you're calling me.'

'Beloved,' Jai translated, a little breathless as her wandering hands stroked across the taut expanse of his flat stomach.

'I like that,' she told him happily. 'I like that very much indeed.'

EPILOGUE

IN AN ELEGANT shift dress the shade of polished copper, Willow studied her reflection in the mirror. The dress was very flattering, the ultimate in maternity wear, and very nearly concealed the bump of her second pregnancy.

A pair of lean bronzed hands settled gently on her hips from behind and she grinned as Jai's hands slowly slid round to caress her swollen stomach. She adored the fact that he was so ridiculously excited about the daughter she carried. They hadn't shared the gender news with anyone else, but Willow could hardly wait to make use of the pretty clothes she had begun to collect.

Even as a toddler, Hari was very much a little boy, stomping through mud and puddles and shouting with excitement as he climbed and jumped and toppled. Of course, their daughter might well be a little tomboy, just as energetic, but Willow knew that she would at least be able to enjoy dressing her daughter in pretty clothes until she became more mobile.

'Happy Birthday, *balmaa*,' Jai husked in her ear, breathing in the rich coconut scent of her tumbling strawberry-blond hair as he pressed a kiss to her shoulder and folded her back against his tall, powerful body.

A split second later, he stepped back to slowly slide a necklace round her slender throat, tipping her head forward to clasp it at her nape. Her fingers lifted to touch the sparkling diamond heart and she whirled with a smile in the circle of his arms to stretch up and find his mouth for herself. Excitement buzzed through her, an ache stirring in her pelvis as he crushed her against him, his urgency only matching her own, because Jai had been away on a business trip for a week and she had missed him.

'I was scared you wouldn't make it back in time,' she confided breathlessly against his shoulder.

'I would never miss your birthday,' Jai censured, watching her finger the delicate heart at her throat. 'That's my heart you hold and it *always* brings me home again.'

Willow giggled. 'You're getting almost romantic,' she teased. 'We should go downstairs and see our guests.'

'My mother was holding the fort when I arrived.'

'Milly is a terrific social asset,' Willow agreed, thinking of the mother-in-law she had never expected to have and her warm relationship with her and Jai's stepfather, Steven, a quiet, retiring older man with a delightful sense of humour.

Over the past two years, their family circle had expanded exponentially, but it was a comfortable and caring expansion, which both of them valued. Jai had dealt with his disillusionment over the father he had once idolised and moved on to develop a strong, deep bond with the mother he had been denied in childhood. He had also become acquainted with his maternal grandfather, the current Duke, who was almost ninety years old. Jai did think, though, that it was sad that his mother had never had another child and that he had no siblings, only stepbrothers and a stepsister, whom they only saw at occasional family events.

Even so, his aunt, Jivika, and her husband were regular visitors, along with various other, more distant relatives. Indeed, Jai and Willow had so many invitations out that they had to pick and choose which they could attend and sometimes it was a relief to return to the tranquillity of the Lake Palace, where life was a little less hectic and they could spend more time together as a couple.

Willow had become broody once Hari outgrew the nursery and turned into a leaping, bounding bundle of energy, no longer content to be cuddled for longer than ten seconds, unless of course he was ill or overtired. She had conceived quickly, and her second pregnancy was proving much easier than the first. She thought that was very probably because she was much less stressed this time and was able to rest whenever she liked.

'You're spoilt rotten!' Shelley had teased her on her last visit to Chandrapur. She was able to see her best friend regularly now because Shelley had more holiday leave in her new job managing a small boutique hotel, which belonged to Jai's cousins. In any case, Willow and Jai spent every spring and summer in London in addition to returning there every year to enjoy a special Christmas at the town house. And when Hari started school, they would be in London even more because Jai did not want his son to board as he had done until he was old enough to make that choice for himself.

And Shelley had spoken the truth, Willow acknowledged with quiet satisfaction, because Jai *did* spoil her and he did make her very, very happy. He also built up her confidence where her father had continually taken her down. Only weeks ago, she had made her first public speech on behalf of the homeless charity she had chosen as closest to her heart from the many supported by the Singh Foundation. Jai's words of praise had made her heart sing and nobody would ever have guessed by his demeanour that he had listened to her rehearse that same speech ten times over.

Now, meeting the arctic-blue intensity of his loving gaze, Willow had everything she'd ever wanted and much that she had not even dared to dream of having, because Jai loved her and their son as much as he loved being part of a family.

'I am crazy about you,' he husked as they descended the stairs to the noisy hubbub of their chattering guests. 'I counted the days until I could come home, and home is always where *you* are, *soniyaa*.'

'I love you too,' she whispered dreamily as his hand engulfed hers, and she whipped round where she stood to claim his sensual mouth for herself again. 'And on *your* birthday promise we'll have a private party for *two*.'

'We're having a very private party for two when everyone's gone home tonight,' Jai assured her, soft and low, running a slow, caressing hand down over her taut spine, making her quiver...

* * * * *

CRAVING HIS
FORBIDDEN
INNOCENT

LOUISE FULLER

To Hugo.
For learning how not to have the last word,
and always being up for a debate about Shakespeare x

CHAPTER ONE

SHIFTING THE PHONE against his ear, Bautista Caine silently dismissed his PA with a sharp upward flick of his head and turned his attention back to his sister's voice.

Not that Alicia was saying anything new in her message. It was more or less a repeat of what she'd said at the weekend—that she was so grateful, and he was the best brother, and she loved him—but it was still good to hear.

His mouth twisted. It had been a difficult, upsetting conversation, but was there any other kind when the subject was Mimi Miller?

He felt his shoulders tense against the fabric of his suit jacket.

Mimi, with her long blonde hair, even longer legs and those silky, soft lips that had melted against his in a kiss he had never forgotten... A kiss that had stifled all common sense and conscience and shaken him to his soul—

He gritted his teeth as his body stiffened like a pointer scenting game.

She was like the proverbial bad penny and probably always would be, given that nothing he'd said to his sister seemed to change her opinion of Mimi. Only a day ago she had told him quite earnestly that Mimi lacked confidence.

Yeah, right, and he was the Easter Bunny.

Nearly two years had passed since he'd dispatched his

sister to New York—ostensibly on the basis that it was a chance for her to learn first-hand about the day-to-day running of the Caine charitable foundation. He'd assumed that the geographical distance and the fact that she would be meeting new and—to his mind anyway—far more appropriate people, would finally bring an end to her incomprehensible and unfortunate friendship with Mimi.

He'd been wrong.

Gazing out of the window at the massed daffodils in the garden of his family's London residence, he narrowed his dark eyes as he mulled over his sister's upcoming marriage to Philip Hennessy.

The news had been neither surprising nor unwelcome, but Alicia's blithe announcement that she wanted Mimi to be her maid of honour had been both. He wasn't sure what had shocked him more: the fact that the two of them were still friends after so many months of separation, or the fact that his sister had chosen to keep their continuing friendship secret from him.

No, that wasn't fair.

He was sure that if he'd asked about Mimi Alicia would have told him anything he wanted to know. But of course he hadn't asked. He hadn't wanted to hear Mimi's name— much less have to face the memory of the last time he'd seen her, or his own part in what had been the narrowest of narrow escapes. It had been easier to assume that out of sight meant out of mind.

Only, despite his concerted efforts to make her so, Mimi Miller was never far from his mind. How could she be? Every time he saw his father he was reminded of the damage caused by her crooked relatives—and, worse, those few hours when he'd let his basest needs overrule his duty to safeguard his family.

He breathed out slowly against the knot in his shoulders.

As usual, when he let himself think about his sister's twenty-first birthday party, he felt the same see-sawing mix of anger and regret. And, as usual, he told himself that it had been a one-off, a momentary lapse of good sense, that he had been caught off-guard by her looking like that, *looking at him like that.* For up until that moment in time he'd seen Mimi simply as a child.

Afterwards he had tried to tell himself that it wasn't her fault. She hadn't chosen to be related by blood and marriage to a pair of crooks, and he hadn't blamed her for what her stepfather and uncle had done.

His lip curled. No, the blame for that lay squarely with him—for introducing Charlie Butler and Raymond Cavendish to his father, for not seeing beneath their urbane charm.

Yet he couldn't completely absolve Mimi of responsibility for her actions.

Even on the night there had been a couple of moments when he'd felt uneasy—something he'd put down to her being Alicia's friend…a friend of the family. Later, though—too late, in fact—it had become humiliatingly clear that she had played a part in her family's deception.

She had almost played *him*—so very nearly played him.

And incredibly, despite everything else that had happened, it was that betrayal—*her* betrayal—and his stupidity that still hurt the most now.

He felt the knot in his shoulders tighten.

At first he'd wanted it to be a coincidence, but her rapid, unexplained exit from the party had confirmed her guilt in his mind, and as events unfolded he'd stopped looking to exonerate her.

Later, for his father's sake and for the reputation of his family, he'd tried to deter Alicia from continuing their friendship—only, of course, his soft-hearted sister had ignored his advice.

He felt a surge of irritation. Not with Alicia. He knew she didn't live in the real world. But he did. And it was bad enough having led the wolves to his door once. Now it turned out that he'd failed again by not insisting she cut all ties with Mimi.

The tension in his shoulders was inching down his spine.

He knew exactly how it would play out if the media ever found out that his sister was BFF with the stepdaughter and niece of the men who had looted the Caine employees' pension funds. It wasn't going to be hard for them to find it out if Alicia made Mimi her maid of honour—and that was why he'd just had to tell his sister that it couldn't happen.

His jaw tensed.

Hearing her so upset had hurt. But the alternative—having Mimi centre-stage at the wedding and in the photos—was just not an option. So he'd used his father's ill-health and the potential damage to the family name to get her to change her mind, and it had worked, but he'd had to come up with something to soften the blow.

He'd done that too, only it was not ideal—far from it. For it would mean letting Mimi Miller back into his life. But he was going to see it through for his sister's sake.

Easing back in his chair, he felt his heart kick against his ribs.

This time there would be no lapses—momentary or otherwise. No loss of control nor lowering of his guard. No having to live with the knowledge that he had come close to putting his family in jeopardy for a second time.

This time it was going to be different. He would be pulling her strings, and he was going to enjoy every second of it.

* * *

Mimi Miller was running late.

Literally running.

Although, thanks to the heels she had unwisely chosen to wear, it was more a stumbling dash than a full-on sprint, and already her lungs were begging for mercy.

Oh, thank goodness.

This was the street. Slowing down to an unsteady walk, she caught sight of her reflection in a shop window and breathed out shakily.

It was her own fault she'd had to rush.

Not because she'd been dithering over what to wear. Clothes weren't really her thing and she only owned two dresses—one of which she hated because it was so tied up with love and dreams and heartache. Her other dress, a navy and white polka dot one, had looked sweet when she'd tried it on at home, but then she'd seen the state of her waist-length blonde hair and, panicking, walked straight into the nearest hair salon for a last-minute and eye-wateringly expensive blow-dry.

But it had been worth it, she thought, her skin tingling with excitement and happiness. Today was the first time she'd seen her best friend in nearly two years and she wanted to celebrate.

Stepping inside the restaurant, she glanced down at her legs, feeling suddenly self-conscious. Jeans and a T-shirt, preferably several sizes too large, was her usual outfit of choice, but Tenedor was a super-exclusive Argentinian eatery, popular with celebrities for its discreet staff and the tinted windows that made life hard for the *paparazzi*. It was definitely not the kind of venue you turned up to wearing faded denim.

Her breathing lurched. Should she even *be* here? It was a long time since she'd moved in these circles—two horrible, hopeless years since Charlie and Raymond had been sent to prison and her life had changed for ever.

But she was being stupid. Nobody was going to connect her with that haunted-looking girl outside the courtroom.

Above the diminishing drumroll of her heart she gave her name to the unsmiling *maître d'* and followed him through the restaurant, her excitement at seeing Alicia overriding her panic at being so conspicuous.

She still couldn't believe that it was two years since she'd last seen her friend. After Charlie and Raymond's arrest they had spoken on the phone—a short, unhappy conversation, with her apologising over and over for what had happened and Alicia tearfully repeating that it changed nothing between them.

Since then they had talked and texted, but after moving to New York Alicia had been busy working for her family's charitable foundation, and then she had met and fallen in love with Philip Hennessy, heir to a restaurant empire, and that had obviously taken up most of her time.

Now she and Philip were engaged, and according to the save the date card she'd received the wedding was going to be in May—less than three months away.

In other words, Alicia was effortlessly hitting all the milestones of adulthood.

Mimi's chest tightened. Whereas *she* was working as a *barista* in a coffee shop at Borough Market, her youthful ambitions to become a film director having stalled before they got started.

And as for her love-life…

It wasn't even a case of the less said the better—there was literally nothing to say. Her one bungled foray into the world of sexual relationships had left her with her virginity intact and her confidence so battered that she'd decided to put that part of her life on hold indefinitely.

She sighed. Early spring made being single seem so much harder. London's parks seemed to be full of pairs of ducks and deer all cosying up together, and it didn't help that the scent of spring flowers reminded her of Alicia's birthday party.

And Alicia's birthday party reminded her of Bautista.

Her breath caught in her throat.

Bautista Caine.

Her best friend's older brother—her first crush. The man who had broken her heart and then walked away without so much as a backward glance.

Bautista…with his curving, lazy smile and steady dark gaze.

She hadn't been alone in fantasising about him. Practically every girl in their school, and probably some of their mothers too, had drooled over him whenever he'd turned up to collect his sister, and it only took the briefest of glances at him to understand why.

He was smart, successful, and so charming that birds didn't just fly off the trees, they dropped like overripe fruit. Not that he was interested in schoolgirls or their mums. His girlfriends were all long-limbed, pouty-lipped models. Hardly surprising, then, that he'd found it so humiliatingly easy to turn down a night with his sister's gauche friend.

Her stomach tightened—only this time not with excitement.

It had been a long time since she'd allowed herself to think about Bautista and the night they *hadn't* spent together. But ever since Alicia had announced her engagement it had been getting harder and harder to hold back the memories and ignore the fact that at some point she was going to have to see him again or forfeit her friend's wedding. Because Alicia worshipped and adored her brother, and he adored her right back.

Unfortunately his feelings for Mimi were somewhat cooler—if complete indifference even had a temperature.

She shivered. It had been one of the few positives about Alicia's absence: not having to face the man who had kissed her and then an hour later looked straight through her as if she didn't exist.

And that had been *before* he'd found out about Charlie and Raymond's appalling abuse of trust.

She felt her stomach contract. Before that night at Fairbourne he'd treated her with measured politeness, but judging by his concerted efforts to keep Alicia on a different continent for the past two years—her friend had let slip that it had been his idea for her to move to New York—he clearly thought she was not to be trusted.

But maybe by the time they did come face to face she might actually have met someone who would compare to Bautista Caine and not be found wanting. Her heart skipped. Maybe she might be able to tell him truthfully that he wasn't all that—

'Mimi!'

It was Alicia, in a beautiful yellow dress, a smile splitting her face, her brown eyes shining with happiness and affection, and suddenly they were hugging and laughing and both talking at once.

'Oh, it's *so* good to see you.' Alicia took a step back and gazed at her with undisguised happiness. 'I thought you might be too busy to fit me in.'

'Doing what?'

'I don't know—you might have been hanging out at some indie film festival.'

Mimi laughed. 'Well, duh, that's *next* month.'

Giggling, Alicia gave her another crushing hug. 'I've missed you so much. I know we talk on the phone and stuff, but it's not the same as having you here.'

Mimi felt her ribs tighten. 'I've missed you too.'

Alicia smiled. 'You look amazing.'

'You mean I'm wearing a dress.'

'*No*, I mean you look amazing,' Alicia said firmly. 'Doesn't she?' She turned to the tall, fair-haired man standing behind her. 'Philip, this is my best friend—the very talented, soon-to-be-discovered filmmaker, Mimi Miller. Mimi, this is Philip. The love of my life and a perfect saint.'

Mimi squeezed her friend's hand. This was what she loved most about Alicia—the way she spoke from the heart. Anyone else would be hiding their feelings, trying to play it cool, making a joke, but Alicia had always been unashamedly open and honest.

Philip stepped forward. 'Hi, Mimi.' He kissed her lightly on both cheeks. 'Alicia talks about you so much I feel like I already know you.'

'And it didn't put you off coming to lunch?' She smiled at her friend. 'You're right—he is a saint.'

'Hardly!' Philip laughed, and then he turned towards Alicia, his eyes softening. 'Alicia's the saint. She makes the world a better place, and I'm the luckiest man alive.'

Mimi nodded. 'Yes, you are,' she said quietly.

But her pulse was beating out of time and she felt a familiar ache in her chest. Would any man ever say those words to her?

It seemed unlikely. She'd only ever really loved one man, and he had made it so dauntingly clear that his interest in her had been nothing more than a moment of indiscretion to be swiftly forgotten that she had decided there and then that she was not ready for love. Maybe she never would be if it involved making herself vulnerable to such unbearable hurt.

Her jaw tightened as she remembered how for a couple of hours she'd let herself believe that her youthful fantasy of love might become reality, only for Bautista Caine to trample her heart and her pride into dust.

Even now, nearly two years later, she could still picture his face as he had stared straight through her, despite having kissed her just an hour earlier with an intensity that had left her blinded, breathless and dazed.

She could feel herself being sucked towards the familiar vortex of unanswered questions.

Why had he kissed her?

No, why had he kissed her *like that*?

With such fierce, consuming hunger.

And why hadn't he come back?

Had she been too eager? Too clumsy?

Her heart balled like a fist.

It had hurt so much. It still did, if she let herself think about it, and what made the pain a thousand times worse was him being her best friend's older brother, for that meant she had no one to confide in.

Her stomach tightened.

She'd have liked to pretend that she hadn't said anything to Alicia purely out of love, and a desire not to put her friend in the middle, but part of her had been afraid. She knew what it was to be cast out into the darkness, and she hadn't been willing to risk losing Alicia as she had lost everything else.

And anyway, there had been too much other stuff going on—important stuff. Charlie and Raymond had been arrested and their two families had been torn apart, so she'd hardly been in a position to just call up her friend and discuss *not* sleeping with her brother.

But now was not the time to be dredging up that particularly dismal part of the past, she told herself firmly. Her best friend was here in London, and she wasn't going to let anything ruin that.

Sitting down, she glanced admiringly around the restaurant. 'This is such an amazing place.'

'Never mind that. I want you to tell me everything you've been doing,' Alicia said, laying down her menu. 'Starting with your film.'

Stalling for time, Mimi picked up her water glass. There was depressingly little to say. Like everything else she touched, it had fallen apart—all her effort and hopes turning to dust just as they always did.

It was true that she had made a film—a short, largely improvised black and white movie about a group of girls on a night out in London—and, incredibly, she had managed to find a distributor for it. Only that had been nine months ago, and she was still struggling to get it released. And, frankly, the chances of that ever happening seemed to be getting less and less likely.

She felt a twinge of tension in her shoulders.

When filming had begun, both her lead actresses had been desperate to grab some arthouse credentials, but since then they had signed on to a high school movie franchise, and now their lawyers were blocking her film's release on the grounds that their clients had only made the movie as a 'favour' to her.

It wasn't true. The real reason those actresses didn't want to see the film released was that some of their 'improvised' comments were not very PG, and they didn't want to damage their new, fresh-faced images.

It was all such a mess—and far too long and boring a story for a celebratory lunch.

She shook her head. 'Later.' Reaching over, she picked up Alicia's hand and turned it over so that the diamond engagement ring glinted beneath the lights. 'Right now I want to hear all about how you two got together.'

Watching her friend talk, Mimi found herself relax-

ing. There was something so innocent and hopeful about
Alicia. Philip was right. She *did* make the world a better
place, and she *wanted* to make the world better for everyone too.

'So, how many people are coming to the wedding?' she
asked as the waiters cleared the table.

Philip frowned. 'We've tried to keep the numbers down
to about two hundred.'

Mimi almost laughed. But of course—their wedding
wasn't just a private exchange of vows. It was a huge event
in the social calendar.

She cleared her throat. 'I'm guessing you're going to
have it at Fairbourne?'

Before her life had been turned upside down she'd been
a regular guest at Fairbourne, the Caines' fabled ivy-clad
Georgian manor. She could still remember her first visit—
how dazzled she'd been by the grandeur and beauty of
the house and the almost ludicrous perfection of everything in it.

Although not nearly so dazzled as she'd been when the
beautiful, dark-eyed heir to the estate had kissed her all
the way to his bedroom, closing the door and pulling off
his clothes first, then hers.

Her stomach clenched.

She felt her fingers twitch against the smooth white tablecloth. Bautista looked sexy as hell clothed. He had the
kind of lean, muscular physique and sculpted body that allowed him to wear anything and make it look better than
anyone else could. But naked—

Her mouth was suddenly dry. Naked, he was just beautiful, gorgeous…all endless, smooth golden skin and curving muscles.

An image of Bautista stretching out over her flickered
before her eyes and she blinked it away as she saw Ali-

cia shake her head, her soft brown eyes suddenly bright with tears.

'Oh, Lissy, what is it?'

Philip took Alicia's hand. 'Bob had a viral infection at Christmas and he's been a bit low since. That's why we've brought the date forward to May.'

Mimi nodded, trying to calm her beating heart. She'd met Alicia's father, financier and philanthropist Robert Caine, many times, and he'd always been a generous, gentle and welcoming host. She felt her stomach knot with guilt. Of course that had been before his already frail health had deteriorated following her stepfather and her uncle's betrayal.

'And it's why we decided to have the wedding in Argentina,' Philip added. 'It'll be autumn there, so warm but not humid.'

Alicia gave him a shaky smile, her face softening. 'And Basa has very sweetly offered to let us use his *estancia* in Patagonia for the actual ceremony, and let guests stop over at his house in Buenos Aires en route.'

Mimi's mouth curved upwards automatically, responding to the joy in her friend's voice, but for a moment she couldn't breathe or speak. Alicia's words were jangling inside her head like the notes on an out-of-tune piano, but she heard herself say quite normally, 'Oh, Lissy, that sounds wonderful.'

The waiters arrived with dessert and, glancing down at her hibiscus jelly and rum baba, Mimi suddenly felt sick. She'd known all along when she'd accepted Alicia's invitation to lunch that it was only a matter of time before Bautista's name came up in the conversation, but even so she was shocked by how much it hurt to hear it spoken out loud.

Was that how he felt when he heard *her* name?

Did he wince inside?

And if so was it with shame at how he'd treated her?

Or, given Charlie and Raymond's actions, was he just relieved that he'd called time before they'd actually slept together?

She doubted that having sex with the stepdaughter of one of the men who had almost ruined his family would be high up on his list of personal goals.

'It's the most beautiful place, Mimi. There's this huge expanse of sky, and the mountains in the distance, and soft golden grass in every direction.' Alicia smiled shyly. 'Basa says it's the first step to heaven.'

Her heart stilled in her chest.

No, that had been the touch of his lips on hers, she thought, heat sweeping over her skin at the sudden sharp memory of what it felt like to be kissed by Bautista.

Her hand shaking slightly, she picked up her glass and drank some wine in a hard swallow. 'I'm so looking forward to it, Lissy,' she said, with a conviction she didn't feel. 'It's going to be the most beautiful day. But is there anything I can do? I mean, I'm sure you've got heaps of people helping...'

'Actually, there is one thing we were going to ask you...'

There was a beat of silence as Philip and Alicia glanced at one another.

'Really?' Mimi leaned forward. 'So ask me?'

'We're going to have a photographer.' Philip grimaced. 'It's not really our kind of thing, all those formal staged shots, but Bob and my parents are a little old-fashioned that way.' He hesitated. 'But what we'd really like is for you to make a film for us.'

'Something personal,' Alicia said quickly. 'You know— like you did at school, with us just talking and being our-selves.' Her mouth trembled. 'You have such a gift, Mimi.

You capture a moment and hold it for ever, and I thought you might be able to do that for us.'

Mimi blinked. Her hands were shaking and her throat felt thick. 'You'd trust me to do that?' she said slowly.

They both nodded.

Meeting her gaze, Alicia gave her a lopsided smile. 'I've trusted you with my life—or have you forgotten playing lacrosse against St Margaret's?'

Mimi grinned. 'It's seared into my brain.'

Glancing over at her friend, she suddenly felt dizzy. More than anything, she wanted to say yes. She loved Alicia, and what better way to prove that than by making her shy, modest friend the star of her own film?

But she knew Alicia too well, and without a doubt this was her way of showing her some support. She didn't need to do that—not publicly, anyway, and especially not on her wedding day. It was enough for her that Alicia had always been such a loyal, true ally.

'Oh, Lissy, I'm just an amateur, really. And this is your big day.' She was trying to gather herself together.

'Isn't that exactly what I said she'd say?' Glancing at Philip, Alicia shook her head. 'I wish I could make you believe in yourself like I believe in you.'

Mimi rolled her eyes. 'You're a good friend, and it's a lovely idea, but you're biased.'

'I knew you'd say that too.'

Alicia smiled, and something in her smile snagged a tripwire in Mimi's head.

'And you're right—I am biased. But it doesn't matter because it wasn't my idea. Or Philip's,' she added as Mimi glanced at her fiancé. 'It was Basa's.'

Mimi froze. Her heartbeat was booming in her ears so loudly she was surprised everyone in the restaurant couldn't hear it.

'I don't believe you,' she said finally. And she didn't.

The Caines might not actually live in a castle, but after her stepfather and uncle had been arrested the family had pulled up a metaphorical drawbridge. Overnight she had simply stopped being invited into their world. There had been no drama about it. They were far too well-bred to make a scene. But she had known from what Alicia *hadn't* said that Robert and Bautista thought she was bad news, and she'd never had any reason to believe they had changed their mind.

Her breath felt jagged in her throat. All she had were those few hours at the party, when she'd mistakenly believed that Bautista felt about her as she felt about him.

'And *that's* why I asked him to join us so he could tell you himself.'

Finishing her sentence, Alicia lifted her hand and waved excitedly at someone across the restaurant.

Mimi glanced in the direction of her friend's gaze and instantly felt the fine hairs at the nape of her neck stand on end. On the other side of the room, with a lock of dark hair falling across his face, his dark suit clinging to his lean, muscular body like the ivy that grew over his family's Georgian mansion, was Bautista Caine.

Her heart seemed to stop beating.

Watching him move, she felt her body turn boneless. There was a swagger to the way he walked, a kind of innate poise and self-confidence that she had never possessed—except maybe briefly, when she was behind the camera. But even in a room like this—a room full of self-assured, beautiful people—he was by far the most beautiful, with his dark, almost black hair and eyes, and his fine features perfectly blending his English and Argentinian heritage.

But his impact on the crowded restaurant wasn't just

down to his bone structure, or those mesmerising sloe-dark eyes, or even that easy honeyed smile that made you forget your own name. He had what directors liked to refer to as *presence*: a mythical, elusive, intangible quality that made looking away from him an impossibility.

To her overstrained senses it seemed to take an age for him to reach the table. Quite a few of the diners clearly knew him and wanted to say hello. Her pulse skipped a beat as a famous Hollywood actress got to her feet and kissed him on both cheeks but Bautista seemed completely unfazed.

Of course he did: this was his world. More importantly, it wasn't hers, and no amount of lunching with A-listers was ever going to change that fact.

Her understanding of that was the difference between now and two years ago when, high on the incredible thrill of finally being noticed by the object of her unre-quited teenage affections, she'd let herself believe that their worlds could collide without any kind of collateral damage.

She knew better now. His abrupt change of heart had been humiliating and devastating—although of course his heart hadn't been the organ involved in that particu-lar encounter.

And that had made her humiliation complete. For al-though she might have been secretly hoping for a declara-tion of love, what she'd offered him had been sex. Simple, no-strings, walk-away-without-so-much-as-a-backward-glance sex.

And he'd turned her down.

Her heart felt like a jagged rock scraping against her ribs.

She had gone to his room willingly, eagerly, hoping, al-most believing, that she could pull it off. But of course all she'd managed to do was prove to herself that, as usual, she was punching above her weight.

'Basa.'

'Philip.'

She watched numbly as the two men embraced.

'No, don't get up, Lissy.' Leaning forward, Basa kissed his sister gently on both cheeks, and then Mimi felt her body tense as finally he turned towards her.

As their eyes met the chatter of the dining room seemed to recede.

Mimi stared at him in silence. It wasn't fair.

It wasn't fair for him to be so devastatingly good-looking. She wanted to hate him. She *needed* to hate him. Only it was hard to treat him as the despicable human being he was when he was packaged so delightfully.

But she wasn't some love-struck girl living out a fantasy, she reminded herself quickly, and there was no excuse for feeling so jittery about a man who had treated her so badly.

'Well, if it isn't little Mimi Miller,' he said softly. 'In the flesh.'

She felt her pulse pool between her thighs. His voice was the icing on the cake. Not some simpering frosted butter but a dark molten glaze—what chocolate would sound like if it could talk.

He leaned down and she breathed in the faint hint of his cologne as his lips brushed against first one cheek and then the other. Her breath stumbled in her throat as he sat down beside her, stretching his long legs out in her direction so she quickly had to tuck hers under her chair to stop their limbs colliding.

He held her gaze for a moment, and then his dark, mocking eyes dropped to her mouth. Instantly she felt her skin begin to tingle, her nipples tightening against the fabric of her dress in a way that made her want to duck under the table and hide.

Breath burning in her throat, she watched him lean back in his seat, and then, turning to face Alicia, he said calmly, 'So, what did I miss, Sis?'

She shook her head. 'Most of lunch. You were supposed to be here at one o'clock.'

He grinned unrepentantly. 'And I messaged you to say I'd be late.' Reaching across the table, he grabbed his sister's hand and squeezed it affectionately. 'Hey, I'm sorry I missed lunch, okay? But, look, I can still have dessert.'

Lowering his ridiculously long eyelashes, he gazed pointedly at Mimi's untouched rum baba.

'Here. Knock yourself out.' Smiling stiffly, she pushed her plate towards him, wishing she could throw it at his head.

'Thank you.' His fingers brushed against hers as he took the plate. 'Now, isn't this civilised?'

Their eyes met, and his cool, unblinking gaze made ice trickle down her spine, for it felt as if they were having a private and far less civilised conversation.

Oblivious to the tension, Philip leaned forward, his eyes seeking out a waiter. 'Do you want coffee with that?'

Basa looked up from his food and nodded. 'I could murder an espresso.'

Philip glanced at Mimi.

'Yes, please.' She smiled stiffly, relief washing over her skin. At least coffee meant this would soon be over and she could escape Basa's taunting gaze.

'So four espressos, then.'

'Actually, could you make that just two?' Alicia nudged her fiancé in the ribs. 'We're meeting your aunt now, remember?'

'We are?' Philip looked blank for a moment and then a

flicker of understanding crossed his face and he nodded slowly. 'Oh, yes, that's right. We are…meeting my aunt.'

Basa rolled his eyes. 'Really subtle, guys.'

He tilted his face towards Mimi and gave her a long, slow smile that sucked the air from her lungs.

'My sister has probably told you that she invited me along so that I could persuade you to film her wedding, but actually that was just an excuse. She thinks we need to have a little chat, just you and me—you know, to clear the air about our families' shared history.'

Mimi blinked.

Absolutely. Not.

She practically shouted the words inside her head, and she was just opening her mouth to repeat them out loud when Basa cut across her.

'And I think she's right,' he said smoothly. 'After all, a wedding is all about moving forward. But obviously if Mimi would rather not…?'

His eyes held hers, dark, uncompromising, daring her to refuse. Beside him, Alicia was staring at her, her own eyes soft and hopeful.

'Please, Mimi. You're two of my favourite people in the world, and I know you're worried about what happened with your family and mine and that's why you don't want to film the wedding.' She bit her lip. 'Look, Philip and I are going to go now, but will you promise me that you'll stay and talk? Please? For me?'

Mimi wanted to say no, to say that there was no point, because Basa wasn't going to listen to anything she said. But the words wouldn't form in her mouth. Not because she didn't believe them or because they weren't true—she did and they were—but because this was the first time she had found herself up against both Caine siblings and she knew she couldn't fight the two of them.

Lifting her face to meet her friend's, she forced her mouth into a smile, and beneath the blood roaring in her ears she heard herself say lightly, 'Okay, I'll stay and talk. I promise.'

CHAPTER TWO

WATCHING ALICIA AND Philip leave, Mimi felt as though she was being left in the playground by her mother on the first day of school. Unlike Basa, she thought, as he leaned back in his chair like a Roman emperor at a feast being held in his honour.

Her heart was thumping like a piston. This wasn't the reunion she'd imagined with Basa—and she'd imagined quite a few of them. The majority had involved the man calmly sitting beside her and apologising, and then begging her forgiveness.

Unfortunately, as with most of her life, the reality was a long way from her fantasy. Her attempt to matchmake for her mother had ended in disaster, her one shot at becoming a film director was languishing in a lawyer's office, and her seduction of Basa had been utterly humiliating.

Was it really so surprising that instead of sticking to her script he was coolly drinking coffee and playing mind-games?

Her breathing faltered. She already knew what it felt like to be played by Basa, and she was in no hurry to be on the receiving end of that treatment again. Clearly the most sensible thing was for one or both of them to make a dignified and swift exit. She would just have to square it with Alicia later.

Trying to ignore the sick feeling in the pit of her stomach, she turned to face him. 'Okay, I know we said we'd stay and talk, but I think we can both agree that was only for Alicia's benefit, so please don't feel you need to stay on my account,' she said quickly. 'Really, I'm not expecting you to.'

His dark eyes glittered. 'What? Not even to pick up the bill?'

Her chin jerked up.

'I didn't come here for a free lunch, if that's what you're implying,' she snapped, and then immediately wished she hadn't, because she sounded defensive and cornered, which wasn't at all the image she wanted to project.

Although, Basa's opinion of her was so low anyway what difference would it make? He might not have said as much but his cool manner and even cooler gaze made it clear he'd made up his mind about her character back when her family had so nearly ruined his, and she doubted there was anything she could do or say to change his view. In his mind she was, and always would be, damned by association.

The waiter arrived with their coffee and she sat fuming, her mind belatedly conjuring up all the various smart put-downs she should have made to his last remark. He was just so insufferable. Sitting there and judging her as though he had the moral high ground, when his own behaviour had been utterly atrocious.

But why should she care what he thought of her anyway?

She watched him reach out and select one of the charming *petit-fours* the waiters had brought to the table with the coffee. Something in the tilt of his head seemed to tug at her memory, and her body tensed as time seemed to roll back on itself and she was in the ballroom at Fairbourne again. And standing on the other side of the dance floor, his dark, dishevelled hair accentuating the precision cut of his dinner jacket, his dark eyes fixed on her as though she was the only woman in the room, was Basa.

And that was why she cared.

In those few hours she had blossomed beneath his unblinking gaze, and then the miraculous, the unbelievable, had happened and he'd kissed her, said words she'd dreamed of hearing and—

Her fingers clenched into fists.

If she was going to indulge herself by reliving the past, the least she could do was do it properly and remember how, just when she'd started to believe he might actually mean those words, he'd got up and left her, and not come back.

The next time he'd seen her he'd looked straight through her. As if it hadn't been him who had cupped her face in his hands, his tongue tangling with hers while his thumbs caressed her aching nipples.

Trying to still the jittery feeling in her chest, she watched mutely as he raised his hands in mock surrender, his dark eyes gleaming. 'Someone's a little touchy. Or did I hit a nerve?'

He leaned forward, his dark hair falling across his face, his mouth curving in a way that made her spine shrink against her chair.

'I sincerely hope it wasn't *my* presence that dragged you away from the charms of Zone Six. I know we had that little "entanglement" at Lissy's birthday party, but if you're thinking we have some kind of unfinished business I'm going to have to disappoint you,' he said softly.

The handle of her coffee cup felt clumsy between her fingers. Her throat was tight and dry, and she was finding it hard to breathe normally.

Of all the arrogant—

Grinding her teeth, she stared at him in silence, a pulse of anger hopscotching over her skin. Did he truly think that was why she had come here? To offer herself to him? After the way he'd behaved.

It was suddenly hard to catch her breath. All the hurt and loneliness and confusion of that night rose in her throat, and when she looked down at her hands she saw they were shaking. Did he have any idea how it had felt? To lie there naked in his bed, her body quivering with longing, filled with disbelief that this beautiful, unattainable man had chosen her, only to discover that he'd changed his mind and not even bothered to tell her.

'I'm sorry to disappoint you, Basa,' she said coldly, 'but I didn't actually know you were going to be here today. And even if I *had* known, any *entangling* with you really isn't that much of an incentive for me to "drag" myself across the road, let alone into the West End.'

He stilled, not just his body but his face, even his eyes, and she felt her heart begin to beat out of time.

'Funny... I don't remember you being so reticent two years ago. In fact, as I recall, you were pretty insistent.'

'*You* asked *me* to dance,' she snapped.

She could still remember her shock, and the sharp tingling excitement as he'd held out his hand. For to her it had felt like the moment when Prince Charming had invited Cinderella to dance at the ball.

Her heartbeat stuttered now.

Maybe if she'd been more worldly she might have seen it for what it was. Thanks to his sister's insistence that he make sure everyone had at least one turn on the dance floor, he had dutifully danced with practically all Alicia's friends by that point. But as he'd pressed her closer she'd been so cocooned in an enveloping, intoxicating happiness that nothing had existed except the muscular hardness of his body and the restless, persistent pulse between her thighs.

His dark gaze rested on her face.

'To dance, yes...' he said slowly.

Her pulse froze, and before she could stop them the images fast-forwarded.

Their 'duty' dance over, she'd thought he would thank her and leave, but somehow they had been on the terrace, the music had faded, and as she'd shivered in the cool night air he'd shrugged out of his dinner jacket and settled it over her shoulders. The silk lining had been warm from the heat of his body, and it had still been warm a moment later, when she'd stood on tiptoe and kissed him...

Her cheeks were hot and her skin suddenly felt as though it was too small for her body. She might have been a virgin—she still was—but she hadn't been completely clueless. There had been a couple of boys at parties, their clumsy lips pulling at hers like overgrown puppies with a chew toy, but nothing and no one had ever made her feel like that.

Her body had seemed to lose all its bones, to become one with his. It had felt as though she was melting into him, everything solid turning fluid, drowning all sense and reason—and, yes, she had been eager, frantic to finish what they'd started without any thought to the consequences.

But admitting that to Basa now wouldn't change his part in what had happened.

He might be blessed with mouthwatering looks and limitless wealth, but that was where his resemblance to Prince Charming ended. Even before Charlie and Raymond had been caught embezzling he'd had no plans to marry a scullery maid—or, in her case, the stepdaughter of an employee. All he'd been interested in was a short, sweet sexual encounter, and that had rapidly lost its appeal when he'd realised he'd have to go hunting for condoms to make it happen.

Of course he'd made up some other excuse to leave, but she knew he hadn't gone to get a bottle of champagne. The truth was that she just hadn't been beautiful or desirable enough to make him want to stay.

'It was a party. I'd been drinking,' she said icily. 'I just wanted to have a bit of fun,' she lied. 'That's what girls want to do at parties, Basa—they want to have fun.'

Around them the air hummed with a kind of anticipatory stillness as his eyes rested steadily on her face. To anyone watching it probably looked as if they were having some kind of intimate *tête-à-tête*, she thought, her fingers tightening around her coffee cup. Only she could feel the waves of animosity seeping across the white tablecloth.

'Mimi by name, and Me-Me by nature,' he said slowly. 'Look, I don't give a toss what you wanted or didn't want. Your life and how you live it doesn't interest me. I just don't want you dragging my sister down to the level of *your* family.' He shook his head. 'I don't know how you have the gall to show your face—'

'I'm not my family, and I would never do anything to upset Lissy.' She felt angry tears spring into her eyes.

He looked at her as if she was an imbecile. 'For obvious reasons I'm not about to take your word for that.' Shaking his head, he leaned back against his chair. 'Much as I want to, I can't stop Alicia being friends with you, but don't think for one moment that I can't see you for the manipulative little hanger-on that you are. And clearly I'm not the only one.'

She stared at his face in confusion.

'I don't know what you're talking about…'

'Of course you do,' he said quietly. 'Your little legal setback?' His eyes flickered over her face. 'My sister might be too sweet and trusting for her own good. Unfortunately for you, though, not all your friends are as naive as she is.'

Her heart bumping unevenly against her ribs, she glared at him. 'They're not my friends.'

'I'm sure they're not.' His dark eyes locked with hers. 'Not *now*. Not after you manipulated them into doing you a favour and then tried to exploit their success.'

She breathed out unsteadily. 'You don't know anything about them. Or me. And I don't have to stay here and listen to this—'

Pushing back her seat, she made to stand up, but before she could move he said quietly, 'Oh, but you do. You promised my sister we would talk. No, sorry—I forgot. That was just for Alicia's benefit, wasn't it?'

'This isn't a conversation. It's just you making vile accusations,' she snapped. 'Do you really think that's what she meant by us talking?'

His eyes rested on her face, and then, tilting his head to one side, he sighed. 'No,' he admitted. 'I don't suppose it is.' He ran a hand slowly over his face. 'Look, Mimi, I'm here because I love my sister, and her happiness matters to me. For some unaccountable reason you being in her life makes her happy, so I'm willing...'

He hesitated, as though he couldn't quite believe what he was about to say.

'I'm willing, for her sake, to call a truce between us— but don't think for one moment that means I want to kiss and make up with you.'

Actually that wasn't true, Basa thought a half-second later. The kissing part anyway.

Picking up his wine glass, he glanced over at Mimi's taut face and wondered if she was thinking the same thing.

Was she remembering that evening, that dance, that kiss? Or, like him, had her mind zeroed in on the moment in his bedroom when he'd slipped the straps of her dress over her shoulders and watched it pool at her feet...?

He shifted in his seat, wishing he could shift the memory of what had happened and what had so nearly happened at his sister's birthday party, but he'd been trying to do that for the last two years and it was still etched into his brain like an awkward tattoo from a gap year in Thailand. And it wasn't just her soft lips or the scent she wore that had burrowed into his subconscious.

Watching her that night, he'd found her beautiful and sexy. But, more than that, intriguing. As a teenager she'd been a regular visitor to the family home, and thanks to her tomboyish clothes, tied-back hair, clunky glasses and gauche manner, she'd been easily distinguished as apart from the 'glossy posse', as he'd christened the rest of his sister's friends.

Of course he'd had no time for anything but work after his father's stroke had forced him to take over the running of the family business. So he hadn't seen her properly for several years when she'd wandered into the ballroom at Alicia's party, looking as apprehensive as an antelope approaching a waterhole.

But that wasn't why he'd done a double take.

Picking up his cup, he downed the rest of his coffee. He needed that hit of raw caffeine to counteract the impact of that moment when Mimi Miller had metaphorically ambushed him and wrestled him to the ground.

She had been wearing a long, high-necked white dress that had seemed to ripple over the heart-stopping silhouette of her body, and her waist-length blonde hair had hung loose over her shoulders like a golden cape. But it hadn't been the duckling-to-swan transformation that had stopped him in his tracks, for at that point he hadn't actually worked out who she was. No, it had been something else—a kind of hesitancy that tugged at a memory hovering at the edges of his mind,

And then, as she'd turned to pluck a glass of champagne from the tray of a passing waiter, he'd felt his heart stop beating. The dress had been backless, provocative without the overt sexiness of a low-cut bodice or short hemline, and, watching her cautious progress around the room, he'd felt a strange mix of resentment and responsibility and an inexplicable need to stay close.

Too close.

Close enough to feel the heat of her skin. Close enough to let his hand slide around her waist and press against the satin-smooth skin at the base of her back. Close enough to get burnt.

His lungs suddenly felt as though they were full of wet cement.

He'd told himself that it was just a dance, and a duty dance at that, but even before the music had ended, and even though he'd known by then that she was his sister's friend, and therefore a complication he didn't need and normally wouldn't choose, he'd pulled her closer, moulding her body to his.

Lost in her scent, and the heat of her bare skin, he'd kissed her all the way to his bedroom. And there they would have finished what they'd started—only he hadn't had any condoms on him. He'd gone back down to the party, to grab a bottle of champagne to console them both, but then, walking back through the ballroom, he'd switched his phone on—the phone he could remember Mimi taking from him and switching off—and the world as he had known it had crumbled to dust.

Gazing down at the list of messages from his law-

yer and his accountant, each one growing increasingly
frantic, he'd felt his heart turn to stone. A brief call to
his lawyer had made it clear that he needed to leave the
party immediately, but discreetly, so as not to alert Alicia, and just as he'd been finishing the call he'd caught a
glimpse of Mimi.

At the time he'd assumed she'd come looking for him,
and he remembered how guilty he'd felt at leaving her
alone for so long.

His heartbeat stalled. Now he would be willing to bet
his entire fortune that she hadn't been looking for him, but
he hadn't known that at the time. Trusting idiot that he'd
been, he'd set off on his way to follow her.

Only it had turned out she'd made other plans.

Mission clearly accomplished, she had been sneaking
out through the back door.

Watching her clutch the arm of a floppy-haired young
man as she climbed into his made-you-look orange Lam-
borghini, he'd been devastated.

He took another mouthful of coffee and swallowed,
wishing it could wash away the bitterness in his heart.

It had only been later, when the scandal had broken and
he'd had time to think, that he'd realised he had been set
up. All of it—her kissing him, her taking his phone—had
just been an attempt to distract him, and as soon as his
back had been turned it had been time for her to go. She'd
even made up some lame excuse to Alicia about feeling ill.

The fact that he had been so easily duped had bruised
his ego, but it had been the disconnect between the seemingly sweet child he'd once known and the woman she had
become that had been most unsettling.

He would never forgive Mimi and her relatives for what
they had done. Their greed and duplicity had nearly ruined his family. But it was the knowledge of how close he'd

come to having unprotected sex with her, and the possible consequences of that act, that had convinced him to come to this lunch.

This time he was going to protect his family—and teach her a lesson for taking him as a fool.

'Okay, fine.'

Mimi's voice pulled him back to the present and, tipping his head back, he met her gaze.

'Okay fine, what?' he asked softly.

'I'm willing to call a truce if you are. But I don't really see any point in us dragging this conversation out any longer.'

'I disagree. We need to discuss you filming the wedding. She's serious, you know?' he added. 'About wanting you to do it.'

She raised her chin, and he felt the shock of her forget-me-not-blue eyes zigzag through his body like a jolt of electricity.

'I know she is, but whatever she said about it being your idea, I know it wasn't, so you don't need to worry. I'm not going to do it.'

She glanced away, and he felt his shoulders stiffen against the crisp white poplin of his shirt. Her desire to leave was so tangible it felt like a living, breathing thing on the table between them, and had this conversation been happening at any point up until a couple of days ago he would have been showing her the door. Hell, he would have been holding it open for her.

But that had been before he'd spoken to Alicia.

His jaw tightened. After his mother's death, and the series of strokes that had left his father's health permanently impaired, he had sworn to protect his sister and do everything in his power to make her happy. And he still felt the same way—perhaps even more so. It was, after all, partly his fault that their father was so fragile and that the business was only just now recovering its former strength.

Clearly he'd rather Mimi wasn't within a hundred miles of the wedding, but Alicia's happiness and his family's reputation were all that mattered to him. Suggesting Mimi film the wedding had been the first thing to come to mind as he had tried to stem his sister's tears and find an alternative to Mimi being maid of honour.

But now that he'd had time to think the idea of her filming the wedding was actually appealing on other levels too—for wouldn't it be safer to have her fully occupied rather than just floating around unsupervised, as she had been at his sister's twenty-first birthday party?

And who better to do the supervising than him? That way he could ensure her behaviour wouldn't bring his family's name into disrepute, *and* make her life as difficult and uncomfortable as she had made his.

'It *was* my idea,' he said softly.

She looked up at him, her blue eyes widening with scorn at what she obviously took to be a bare-faced lie.

'Of course it was. I mean you *love* having me around. That was obvious after—'

She broke off, frowning.

'After what?' he asked slowly.

Inhaling a shaky breath, she shook her head. 'So tell me, then, Basa, why exactly do you want *me* to film your sister's wedding?'

He shrugged. 'Why not?'

'What do you mean, "why not"?'

'I mean why wouldn't you do it?' he said patiently.

She stared at him suspiciously. 'You *do* realise you said that out loud?'

He smiled. 'I am aware of that, yes.'

She bit her lip and, watching her bite into the soft pink flesh, he felt his heart-rate double as his brain unhelpfully offered up an image of those same soft pink lips parting beneath his mouth.

Suddenly the need to have her commit to the project became as intense as the ache in his groin.

'She's your friend—your best friend—and I know she doesn't ask much from you because she doesn't ask much from anyone,' he said bluntly, watching a flush of colour seep over her cheekbones. 'But she has asked you to do this one thing.'

He could see by her expression that she was confused by his words, and then abruptly her face cleared.

'Oh, I get it. This is you trying to persuade me so that you can tell your sister what a good brother you are.' Her chin jutted. 'Well, if that's all you're worried about you don't need to pretend. I'll tell her you tried and I wouldn't listen.'

'I'm not pretending. I think you'd do an excellent job. You're a good filmmaker.'

'Right...'

She shook her head, and the defensive expression on her face chafed at something inside him.

'And you know that *how*, exactly?'

'Alicia showed me some of the films you used to make at school.' His eyes met hers. 'They're clearly amateur, but you really capture that teenage sense of waiting and wanting. There's not a wasted breath,' he said softly.

There was a beat of silence, and then his breathing stalled as she looked up at him with such sweet, desperate hope in her blue gaze that for a few half-seconds he forgot the past, and everything that had happened, and he was simply fighting against the insane urge to reach over and pull her closer, until her body fused with his just as it had two years ago.

Across the room, a champagne cork popped, and they both blinked at the same time.

Tuning out the heat pulsing over his skin, he regulated his breathing. 'Like I said, you're a good filmmaker, and this is your chance to be a good friend as well. So please say yes and make some happy memories for my sister.'

There was a beat of silence and then her shoulders slumped. He knew he'd won even before she began to nod her head.

'Okay, I'll do it.'

'Good.' Brushing aside the relief warming his skin, he glanced at his watch. 'I'll get your number from Alicia and then my PA can call you and talk flights—'

'Flights?' She cut across him, her eyes narrowing. 'What flights? To where?'

'Buenos Aires,' he said calmly. 'Don't worry, I'm paying. First class ticket, and obviously you'll stay at the house before we go to Patagonia.'

She began to shake her head. 'No, no, no. I'm not doing that. I'm not going to Argentina.'

'Really?' He frowned. 'So, have you got some kind of satellite camera on loan from NASA? Because London to Buenos Aires is one hell of a long shot.'

Ignoring her outraged expression, he pulled out his phone and swiped casually through his diary.

'I can't do anything for the next couple of days, but I can fly down from the States on Friday.'

Her eyes flashed. 'I don't care if you can fly to the moon and back. I'm not going to Buenos Aires on Friday. Or on any day you care to mention, in fact.'

'Oh, but you are—and I'll explain why. The wedding is in less than three months, and Alicia is flying out with my father in a few weeks to settle in. She's going to have enough on her to-do list without you wandering in at the last minute with a hundred and one questions that could have already been answered in advance. By me.'

He was impressed by the plausibility of his words, and he could see they had taken the wind out of her sails.

'It's got nothing to do with you,' she managed finally. 'It's not your wedding and you don't know anything about film making.'

'Oh, I think it's got *everything* to do with me,' he said mockingly. 'Given that the whole event is going to be happening in my homes, and I have very specific and inflexible house rules.'

He saw her teeth clench.

'You can't expect me to make up my mind now. I'll need time to think about it.'

'I'm not selling you a car, Mimi.' He let his gaze drift over her face, enjoying the mix of frustration and fear in her blue eyes. 'Look, I'm a busy man, so I'm afraid you're going to have to work around my schedule—and that means you coming to Buenos Aires this Friday.'

'What about *my* schedule?' she snapped.

'I think Crema will probably be able to fill your shifts quite quickly, don't you?'

He'd deliberately made his voice condescending, and it was a measure of her fury that she didn't even register the fact that he knew where she worked.

She glared across the table. 'You are so unspeakably arrogant.'

'No, I'm just honest—but I guess that's a bit of an alien concept to you.' Their eyes locked, hers furious, his taunting. 'How *are* Charlie and Raymond, by the way? Still enjoying their stay at Her Majesty's pleasure?'

She stared at him, a flush of pink spreading like a

sunset over her incredible cheekbones. 'You are a horrible man.'

'And *you* are bad news.' He held her gaze, ignoring the pull of her scornful pout, wishing she didn't look quite so sexy when she was angry. 'So, if we're done trading insults, let me tell you how this is going to work. The last thing my family needs on my sister's wedding day is a scandal.'

And it wasn't going to happen on *his* watch. He'd learned his lesson two years ago, when his hasty, mismanaged, ego-led decision to employ Charlie and Raymond had so spectacularly backfired. He'd been responsible for that disaster, and the collateral damage it had caused, and it was his job—his duty—to prevent anything like that happening again.

He looked up, his eyes holding hers. 'Particularly one involving *you*. So I need you to conduct yourself in a proper manner. That means following my rules, and it'll be easier to explain those rules on-site. But if you don't think you're mature enough to handle one little fully paid trip to Buenos Aires, then call Alicia.' He held out his phone. 'And break her heart.'

She stared at him mutely. 'You really are quite something. All that guff about moving forward was just for Alicia's benefit.'

'Don't push it, Mimi. I'm not going to fall out with my sister over this, but if you think that means you get a free rein in my home then you really don't know me at all.'

'Thankfully, no,' she spat. 'But if you feel that strongly about me then why don't I just stay in a hotel? Don't worry. I'll pay.'

Her skin was flawless, and the soft curl of her mouth was making him lose concentration. She was beautiful and angry and he badly wanted to kiss her.

And that was what gave him the strength to lean back in his chair.

'Sadly, that wouldn't work for me,' he said softly. 'You see, I prefer to keep my friends close but my enemies closer.'

CHAPTER THREE

LEANING FORWARD, MIMI gazed out through the limousine's tinted window, a pulse of excitement scampering over her skin as the unfamiliar streets of Buenos Aires spun past her eyes.

Bautista Caine might be the most annoying, self-satisfied and judgmental man she had ever met, but right now she couldn't help grudgingly feeling just the teensiest bit grateful to him—for had *she* been paying for this trip it would have been a far less comfortable experience.

Travelling first class, with the added bonus of being a 'friend' of the Caine family, had not only made the thirteen-hour flight pass with surprising speed, but there had been a few other surprises too—like a complimentary facial and this chauffeur-driven limo waiting for her at Ezeiza Airport!

Her mouth twisted. Once, that kind of luxury had been normal to her. Her stepfather's job at Caine's, the private bank founded by Basa's great-grandfather, had given her family an enviable lifestyle. They'd moved to Chesham Place and she'd been sent to the same exclusive school as Alicia. There had been summer holidays in the Caribbean and skiing breaks in Aspen and Verbier.

But, really, enjoyable as it had been to have so much money, the best thing for her had been seeing her mother

Nancy free of her habitual disappointment in being married to a man she didn't like and certainly didn't love.

And then, almost overnight, it had gone. Everything. The house. The holidays. Her mother's happiness. And suddenly she had gone back to being one of the have-nots.

Charlie and Raymond had both been sent to prison, and she and her mother had wound up in a small terraced house in Bexley. Not that she'd minded much by then. She'd been desperate to escape the clumps of photographers lurking outside the house, and the neighbours who had gossiped about her behind their hands.

Only Alicia, the one person who had every right to reject and resent her, had stayed loyal. And that was why she was here—whatever her brother might choose to tell himself.

Her shoulders tensed against the smooth leather, the memory of their last meeting replaying inside her head. It was galling how easily he had got his own way—and, truthfully, that was what this trip was about. However Basa might choose to dress it up, he'd been throwing his weight around. Even now, two days after it had happened, it still made her go hot and cold.

The cold was understandable. On its own, his last remark had been enough to send icy shivers down anyone's spine, but the heat...

Lip curling, she blanked out the memory of her body's involuntary and mortifying response to his and sat up straighter in her seat.

It had not been the most satisfactory encounter, although it had certainly been an improvement on their previous one. At least she hadn't ended up taking off all her clothes and making a complete fool of herself.

It was not exactly a high bar to set, though, was it? Staying clothed and not offering herself on a plate to a man who clearly despised her?

Her phone rang inside her handbag. Reaching in to find it, she frowned. It was probably her mum. She'd told her she'd call her when she landed, but she really couldn't face talking to her just now.

She felt a nibble of guilt. She had yet to tell her mother what she was doing in Argentina. Nor had she told her about Alicia's wedding—mainly because anything to do with the Caines was a no-go area. She knew from experience that hearing their name would start her mother on that downward spiral of 'if only', so when her mum had assumed she was in Argentina for work she hadn't corrected her.

Glancing out of the window again, at the faded, elegant architecture, she felt her heart contract. She hated lying to her mother, and resented having to do so, but there was no point in blaming anyone but herself for this uncomfortable arrangement. If she hadn't encouraged her mum to marry Charlie, none of this would be happening.

Pulling out her phone, she glanced down at the screen and exhaled in relief. It was Alicia. 'Hi, Lissy. I was going to call you later, to thank you for the bikini.'

It was so typical of her friend, she thought, some of her panic fading as she remembered the beautiful black and white bikini she had received in the post, together with a note telling her to relax and enjoy the sun and the pool.

'Oh, I just saw it and I thought...' Alicia hesitated. 'I can't really talk for long. I'm on the way to meet Philip's aunt—for real this time. I just wanted to make sure you're okay.'

'How could I not be okay?' Mimi said quickly. 'I've got people falling over themselves to be nice to me.'

She managed to inject a teasing note into her voice, even

though right now she felt as if she was about to spend the weekend in a lion's den rather than some opulent mansion.

Basa might have insisted that she stay at the Caine family home, but his decision had nothing to do with wanting to be hospitable. He just wanted to make sure she did nothing to bring his family's name into disrepute.

It didn't matter that he'd treated her appallingly. To him she was Charlie Butler's stepdaughter and Raymond Cavendish's niece. She was, and would always be, tainted by association.

'Good.' Alicia said quickly. She sounded a little breathless, as if she was rushing somewhere. 'I'm sorry about lunch. I should have told you Basa was going to be there. It wasn't fair to drop you in at the deep end like that, so thanks for staying and thanks for making all this effort for me.'

'Yeah, travelling first class and being chauffeured around is a hard ask,' Mimi said lightly. 'But, hey, someone's gotta do it.'

'I didn't mean that. I meant…' Alicia paused. 'Look, we never really had a chance to speak after the party…you know…because…'

She hesitated again, and Mimi felt her stomach clench like a fist.

Because my stepfather and uncle had helped themselves to a bunch of pensioners' savings, she finished silently.

'Anyway, I just thought we should talk about it.'

'About what?'

For a moment Alicia didn't reply, and then she said quietly, 'I know what happened with you and Basa, Mimi. At my twenty-first.'

For a moment her mind went completely blank. She felt numb. Her heart was beating with unnatural slowness, like a clock that needed winding, and she knew that her face was constricted into an expression of horror.

'I don't know what you mean,' she said slowly. 'Nothing happened.'

'Oh, Mimi, please don't.'

The hurt in her friend's voice made her stomach squeeze into a knot of misery. She swallowed. Her mouth felt dry. She couldn't believe it. She couldn't believe that after all this time Basa had told Alicia about that night.

Imagining the spin he'd have put on the story, she started to feel sick. 'What did he say?' she croaked.

'Who? Basa? Nothing. I didn't talk to him about it. I didn't have to. I saw how the two of you were together at the restaurant.'

Mimi felt her skin squeeze her bones. She was starting to shiver with shock and panic. 'We were fine,' she said quickly.

'I'm not stupid, Mimi.'

She heard Alicia take a breath.

'I know you two had an argument, and that's why you left the party without saying goodbye. Only you didn't say anything to me because you thought it would upset me, so you said you felt ill.'

'I did feel ill.' Mimi swallowed past the ache in her throat. It wasn't a complete lie. She *had* felt sick at the mess she'd made of everything. 'And I just wanted to go home.'

'But Basa thought you should stay and he had a go at you?' Without waiting for confirmation, Alicia said quickly, 'I'm sorry. He's always been protective, but since Mummy died he just wants everything to be perfect for me.'

Mimi breathed out unsteadily. She felt almost lightheaded with relief, but also guilty that Alicia was blaming herself for something that hadn't even happened. But what purpose would telling her the truth serve except to make herself feel better in the short term?

'I'm sorry,' she said quickly. And she was—although not for concealing a fictional argument with Basa, but for letting Alicia believe a lie.

'For what?'

For probably the first time in her life her friend sounded exasperated with her.

'For feeling sick? For standing up for yourself? *I'm* the one who should be saying sorry. I know he's my brother, and I love him to bits, but you could have told me. I wouldn't have taken his side, you know.'

'It's okay to take his side,' Mimi said gently. 'He's your family.'

'And *you're* my family too. I know what your stepfather and uncle did was wrong, but it had nothing to do with you.'

Mimi's fingers tightened around the phone.

Except that it did.

Maybe not here in Buenos Aires, where nobody knew her, but back in England, she was always on edge—always expecting the past to suck her back into that dark place she'd been two years ago. It didn't matter if she was on the bus or in a café. She would look up from her magazine or her coffee and find someone looking at her curiously, and instantly she would be terrified that they were putting two and two together and coming up with a headline.

It was that fear of losing her anonymity that was the reason she hadn't really fought back against those actresses. She had been too scared that if she escalated things inevitably her name would pop up in some internet search and her scandalous past would suddenly be current news again.

'I know,' she lied.

Alicia breathed out shakily. 'And who I choose to have

in my life has nothing to do with anyone—including my brother. You're my friend, and I think Basa accepts that now.'

Like hell he does, Mimi thought, remembering Basa's parting remark about keeping his enemies close.

Injecting her voice with a note of brightness she didn't feel, she said, 'Did he say that?'

'Well, not exactly,' Alicia admitted. 'But he did say you two had had a very productive talk and that you had reached an understanding. And that's the thing about Basa: if you're on his team he'll do anything for you.'

Having arranged to call back later, for a longer chat, Mimi promised to send Alicia a photo of herself in the pool and hung up. She felt as if she'd just run a marathon, but at least one positive had come out of the conversation. Alicia believed that she and Basa had 'reached an understanding'.

As if!

The only thing he wanted was to toss her into the Thames.

She could just picture his dark eyes gleaming as he fed Alicia his carefully edited version of their conversation. Her jaw clenched. All that rubbish about them having a 'productive talk' when he'd basically told her that he didn't like or trust her. He was a disingenuous, loathsome man.

Unfortunately for her, she was going to be staying in his house, with him, for the next forty-eight hours...

She turned her glare back to the window. Outside, clusters of extraordinarily beautiful *porteños* were making their way to work—or perhaps, given the reputation of the city's nightlife, on their way home to bed.

Glancing at the back of the chauffeur's head, she wondered what would happen if she asked him to keep driving around? She would book into some anonymous little hotel off the main strip and then maybe head out to a café and sit outside in the sun with a coffee and pastry, just watch people going about their day-to-day lives.

But there was no escaping her destiny—not least because she'd promised herself that she would see this thing through to the end. Whatever Basa said, and however he behaved, she was going to stay cool and let it wash over her—for Alicia's sake.

The air bounced out of her lungs. Who knew? Maybe if they spent some time together he might alter his harsh opinion of her and start to see the person she really was.

And there were some upsides to the situation. She hadn't been on holiday for so long, but now she was in Buenos Aires, and she was going to stay in a beautiful mansion with a swimming pool.

An image of Basa in swim-shorts, water dripping slowly off his smooth, contoured body, parachuted into her head, and instantly she felt that familiar rushing sense of vertigo, as if she was standing at the top of a skyscraper and looking down. And then her heart twitched against her ribs as finally she asked herself the question she'd been dodging since the moment she'd watched him swagger into the restaurant.

Why did she still feel this way about him?

For a start, it wasn't logical or dignified. How could she feel anything but contempt and loathing for someone who had treated her as he had? It wasn't as though it had been a mistake. He had stripped her naked and kissed her until her body had felt as though it was going to combust, and then he'd got up, got dressed and never come back.

And the worst part was that she had waited for him. She had lain there in his four-poster bed like some stupid sacrificial virgin and waited.

She could still remember how it had felt. That dizzy, disbelieving euphoria. And then, as the minutes passed—

first five, then ten, then twenty—her happiness had started to ooze away like air from a punctured football. Uncertainty and panic had begun to creep in, until finally she'd been able to bear it no more and she'd found her clothes and got dressed.

Her heart began to thump. Even then she hadn't really taken his disappearance at face value. Incredibly, she'd actually been *worried* about him—she'd thought something must have happened for him not to return. But of course nothing had happened.

He'd been standing in the ballroom, talking on his phone, and then he'd turned towards her. And this was the worst part—this was the part that had finally made her understand what had happened. Not by the slightest curve of his mouth or tilt of his head had he acknowledged her. He'd looked straight through her as if she wasn't there or he didn't know who she was.

Maybe if she'd been older, or more experienced, she might have felt and behaved differently. But she'd been young and desperately in love and so unsure of herself, and her self-doubt had flared beneath his dark, blank-eyed gaze. All she'd wanted to do was crawl into a dark hole and lick her wounds.

And then she had seen Alicia there, dancing and laughing, and that was when she'd turned and walked away from the ballroom, begged a lift back to London. She'd known she couldn't face her friend, for if she had she wouldn't have been able to stop herself from telling Alicia everything. Having lost so much in her life already, she hadn't felt able to risk having that conversation and losing her best friend too.

She shivered. Sometimes she felt as if she was jinxed. What other explanation could there be for the way her world so frequently and effortlessly imploded? She was the common denominator in all of it. Her father leaving, Charlie and Raymond creating the wrong kind of headlines, and now her film, idling in some lawyer's office.

She felt the car begin to slow, and as it did so her pulse began to accelerate. For the last few minutes she'd been distracted by thoughts of Basa, so she hadn't really been paying attention to what was happening outside the window, but as she looked nervously through the glass she realised that they were driving down a wide, tree-lined boulevard. Set back from the road, some concealed by decorative walls, others by perfectly trimmed hedges, were several houses the size of hotels.

Oh, my goodness, this must be it.

Through the window she watched nervously as wrought-iron gates as tall as they were wide swung open smoothly. The car slid between them and a moment later stopped in front of one of the most beautiful houses Mimi had ever seen—and the biggest. The cream-coloured building seemed to stretch endlessly in both directions, and she had to tip back her head to see the rooftop.

She stepped out of the car, feeling horribly underdressed in her cargo pants and faded sweatshirt, just as a beautiful middle-aged woman appeared in the doorway. She had shining dark hair, and eyes the same colour and shape as Marcona almonds, and she was clearly expecting Mimi.

'*Buenos días*, Señorita Miller. I hope you have had a pleasant trip. My name is Antonia and I'm the housekeeper here at Palacio Figueroa.'

Mimi felt her breath catch. *Great, Basa owns a palace.* No wonder his housekeeper looked like a movie star.

Inside, there was no point in pretending she was anything but dazzled. The house was gorgeously over the top, with cornices and swags everywhere, and a rich, vibrant colour scheme that perfectly complemented the opulent velvet furniture and Savonnerie rugs.

'I'm sure you want to freshen up, so let me show you to your rooms,' said Antonia, and smiled. 'I gather this is your first visit to Buenos Aires? I hope you enjoy your stay in our beautiful city.'

Mimi managed to smile back at the other woman, but inside she was thinking that it would be a lot easier to enjoy her stay if she didn't have to spend it twitching inwardly beneath Basa's dark, critical gaze.

Thank goodness he wasn't arriving until this evening. With luck, she might even be able to plead exhaustion and turn in early, and then she wouldn't have to see him until the next morning.

Antonia stopped beside her. 'These are your rooms.'

Smiling politely, Mimi stepped through the door—and stopped. Her heart began to thump against her ribs. Mid-morning sunlight and a warm breeze were seeping through the open windows. The walls were painted ballet-slipper-pink, and there were several sofas and armchairs all covered in gold and pink striped silk.

'This is your sitting room. Your bedroom is through that door, and then you have a bathroom and dressing room next door. I'll let you settle in. Please treat the house as your own, and if you need anything at all, just ask.'

Clearly Antonia hadn't received the memo about Mimi being the enemy within, she thought as she tiptoed into the bedroom and gazed in delight at the vast, ornate four-poster bed.

After ten minutes of wandering from room to room, she decided that she liked the dressing room best. It was just so indulgent. A huge gilt-edged mirror ran the length and width of one wall, and opposite there were two beautiful chaises-longue—presumably so someone could sit and watch you get dressed.

Or undressed.

Without warning, an image of Basa lolling on that sofa, his dark gaze intent on her body as she slowly stripped in front of him, slid into her head and, gazing at her reflection, she felt her skin start to tingle.

Oh, for goodness' sake!

Her heart beating out of time, she turned away from the mirror and stalked out of the dressing room, cursing herself for being every kind of idiot and then some. This weekend was going to be challenging enough without her fantasising about a man who had made it perfectly clear that his attraction to her had been brief, and based on nothing more flattering than opportunity.

A slight breeze lifted the curtains and, crossing the room, she gazed down at a beautiful rectangular pool of perfect turquoise water. It looked so tempting, and it was exactly what she needed to cool off her overheated body and imagination.

Alicia was expecting a photo of her in her new bikini, and even Antonia had suggested she might like to go for a swim. Besides, Basa wasn't arriving until this evening so how would he even know?

Fifteen minutes later she had completed maybe a dozen or so languid lengths of the pool and was floating in the shallow end, her eyes closed against a sun that was gratifyingly brighter than the one at home. From the house, she heard a door open and the sound of footsteps—it would be Antonia, coming to find out if she wanted anything.

Not wanting to look as though she was taking any of this for granted, she forced her eyes open and swam over to the edge of the pool…and froze. Breathing out shakily, she squinted into the sunlight at a man she recognised only too well.

Except it couldn't be him, she thought, her heart doing a series of violent backflips. He wasn't supposed to be here until this evening.

But, whether he was supposed to be there or not, it *was* Basa, standing at the top of the steps leading down to the terrace, his dark eyes hidden beneath a pair of sunglasses, his dark suit incongruous among the loungers and sunlight.

For a moment he didn't move, and then to the loud and irregular accompaniment of her heartbeat, he made his way slowly down the steps to the pool.

She stared up at him mutely as he came to a halt in front of her upturned face.

'So,' he said, in a voice that stopped the breath in her throat, 'I see you've already made yourself at home. Having fun?'

Basa gazed down at Mimi, his eyes narrowing as he slipped off his sunglasses.

Walking into the house, he'd been talking on the phone to his PA and had simply mouthed a greeting to Antonia and gone straight up to his rooms. He had a headache that was threatening to split his skull in two, and he was tired after a night spent in transit and on his laptop. Still talking, he'd been in the process of loosening his tie when he'd glanced out of the window to the terrace below.

Instantly his brain had dropped into neutral and he'd begun spouting gibberish—much to the confusion of his assistant.

He'd hung up and, without pausing to consider the consequences, strode back downstairs, past his startled housekeeper and out onto the sunlit terrace.

Normally on a day like this he would have taken a dip

himself, but the fact that Mimi was in the pool and there-fore depriving him of that pleasure seemed to justify the anger boiling in his chest.

An anger that was doubly vexing because Mimi's near-naked presence in his pool was down to his own impulsive and unthinking behaviour.

His chest tightened. Ever since he'd walked out of that restaurant he'd been questioning his logic, his motives—hell, even his sanity—in arranging this weekend with her. But, confronted by Alicia's stubborn attachment to the woman now in his swimming pool, and by the memory of what had so nearly happened at his sister's birthday party, he'd acted with uncharacteristic rashness.

Firstly by suggesting that Mimi film the wedding and then by insisting that she come to Argentina.

Ostensibly, both were based on clear and infallible rea-soning.

Mimi would be less visible behind a camera than in front of it, and by demanding that she came this weekend he was putting their relationship on a more formal footing. He wasn't her boss, exactly, but he wanted to make it clear that she was answerable to him. That way there could be no blurring of lines when it came to how they interacted with one another.

His heart began to beat faster.

But that was only a part of why he wanted her here. That night in Fairbourne his hunger for her had blinded him to what lay beneath that beautiful creamy skin. Now, though, he knew her true character, and he wanted her to know that he was in full possession of the facts and her charms no longer held any attraction for him.

He'd fully expected his first meeting with Mimi at his home to prove him correct. By rights he should be standing here feeling immensely satisfied at having summoned her across an ocean, his body stone-cold.

Unfortunately the ache in his groin suggested that hope might have been a little premature.

Gazing down at Mimi, devastating in a black and white striped bikini, he felt his breathing unravel, and wished he'd had the sense to keep his sunglasses on.

'I'm just taking a dip...'

Her blue eyes were watching him warily, and that together with the fact that her bikini-clad body was making him feel like some idiot in his suit only seemed to increase his irritation.

'Yes, you are,' he said softly.

'Antonia said it would be okay.' She frowned. 'I thought you weren't going to be here until later?'

'Oh, I see. So this is a case of while the cat's away?'

'No, it isn't.'

Her gaze narrowed, and he could tell she was trying not to lose her temper.

'It's fine,' he said. 'Like you say, you're just taking a dip.' Crouching down, he scooped up a handful of water, checking the temperature. 'Feels great. Maybe I'll join you.'

She shrank away from him like a vampire being offered garlic. 'Actually, I was just going to get out.'

He watched in silence, his stomach clenching with a combination of lust and anger, as she swam a couple of strokes and rose up out of the pool, droplets of water trickling down her neck and back. His breathing shifted. It was an all too familiar view—not from life, but from memory... the memory of that evening and that dress. Even now he could remember how it had felt. He wanted to touch her so badly that night, to run his fingers down the smooth curve of skin...

Not any more, he told himself, blocking his mind to the rush of heat tightening his muscles. Not in this lifetime.

'Here.' Catching sight of her robe, hanging from the back of one of the loungers, he picked it up and held it out to her, keeping his eyes locked on hers as she shrugged her arms into it.

'Thank you,' she muttered.

'No, thank *you*,' he said with mocking courtesy, wanting to make her feel as off-balance as she was making him. 'For coming out here at such short notice. It was very kind of you to juggle your busy schedule for me.'

Her eyebrows shot up and, lifting her chin, she said coldly, 'Let's get one thing straight, Basa. I'm not doing this for you. I'm doing this for Alicia, because she's my friend and her happiness matters to me more than anything else.'

Her mouth softened into the slightest of smiles as she spoke Alicia's name, pulling his gaze to her lips and the blood to his groin so that he suddenly felt lightheaded.

'Finally we have something in common,' he said,

Her eyes widened, her smile shifting into a scowl. 'You and I have nothing in common, Basa. I wouldn't treat a dog the way *you* treat people.'

Basa stared at her in silence, his jaw clenching. He could hardly believe that Mimi Miller—*Mimi Miller*, of all people—was saying this to him.

'And how exactly *do* I treat people? Actually, forget about me—let's just look at how *you* treat people. How you present yourself as someone to be trusted when all the time you're playing out your own agenda.'

She rolled her eyes. 'Oh, here we go again. You do realise I'm actually a completely separate person from my stepfather and uncle?'

'I do—and I wasn't talking about them. But since

LOUISE FULLER 61

you've brought them up...' His mouth twisted. 'What is it
they say? The apple never falls far from the tree? But even
if it did, you also had Charlie as a role model. You probably learned how to grift before you could walk.'

'If you would just listen to me for five minutes I could
explain—'

'You mean lie.' Shaking his head, he dragged his eyes
away from the three sopping wet triangles of fabric mas-
querading as her swimwear. 'What did you think? That if
you sashayed out of the pool in your itsy-bitsy bikini I'd
be too busy drooling to listen to what came out of your
mouth?'

He watched the colour spread over her cheeks. She was
staring at him open-mouthed, as if she couldn't quite believe what she was hearing, and he couldn't say that he
blamed her. His accusation had been harsh and gratuitous,
but with her body so tantalisingly close to his, and his own
body acting as if it had only recently woken from hibernation, he needed to remind himself of the kind of woman
she was beneath that delectable skin.

And he was still smarting over her remark about how
he treated people. How *he* treated people! She might have
conveniently forgotten her behaviour, but he hadn't, even
though part of him wanted to forget everything about that
night.

But he could still remember every second.

Her soft, teasing laugh when she'd taken his phone and
switched it off...the feverish, almost clumsy way she had
kissed and caressed him, as if she was nervous about something. And, of course, the cherry on the cake: the fact that
she hadn't given any thought to protection. She should
have told him she wasn't on the pill and didn't have any
condoms with her.

His shoulders stiffened. If he hadn't double-checked,

who knew what might have happened? The media would have had a field-day. His body tensed as he imagined the gleeful, screaming headlines and, worse, his father's devastated expression as the news spread around the world that his son had impregnated the stepdaughter of the man who had almost destroyed his family.

She took a step forward, shoving her hands on her hips and unintentionally pulling the edges of her robe apart. He breathed in sharply, his anger forgotten as he caught a glimpse of her marvellous body. He gritted his teeth. It was beyond his comprehension why he should still feel like this. It had been two years. So much had happened in that time—so many good and amazing things, with good and amazing people—so why was he endlessly reliving a moment that should never have happened in the first place with a woman he didn't trust or like?

'I'm guessing you don't suffer from vertigo, do you, Basa?'

Her words caught him off-guard and he frowned. 'What has that got to do with anything?'

'Just that it must be so very high, up there on your horse, sitting in judgement over everyone, making assumptions about who they are based on nothing more than your own prejudices.' Her gaze rested scornfully on his face. 'It's a good job you gave up law. You clearly haven't mastered the basic principle of innocent until proved guilty.'

Wrong, he thought silently. He understood innocence, and there was nothing innocent about how Mimi had acted that night.

He shook his head. 'I was interested in corporate law, not criminal law, but I don't need to be a barrister to know that there are two kinds of people in this world. Those who need the judgement of a court to know whether they're guilty of a crime, and those who have a conscience. I think we both know that you fall into the former.'

She lifted her chin, her hands clenched into fists, and he knew that she was itching to thump him.

'I *do* have a conscience, and I *don't* feel guilty about anything I've done.'

'That doesn't surprise me.'

He took a step forward, almost enjoying the flare of fear and anger in her blue eyes as she backed away unsteadily. That was why he'd invited her here, wasn't it? To let her know where she stood and to demonstrate his complete and utter contempt for her.

'But let's forget about the past for the moment. I want to talk about the present, and how you're going to behave for the next few months.'

'I know how to behave.' She glared at him.

'Good. Make sure you keep it that way. Because I'm only interested in two things, sweetheart: my sister's happiness and my family's reputation. And if you do anything—anything at all—to jeopardise either of those, you will wish you had never crossed my path.'

'I wish that already,' she snapped.

They were so close he could see her flawless skin and the flecks of green and gold in the blue of her eyes. As he took another step forward he heard her breath catch, and instantly his blood was beating a path to his groin. For a split second he forgot everything—his anger, her family's crimes. All he could think about was how badly he wanted to slide his hands over the damp skin of her waist and pull her against his tense, overheated body…how desperately he wanted to kiss her.

'Tough,' he said coolly. 'I'm going to be your shadow at this wedding, Ms Miller, so get used to it.' Pushing back the cuff of his suit jacket, he glanced at his watch. 'Antonia has prepared lunch. We eat at one. Make sure you're on time.'

He let his gaze drift over her damp skin.

'And make sure you're properly dressed. Or I might accidentally confuse you with dessert.'

CHAPTER FOUR

HAVING SHOWERED AND CHANGED, Mimi made her way down to the dining room at exactly one minute past one o'clock. She would have liked to make Basa wait longer, as a sort of tit-for-tat for making her wait for him at Fairbourne, but even if he made the connection it would only make her look petty.

Lunch was somewhat strained. She was itching to tell Basa exactly what she thought of him, and only by constantly reminding herself that she was here for Alicia did she hold back her indignant words.

Obviously she got it that he hated her stepfather and her uncle. They weren't exactly top of *her* Christmas card list either. But it wasn't as if you got to choose your family, and his constant sniping was getting on her nerves. Besides, what gave him the right to have a go at her anyway? It wasn't as though *his* actions had been beyond reproach.

Picking up her glass of water, she took a sip, concentrating on the chill of the liquid and not on the heat that always accompanied her memories of that night at Fairbourne. Memories of the heat of a passion that had left her breathless, swiftly followed by a different kind of heat— the warm, sticky flush of shame at knowing that Basa would rather disinherit himself than tangle with the woman whose family had brought scandal to his doorstep.

And, judging by his comments earlier, and at that lunch with Alicia and Philip, he still felt the same way. No doubt this lunch was just another opportunity for him to lay down the law. But could he not just be civil for five minutes, given that this stupid weekend had been his idea anyway?

She felt another wave of irritation rise up inside her. It wasn't as if he was the only one who had a reason to lash out. She could just as easily be giving *him* a hard time—and about his actual behaviour, not the actions of some of his relatives.

It was so tempting to tell him some home truths, and for a few highly enjoyable moments she imagined telling Basa exactly what she thought of him—with a crushing eloquence she didn't actually possess. But for now she was just going to have to think it, not say it. Getting into some kind of slanging match with him might be gratifying in the short term, but she would end up hurting Alicia.

Her shoulders tensed. These next two days were going to be a very challenging exercise in self-restraint, but thankfully there were some positives, she thought, glancing down at her starter of smoked aubergine in a *criolla* sauce.

Picturing what she would be eating if she was at home, she almost smiled. Her lunch was usually some kind of panini, bolted down with a bottle of water. Clearly, though, people like Basa didn't have toasted cheese sandwiches for lunch.

It was just a shame *he* had to be here, casting a cloud over her with his cool, assessing gaze, but at least now that she had swapped her bikini for a denim shirt dress and ankle-high western boots she felt far less exposed.

However, compared to Basa's minimalist dark suit and perfectly knotted Windsor tie, she still felt a little under-dressed. Did he dress like that out of habit? Or was it a conscious choice? A sort of modern armour designed to intimidate and inspire respect using French cuffs and hand-sewn buttonholes instead of steel plates?

She glanced furtively over to where he was discussing wine options for the evening meal with Antonia. Not that it would matter what he wore. To add to his already overflowing list of advantages in life, he had the kind of beauty that elevated him above the ordinary.

Fortunately, she had plenty to look at other than his annoyingly handsome face. Like the rest of the house, the dining room was effervescently decorated, with walls sheathed in shimmering green silk, not one but five chandeliers, and a huge transparent acrylic table that looked as though it was made of moving water. But it was the two vast Basquiat canvases that dominated the room, their striking skulls and hieroglyphics making her forget to eat.

'Do you like Basquiat?' he asked suddenly.

She nodded, her face stiffening automatically into an expression she'd perfected during her stepfather and uncle's trial.

In the restaurant and outside in the pool, she'd been so stunned to see him that it had been hard to do anything but gape. Now, though, the fact that she was fully prepared, and fully dressed, meant that she could compose her features, for she'd learned the hard way that self-preservation required composure.

In the beginning, when Charlie and Raymond had been arrested, she'd tried to hide her face as the photographers rushed forward, shouting her and her mother's names, but she'd quickly realised that there was nowhere to hide. So she'd learned to school her features, to blank her gaze and give nothing away.

It was just a pity that she hadn't been equipped with

that skill on the night of Alicia's birthday—the night when she'd stripped, both literally and metaphorically, for Basa.

Pushing the memories aside, she glanced up at the Basquiats.

'They're incredible. But I would have thought they were a little too edgy for your taste.'

His level gaze rested on her face. 'Perhaps. But art is like dining. If you always eat the same food, you never expand your palate. Besides...' he smiled slowly, his dark eyes drifting down over her dress '... I like sampling new flavours.'

Her heart jerked inside her chest. Was that what had happened that night? Was that how he had seen her? As a 'new flavour'? She thought back to his parting remark by the pool, and the ache in her chest solidified into a hard ball of anger.

He was so entitled and arrogant. Lumping her in with every other woman in his sexual back catalogue. But she would see if he liked having the same treatment himself.

Lifting her chin, she held his gaze. 'I like sampling new things too.'

The lie made her heart race faster, but what did it matter? She'd tried telling him the truth, and it had done nothing to change his low opinion of her, so frankly he didn't deserve the truth. She watched his eyes darken, felt a pulse of satisfaction and unease bumping over her skin.

For a moment he didn't reply and then, laying his cutlery down, he said softly, 'I'm sure you do. Just make sure you don't sample any at my sister's wedding.'

Mimi stared at him in silence, trying to remember her private promise to Alicia, but as she looked up into his face something inside her snapped. Thanks to his careless treatment of her she hadn't had the confidence to so much as kiss a man, much less have sex with him, for two years, and now he was warning her off.

'It's none of your business what I do or who I do it with,' she snarled. 'You are not my keeper.'

It was the wrong answer—she knew that even before he leaned forward, his gaze narrowing as though he was tracking her with a long-range rifle.

'It is my business if you start hitting on my guests.'

Her heart was beating so hard she could feel her ribs quivering. Was he for real?

'If anyone's going to start hitting on the guests it will probably be you,' she snapped, the words spilling from her mouth like milk boiling over in a pan. 'Or have you forgotten what happened at Alicia's party?'

He stared at her in silence and she felt her pulse accelerate, the palms of her hands grow damp. It was like being in some horrible nightmare when you couldn't wake yourself up. Only she wasn't asleep, and this conversation was going nowhere—unless reliving the humiliation of that night was her goal.

But what would be the point of rehashing the past? It was history, fixed for ever in time. What mattered was what was happening here and now—or rather, what wasn't happening. Not any more anyway.

'You know, I'd have thought a busy man like yourself wouldn't have time for playing games,' she said, leaning back in her chair, wanting more distance between herself and his unsettling dark gaze.

'I'm not playing games,' he said softly.

'Oh, but you are. Nasty, horrible, bullying games.'

He laughed, the sound echoing harshly around the beautiful room, and her heart began to thump hard inside her chest.

'How exactly am I bullying you, Mimi? Please, I'm curious. Was it your first-class flight? Did you find that too *oppressive*?' he said mockingly. 'Or does coming here to my beautiful home and being waited on by my staff make you feel *threatened*?'

She glared at him. 'I didn't want to come out to Argentina. You made me feel like I had to.'

'You did have to,' he said coolly. 'I have—'

'*Rules*. Yes, I know.' She spat the words at him dismissively. 'You told me. And I believe you. A stuffed shirt like you probably has a library of rule books—but surely none that required me to come out here in person.' Meeting his eyes, she shook her head. 'No, there's only one reason you dragged me out here, and it's got nothing to do with how I conduct myself in your Patagonian home.'

His face didn't alter, but something shifted in his eyes, and she felt her breathing lose its rhythm as she realised that her hunch was correct.

'You hate it, don't you? The fact that Alicia is my friend. And you can't bear it that you haven't been able to change her mind. That's why you want me out here—so you can spend two days trying to make me walk away from our friendship. To make me look like the bad girl. Well, it's not going to happen.'

She breathed in sharply, her pulse accelerating, as without warning he scraped back his chair against the marble floor. The force of his action nearly tipped it over and then, with swift, purposeful intent, he strode around the table until he was standing in front of her.

'It already has,' he snarled. 'You might look like an angel but you're just like the rest of your family: rotten to the core. Unfortunately, my gentle, big-hearted sister has yet to discover the *real* Mimi Miller, so I thought I'd speed up the process a little.'

Her chair rasped backwards as she stood up too, her

hands curling into fists, shocked by his admission, shocked too by how desolate it made her feel to know that there was nothing she could do, much less say, to sway his mind from the view that she was just as corrupt and manipulative as her stepfather and uncle.

But it shouldn't hurt this much. After all, it wasn't as if he was the only person who believed in the no-smoke-without-fire argument. Even before the guilty verdict many of her friends and acquaintances had vowed never to speak to her again. Yet for some reason his judgement hurt more than anyone else's.

'That's the difference between you and Lissy. You. Don't. Have. A. Heart.' Lifting her hand, she punctuated each word with a jab to the taut muscles of his chest.

She gasped when he caught her hand and jerked her closer—so close she could feel the heat of his body and his anger pulsing under his skin in time with hers. Only it wasn't his anger that was scaring her. It was what lay beneath…the curling, confusing pull of desire that was quickening her pulse and making her legs shake.

Her heart jumped. He felt it too. She could see it in the sudden shrinking of his pupils. For a few quivering seconds she stared at him dazedly. They were close enough that if she tilted her head just a fraction her lips would brush against his, and she felt her body lean forward even as her mind rebelled at the thought.

She jerked her eyes up to his face as he took a step closer, his grip tightening, his beautiful curving mouth distorted into a sneer.

'My heart doesn't need to get involved when I'm dealing with a self-serving little witch like you—just my instincts. And they tell me that sooner or later you won't be able to help yourself. You'll see something you want, something bright and shiny, and you'll throw my sister under a bus to get it.'

She shook her hand free. 'That's not true. I love Alicia and I would never do anything to hurt her.'

'An admirable sentiment, I'm sure. Unfortunately,' he said slowly, 'you already have.' His eyes held hers, their dark pupils relentless and unforgiving. 'And that's the worst thing about people like you and your stepfather and your uncle. You don't understand love and loyalty, so you don't know what it feels like to have it thrown in your face.'

He was wrong. She knew exactly what that felt like—so much so that she could still feel it now, the hot ache of humiliation and a hollowness inside that sucked in every hope and dream like a black hole in space.

For a moment she couldn't speak. The pain was blocking her ability to think straight. Didn't he realise that she'd been in love with him? That her heart had been broken that night…by him?

She took a deep breath. He had recognised her hunger for it had reflected his, but he hadn't been in love so of course he hadn't seen her desperate, hopeful yearning. Her stomach tensed. She'd been a fool to come here, but she would be an even bigger fool to stay.

'And the worst thing about people like *you*,' she said, 'is that you always think you're right. Even though statistically you have to be wrong sometimes, you think you're better than everyone else—that you're one of the good guys.' Breathing out shakily, she shook her head. 'What a joke!'

A part of her could hardly believe what she was saying, but she was sick of him playing judge, jury and executioner.

'You know what, Basa? Back in England, I thought maybe just a tiny part of you meant what you said to Lissy about clearing the air. That you might be willing to give me a chance to show you who I really am. But you don't want to do that, do you?'

'No, I don't,' he said softly, his eyes locked on hers. 'What would be the point? You see, I already *know* who you are.'

Actually, you don't.

The words formed inside her head, but before she had a chance to say them out loud her eyes snagged on the heat in his gaze. And without pausing, much less thinking, she took a step forward and kissed him.

Her mouth melted under his, her hands pulling him closer, carelessly crushing the fine wool fabric of his jacket and then moving up around his neck as naturally as if they did it every day.

He tensed, his breath backing up in his throat, and then he gathered her closer, pressing her against him as if he was scared she would slip through his fingers. She felt her body loosen, so that there was nothing holding her together except his arm around her waist and his lips on hers.

She moaned, and as if he'd been stung he jerked away from her, his eyes widening as he gazed down into her face.

'What the—?'

Later, she would question the rawness in his voice, but in that moment she was too stunned, too devastated by the incredible stupidity of her actions, to register it—too focused on the need to escape from this house, and this man, and the tangle of suffocating emotions that had caused a thick, choking panic to fill her chest.

She took an unsteady step backwards.

'You think you know me, but you don't know me at all. So let me introduce myself. Hi, my name's Mimi Miller, and my life is miserable enough as it is without having to put up with some cold-blooded arrogant bully sitting in judgement over me for the next two days. I wish I could say it's been a pleasure meeting you, but it hasn't. So, if you'll excuse me, I'll skip dessert.'

And before he had a chance to reply, much less react, she darted past him, narrowly sidestepping a startled Antonia. She registered the housekeeper's dazed expression, heard Basa call her name, but she didn't stop. She just kept moving through the hall and up the stairs, until finally she reached the sanctuary of her bedroom.

Slumping back against his chair, Basa picked up his coffee cup and then put it down again, an expression of disgust twisting his handsome face. After Mimi's exit he'd left the dining room as usual, to take his coffee in the lounge, but he didn't want coffee. He wanted to know what was happening to his perfectly ordered life.

Except that whatever loosely passed as his brain these days was struggling to form a sensible thought.

But how was he supposed to think straight when life had thrown a curveball like Mimi Miller at him?

He gritted his teeth. The answer to that should be *easily*. He was a twenty-nine-year-old billionaire businessman who also happened to be the head of one of the largest charitable foundations in the world. So why, then, had he just let a woman he didn't like or trust or respect turn him inside out as effortlessly as if he was some adolescent schoolboy, barely in control of his hormones?

All he knew was that nothing was turning out as he'd planned and that today's encounter with her had left him almost as stunned as the one at Fairbourne two years ago— and that her anger and her accusations had shaken him almost as much as her kiss.

His body stiffened predictably as he remembered the urgency of her mouth on his and the melting softness of her body. That certainly hadn't been on the menu, and he still had no real idea how it had happened. One moment they were eating lunch, the next arguing. So how had they ended up clasping and kissing one another as though the world was about to end?

He sure as hell didn't know, and the only person who might be able to answer the question was upstairs, probably wishing all manner of plagues upon his head.

When Mimi had stormed off he'd had to fight an almost overwhelming urge to go after her and introduce himself to *her* properly. And by *properly* he meant with both of them naked and in her extremely large four-poster bed. Or his. Then he'd show her exactly how little he had in common with a stuffed shirt, he thought savagely.

From the moment her lips had touched his he hadn't cared about her family, or her lies, or the fact that she represented everything that was wrong with the world—the greed, the solipsism, the lack of responsibility for one's actions. All he'd cared about was tasting more of her.

Thankfully Antonia had been there, and despite the feverish hunger gripping his body he'd been conscious of his housekeeper's carefully averted gaze and had sat back down and finished his meal.

His fingers tightened against the thin porcelain handle of the coffee cup. He shouldn't care about what she'd said, and yet he could still hear Mimi's words inside his head. And each time he thought about them, and the accompanying expression on her maddeningly beautiful face, his anger seemed to grow exponentially, so that he could feel it rising like a dark wave inside him.

He wasn't a bully, or arrogant, and he certainly wasn't cold-blooded—not around *her* anyway. And why had she said that her life was miserable enough already?

He shifted in his seat. He didn't know the answer to that

either, but he *did* know that it wasn't fair for her to look like that. She should look like a gargoyle, so that no one—particularly not him—would be deceived by the softness of her mouth or her wide blue eyes.

Jerking his elbow to reveal his wrist, he glanced down at his watch and frowned. He'd assumed when she ran upstairs that she needed time to cool off, and that after an hour or so of sulking she would reappear. Not crushed—that would be too much to hope—but suitably chastened.

His heartbeat slowed. Time was running out.

Alicia would undoubtedly call soon, to check how everything was going, and what was he supposed to say?

Yes, everything's going really well. She kissed me, and I kissed her back, and then she stormed off and now she's hiding in her room.

Picturing his sister's face, her soft brown eyes wide with worry, he cursed his sister's so-called friend in both English and Spanish. He hated it that she had this power over him, but he wasn't about to lie to Alicia so...

He drained his coffee, put down the cup and stood up.

Upstairs, he stood outside Mimi's bedroom door, his jaw so tight it felt as if it might shatter. Damn her. She was going to pay for making him climb the stairs and seek her out.

He knocked and waited.

But why was he waiting? This was *his* house, he thought irritably. And, turning the handle, he opened the door and stepped through it.

The sitting room was empty and, feeling irritation swelling against the stretch of silence that greeted him, he stalked across the hand-knotted rug towards her bedroom.

'Okay, you've made your point,' he said, glancing over at the bed. 'But I think—'

He broke off mid-sentence. The bedroom was empty,

and so was the bathroom and dressing room, and the lack of any clothes or luggage confirmed what the knot in his stomach had already told him.

She had gone. Left. Fled.

His pulse soared, panic blotting out any residual anger.

Where had she gone?

This was not one of her better ideas, Mimi thought, hugging her bag against her chest as she glanced wearily around the crowded side street.

But the word *idea* suggested some kind of thinking had taken place, when in reality she had spent fifteen minutes working herself up into a lather about Basa's rudeness, and her own utterly incomprehensible and humiliating decision to kiss him, and then in a rush of panic simply grabbed everything that belonged to her and sneaked out of the house.

At first, as she'd stomped down tree-lined boulevards in the warm sunshine, she had felt quite pleased with herself. It had been immensely gratifying, picturing the shocked expression on his handsome face when he discovered she was missing. Easy to picture herself staying in some little hotel, just as she had imagined on the limo ride to Basa's home.

Now, though, she was hot and tired, and for some inexplicable reason all the hotels seemed to be full.

Glancing up, she spotted another one, the sixth she had tried, and edging through a large group of men, she made her way to the front desk.

Smiling at the receptionist, she glanced down at her phone at the Spanish phrase on the screen. *'Hola! Tienen una habitación para dos noches?'*

The receptionist smiled. 'You are English, yes? I am sorry, we have no rooms available. I think you will need perhaps to go further out from the centre.'

Mimi leaned against the desk, a quiver of apprehension pulsing down her spine.

'Why is it so busy? Is something happening?'

'Yes, today is the Superclásico.' Catching sight of Mimi's baffled expression, the receptionist laughed. 'It is a football match. A very important game today.'

A football match. Of course.

Leaving the hotel foyer and gazing around, she felt her cheeks grow warm. She was such an idiot! She'd noticed earlier that everybody seemed to be wearing identical co-loured shirts, but she'd been too distracted to give it much thought. Now she realised that the streets seemed to be filling up with crowds of people wearing blue and yellow shirts, some wrapped in flags, others waving them. Even moving forward was suddenly so much harder, for there were so many people.

Where was she going to stay?

Across the square, she glimpsed a flash of red and white, and above the chanting she heard the sound of po-lice sirens. Just like that, the crowd began to move. She didn't want to go with them but it was impossible to resist the tide of bodies. Telling herself that if she just went with the flow everything would be fine, she tried not to panic. But she could feel herself losing her balance.

And then, as she started to fall forward, someone grabbed her arm from behind and hooked her through the surging tide of fans.

Head spinning, pulse racing, she was about to turn and thank her rescuer when she found herself face to face with Basa and her words of gratitude turned to ashes in her mouth.

'What the hell do you think you're doing?' he snarled.

CHAPTER FIVE

Gazing down into Mimi's stunned face, Basa felt his pulse surge.

For a moment his relief that he had found her and she was safe fought with anger at her reckless, impulsive behaviour, and then almost immediately his anger won and, oblivious to the security team hovering behind him, he crowded her back against a shopfront, his dark eyes locking on hers.

'Have you completely lost your mind?' He almost spat the words at her.

Breathing in, he mentally replayed the fraught minutes that had accompanied his swift, discreet search of the house and grounds after he'd found her rooms empty. His initial shock had hardened to an icy fury as he'd realised he was right. She had cut and run. Packed her bag and left, without so much as a note. But then she was good at sneaking off...

His mouth tightened.

It had taken an hour to find her. An hour of driving down street after street, his eyes feverishly hunting the crowds for a tell-tale glimpse of a blonde ponytail among the mass of mostly dark heads. It had been the longest, most stressful hour of his life, and the bar was set high.

It was pure chance that he'd spotted her, and the randomness of that fact only made him feel more agitated, for with each passing minute his imagination had grown ever more flexible—particularly when it had dawned on him that the Superclásico was happening in the city.

The match was a legendary fixture in the football season. There was a fierce rivalry between Boca Juniors and River Plate fans that frequently erupted into violence, and the sight of Mimi being swept along on a sea of blue and yellow had made panic hum in his veins.

Shouldering his way through the crowd, he had only just managed to haul her to safety. But now, instead of thanking him like any normal person, she was glaring up at him as though he had just stopped her winning gold in the Olympics.

'No, actually, I haven't. Unless you think looking for a hotel room is a sign of madness.' She shrugged her arm free and took a step backwards, her wide blue eyes resting on his face.

He stared at her in silence, trying to swallow the adrenaline and ignore the scent of her warm, jasmine-scented skin at the same time.

Much as he would like to bury his face against her throat and forget what was happening, right now, there were more pressing matters to address. Like the fact that she would almost certainly have been trampled underfoot had he not found her when he had.

'Do you have any idea what's going on here?' He gestured past her head to where clumps of police officers were shepherding fans away from the square.

She lifted her chin. 'Yes, of course I do. It's the Superclásico.'

Stunned—maddened, in fact, by the tilt of her chin and the irritatingly condescending note in her voice—he said slowly, 'And what exactly is that?'

'It's a football match.'

'*Wrong.*'

Her eyes widened and flicked to his face, and he felt a juvenile twitch of satisfaction at having taken the wind out of her sails.

'It's not just *a* football match, it's the derby between two of Argentina's best teams, who also happen to hate each other and are not shy about showing it. People get hurt. *You* could have got hurt.'

Saying the words out loud made him feel sick, but the impulse to pull her into his arms and hold her safe swiftly evaporated as he glanced down at her. She was staring up at him mutely, and the truculent expression on her face, coupled with the fact that a group of men across the street were staring at her with undisguised admiration, made his already fraying temper unravel further.

'More importantly,' he said tersely, '*if* you had been hurt it might have got out that you are here as my guest—and, frankly, that's not something I want to be made public.'

She went pale and, watching the colour drain from her cheeks, he felt a twinge of guilt at the brutality of his words. But he told himself that he didn't care. Mimi had been more than willing to play her part in deceiving his family, not to mention permanently depriving a bunch a pensioners of their savings, so she had no right to get upset at hearing a few home truths.

'The Vázquez family is as high-profile and respected here as the Caines are in England, and I don't need you jeopardising either one of my good names—particularly with the wedding so close.'

Her incredible blue eyes flashed with barely concealed scorn and, shaking her head, she gave him the sort of smile that could turn water into ice.

'And that's all that matters to you, isn't it, Basa? Your

name. Sorry, I mean your *names*.' Her lip curled. 'And I thought philanthropists were supposed to care about the welfare of others…'

He held her gaze. 'Oh, I care—just not about rude, self-absorbed little troublemakers like you, who act first and think later.' His jaw clenched as he remembered the slippery rush of panic when he'd realised she had bolted. 'And who have no qualms about lying or stealing or sneaking off, but still expect some poor mug to roll up and rescue them from the mess they make.'

'That's not fair. I didn't ask or need to be rescued!'

She was gazing at him with a combination of loathing and disbelief, as if he'd just turned into a toad in front of her.

'And you are definitely *not* my idea of a knight in shining armour.'

Her voice was growing shriller, and he could see more of the men glancing curiously at them.

'Yeah, well, you're definitely not *my* idea of a damsel in distress.'

She might be young and female, and in need of rescuing, but she was hardly innocent. In fact, he doubted she knew the meaning of the word.

Shaking his head, he swore softly under his breath as a couple more men glanced over. What was he doing? He should be getting her off the street, not engaging with her in some kind of slanging match.

'Okay, that's it,' he said irritably. 'I am done with this stupid conversation.'

'That makes two of us,' she snapped.

He couldn't be sure if it was the petulance in her voice or the way she was holding her battered overnight bag in front of her like a shield that finally caused his temper to snap, but without consciously planning to do so he reached out and plucked the bag from her hands.

'Hey! What are you doing? Give that back.'

She made a grab for it and instantly he caught hold of her, wrapping his fingers around her wrist.

'Let's go!'

'I'm not going anywhere with you.'

She struggled against him, her long blonde hair slipping free of the ponytail at the base of her neck, but he simply tightened his grip and began propelling her past the determinedly blank faces of his security team towards the first of the two large black SUVs idling down a side street at the edge of the square.

'What are you doing?'

She was struggling to break free of his grip, and a voice inside his head was telling him that he was acting like some Stone Age throwback—only his fingers refused to let go of her arm.

'Escorting you to the car,' he said through gritted teeth. 'Before someone recognises you.'

Eyes narrowing, she tugged at his arm. 'This is not escorting…it's abducting.'

'Yes, I suppose it is.'

He stopped so abruptly that her flailing body collided with his, and desire, hot and potent, punched him in the stomach as she grabbed at his shirt to steady herself. For perhaps twenty seconds his exasperated eyes met her furious ones, and then she snatched her hand away as if she'd been stung, in a way that utterly infuriated him.

'Either way, I don't much care.' Glancing past her at the departing crowds, he gave her a small, mocking smile. 'And I'm not getting the feeling anyone else does either. So I suggest you get in the car—or, so help me, I will put you over my shoulder and carry you there myself.'

And then what?

The question slid into his head and his breath caught in his throat as he remembered her body twined around his as he'd carried her onto the bed in his room at Fairbourne. Blanking his mind to the memory of her bare thighs sliding around his hips, he tightened his grip on her wrist.

'You wouldn't dare,' she said. 'You're far too worried about what somebody might see or say.'

'Try me,' he said softly.

He watched her eyes narrow.

'I already did.' She was shaking with anger, her cheeks flushed with red flags of defiance. 'And it wasn't worth the effort of stripping.'

Basa stared at her, shock and anger flooding through him. No, not anger. It was rage—the kind of white-hot fury that blanked out everything but the darkening bruise around his heart and the blue of her eyes.

'And yet you still did it,' he said, his fingers squeezing around her arm. 'You went up to my room, took off your clothes and got into bed with me.'

His throat tightened. There had been a honeyed sweetness to her eagerness. Her skin had been smooth, her mouth soft and her body even softer as she'd melted into him in a way that no other woman had.

'I guess the thought of spending your share of the pension pot helped you overcome whatever limited scruples you possess.'

Her face was so white it looked as if it was ossified.

'That's not why I went to your room.'

He heard the catch in her voice and knew he had the upper hand.

'Of course it wasn't.' His mouth curved into a sneer. 'You'll be telling me next you wanted to look at the view from my window.'

She took a quick breath. 'I went up to your room because I wanted to have sex with you.'

The bluntness of her words momentarily caught him off balance, but, recovering his composure, he shook his head. 'That's not true. You had no intention of sleeping with me; you were just there as a decoy.'

Her pupils flared with anger. 'It *is* true.'

'Then why weren't you prepared?' he snarled.

'Because I'd never slept with anyone before, that's why,' she said, and the shake in her voice made it sound as if she was close to tears.

The pavement seemed to ripple beneath his feet as her reply ricocheted around his head like a firecracker. In the square, the excited crowd were setting off flares, and he stared at her in confusion as trails of blue and yellow smoke began swirling around them. His head was spinning and he was struggling to keep his face composed. Shock— raw, unfettered shock—vied with disbelief.

Why hadn't she told him that on the night?

Was it true? Or was she just playing with him?

Her cheeks were flushed, but he didn't know if that was down to anger or chagrin at having blurted out something she would likely rather have kept hidden from him. All he knew was that this wasn't a conversation he wanted to have in the street, in front of hundreds of strangers and the averted gaze of his bodyguards.

He wanted answers. He wanted the truth. And once he had her safely inside the car, he intended to get it.

'We're not talking about this here,' he said curtly.

'Actually, I don't want to talk about it anywhere.'

Seriously? He stared down at her, a beat of exasperation pulsing over his skin.

'So you think you can just toss that grenade into the

conversation and then—what? Bat your eyelashes and swan off into the sunset?'

She glared at him. 'I don't want to talk about it,' she repeated.

'In that case, you can *not* talk about it in the car.'

'I don't want to get in the car.'

Glancing from her face to her tightly closed fists, he swore softly. But, even though her stubbornness was exasperating, he found himself admiring her defiance. He was six foot four and, thanks to his head of security, Arturo, he knew how to handle himself. But Mimi was fronting up to him like a boxer.

'Tough. You don't have a choice. Because I'm sure as hell not leaving you here.'

Their eyes locked. Eventually she lowered her gaze and he felt her body go limp.

'Then let go of my arm,' she muttered.

Her sudden capitulation chafed at something inside his chest and again he had to suppress a swift, incomprehensible urge to pull her against him.

'Fine. But don't mess me around,' he warned.

Slowly he uncurled his hand and, giving him a baleful glare, she stalked towards the waiting SUV like a cat on a hot tin roof.

He breathed out through gritted teeth and then made his way across the street, stopping to give instructions to his driver. He climbed into the car, glancing over at Mimi. As expected, she was scrunched up in the opposite corner, pointedly staring out of the window. Short of sitting on the roof, she couldn't have put any more distance between them, but that was fine with him.

He needed space to bring order to the chaos of his thoughts, and time to adjust to the revelation she had so casually tossed into the conversation.

His heartbeat accelerated. He couldn't comprehend that he might have been wrong about her. Surely she couldn't have been a virgin that night? It didn't make sense; she must be lying. But there had been a tension in her voice that had sounded real…

With an effort, he forced himself to replay that night at Fairbourne. He tried to remember whether she had been tense or apprehensive, or had acted in a way that might have suggested she hadn't had sex before. Could he have been so stunned by his own febrile reaction to her that he'd missed it? Had there been a moment, just a fraction of a second, before he'd asked her if she had protection, when he'd pushed against the slick warmth between her thighs and she'd gripped his arm tightly…? With what?

At the time it had felt like hunger, urgency. Now he wondered if it had been uncertainty and panic.

At the time she'd said nothing. In fact, she'd pulled him closer, kissing him frantically and—

It had never crossed his mind that he would have been her first lover. He'd thought he had her all figured out— that in the years when he'd been studying at university and then taking over from his father she'd done a lot of growing up. With that heart-stopping body, her mass of blonde hair and soft pout, he'd had no trouble imagining her being most men's fantasy come to life, so he'd assumed that she knew what she was doing, knew what men liked, and that was why she was being so responsive, so hungry, so uninhibited.

Only…what if it had been nervousness about losing her virginity that had made her so frantic?

His stomach felt as if it was full of stones.

For so long he'd been certain that she had cold-bloodedly lied to him, with that same soft mouth that had kissed him so sweetly. He had thought she was the kind of woman who would effortlessly seduce a family friend to give her crooked relations time to cover their tracks. A woman who would have thought nothing of having unprotected sex with him even though she must have known indisputably that any future baby would have been born into an irreversible feud between their two families.

That she had acted like that, with such determined ruthlessness, had been as shattering as it had unfathomable. But now he was finding out that he had been wrong about how sexually experienced she was. And the fact that he'd been wrong about that was making him question everything else he'd thought to be true about the woman sitting next to him.

His jaw was suddenly so tense it was difficult to release the breath he'd been holding in.

Had he been wrong?

Rather than questioning the 'facts', had it just been easier to accept them at face value?

Maybe… But if she really had been a virgin surely she would have said something?

'Mimi—'

He started to speak, but as the car began to move she cut him off.

'I have nothing to say to you.'

He shrugged. 'Then I'll do the talking.'

'But just so we're clear,' she said, and carried on speaking as if he'd not said a word, 'I am not stepping foot in that house again. So if you could just drop me at the airport…?'

He stared at her, his body tense with incredulous anger. Did she really think she could just explode a bomb into his world and then walk away without so much as a word of explanation?

'This is not a taxi service, and you will go where I take you.'

The hostile expression on her face did nothing to improve his mood.

'I'm not going anywhere with you except to a hotel or the airport,' she snapped back.

Her eyes were the same shifting capricious blue as the lake surrounding his house in Patagonia, and just looking into them made him want to strip naked and dive in. Or maybe it was the smooth skin of her bare legs, or her pink, kissable lips that were making him want to tear off both his clothes and hers?

'There's no point going to a hotel. None of them will have any rooms,' he said curtly.

'Then I'll wait at the airport.' Her soft mouth was fixed into a steely line.

'You won't need to wait.'

Rolling her eyes, she muttered something under her breath that sounded like 'entitled, arrogant jerk', and turned towards the window. But less than thirty seconds later she turned back to face him, a frown creasing her beautiful face.

'I don't understand…we just passed the sign to the airport.'

'Yes, we did,' he said evenly.

'But you said you were taking me there.'

He shook his head. 'No, you just made that assumption.'

As he had assumed she was sexually experienced?

The question popped into his head without warning and, gritting his teeth, he pushed it to the back of his mind. He would get answers, but with the aftershock from her revelation still juddering inside his head he didn't know up from down—knew only that it would be a bad idea to try and resolve this now.

'So where are we going, then?'

Her hands had curled into fists and he could hear the undercurrent of panic in her voice.

'Somewhere private.' He stared at her steadily. 'Somewhere you won't be able to embarrass my family. Somewhere a long way from civilisation, where nobody knows who you are. Somewhere you and I can have a nice long chat without any interruptions.'

'What do you mean by a long way from civilisation?'

It was testament to the level of her panic that she didn't even blink at his threat of a chat. He watched as she stared at him blankly, and then a flicker of alarm travelled across her face and she started shaking her head.

'No, Basa. I am *not* going to your house in Patagonia now.'

'Too late,' he said calmly. 'We're already on our way.'

Mimi felt as though a bucket of icy water had been up-ended over her head, like in one of those internet challenges. But at least with those you knew what to expect. How could she possibly have foreseen that he would pull a stunt like this?

She bit her lip. He couldn't be serious. Patagonia was hundreds of miles away, and he'd already told her he couldn't put his job on hold like she could.

Relief flooded through her veins.

Surely this was just part of his ongoing mission to show her who was the boss—or maybe he was trying to scare her, to punish her for sneaking off. But whatever it was, it couldn't have anything to do with wanting to talk about her virginity. Why would that matter to him?

Her skin felt as if it was melting.

It was awkward enough that she had admitted her inexperience to one of the most eligible bachelors in the world, but any conversation about her sex life was quickly going to reveal that she was still a virgin—and, frankly, that wasn't something she wanted to share with Basa Caine right now.

Actually, make that *not ever*.

It wasn't that she was embarrassed. All her closest friends, including Alicia, knew that she hadn't slept with anyone yet, but she would rather set fire to her own head than open her mouth and share that particular piece of information with a man who had kissed her and found her wanting.

For a moment she considered her options.

It didn't take long as there was only one.

She gritted her teeth. She didn't want to do it but she had to do something—and she was willing to do anything to derail his plan to take her to Patagonia…including apologise.

Taking a steadying breath, she gave him a small, taut smile. 'I know you're angry with me, and I'm sorry for disappearing like that. I probably shouldn't have left without telling you first—'

His gaze rested on her face. 'There's no "probably" about it, but I suppose I shouldn't be surprised. You're good at sneaking off when nobody's looking.'

Her heart began to beat a little faster. It was the second time he'd said that, and she still didn't know what he meant by it, but now was not the time to get distracted.

'Like I said, I'm sorry, okay? I just thought there wasn't much point in my staying when every time we talk we just end up arguing.'

And, of course, there had been the small but embarrassing matter of her kissing him, and it would be even more embarrassing if he realised she was still a virgin.

His dark eyes rested on her face. 'We don't only end up arguing,' he said softly.

She blinked, and breathed out unsteadily. She was still shocked at her own behaviour—the kissing part, anyway. Obviously running away after she'd kissed him was completely understandable, but of course that didn't mean she could pretend it hadn't happened—particularly when he was sitting approximately three feet away from her.

Forcing herself to meet his gaze, she shrugged with a casualness she didn't feel. 'That was a mistake.'

'Define mistake,' he said softly, his eyes glittering.

Her breath seemed bottled in her throat. That would be because of getting in the car with him. It was too small a space, and he was too close, and when he looked at her like that it seemed even smaller.

Ignoring the prickle of heat seeping over her skin, she sucked in a breath, trying to stay calm. 'It was stupid and rash and I don't know why it happened,' she lied, keeping her eyes locked on his and away from the tempting curve of his mouth.

Earlier, in the crowded city streets, it had been easy to blank out the kiss he had so helpfully brought up, but now, with his lean, muscle-packed body sprawled only a few feet away from hers, she could feel the same insistent hunger curling through her body that had been her undoing in the dining room.

'I promise you don't need to worry about me doing anything else stupid or rash that might embarrass your family.'

'Oh, but I do worry, and that's why we can't stay in Buenos Aires.' His dark eyes locked onto hers, holding her captive. 'That and the fact that I intend to have a conversation that clearly needed to happen two years ago.'

Her chest was pressing so tightly against her lungs it was difficult to breathe.

'No, that's not—' she began, but he cut her off.

'I'm not going to let you draw me into another argu-

ment, Mimi. This is the airfield and that—' he gestured
to a sleek white plane sitting on the runway '—is my jet.
And now you have a choice to make. Either we use my jet,
which will take approximately three hours, or we drive.
That will take nearer eleven hours, so—'

She stared at him, her heart beating in her throat.
'You're joking. This is a joke, right?'

'No, it's not.' His dark gaze rested impatiently on her
disbelieving expression. 'One way or another we are going
to Patagonia as planned.' As she pulled out her phone, he
sighed. 'There's no point trying to call anyone. You won't
get a signal here, nor where we're going either.'

Glancing down at the screen, she tightened her fingers
around the phone. He was right.

'I can't believe you're doing this.'

He shrugged. 'You're not going anywhere without me
until this is resolved.'

Mimi felt dizzy. This couldn't be happening. It was too
crazy, too preposterous to be real, and yet the expression
on his face told her he meant what he said.

Her heart began to pound. Fifteen long minutes ago
having a conversation with him in the car about her non-
existent sex life had seemed like a form of torture, but
compared to being trapped with him for who knew how
long, in the middle of nowhere, it was clearly the lesser
of two evils.

Her heart thumped inside her chest. She could refuse to
go, or try and persuade the chauffeur to intervene on her
behalf, but somehow she didn't think either course of action would get her what she wanted. Nor did she want to
issue him a challenge, like she had earlier. The last thing
she wanted was for Basa to make good on his threat to put
her over his shoulder.

She stared out of the window. The instinct to run was nearly overwhelming, but where would she run *to*?

And yet she couldn't spend an indeterminate number of days—*and nights*—with him on an island in the middle of nowhere. Surely there was another solution?

'Look, we don't need to go to Patagonia to talk. You want to talk—then, let's talk now,' she said quickly. 'What is it that you want to know?'

'The truth,' he said softly.

She stared at him in silence. Somewhere deep inside she could feel a long-buried, festering anger roiling up inside her, after two years of being ostracised and judged and condemned without trial.

He made it sound so simple, but for the last two years there had been no single absolute truth—just a shifting kaleidoscope of other people's opinions and beliefs that had nothing to do with who she was or what had happened—and not once had he been interested or willing to listen to her version.

'Don't make me laugh! You don't want the truth. You've *never* wanted the truth. You've never once given me the benefit of the doubt. You're just like everyone else. You just want to judge me.'

Her chest pinched as she remembered all the assumptions that people had made about her and her mother. The neighbours and friends and journalists and lawyers and all those people she had never even met, who had read and repeated and believed that she was guilty on the basis of nothing more than whispers and assumptions.

But it was his judgement that hurt most of all.

'Mimi, listen—'

'No, *you* listen, Basa.'

She took a quick breath, pushing past the ache in her chest.

'If you want to force me to go all the way to Patagonia with you then *fine!*' She filled the word with all the frustration and fury that was filling her body. 'But you're wasting your time. I'm done talking to you. So I hope you're comfortable with silence, because that's all you're going to get from me.'

CHAPTER SIX

SHE KEPT HER WORD, smiling politely at the crew as they showed her to her seat, and then turning her face towards the window as soon as they were alone. It was deeply childish, she knew, to act that way, and judging by the look on Basa's face he thought so too, but she'd had enough of worrying about what he thought of her. Accommodating his stupid demands and apologising hadn't done much to change his opinion of her, so why not just be the rude, self-absorbed little troublemaker he thought she was?

Her head was aching and, overwhelmed with the tension and drama of the day, she leaned back against the leather headrest and closed her eyes.

What felt like thirty seconds later she heard the soft whine of wheels dropping into position and, opening her eyes, realised that she had fallen asleep.

She glanced out of the window and felt her heart bump against her ribs. They were getting ready to land.

Moments later the wheels hit the ground, and then she was climbing into another SUV.

It was late evening, and the sun had only recently set, so there was still a thin ribbon of gold on the horizon. But even with the headlights of the car at full beam she could see that beyond the darkness there was nothing except more darkness. And there was a threatening heaviness to the air, so that the night sky felt as though it was just inches away from swallowing her whole.

It felt as if they had reached the edge of the mapped world, and her stomach flipped over as the reality of her situation hit home.

Why had she allowed this to happen?

She couldn't be stuck out here with this beautiful, furious man, who disliked and distrusted her in equal measure— the same man she had kissed just hours earlier, without any regard for the consequences, just as she had two years ago.

Shivering against the cool chill of the memory of that night, she steadied her pounding heart. Two years ago she would have followed him barefoot and naked into the wilderness, for then she had been willing—impatient, even— to give him her body and her heart. But back then he hadn't wanted either, and nothing had changed except that now he wanted the truth.

She knew he was talking about what had happened that night at Fairbourne. But what if in exposing one truth he uncovered the real truth? That everything she touched turned to ashes?

He already knew about her stalled career; he didn't need to learn that the rest of her life, including her love life, was similarly stunted.

The car stopped, and when she climbed out she saw that they were parked by the side of a lake. A series of low-level lights illuminated a wide wooden jetty, at the end of which was moored a large motorboat.

Refusing to give in to the slippery panic sliding over her skin, she ignored Basa's outstretched arm and climbed into the boat. Soon they were moving smoothly across the water, the slow tick of the outboard engine blending with the gentle lapping of the water.

Around fifteen minutes later they reached the island.

She had a fleeting impression of a curving silhouette of silvered wood and long low windows before Basa hustled her inside.

'I gave my staff the evening off, but I'm sure there will be something in the kitchen if you're hungry.'

When she didn't reply he shook his head.

'Okay, you've made your point, Mimi. Can we stop with all the silent treatment now? It's not as if refusing to speak to me is going to change anything, or make me disappear. And it's certainly not going to make our stay here particularly enjoyable.'

Their stay!

His words echoed loudly inside her head as she stared at him in disbelief, curling her toes inside her shoes to stop herself from throwing his remark back in his face—or, better still, throwing him into the lake outside.

He was making it sound as though this was some kind of mini-break, when in fact he'd forced her into coming here against her wishes. And now he had the gall to complain that she was going to ruin the enjoyment of *their stay*.

A pulse of anger beat over her skin as she met his gaze.

'So you're going to keep this up the whole time?'

He was looking down at her with barely concealed impatience, and as she glared back at him his eyes narrowed.

'Actually, you know what? Forget it. I mean, what was I thinking? How could I even consider having a civilised conversation with someone who was raised by wolves?'

Mimi gaped at him, momentarily winded by the injustice and hypocrisy of his statement.

'And abduction and coercion are just *so* civilised, I suppose,' she snapped, her vow to remain silent forgotten in a white flash of anger that blinded her to everything but the need to wipe that dismissive sneer from his handsome face.

He stared at her, a muscle ticking in his cheek. 'I am not doing this now. I'll show you to your room.'

Turning, he picked up her bag. She stared at his broad back and felt her body start to shake. Funny, that. She started talking and immediately he wanted to leave.

Her heart felt like a lump of lead inside her chest. All that stuff he'd said about wanting a conversation had really been about him pulling her strings, making her dance to his tune. He didn't care about her, or what had happened. Or about the anxiety he'd caused by dragging her out here and holding the threat of an inquisition over her head. And now he thought he could just send her to her room like some truculent child.

'That's right. Walk away, why don't you?' she snarled. 'That's what you do, isn't it, when you can't get what you want? Why don't you pretend you're looking for a bottle of champagne while you're at it?'

He swung round, his dark eyes glittering with fury. 'Keep your voice down.'

'Don't talk to me like I'm one of your staff.'

'I'm not. But then, my staff don't stand around screeching like a fishwife when everyone else is trying to sleep.'

'I'm not screeching.' She stabbed a finger in his direction. 'You're just so used to bullying people into doing what you want that you can't bear me standing up for myself! Oh, and by the way, I'm not a fishwife. In fact, I'm not anyone's wife. I'm actually very happy being single. But *if* I did get married it definitely wouldn't be to an insufferable jerk like you.'

He dropped her bag onto the smooth wooden floor, and walked purposefully towards her, his gaze fixed on her face. 'I wasn't proposing,' he said coldly. 'I'm not looking for a wife right now. And when I am ready to marry, it will be to someone who understands my world. Someone who shares my values.'

She stared at him mutely. For so long, right up until that night at Fairbourne, she'd imagined herself in love with this man. But whatever had possessed her to think that he might love her back? Even before her stepfather and uncle had knocked her life off course they had been from different worlds—his old money versus her newly acquired wealth.

And of course she knew exactly what kind of wife Basa would choose. Beautiful, smart, successful in her own right... And she would also have one of those names that mattered—the kind of name that got you the best table in the restaurant.

In other words, nothing like her. Or the version of her that he and practically every other person except Alicia believed her to be.

Her hands curled into fists. 'For the last time, I didn't know what Charlie and Raymond were doing. It was as much a shock to me and my mum as everyone else. You might not want to believe that, but that doesn't stop it being true, and the truth is what you said you wanted.'

His face looked as if it had turned to stone.

'Oh, what's the point? I need some fresh air.'

Fresh air and a much-needed reprieve from his presence.

She stormed back the way she'd come, through the front door and out onto the deck.

Basa swore with frustration, and then, without having had any thought of doing so, he was striding after her. 'Why should I believe you?'

A cool breeze accompanied the silence that followed his words and then she spun round, her eyes blazing in the darkness. 'Why wouldn't you?'

There was an ache in her voice like a bruise, but he ignored it. 'Evidence!'

'What evidence?' she snapped. She was staring at him as if he'd grown two heads. 'You mean being related to Charlie and Raymond?'

'No, I don't mean that. That would be petty—not to say unfair.'

He shook his head. Tension was swelling around them, crowding them as he had crowded her earlier in the street, and then in the car, and suddenly he was fighting to stay calm.

'None of us gets to choose our relations, Mimi, but we do get to choose how we act, and that's how other people judge us. On our actions.'

She breathed in sharply. 'Well, in that case, if you would stop slinging mud in my direction for a couple of seconds, you should take a good, long look at yourself.'

He took a step forward, his eyes fixed on her small, pale face. 'Meaning?'

'You took me to your room and stripped off my clothes and then you lost interest. Only you didn't even have the common decency to tell me to my face. You just left me lying there, like some half-eaten dessert, while you pretended to go and find a bottle of champagne.'

The ache in her voice made him flinch inwardly, and he felt a dull flush of colour spreading over the contours of his cheekbones as, inevitably, they reached the crux of the matter.

'But why were you even there? In my room? In my bed?'

He felt a stab of shame. It had been his decision to employ Charlie and Raymond, and his lack of judgement had caused untold suffering to so many people—not least his own father. And yet here he was, fixating on Mimi's motivation for turning that sweet smile his way.

'I told you why.' She stiffened. 'I wanted to have sex with you.'

His body hardened at the frankness of her words, his eyes dropping instinctively to the lush pink mouth that had spoken them.

'But you say you were a virgin.'

Her chin jerked up, her eyes widening with shock and hurt, and for one tiny insane moment he wanted to reach out and pull her into his arms.

'I don't just say it, Basa, I *was*. I st—' She broke off, stepping back unsteadily.

It was the second time she had made that claim, and once again he found himself questioning both her and himself. There had already been so many false positives that he didn't know whether to believe her. Could she really be telling the truth? Or was she just playing him again? Trying to soften his resolve?

'So why me? Why that night?'

It was the question he'd asked himself on so many occasions—a question he'd even considered asking his sister over the many months that had passed since that night. A question that seemed to matter even more now that she was claiming to have been a virgin.

'Why does it matter?' Her voice was unsteady now too. 'It was two years ago. Why do you care?'

He took a step closer, the taste of anger and frustration bitter in his mouth.

'The reason I left you lying there was because I was talking to my lawyer—the lawyer who had been calling me and leaving messages all evening about a "discrepancy" in the accounts.'

She stilled, her blue eyes suddenly like saucers. He could almost track her thoughts as she worked back through the timeline of those hours and days before news of the embezzlement broke.

His own thoughts stalled. No, that didn't make sense. She shouldn't need to work back through anything. According to his argument she would already have known that time was running out for her stepfather and her uncle, and that was why she had made a play for him.

Unless… *Unless he'd been wrong.*

Blanking his mind to that possibility, he leaned forward, the muscles in his arms swelling against the fabric of his jacket. 'Thanks to you, I never got those calls or messages—because you took my phone and switched it off. Or did you forget that little detail from the night? *"Oh, please, Basa, let's shut the whole world out."*'

Watching the colour drain from her face, he wanted to stop and rewind, erase his remark, but another part of him—the part that still stung from being played—wanted to hurt her.

'You know, I actually thought it was poetic.' He shook his head. 'It didn't occur to me that you meant it literally—that you were shutting the world out to give Charlie and Raymond time to cover their tracks.'

Mimi stared at him in silence. She looked stunned.

'That's not what I was doing,' she said shakily.

'Really?' Basa shook his head. 'So why didn't you come and find me to say goodbye?' He felt a spasm of fury, remembering the moment when he'd seen that nameless guy with his hand resting on Mimi's back. 'Oh, sorry—I forgot. I already know the answer to that one. I saw you with him. About five foot eight, stupid floppy hair, even stupider orange car…'

His voice sounded raw, and he hated the note of jealousy that had crept in beneath the anger, but he didn't care about anything now except getting her to admit the truth and prove he'd been right about her all along.

'Do you see my problem, Mimi? You want me to believe you wanted me so much you were willing to give me your virginity—but if that's true, if you really were innocent, why did you sneak off with lover-boy?'

Her face was as white as paper now.

'I did want you.' She took a step closer, her hands trembling by her sides. 'And he wasn't my lover. I just overheard him saying he was going back to London. I wanted to go home so I asked him for a lift.'

'Right. So I'm supposed to believe that the pair of you driving off into the sunset was just a coincidence?'

'No.' She shook her head. 'It wasn't a coincidence. It was a necessity.'

'I don't understand.'

Her eyes flared, a sudden flash of blue in the darkness.

'Of course you don't. You're Bautista Caine. You have women chasing you on every continent. Nobody leaves you—nobody walks out of your life as if you don't matter. When you didn't come back I thought you'd changed your mind.' She breathed in sharply. 'That you'd been curious but I'd been a disappointment. I just wanted to get away.'

She stared past him into the darkness, and through the confused tangle of his feelings for her, the anger and the hurt, he heard the shake in her voice and knew she was an inch from tears.

'You weren't a disappointment,' he said quietly. How could she think that? 'And I wasn't just curious. I was captivated.'

He could still remember every pulsing second with punishing clarity. The slow slide of her skin against his, the urgency of her mouth. Had she no idea of how sweet she had been? How desperately he had wanted to fuse his body with hers and the weight of his disappointment when he'd had to bring it to a halt?

But how could she? If she was telling the truth then she'd had nothing to compare it to.

His breathing slowed. He could remember his own first time—how nervous he'd been, how anxious to do it right and to give pleasure as much as to receive it. What would he have thought if he'd been in her position?

He frowned. 'But why Alicia's birthday party? If that was to have been your first time, why did you choose that night?'

'When else was it going to be?'

In the still night air her voice scraped against his senses. Her eyes were deep blue on his, and she was so close now that he could see her whole body was trembling.

'I know Alicia's my friend, but I didn't mix in your circles. I knew you'd be at the party, and when you asked me to dance I thought it was our one chance to be together. That's why I took your phone and turned it off so...' She hesitated. 'So we didn't lose our chance.'

He knew it was what she would say if she was trying to manipulate him, but her words made sense in a way he didn't want or need to question.

'Why didn't you say something? Why didn't you tell me you'd never had sex?'

Her eyes slid away from his. 'You could have anyone. I thought if you knew I was a virgin it might put you off.'

His chest felt as though it was in a vice and he took a step closer, feeling again that need to take her in his arms.

'When I left you I did go and look for some champagne. I had every intention of coming back. And I would have done except—'

'It doesn't matter now,' she said quickly. 'It's all in the past.'

There was nothing between them now but a sliver of

silence and the muscles tightening beneath his skin. He took another step closer.

'Is it?'

She blinked, and he knew without looking that his question had hooked her. He heard her swallow and suddenly his heart was hammering. His eyes were drawn unwaveringly to the heat in her eyes as she let out a staccato breath.

'Yes—yes, it is.'

'I don't believe you.'

The air was humming now.

Her lips parted. 'You never do.'

'Would now be a good time to start?' he asked hoarsely.

She stared at him, motionless, the darkness swelling around her. And then she was shaking her head, and before he had a chance to consider what that meant she'd drawn in a quick breath, stood up on her toes and kissed him.

His body tensed momentarily and then he pulled her against him, one hand splaying against her spine as he buried the other in her hair and kissed her back, pleasure spreading over his skin like ripples in a pond.

Her lips felt soft and she breathed jerkily into his mouth, catching his lip with her teeth as he clasped her head, tightening his hand in her hair as he tilted her face to deepen the kiss, wanting to taste her sweetness, to satisfy his hunger.

He could feel his tongue inside her mouth and she arched against him, moaning softly. He felt his groin harden, and instantly the need to touch more of her was urging him on like a jockey with a whip.

His fingers found the buttons of her dress and, popping them open, he breathed his way down over the skin of her throat and collarbone to the swell of her breasts. He lowered his face, blindly brushing it against the soft cotton of her bra, feeling his body harden as the nipples grew taut.

He wanted to hear her moan again and, pushing the

fabric to one side, he sucked a nipple into his mouth, nipping and licking, his heartbeat filling his head as he felt her shiver against him.

He was harder than he'd ever been, and yet liquid too, so that he could feel himself melting into the darkness around them.

Raising his mouth, he found her lips with his, kissing her, tasting her, kissing the soft skin of her cheeks and throat, then back to her mouth, wanting, needing, to drain the sweetness from her lips.

Gently, he pushed up the hem of her dress, running his hand over her thigh, and as he flattened his palm against the damp cotton of her panties she moaned again.

'Mimi...'

He whispered her name, but even as his voice echoed in the darkness she was pushing him away.

Looking down at her, he saw a pink flush seeping over her cheeks. Her eyes were wide with a mixture of shock and hunger that he knew must be mirrored in his own dark gaze.

'I—' Her voice bled into the darkness. 'We can't.'

Gritting his teeth, he took an unsteady step backwards. He had never wanted to disagree with anyone more in his life, but despite the solid evidence pressing against his trousers he knew she was right. As tempting as it was to have sex with Mimi, out here in the darkness, at some point the sun would rise, and in the daylight they would both regret their hasty surrender to the heat and hunger of the moment.

They'd had their chance at Fairbourne but it wasn't meant to be—and that had been before they'd had all this history between them.

Besides, no amount of desire could blot out the facts: Mimi was related to the two men who had almost ruined his family's business, not to mention the lives of several thousand pensioners. An affair, however brief, would certainly alleviate the sexual tension between them—but at what cost? If it ever got out that they had slept together even once the media would pounce on the story and the Caine name would be dragged through the mud again.

'I know,' he said.

The relief in her eyes stung, but at least it took the edge off the ache in his groin.

'It's been a long and emotional day. Lines have got blurred.' He forced himself to hold her gaze. Injecting coolness into his voice, he said, 'You must be exhausted. Let me show you to your room.'

His senses were jangling, and the shift from passion to pragmatic almost blew his mind, but somehow he managed to find his way back into the house and to the bedroom door.

'It's all fairly straightforward. I'm just down there if you need me for anything.'

The expression on her face suggested that was about as likely as him finding mermaids in the lake tomorrow morning.

'Goodnight, then,' he said evenly.

Turning, he strode down the hallway before she could close the door in his face—or, worse, before he did something unutterably stupid, like capturing her mouth with his and finishing what they had started out on the deck.

CHAPTER SEVEN

WHEN MIMI WOKE, her room was in darkness, so that for a couple of moments she thought it was still night-time. Then, as her eyes began to adjust, she realised there was a thin line of daylight around the edge of the curtains. And with the daylight reality came rushing in.

Rolling onto her back, she stared up at the ceiling as her face flushed with heat.

Last night she had kissed Basa.

Twice in one day.

Skin tightening, her mind replayed the slow, pulsing hunger in his dark gaze and the bone-melting heat of his response when she kissed him. Thankfully she had come to her senses, pulling away from temptation before she'd done anything more. But she hadn't just wanted to kiss him. She had felt hollow with desire, as if everything solid inside her had dissolved and she was made of nothing but air. She had wanted him...wanted him to fill that aching emptiness.

She might be weak and reckless, but she wasn't completely stupid. She knew that even if they only slept together once, to satisfy their mutual hunger, it would be asking for trouble. There was no way she could cold-bloodedly file that particular experience away. Not when it would first involve admitting the small matter of her virginity to Basa.

Her cheeks felt suddenly hot.

She had almost told him last night, when he'd been grilling her about her motives for going to his room, but she was glad she hadn't. She didn't want him thinking she was holding out for him. She just hadn't met anyone else who made her want to take that next step. He was an impossible act to follow.

But she sure as hell wasn't about to admit that to him. He might be attracted to her, but she had known even without his not so subtle reminder about his preferred future Mrs Caine that she was not his type, and the speed with which he had showed her to her room suggested buyer's remorse at having responded to her so fervently.

Pushing back the duvet, she slid out of bed. Using the light creeping into the room, she made her way to the window and cautiously pushed the curtains aside.

She stared through the glass, not breathing.

Whatever she had been expecting, it had not been this. The view was epic, staggering, intoxicating.

The lake looked like a vast blue mirror, and a dark fairytale wood hugged the edges of the water. It was difficult to make out the individual shapes of the trees that lay beyond. Further away, a lemon-coloured sun was warming a flotilla of snow-tipped peaks.

She bit into the smile that was curving her lip. It was beautiful, but she was not here to sightsee. And after last night Basa would probably be desperate to get back to civilisation, so there was no point getting too excited about the scenery.

She showered beneath what felt like a waterfall of warm water in the state-of-the-art bathroom, then pulled on a pair of trousers and a sweatshirt and tied her hair up in a loose bun before making her way to the living room.

The house was quiet and beautiful in a completely different way from the mansion in Buenos Aires. That was all drama and gilded glamour, whereas this was all about tapping into the surroundings. The decor was understated, but casually opulent with an emphasis on natural materials. It was also messier than the other house, she thought as she looked about, glancing at the rows of shelves that were curtseying gently beneath the weight of books.

How could one man live in two such diametrically opposed homes?

She was curious—more curious than she had a right to be or the good sense not to be. She tilted her head on one side to read the spines, looking for clues.

'Take one if you want,' said a cool, refined voice from somewhere behind her.

Cheeks burning, Mimi turned to find Basa watching her from the doorway. She felt her pulse quicken. He was wearing jeans and a dark jersey that hugged the muscles of his chest. The sleeves were pushed up to his elbows, revealing a tantalising stretch of smooth, golden skin. Against her will she found herself picturing the rest of his body.

Horrified by the direction of her thoughts, she shook her head. Her eyes darted around the room, looking for some means of escape, but there was only one door and his shoulder was wedged against the frame, his body filling the opening. It was the perfect pose, both owning the room and blocking her exit, and as if he could read her mind his mouth curved up into one of those rare smiles that made her feel as if she was drowning beneath her own heartbeat.

'Really, I mean it.'

Pushing away from the doorframe, he came and stood beside her, his dark eyes flickering over her face. 'It's one of the pleasures of coming here—the chance to lose oneself in a book.' He held up the one in his hand. 'I'm reading this at the moment.'

Mimi frowned. On the cover a woman's profile was silhouetted against a pale green background; she had a bun like hers, but much neater, so she guessed that it was either a magical fantasy or a historical romance—two genres she wouldn't have thought appealed to a man like Basa.

Catching sight of her expression, he smiled crookedly. 'I think Alicia must have left it here last time she came. It's not my usual thing, but I realised I've been complacent in my habits and I thought it was about time I stopped judging a book by its cover.'

Her pulse scampered as his gaze rested on her face and she replayed his words inside her head.

'Do you like reading?'

She blinked. After so many tense, panic-inducing conversations it felt strange talking about something as ordinary as reading.

'Yes, but I'm really bad at choosing books.'

He looked up at the shelves, frowning, his gaze narrowed as if he was searching for something specific.

'Here, try this one.' He pulled a book free and handed it to her. 'It's a translation, but a good one. I think you'll enjoy it.'

'And why's that?' She glanced at the cover suspiciously.

'It's a well-written contemporary novel.' His eyes were steady and unblinking on her face. 'Oh, and it has a heroine who's been wrongly condemned by society.'

She kept on staring at the cover, his words repeating inside her head. *Wrongly condemned.* He had definitely said 'wrongly'. Her heart bumped against her ribcage. Was he trying to say something? Or was she reading more into it than was there?

Looking up, she met his gaze. 'Is that your way of saying sorry?'

He stared at her for a moment and then sighed. 'I'm not often wrong.'

She rolled her eyes. 'I guess that must be why you're so bad at apologising.'

There was a pulse of silence and then he spoke again. 'I'm sorry.'

Her chest tightened. 'For what? Being bad at saying sorry or for thinking I was part of the criminal underworld.'

'Both.' Basa's mouth twisted into something between a smile and a grimace. 'I'm sorry that I'm so bad at apologising, but mostly I'm sorry for lumping you in with your stepfather and uncle. You don't deserve that.'

His eyes were fixed on her face as if her reaction mattered to him, as if he cared what she thought of him. She felt an inexplicable lightness fill her body.

'I was wrong.'

He took a step closer, close enough that she could see the rise and fall of his chest, and her heart squeezed tight with panic. Suddenly she wanted to throw his apology in his face, to stay good and mad with him. Because if she let herself feel tenderly towards this man she would end up getting hurt, just like two years ago. It wouldn't matter that she didn't love him—she was still too vulnerable where he was concerned. For he was both a symbol of her hopes and dreams and a reminder of her failures.

'I accept your apology.'

He stared at her for a moment. 'In that case would you like to join me for breakfast? I know Claudia, my housekeeper, is looking forward to meeting you.'

He was speaking with a kind of detached courtesy, as if she was a guest at his hotel, and she stared at him warily.

It was at least something that he no longer saw her as public enemy number one, but in another way she almost preferred the intensity of his anger. Anything would be better than this careful politeness.

But it would sound utterly mad to say any of that out loud, so instead she just nodded.

Breakfast was delicious, and she ate hungrily.

Across the table, Basa drank coffee. He seemed distracted, and she guessed he was trying to work out how to tell her that they would be returning to Buenos Aires without losing face.

Thankfully the view from the dining area was as spectacular as the one from her bedroom.

It was not hard to see why Alicia was so excited to be having her wedding here, she thought, her eyes drawn to the smooth blue lake and then up to the vast blue sky. Getting married here would be like receiving nature's blessing on your life together.

'Would you like to go for a walk?'

Basa's voice brought her head around and she turned towards him, her eyes finding his. And with thoughts of Alicia's happiness uppermost in her mind, it was easy to nod and say, 'Yes, I would—very much.'

The sun was high in the clear blue sky, and there was no breeze to move the leaves of the sturdy *lenga* beech trees that grew right up to the edge of the lake.

Basa glanced over to where Mimi was staring across the lake, her blue eyes exactly the same colour as the water lapping over the stones.

It was a beautiful day, the perfect introduction to this majestic jagged land that he loved so much, even when the wind tore across the lake, sending waves crashing to the shoreline. There was something raw and real about life so close to the clouds, an unchanging, impervious essentiality that was a welcome contrast to the artifice and embellishment of the rest of the world.

And, judging by the smile tugging at the corners of Mimi's mouth, she thought so too—although he wasn't completely sure why that should make him feel quite as happy as it did.

'So what do you think?' He was careful to keep the curiosity out of his voice but his heart began to beat faster.

'I think it's the most beautiful place I've ever seen,' she said quietly. 'However did you find it?'

For a moment he considered whether to tell her the truth. But the fragile peace he had brokered this morning was still holding and he didn't want to do anything to put that in jeopardy. Then again, he was tired of all the misunderstandings between them—unnecessary and upsetting misunderstandings that had been caused by both of them being less than forthcoming with the truth.

He thought back to their conversation last night. Afterwards he had found it hard to sleep—and not just because of that kiss, although that certainly hadn't helped. For two years he'd convinced himself that he knew Mimi and that she was guilty, duplicitous, and self-serving. Now he was having to rethink his opinion of her.

And of himself.

He'd always believed that he was basically a good person: fair, rational, kind. Except he had been none of those things with her. He had been angry with himself for welcoming Charlie and Raymond into the business, and Mimi into his bed, and he'd turned that anger on her to punish her for his own ineptitude. Bullied her into coming to Argentina and Patagonia, and demanding a truth he had forced her to hide.

The least he could do now was tell her the truth.

'After the trial ended I brought my father and Alicia to Argentina to get some breathing space.' Seeing Mimi's face stiffen, he hesitated. 'It was Antonia who told me about this place. Her great-uncle owned some land up here, and he had a little fishing shack on the island, only he was getting too old to make much use of it. So I made him an offer. A good offer,' he added. 'I might be an insufferable jerk, but I'm not a greedy one, and I wouldn't exploit an old man's ill health.'

Her eyes darted to his face, and he winced inwardly. He had wanted Mimi to know that he hadn't taken advantage of the old man. She already thought he was manipulative and bullying and he hadn't wanted to say anything that reinforced that view of him. But, spoken out loud, his words had sounded less like an explanation and more like another accusation.

He frowned. 'That wasn't a dig at you.'

'I know.' She gave him a small, tight smile. 'You don't pull your punches, Basa. If you wanted to bad-mouth Charlie and Raymond you wouldn't be coy about it.'

She was right. He thought back to how he had spoken to her before. He had been so harsh, so unforgiving, both in his manner and in his choice of words.

'I was angry. I still am angry with them. They had no reason to steal.' A hardness crept into his voice, and his hands were suddenly clenching so tightly that his knuckles felt as though they were about to split apart. 'They had so much more than so many other people—so much more than those pensioners.'

She hesitated, and then she reached out and grasped his fists, gently uncurled his fingers. 'I know.'

Her soft expression pulled at some thread inside him and he glanced away. 'They hurt my father, Mimi. He's never been strong, and he was shocked and devastated by what they did. He had another stroke—a bad one. I had to take over the business, the foundation...'

Charlie and Raymond had stolen more from him than money. He'd lost the freedom and independence that most twenty-somethings enjoyed and, more importantly he'd lost his father.

There was a moment of silence and then she said quietly, 'I'm so sorry, Basa.'

Her eyes were clouded with sadness and he could hear the ache of regret in her voice.

'It's not your fault, truly, but it was a difficult time.' He glanced past her at the ridge of mountains in the distance. 'That's why I bought this place. To have somewhere away from the world. Somewhere tranquil and safe.'

He hesitated. As a general rule he didn't talk about himself, and he had never told anyone that before. He'd told his father and Alicia that he'd bought the land as an investment—he hadn't wanted them to think that he couldn't cope, or that he was scared, though in fact both had been true.

'It must have been hard for you,' she said gently. 'Being thrown in the deep end like that.'

They were walking now, and he stared at her profile in silence, caught off balance by the note of concern in her voice. He knew his family loved him, but nobody ever really asked him about his feelings, and he'd always been glad, even proud about that, for it meant he was doing his job properly. Now, though, with Mimi's blue gaze searching his face, he realised that he wanted to share those buried emotions with her.

'It *was* hard. It was all such a mess. For months I wasn't sure if I could save the business. I even thought we might lose Fairbourne.'

He could still remember the cold grip of panic, the need

to confide in someone and yet the pressure to stay silent. He'd been so scared, and he'd felt so alone—just like after his mother died.

'It helped that it wasn't the first time I'd had to take over. After the accident I was acting CEO for a while—just until my dad got back on his feet.'

He felt her fingers tighten around his.

'I didn't know.'

'It was a long time ago.' The worry in her eyes and the fact that she cared was messing with his head. 'Anyway, everything was fine in the end. I managed to sort it.'

'You didn't just sort it,' she protested. 'You saved it.'

'It was my responsibility.' His mouth twisted. 'It was my fault it happened. I hired Charlie and Raymond. I trusted them.'

'Why wouldn't you?'

'I should have known.'

He felt his shoulders tense, the shame and shock of his stupidity as fresh now as it had been when he'd met his CFO the morning after Alicia's party.

'There were signs, little things, but I was so desperate to prove myself, to show my father he could trust me that I just ignored them.' His eyes rested on her small pale face. 'After it all fell apart I was so focused on turning everything around I didn't realise how much it affected the way I interacted with people, but trust is hard to recover once it's lost.'

'Yes, it is,' she said quietly.

Mimi looked away. It hurt too much to see the pain in his eyes—pain caused by *her* family, by her stupid, selfish stepfather and equally stupid, selfish uncle.

She stared across the water to where small waves splashed against a series of sharp black rocks. Against the placid surface of the lake, it was easy to focus on their jagged threat—just as she had chosen to focus on Basa's outward hostility rather than the trauma that had created it. He'd lost his mother when he was not much younger than she was now, and for a time he had been responsible for looking after his family.

Remembering Alicia's remarks in the car, she felt her heart beat a little faster. He still was.

She could see now that it hadn't ever really been about him. It had been about herself, and the private fear that once again she had jinxed something that might have been perfect.

Basa seemed so strong, so determined, and she'd judged him as he had her: on outward appearances. Hearing him talk about his family's name, she had thought he was a snob; when he'd spoken about having rules, she'd thought he wanted to be in control without understanding why he needed to be. She hadn't understood his deep-seated sense of responsibility for the scandal that had so nearly ruined his father and Alicia.

She knew what it must have taken to turn his business around and restore his family name, and there could be no doubting his love for his family or his sense of responsibility for them and for the pensioners who had been robbed. He had stepped up, and it was incredible what he'd done, given how young he was.

But all injuries left scars: some visible, others less so. And she understood why he found it hard to trust people—her in particular.

All her life she had struggled to trust herself, to trust other people. Her father had started that particular ball rolling. He'd left shortly after her tenth birthday and, devastated by his rejection, her mother had turned for support to her charming but irresponsible brother Raymond, who had introduced her to his best friend Charlie.

Had she ever liked Charlie? Not really—but she'd been desperate to see her mother happy again, so she'd encouraged the relationship.

'We trusted them too. My mum and me. *I* trusted them,' she said slowly.

'You were a child.'

'At first, yes. But later I think I knew they weren't be trusted. Raymond was lovely, but he was always a chancer, and Charlie was so clever at making you believe what he said.'

His face tensed and she braced herself, expecting him to pull away, but instead his fingers locked more tightly around hers. 'But you didn't know.'

Yesterday he would have phrased it as a question, but today it was a statement, and she squirreled that away, scared by how happy it made her feel.

'No,' she agreed. 'But I still felt responsible, and stupid, and scared. Especially during the trial.'

His eyes searched her face. 'It must have been hard.'

Mimi swallowed. Thankfully, it was all a blur. There had been so much happening—so many changes in such a short time. Mostly it had felt like riding a rollercoaster— slow stretches of normality and then a sudden, plunging, terrifying dip.

'It was exhausting. And confusing. And we were so naïve—or maybe I was naïve. My mum was just out of it.'

'What do you mean by naïve?'

'I mean stupid. Dopey.'

She bit her lip, remembering the first time a news story about her had popped up on her phone. It had been like the kind of dream in which you're naked in public—except she had been awake, and there had been nowhere to hide.

'I knew it would be bad for Charlie and Raymond. I just never thought me and my mum would be on trial too. But we were, and we didn't have a barrister to speak for us.'

She looked across the lake to where a bunch of ducks and swans were mobbing a smaller bird.

'I hated those photographers. They were so insistent, so bullying. But it was never knowing how people were going to be that was the worst.' Her smile felt as if it was made of *papier-mâché*. 'Sometimes they'd be nice to my face, then talk about me behind my back, and other times they just crossed the street really pointedly.'

His jaw hardened. 'I'm sorry.'

'It's not your fault.'

'I didn't exactly help, though, did I?' He stared down at her, his dark gaze fixed on her face. 'And now? How is it now? Is it better?'

The genuineness of his concern made her feel a little dizzy. 'Most of the time.'

They were back at the house now, and as she gazed across the deck, she searched for the right words.

'I guess if it hadn't happened I would have argued more with the lawyers about my film. But I didn't want to risk someone working out who I am and going to the newspapers.' She met his gaze. 'Like you said, trust is hard to recover once it's lost.'

'But your life is okay?'

He seemed tense again, and her heart began to pound. Just for a moment she had felt a connection beyond the sexual—a shared understanding of the burden of guilt and responsibility. Now, though, he seemed on edge again, and she didn't understand why.

'Yes, it's fine. I live at home, and that's okay for now. I have a job I hate, but I like my colleagues, and I have Alicia.'

His eyes were steady and unblinking.

'Alicia thinks you deserve more. She thinks you need a man in your life.'

'Alicia's in love.' She managed to laugh. 'Of course she thinks that.'

'But you don't?'

She felt a rush of panic at both the dark intensity of his gaze and the unedited answer hovering dangerously on the tip of her tongue, like a swimmer poised on the high-dive board.

'I don't really think about it,' she lied.

She thought about it a lot. Even before her teenage crush on Basa she'd worried about whether she would ever be able to sustain a loving relationship, or if she would mess it up. The thought made her entire body grow tense.

'Look, I know Alicia wants me to have what she has, but I haven't met anyone I want to be with in that way…' She stumbled over the lie. 'And I don't want my first time to be with some random man…'

She froze, and there was a long, pulsing silence as her words echoed loudly back and forth across the still stretch of water.

'Your first time?' He frowned. 'What do you mean *your first time*?'

Her heart was pounding and she could feel the blood rushing to her face.

'Are you saying you haven't had sex with anyone?'

She pulled her hand away, flustered as much by his sudden intense focus as by her slip of the tongue. 'It doesn't matter.'

'It doesn't matter…?'

He sounded confused, and she felt more panic, followed by a rush of irritation.

'Yes, Basa, it doesn't matter.'

'It matters to me.'

'Why would it? Oh, right.' She stopped abruptly. 'I get it. You didn't believe me yesterday.'

'That's not true. I did believe you.'

'So why the shocked expression?'

His dark gaze narrowed. 'I don't know…maybe because you said all that stuff about sampling new flavours.'

She felt her face grow hot. It was true, she had—but only so as not to lose face.

'Why would you lie about that?' His mouth tightened.

'My sex life was…*is* none of your business. And, frankly, I don't see how my being a virgin then or now has any effect on this.' She couldn't keep the shake out of her voice. 'Unless in some mad way you think being one makes me some kind of innocent?'

'No, of course I'm not saying that.' His eyes narrowed. 'I'm saying that you being a virgin changes the facts, and if you'd just told me that, right at the beginning at that stupid lunch with Alicia and Philip, we wouldn't have had to go through all of this.'

A red veil was slipping in front of her face. Was he blaming *her* for his actions? 'That's not fair…' The injustice of his words felt like a blow to the head. 'You didn't want to listen to anything I had to say.'

'Oh, I promise you, Mimi, if you'd told me that I would have listened.'

'Okay, maybe you would.' Her pulse was dancing with indignation. 'But you wouldn't have believed me, would you?'

He didn't reply, but she felt no satisfaction at having been proved right. Instead, she was feeling slightly sick—and trapped.

'So now you know everything there is to know about me, Basa,' she lied, 'so this conversation is officially over.'

Spinning around, she walked quickly back into the house, wanting to get as far away as possible from the truth that had followed her halfway around the world. Not the fact that she was a virgin, but the fact that he didn't trust her and never would.

Watching her leave, Basa felt his whole body tense. He'd made such a mess of this. And he couldn't blame Mimi. Although, true to form, he had done exactly that.

He breathed out unsteadily, a splinter of guilt stabbing between his ribs. It had never occurred to him that she might still be a virgin and her admission had caught him off balance. He'd felt angry with her for not telling him, so it had been easy to blame her for making him act irrationally.

But really he was angry and disgusted with himself.

For not bothering to check her level of experience and not letting her give her side of the story.

For not completely believing that she had been a virgin that night.

And for blaming her for his own selfish and shoddy behaviour.

Without realising it he was walking through the house, driven by a sense of purpose he hadn't felt since the morning after Alicia's birthday party.

He was going to make this right. And he was going to do it now.

He caught up with her just outside her bedroom door.

'Mimi—'

'I don't want to talk any more, Basa.' She stepped into her room, holding up her hand to halt him.

'I know, but I have to say this—please, Mimi.'

He watched her hand tremble as she lowered it.

'You were right. I didn't completely believe you and

I'm sorry for that—I'm sorry for all of this. I brought you here to prove I was right about you. But I wasn't. I was wrong.' He breathed out unsteadily. 'And you were right about me. I never gave you a chance. I ignored everything Alicia said about you because it was easier—'

Her blue eyes widened. 'What do you mean?'

He hesitated. It was a secret he'd always kept to himself: that the shock of Charlie and Raymond's betrayal had hurt less than believing Mimi hadn't wanted him that night.

'That night at Fairbourne I wanted you so badly it hurt, and I thought you wanted me.'

'I did,' she said shakily.

'I know.' He corrected himself. 'I know that *now*. But that night I thought you'd played me. And then, when everything came out, I was so angry with you, with myself, I let that anger blank out everything else. Only, this is not who I am, Mimi, and I'm ashamed of myself for behaving like this. I'm so sorry if the way I acted that night put you off getting involved with anyone else.'

She was staring at him, her face framed in the light from the window.

'It didn't. Not in the way you mean. I could have had sex with other men, but I didn't want to because...' She hesitated. 'Because none of them made me feel the way you did just by looking at me.' Her mouth trembled. 'The way you still make me feel.'

His heart seemed to have doubled in size. 'Do you mean that?'

His pulse jumped as she nodded slowly.

He lifted his hand and gently caressed her cheek. 'I haven't been able to get you out of my head,' he said softly.

Her eyes widened. 'Really?'

Staring down into her face, he nodded. 'Really. I wish

I'd said something sooner, but mostly I wish I'd done this…'

Capturing her head, he lowered his mouth and kissed her lightly, moving his lips across hers, his body hardening as he heard her breath catch in her throat.

Mimi felt her stomach clench with need. Her head was spinning. His lips were soft but firm, and he smelled of clean air and beech leaves. He was all she'd ever wanted— but she'd been here before and it was hard to forget how it had ended.

She felt her body stiffen at the memory of those long minutes of waiting for him to return.

'It's okay.'

Sensing her hesitation, he broke the kiss, his dark gaze searching her face.

'It's just a kiss,' he said soothingly.

'I don't want it to be just a kiss. But I don't want it to go wrong again.'

'Easy…' He pulled her closer, cupping her face. 'It won't go wrong. But there's no rush. Do you need time to think?'

'I've had time.' Shakily, she reached out and rested her hand on his chest, feeling the swift, unsteady beat of his heart. 'A long time. And I want to make love with you. Here. Now.'

His breathing jerked and she felt his heart accelerate beneath her palm.

'I want that too,' he said hoarsely.

His gaze slid slowly down her body and then he began to kiss her again, nudging her gently back towards the bed, his fingers slipping under her top, sliding over her skin, slow and soft and sure.

'Okay?'

He lifted his face to hers and she nodded. Then, with fingers trembling, she pressed her hand against the hard push of his erection. He sucked in a breath and her stomach clenched at his obvious hunger for her, at the size of him. How could she give this man what he needed?

He caught her hand with his, his breathing unsteady as his eyes met hers. 'Don't be scared. I won't let it hurt. I don't ever want to hurt you.'

'I'm not scared…just a bit nervous.'

'So let me help you relax,' he said softly.

He stripped off his clothes, and then hers, gently peeling off her bra and panties, kissing her the whole time, his hands caressing her hip, her waist, the underside of her breast, until she was shaking with need, wanting him to touch the fluttering pulse between her thighs.

When they were both naked she felt her stomach tighten with nerves. He was so solid and aroused, and his dark gaze was so intense she could feel it deep inside her.

'Why are you looking at me like that?'

'You're beautiful.'

Saliva pooling in her mouth, she stared at his lean, beautifully muscled body, her eyes lingering on the smooth length of his erection.

'So are you,' she said softly.

He smiled, and she smiled back at him, and then she felt her whole body start to throb as he pulled her gently towards the bed.

His skin was just as she remembered it—smooth and warm and firm. Greedily, she caressed the contours of his back, her breathing losing its rhythm as his hands dropped to her waist. He pressed her against the thick ridge of his erection and she felt her heartbeat accelerate in time with the oscillating ball of heat low in her pelvis.

He began moving against her slowly, his hot mouth

seeking the bare skin of her neck, kissing and licking the raised line of her clavicle until she was drowning in the dark, teasing currents surging through her body.

She gasped as his hands caressed her eager, straining body, her head swimming as they slid over her ribcage to capture her breasts. His fingertips skimmed over her taut nipples, and then her stomach clenched sharply as those same fingers slipped down to the triangle of blonde hair and the slick heat between her thighs. His breathing jerked and she parted her legs, letting him take the weight of her in his hand, moving against the insistent press of his palm.

'I want you,' she whispered, her hand closing around him.

He groaned against her throat. 'Wait a minute,' he muttered.

She watched dazedly as he reached for his trousers and pulled out his wallet.

'Are you sure you want this?' He was holding a condom packet, but loosely, and she knew he was waiting for her consent. 'Are you sure you want me?' he said hoarsely.

She nodded. 'I've never been surer.'

And suddenly he was there, his big body warm and solid against hers. She locked her hands around his neck as he shifted against her, lowering his hips to hers, his erection hard and hot. And then her pulse accelerated as he pushed forward.

She took a breath, trying to relax, but her face must have given her away because he stopped moving.

'Don't stop,' she whispered.

'I'm just letting you get used to me.'

She felt his hand slide to her hip, shifting beneath her to raise her up, and suddenly it was easier, smoother. Now her body was welcoming him, and she was rising up to meet his thrusts.

Letting her arms curl around his shoulders, she pressed up against him, breath quickening, muscles clenching as a pulsing heat gathered inside her and exploded like a supernova, and then she felt him clamp her closer, his body erupting into hers with a groan.

CHAPTER EIGHT

BREATHING OUT UNSTEADILY, Mimi buried her hands in Basa's dark hair, her heart racing in time with his, lost in the aftershocks still quivering through her body, in the scent of his skin, and in disbelief at her own uninhibited passion.

No one had ever held her like this...so close.

If only they could stay like this for ever.

She felt him shift against her and her heart gave a little jump as he raised himself up onto his elbows and stared down into her flushed face.

'Was it okay?' He stroked her tangled blonde hair away from her forehead.

She nodded, then smiled. 'It was a lot better than okay.'

Something flared in his dark eyes. He lowered his mouth and she arched upwards as his lips brushed her neck, her collarbone, the curve of her breast.

Raising his head, he gently eased himself out of her. 'I'll be right back.'

Pulling the rumpled sheet up over her legs, she watched him walk into the bathroom, her breath catching in her throat. Earlier, she'd been too caught up with nerves and expectation and desire to take in his beauty, but he really was absolutely gorgeous, she thought, her eyes running down his spine to the muscular swell of his buttocks.

Rolling onto her side, she buried her face in the pillow, inhaling the faint trace of his aftershave. She felt stunned, happy, her body soft and loosened. She was suffused with a tranquillity very different from the sharp, sweet spasm of pleasure that had so recently swamped her, and she lay for a moment, trying to remember how she had felt before.

Did she feel different?

Her mind was still hazy from climaxing and it took a moment for her to bring order to her thoughts.

Yes and no.

Physically, she ached a little, but there had been no actual pain, just a sense of being stretched—and, frankly, her head had been spinning, her body rippling with other more urgent and pleasurable sensations for her to register the actual moment.

And yet she did feel different—though not because of some shift in status to 'full womanhood'. Maybe she would have had that kind of transformative moment if she'd still been an adolescent, but for her this was not just about having sex for the first time...it was about what it felt like to surrender, truly surrender, to desire. It was about discovering a different side to herself—a passionate and fearless self so unlike the woman who had been living her life in the shadows for the last two years.

It had felt so right, beginning her sexual awakening with Basa. But not out of any lingering, sentimental attachment to her teenage fantasies—that fairy-tale prince of her dreams had never existed except in her imagination.

The man who was here with her now was not perfect at all. He was stubborn, and ruthless, but he was also loyal and caring and he had a deep-rooted sense of responsibility for his family, friends, and employees. Most importantly of all, he was real, and together the two of them had faced their shared past, here in this beautiful wilderness.

She glanced out of the window. The sun was shining, birds were singing—everything was carrying on without any thought of what had just happened in this room.

What would happen next?

Her breath swelled in her throat. It was stupid, really. She'd spent so many years dreaming about Basa and it was only now she realised that her fantasy had stopped at the moment of climax.

Her eyes darted towards the discarded clothes on the floor. Was he going to come out of the bathroom and just start getting dressed? She sat up. Should *she* be getting dressed?

Before she had a chance to move he walked back into the room and slid in beside her, gathering her against him.

Her heart rebounded inside her chest and she breathed in against a rush of emotions. But it was okay to feel a little emotional, she told herself. It was her first time, and the sex had been so good; Basa had made it good for her.

For a moment she lay listening to his breathing, savouring the heat and solidity of his body next to hers, and then she turned and looked up at him. 'How about you? Was it okay for you?'

He stared at her for a moment. 'It was a whole lot better than okay.' His face softened, and he laughed. 'Do you know, nobody has ever asked me that before?'

She laughed too. 'There's a first time for everything.'

'Yes, there is.' He touched her cheek gently, his face growing more serious. 'Did you mean what you said about why you waited?'

When she nodded slowly, he dipped his head and kissed her, his hand hugging the curve of her hip.

'I really am sorry, Mimi, for how that evening ended between us, and for leaving you up in my room like that.'

'It doesn't matter any more.'

'But it did then,' he persisted. 'And I think it's stayed with you.'

She was about to tell him it hadn't, only she didn't want to lie to him any more. 'A bit,' she confessed.

She hesitated, the impulse to make light of her feelings fighting with her need to be truthful.

'But I can't blame how I felt entirely on what happened at Fairbourne.'

A minute ticked by and then he frowned. 'What do you mean?'

She felt suddenly aware of his gaze, and of the pulse beating in her throat.

'There were things before that. Like my parents. They had an incredibly passionate relationship and I wasn't planned.'

Body tensing, she took a shallow breath. It was the first time she'd told anyone that—not even Alicia knew—and it made her feel horribly exposed.

'I wasn't either. Apparently my father was astonished when my mother told him.'

He spoke matter-of-factly and, looking up, she felt some of the tightness ease from her shoulders.

'My dad was astonished too—but not in a good way.' She dropped her gaze. 'Me being around changed things— for my dad anyway. He left, and my mum never really got over it. That's why I was so happy when she and Charlie got together.'

His face stiffened, but it was too late to take it back.

She swallowed. 'Actually, I wasn't just happy... I encouraged her.'

She held her breath, expecting to see contempt or confusion in his eyes.

But after a moment he said quietly, 'For the right reasons.'

'I suppose...'

His words had made warmth snake across her skin, and for a few quivering seconds she wanted to tell him more. But surely it was better to quit while she was ahead, so instead she shrugged.

'Anyway, I got on with my life, and you had a good reason for not coming back to me that night.'

He hadn't told her much, but it was easy to embellish the bare bones he'd given her—the nightmarish hours following that call to his lawyer, his escalating shock and disbelief at each emerging revelation.

'I don't know how you dealt with all of it,' she said quietly. 'You were so young.' Just twenty-seven. 'But you took care of everything…you righted the wrongs.'

'Not all of them,' he said softly.

His fingers twitched against her skin. Leaning forward, he caught a handful of her hair and wrapped it around his fingers, using it to draw her closer to him. She felt her insides grow liquid and hot as he stared down into her face, his breath warm against her skin.

'But I'm planning on making up for lost time.'

'You are?' Her voice sounded far away, muffled by the uneven thud of her heartbeat.

'If you want me to.'

She could feel her body rippling back to life as his dark gaze roamed her face. He was answering her unasked question, offering her a next step. What should she say?

He was talking about sex, and though she wanted to make up for lost time as much as he did, she couldn't help but be a little nervous. She didn't need to ask, didn't *want* to ask about his previous partners, but it was clear that Basa was sexually experienced—certainly experienced enough to be able to separate his emotions from his libido.

But how did she know she could do the same?

She'd only had sex once, and maybe if it *had* been just

'okay' then it would have been easy to walk away—to treat this as a one-off, her first and last time with Basa. Maybe if it *had* been just 'okay' she would honestly have said that sex was just a physical activity, involving bodies.

But sex with Basa had been astonishing, frantic, miraculous. And, although her one experience hardly qualified her as an expert, she knew already that for her it had been more than just bodies moving in time with one another. There had been tenderness, and with tenderness came vulnerability, and she was already vulnerable enough where Basa was concerned. She wasn't sure if she would be able to stop herself from making the physical attraction between them more than it really was, and yet...

His skin felt so deliciously warm and smooth, and she couldn't resist running a hand over his stomach, her fingers tracing the contoured lines of his muscles, her head dizzy with the freedom of being able to reach out and touch him, of not having to hold herself in check.

He sucked in a breath, his hand catching hers.

'What's the matter?' She looked up at him.

'Nothing.' He shook his head. 'I'm trying to play it cool here, but my body's acting like it belongs to some horny teenager.'

The air between them seemed to thicken, and her pulse quickened at his confession, at his open acknowledgement of her power to arouse him.

'I thought you wanted to make up for lost time?' she said softly.

Her hand slid lower down over his belly, trembling slightly, and she wrapped her fingers around his hard, straining length, her breathing losing its rhythm as his pupils flared.

'Oh, I do,' he said hoarsely as he reached out and cupped

her breast, his thumb brushing lightly, maddeningly, across her rigid nipple.

Somewhere low down and deep inside she could feel herself melting, and she squirmed against his hand, moaning softly. She felt his breathing change as he pulled her close and rolled onto his back, taking her with him, anchoring her aching, hollowed-out body to his with not quite steady hands.

Shivering, she arched, pressing down against him as his fingers caressed her breasts, their teasing touch sending ripples through her body so that she could think of nothing but him, nothing but her need to feel his heat and power again, to feel him inside her.

She shifted against him, parting her legs further, chasing the fluttering beat of heat that was just out of reach. Groaning, he leaned sideways, fumbling on the floor for his discarded wallet, his other hand gripping her against him.

'Here.'

He handed her the condom packet and she tore it open.

'Pinch the end.'

His jaw was clenched, the muscles bunching in his arms as she rolled it onto his hard length. She felt a wet heat flood between her thighs at the barely checked hunger in his eyes, and then she lowered herself onto the blunt head of his erection.

His fingers grazed her stomach, strangling the breath in her throat.

'Don't be scared,' he whispered, sliding his hands under her bottom and lifting her up. 'Just take it slow. I won't move until you're—'

He breathed in sharply as she reached down and took him in her hand, guiding him slowly. A moan climbed up her throat as she pushed down, her body stretching, filling with what she wanted. His fingers reached for her breasts and then, raising himself up, he took first one and then the other nipple into his mouth, tonguing and licking them in turn, his breathing ragged as she started to rock against him.

Her body was contracting, tightening and pulsing around him, and then he started to move beneath her. She was moving in time with him, torn between the soft press of his mouth and the hard push of his body.

He made a rough sound and fell back against the pillow, his dark eyes resting on her face. His hands moved over her thighs, and then between them, his fingers oscillating in time to her heartbeat until she was shaking with need and pleasure.

'Look at me, Mimi,' he whispered.

She stared down into his face, her breath jerking from her throat as he eased himself in and out of her body with ever-increasing urgency. His hands gripped her waist and she cried out, her body splintering apart, gripping him tightly as he groaned and thrust up inside her.

Her heartbeat was filling her head and she shuddered against him as he breathed out unevenly, his chest rising and falling. Heart pounding, she stared down at him, trying to imprint the moment into her memory, wanting to remember the shape of his mouth, the pull of his gaze, the feel of his body inside hers.

'Come here.' Pulling her forward, he kissed her, and then, cupping her face, pressed his forehead against hers. 'You're smiling,' he said softly.

Mimi tilted her head back. 'I'm happy.'

Happier than she could ever remember being. Except she couldn't help but feel a flicker of apprehension—because in her world happiness came with an inbuilt risk that at some unspecified point in the future all of it could be taken away.

His eyes were dark and unwavering. 'What a coincidence. So am I.'

Pulling her closer, he smiled, and instantly she forgot her fears and was lost in his smile, lost in him, so that nothing mattered except the press of his lips against hers...

Basa shifted forward in his chair. As he scrolled down his laptop screen he tried to concentrate on what his PA had written. Rebecca was an excellent PA, and normally he enjoyed her concise and meticulous reports, but today he was struggling to focus on anything other than the woman standing on the deck outside his window.

Mimi was staring across the lake. She was holding up some kind of video camera, so he couldn't see her face. She was wearing nothing that could be described as even vaguely attention-seeking, and yet his gaze kept returning to her approximately every ten seconds.

Sighing, he closed his laptop and leaned back, frowning at his uncharacteristic lack of focus. On an average day he would have worked through a report like this one in a couple of hours, and his recommendations would already be winging their way back to Rebecca.

Only this wasn't an average day. It was the day he and Mimi had become lovers and he was still coming to terms with that new and incredible reality.

His pulse jumped. He was Mimi's first lover, and he was a little confused—ashamed, even—by how much that mattered to him. He'd always thought of himself as modern and urbane, but against his will—against that image of himself—he could feel himself liking the fact that he was her first.

He breathed out slowly. It felt weird not to recognise his feelings—but why should his feelings be immune to change? Over the last forty-eight hours he and Mimi had more or less rewritten their shared history, and it appeared that he'd spent the last two years spectacularly misjudging her in about as many ways as it was possible to misjudge a person.

Remembering her remark about the view from his high horse, he felt his mouth twist. That horse had bucked him off—big-time.

A movement out on the deck tugged at his gaze and he glanced over. His eyes narrowed and his body hardened with crashing predictability at the sight of Mimi leaning over the table. She was obviously just playing around with angles, as she had been doing most of the morning, but thanks to the feverish desire gripping his body it took less than thirty seconds for his brain to summon up a vision of her leaning in much the same way over his bed…wearing nothing but those heels she'd had on in the restaurant…

Breathing in sharply, he stood up. He needed to move— get some fresh air, get some perspective. Or at least stop what Alicia would call objectifying women.

Alicia.

He gritted his teeth. He had completely forgotten about his sister in all this, but now he felt his chest tighten. He was fairly sure he knew how Alicia would react. With her wedding so close, she was predictably loved-up right now, and he could imagine that nothing would give her greater happiness than for her brother and best friend to fall in love.

Except they weren't in love.

In lust, definitely—but love? That feeling of being in-tertwined with someone else's essence? That was something he had never felt.

Of course in a perfect world he would choose what Alicia had with Philip, what his parents had shared for twenty-two years. But it was the aftermath of his mother's tragic death, not his parents' happy life together, that he remembered the most.

In the weeks and months following the accident all their lives had been knocked off course. Alicia had been just fourteen, and she had been devastated, but his father had never recovered from losing the woman he loved, and for a time it had felt as if they were orphans.

He'd hated seeing his sister so upset and his father so broken. All he'd wanted to do was take away their pain, to protect them from a cruel and unjust world, and now he wanted to do the same for Mimi.

He could protect her here. Here, they were safe—*she* was safe—from the predatory press and a public hungry for gossip.

But they couldn't stay on this island for ever.

He glanced down at his laptop. Back in the real world he had responsibilities—a business to run, a family who needed him. What was happening here with Mimi wasn't real, and it wouldn't—couldn't—survive any kind of brush with reality.

And yet this thing with Mimi felt more real than any relationship he'd ever had, and although it might sound crazy he felt closer to her than to all the other women he'd dated.

But was it that surprising?

One way or another Mimi had been in his life for the best part of a decade.

And now she was in his bed.

Only, what did that mean?

For him? For her? For both of them?

It was a question he'd been asking himself in a variety of ways since leaving her bedroom, and he was still no closer to answering it. But maybe he didn't actually need to know what any of it meant when they would both be back in England tomorrow.

Ignoring the tension in his back at that thought, he made his way outside.

On the deck, Mimi was now talking to Claudia. There was nothing remarkable about that, except the fact she was speaking in Spanish. Agreed, she was not particularly fluent, but he found it oddly endearing that she was bothering. In fact, he was surprised that her making such an effort mattered so much to him.

He stopped beside her. *'Muy impresionante!'*

Turning she blushed. *'Gracias...* I think.'

He felt his own skin prickle as she met his gaze. 'I didn't know you spoke Spanish.'

'That would be because I don't.' She turned to the housekeeper, smiling. 'As Claudia can confirm.'

Claudia shook her head. 'I was the same as you when I started speaking English. What is important is to try.'

From the direction of the kitchen a buzzer went off, and she excused herself and went back into the house.

For a moment neither of them spoke, and the silence was broken only by the gentle rhythmic splash of water against the side of the deck.

After the fierce intensity of their naked coupling it felt strange seeing her clothed, out here in the daylight, and he could tell from her stillness that his feelings mirrored hers.

His mind rewound an hour, his blood beating hot and fast as he remembered how she had felt and tasted, her lack of inhibition, her curiosity and hunger. Before today he would have said that sex was just sex, for typically the hunger that possessed him passed as quickly as early-morning mist when it was satisfied, but with Mimi the opposite seemed to be true, and instead of fading his body was still hard and aching.

He looked down at her. She looked so young, so wary, and he felt the ache of guilt at the part he had personally played in robbing her of her confidence. It might not have been intentional but, whatever she had said earlier, he could tell from the tension in her shoulders that she was waiting for things to fall apart.

He felt a sudden need to reassure her, to rebuild her trust in people. In him. There had been too much confusion between them, too many lies in her life already, so he needed to be honest.

He hesitated before taking hold of her hand and pulling her closer. 'Are you still happy?'

Her blue eyes were searching his face.

'Yes, but…' She paused. 'I don't know how this part works.'

'I don't know either,' he said softly. Watching her frown, he shrugged. 'I like women, and I like sex, but the aftermath is not my thing. Usually I have a reason to leave—or I create one.' Lifting her hand to his mouth, he kissed the palm. 'But I'm not ready to leave just yet, and I thought you might not be either, only—'

His pulse twitched. Since when had he decided on extending his stay? Or asking Mimi to join him?

She blinked. 'Only what?'

'Only I didn't give you much choice about coming out to Argentina, and no choice whatsoever about coming all the way out here. I was out of order, and I'm sorry for how I acted.'

She bit her lip. 'It *was* out of order, but I can understand now why you did it. You had your reasons, and you were right.' She held his gaze. 'We did need to talk.'

'And now we have…so theoretically there's no reason for us to stay any more.' He stared down into her eyes. 'I guess what I'm asking is do you want to go back to England? Or do you think you might have a reason to stay for a couple more days?'

He could almost follow her thoughts, fear battling with longing.

'I don't know if that's a good idea.' She hesitated. 'But I really want to make this wedding film sing, and if I had more time here I think that would help me get a feel for what will work best. But I suppose I just need to know what's happening…' A flush of pink suffused her cheeks. 'With us, I mean—'

His heart kicked against his ribs. At least one of them was being honest. He stared at her in silence, fighting against the protective feeling produced by her words, concentrating on the facts. It had taken guts to ask that question—more guts than he had, apparently—so the least he could do was be brave enough to answer it.

Pulling her closer, he smoothed her hair back from her face. 'It's simple, really. I want you and you want me. We both know it's not permanent, but that doesn't mean it's not real, Mimi.' He took a slow breath, recalling his earlier thoughts. 'And it *is* real for me—as real as you are, here in my arms.'

She nodded. 'For me, too.'

His heart beat faster—not just with desire but relief. 'So will you stay?'

She hesitated, then nodded again.

Lowering his mouth to hers, he kissed her quickly, closing his eyes to block out the uncertainty in hers. He didn't do love and he couldn't love Mimi. She was too young, too much of a responsibility, and he already had enough responsibilities to last a lifetime. He could never truly right the wrongs of the past—his or anyone else's—but she deserved to be happy, and for the next few days he was going to do everything in his power to make that happen.

'Where are we going?'

Frowning, Mimi glanced over to where Basa sat beside her, his dark hair blowing in the wind. One of his staff, Lionel, was driving them up a bumpy and quite steep grassy hillside, and she was having to grip both the underside of her seat and Basa's hand, just to stop herself from sliding sideways.

Turning, he squeezed her hand. 'It's not far now.'

'That doesn't answer my question,' she complained.

He smiled, and as she watched his lips curve upwards her heart felt too big for her ribs and her question seemed suddenly irrelevant.

'I don't want to risk spoiling the surprise,' he said.

'It would have been a lot easier choosing what to wear if you'd given me a clue,' she grumbled. 'Now I don't know if I'm underdressed or overdressed.'

His dark eyes rested on her face, then dropped over the curve of her breasts beneath her wrap top. 'As far as I'm concerned if you're not naked then you're overdressed.'

Mimi felt her skin grow warm. She still found his hunger for her incredibly exciting, and just thinking about his hands and mouth exploring her naked body made her mouth turn dry. The last two days had passed with incredible speed, and this was their final morning in Patagonia. Basa had woken her before the sun had even risen and her body had instantly softened in response.

But he'd rolled them both out of bed and dragged her into the shower.

She'd felt disappointed…a little crushed, actually…until he'd pulled her closer, and kissed her fiercely. Then he'd dropped to his knees and she'd felt his hands grip her hips before he'd started kissing the tops of her legs.

Her breath fluttered in her throat as she remembered the feel of his flickering tongue as it had eased between her thighs, nudging against the tight ball of heat there, his warm saliva mixing with the warm water.

She'd had no idea that she would feel as if her actual

bones were melting, and afterwards, when he'd gently turned her away from him and thrust into her, his arm around her waist, anchoring her to his body, she had felt both his power and his tenderness.

Now, pressing her knees together, she glanced over at Basa's profile. She couldn't imagine any other man being so expert, so fierce, so generous—couldn't imagine being with another man. But that would change, she told herself. It would have to change. And at least this way there was no time for her to mess it up.

As they reached the top of the hill the ground flattened and she saw there was another car already parked. Two men were leaning against the car, and spread out over the springy grass was a huge pale blue and white hot air balloon.

She swallowed a breath.

'We haven't left the island since you got here, and I can't let you go back to England without seeing something of my second homeland,' Basa said quietly. 'This way you'll get to see so much more.'

The thought of going back to England made her chest feel too tight, and suddenly her eyes were burning with tears.

But she smiled past the ache in her throat. 'I've always wanted to do this…'

His eyes held hers. 'So let's go sail along the silver sky. Here—' he handed her a quilted jacket '—you'll need this.'

It took thirty minutes to inflate the balloon. Their pilot, Butch, spoke very good English, but with a strong Spanish accent.

Mimi frowned as Basa helped her into the basket. 'Butch isn't a very Argentinian name.'

Butch laughed. 'My real name is Gonzalo, but everyone calls me Butch because I am from Cholila.'

'Cholila is outlaw country,' Basa explained. 'Butch Cassidy and the Sundance Kid hid out there for a while when they were on the run.' His eyes hovered over the pulse-point in her throat. 'Since Butch is in charge, for this ride at least, maybe that makes you and me outlaws too.'

His smile transfixed her, slowed her pulse and stilled all thought, so that it was perhaps a full five minutes before she realised that the balloon was slowly rising up.

Her head began to spin. Basa had been right. The sky was silver up here—and blue and pink and gold. The air was crisp, but the rising sun was warm, and then Basa wrapped his arms around her waist and the heat of his body quickly enveloped her.

'There's the island,' he said, leaning in, his cheek brushing against her.

'Look at the lake—it's so blue.'

From so high, the translucent water was jewel-bright, studded with the dark shapes of ducks and swans. Heart thumping, she gazed down. Beneath them she could see grazing cattle, and Basa pointed out an eagle soaring in the air currents. It was so vast, so open, with huge, grassy plains spreading in every direction, right up to the foothills of the mountains, and all of it was gilded in sunlight.

She turned to look at him, a painful heat filling her chest. 'Alicia said you call this place the first step to heaven.'

'I do.' His eyes, dark like the rocks in the lake, met hers. 'And now I have my very own angel.'

Was it the poetry of his words making her feel so dizzy? Or the fact that he wanted to share this beautiful place with her even for a moment? She didn't know, but it was a bittersweet feeling to remember that tomorrow this would all be just a memory.

Her heart felt as though it was being squeezed. She

thought she had known loss and sadness, but this was a new kind of feeling—an emptiness that made her feel as if she was hollow inside. Her hand gripped the side of the basket. Her pulse was pounding, and she was torn between wanting to capture this moment for ever—his face, his voice, the way he filled not just the basket but this endless sky—and forgetting they had ever met.

The rest of the flight seemed to pass in seconds, and then Butch brought them down with little more than a bump. Within minutes the two SUVs were powering through the grass towards them.

Back at the house, she spent the rest of the day trying to ignore the ache that had started inside her up in the silvery sky. She packed, and talked and smiled with Claudia, and watched Lionel build a vast willow frame above a circle of fire for an *asado* later.

And then she and Basa walked around the island until the ache became unbearable and she was suddenly frantic for the feel of his body on hers, and in hers, and she towed him back to the bedroom where they made love for the rest of the afternoon.

Later, they sat by the fire, drinking ice-cold champagne while Lionel and Claudia cooked the meat.

'What you were talking about earlier,' he said abruptly. 'About you not being planned by your parents. I don't understand what my not coming back to the room that night has to do with the way that made you feel.'

For a moment her mind was utterly blank, but then, as she tried to think of a way to answer his question, she felt something stir inside her. When they made love they held nothing back, so why was she still hiding herself from him?

'Sometimes it feels like it's my fault,' she said carefully. 'That if I hadn't been born my parents would still be together.'

'Maybe they weren't meant to be together.'

She wanted to believe him, and she was sure he believed what he was saying, but he only knew some of the facts.

'I mess things up.' Her mouth began to tremble and she twisted it into a mangled smile. 'Not just my parents' marriage. I messed up with you. And the film I made has never been seen by anyone except lawyers.'

'You didn't mess up with me. It was just as much my fault as yours. And whatever those lawyers are arguing, I bet I could find ten different lawyers to say the opposite.'

Suddenly there were tears in her eyes. 'It wouldn't make any difference,' she said wearily. *'I'm* the problem. I ruin everything.'

'Not everything,' he said gently.

She felt her heart contract. He was being so sweet, and she was ruining their last night together. With an effort she smiled up at him. 'No, not everything.'

It was getting dark by the time the food was ready, and they ate greedily, licking the meat juices from their fingers. There was also trout from the lake, whole squashes and potatoes cooked in the ashes, and for dessert slow-roasted peaches that seemed to melt in her mouth.

'Like it?'

Mimi looked up. Basa was watching her, his face half in darkness, his eyes like stars.

She nodded. 'It's amazing. It's all amazing.'

He was amazing.

She had thought he was cold-hearted and judgmental, but she knew now that he was neither. He was kind and loyal and strong, and the idea of being apart from him for even a day was unbearable.

All of a sudden she felt dizzy—the same dizziness she

had felt in the balloon, when she'd been trying to commit Basa to memory.

Only, there had been no need. Her heart had got there first. She didn't have to try and remember him. She already knew everything about him by heart—the good and the bad—and that was why she loved him.

For a moment she sat gazing across the dark stretch of water, stunned by the truth. In a few short days he had become not just familiar, but necessary to her life. It was new and thrilling to feel like this, and yet so old, for she had never really stopped loving him. Why else had she agreed to come out to Argentina in the first place?

She wanted to tell him. To share her feelings. After all they had shared everything else: their bodies, their fears, their anger and pain. And now their love?

Except it wasn't *their* love, it was only *hers*, in spite of the intensity of their lovemaking and the romantic appearance of these last few days.

She knew all about Basa's deep-seated sense of responsibility for those around him, his need to right the wrongs. And that was all she was to him—a wrong to be righted.

The ache in her chest was spreading and, needing to make it stop, she leaned forward and took his face in her hands, kissing him fiercely.

'I need you,' she whispered.

And he pulled her to her feet and led her back into the house, where they stripped one another naked and she welcomed the wordless oblivion of her body's response to his.

CHAPTER NINE

GAZING DOWN INTO the lake, Basa stood shivering for a moment in the crisp morning air and then, tipping forward, he executed a perfect forward dive.

His heart jolted, and he felt the chill of the water like a punch. Striking out, he began to swim towards the distant shore. Normally he loved swimming in the lake—loved the sense of freedom and peace, the chance to connect with nature in its raw state—but today he just needed to move, to lose himself in the rhythm of his body and briefly suspend the conflicted thoughts that had dogged him since waking.

Last night had been incredible— He frowned. No, that was wrong. There were no words, or none in *his* vocabulary, to describe what it had been like, but he did know that it would never be as good with any other woman.

They had made love repeatedly, feverishly at first, with his body responding to the white heat of her desire and the urgency of her mouth, and then more slowly, each of them holding back, letting their hunger build in time with their accelerating heartbeats, neither one wanting that time to be the last, so that even before their shuddering bodies had stilled they were reaching for one another again.

He had fallen asleep with Mimi's body caught against his and woken early with a cramp in his arm. Shifting free, he had found it impossible to doze off again, with his body tuning in to the tension in his head, so he had quietly rolled off the bed, found his swim-shorts, and made his way onto the deck.

Slowing his stroke, he lifted his head from the water. He was more than halfway across the lake and his muscles were warm now, and aching. Using the glow from last night's *asado* as a beacon, he headed back towards the deck, his arms working in time with the arguments and counter-arguments firing back and forth.

Logically, he knew that he and Mimi had no future, and that the only reason it felt as if they did was the fact that they had been cooped up together with a barrel-load of heightened and complicated emotions and a shared history for company.

A shared history that was still mired in scandal…a scandal that definitely hadn't yet reached its sell-by date. And he couldn't risk exposing his family, or Mimi, to any more unwanted media attention.

His fingers grazed the wooden underside of the deck and, reaching up, he pulled himself out of the water, smoothing his wet hair back, feeling his skin burning in the cool air.

This time tomorrow his life would be back on track, he told himself. Okay it was going to feel a little odd, her not being there, but with the benefit of time and distance it would soon seem like nothing more than a fantasy frozen in time.

Only, having steeled himself to face a future without her, now he was floored by the reality of what that would mean.

He couldn't picture a bed without Mimi in it—and it wasn't just sex. He loved to lie and watch her brush her hair. Loved to hold her in his arms while they read to one another out loud from their books.

How could he walk away when every thought, every action came back to her?

Breathing out unevenly, he made his way back into the quiet of the house and to her room. She was still sleeping, and for a moment he stared down at her, his body loosening with desire, his heart pounding out of time, as he watched the steady rise and fall of her shoulders.

Then, as though sensing his presence, her eyes opened and she looked up at him drowsily. 'Basa...'

'I'm here.'

She shivered when he reached out and touched her bare collarbone, her eyes more grey than blue in the hazy morning light that was inching into the room. 'You're cold.'

'Sorry. I couldn't sleep, so I went for a swim in the lake. I'll go take a shower...warm up.'

'I've got a better idea.'

Her fingers slid up his thigh and his muscles bunched as she pressed her hand flat against the erection that was pushing against the damp fabric of his shorts.

'Come back to bed,' she whispered. 'Body-to-body heat is the best way to get warm.'

It wasn't heat he wanted—it was her. And not just to warm up his body. But what he wanted was complicated, fraught with risk.

He watched her slide his shorts down over his hips, and as he slipped beneath the sheets he let his hunger blot out everything else.

'Forgive me.' Switching off his phone, Basa ran his hand over his face, grimacing apologetically at Mimi. 'That was my head of HR in New York. She's been sitting on something for a few days now and I really needed to sign it off.'

They were on the plane now—somewhere over the

North Atlantic. Both of them had slept on the overnight part of the flight, but since breakfast he had been trying to resolve this issue with his North American office.

Mimi looked up from her book and smiled. 'It's fine. It gave me an opportunity to get stuck into this.' Her blue eyes rested on his face and then dropped to the book in her lap. 'I'm nearly finished, so I should be able to give it back to you before we land. Or I can just give it to Alicia,' she added.

Her remark was innocuous enough, the kind of polite comment anyone might make about a book they had borrowed, but he felt his body still, saw her still too, and knew that she had picked up on the unspoken implication of her words: when they stepped off the plane in London they would be going their separate ways.

'Keep it.' He managed to smile, his body tensing in ever-tightening anticipation of a moment he was dreading. 'Please, I'd like you to keep it.'

'Okay, well…thank you.' Looking up at him, she bit down on the corner of her lip. 'Was it a big problem? Your call?'

He shook his head. 'No, not really. It's a bit of a headache, but it's nothing major, and certainly nothing that can't be sorted. It's just that I have to be the one to sort it, and I don't normally drop off the grid so comprehensively.'

She frowned. 'But doesn't that happen every time you go to Patagonia?'

He held her gaze. 'No, actually, it doesn't. Usually, I crack and end up calling in.'

Her eyes narrowed. 'You told me there was no Wi-Fi.'

'There isn't,' he said quickly. 'But I do have a satellite phone.'

'That you forgot to mention?'

'No, I didn't forget. It was deliberate.' He sighed. 'In

the beginning I didn't want you radioing home for back-up, and then later...'

He hesitated. Making love to Mimi and then sorting out this mess in New York had temporarily stifled the debate in his head over what he *should* do and what he *wanted* to do. He had done this journey so many times, and he knew that they were probably less than an hour away from land-ing. Now that they were so close to England he could no longer avoid the bruising reality of the facts.

If he didn't do or say something in the next sixty min-utes then he was going to end up sleepwalking into a sit-uation he didn't want—namely, Mimi's abrupt departure from his life.

But not from his head.

He felt his chest tighten, the impossibility of it all mak-ing his whole body tense with a panic he had never felt before.

When his mother had been killed he'd been too numb with shock to feel anything, and later the need to care for his sister and father had overwhelmed his own desperate loneliness and loss. And that night at Fairbourne when he'd called his lawyer had been the same. There had been no time to think about his own feelings; that had come later, after the dust had settled. And however terrible it had been—and it *had* been terrible—both times had been played out in public, shared with family and friends and police officers and lawyers.

This feeling was his alone, and he had to deal with it on his own.

His heart began to pound. It was an unsolvable di-lemma. He and Mimi might work on an island on a lake in Patagonia, but they weren't outlaws. They couldn't run away and hide out at the edge of the world for ever.

Back in London—make that anywhere people had

smartphones—his relationship with Mimi would be news, and once it was out there he wouldn't be able to control it.

He knew exactly how bad it might get. His body tensed as his mind recalled how bad it had been before. For a full year he hadn't been able to open a newspaper or search for his family's name on the internet without wanting to dig a hole and bury himself.

He couldn't unleash that kind of abuse on his loved ones.

'And then later, what?'

His head snapped up at the sound of Mimi's voice. He'd forgotten they were in the middle of a conversation, but now, looking down into her wide, blue eyes, he realised he was fighting a battle that had been lost the moment they had arrived on the island and given in to the inexorable sexual pull between them.

He took a breath. 'Then later... I didn't want you to leave.' Reaching out, he took her hand. 'I don't want you to leave now.'

Somehow saying it out loud made it more real, more urgent, and instantly he felt his mind refocus. He'd been thinking about this the wrong way—seeing their time together in Patagonia as an exception. But they didn't need an island to make this keep on working for however long it took for the fire between them to die. He had plenty of homes scattered across the globe, all of which were well protected from the public's curious gaze. Homes with high walls, large grounds and loyal staff, including well-trained and highly efficient security teams. With a little effort on both parts they could carry on just as before. All he needed to do was find out if Mimi was willing to make that effort.

'I don't want this to end. You and me...what we have. I thought you might come and stay at my townhouse... maybe we could talk it through.' He hesitated. 'I suppose what I'm trying to say is that I'm not ready to say good-bye just yet.'

For a moment the only sound in the cabin was the hum of the engine and the faint chatter of his crew, and then Mimi looked up at him, her mouth trembling.

'I'm not ready to say goodbye yet either.'

He pulled her against him, his mouth finding hers. There was a fullness in her chest, a relief that seemed stupid now she had agreed, but he couldn't stop himself from pulling her closer, then closer still, until there was no gap between them.

It was raining, and after the wide open skies of Patagonia, London felt like a toy town. Glancing up through the tinted glass at the grey English clouds, Mimi felt her stomach flip over. Since that moment during the flight, when Basa had told her that he wanted her to come and stay at his house, her emotions had been swirling inside her like a tornado. She was happy and scared, excited and stunned, and nervous—absurdly and acutely nervous.

Every time she opened her mouth she thought she was going to blurt it all out: her feelings, her love for him. She could feel it swelling up inside her, pulsing between them.

She clenched her hands in her lap. She loved him so much, but telling him would be an act of madness. He might have feelings for her, but he'd never so much as hinted that they were of a permanent or romantic variety, and him not wanting to say goodbye yet didn't change anything. What he was offering was merely an extension of their current arrangement, not a declaration of eternal love.

'What are you thinking?'

Her pulse jumped as Basa leaned over and put his hand on hers, pulling her fingers apart and then slotting them between his own.

She smiled. 'Everything feels so small.'

He nodded. 'I know. It's crazy, isn't it? Thirteen million people live in London, but right now it feels like a village.'

His dark eyes rested on her face, his mouth curving up into a smile that made her forget to breathe.

'Are you okay with this, Mimi?' he said abruptly. 'About coming back with me to the house? I mean, I threw it at you at the last minute.' He grimaced. 'And it's not as if I've been considerate of your wishes so far.'

Her stomach somersaulted. 'Are you *not* okay?' she asked. Was he trying to be fair? To atone for his behaviour? Or had he changed his mind?

'Yes. I mean, no.' He frowned. 'Or do I mean yes? Whatever.'

She felt his fingers tighten around hers and, lifting her hand to his mouth, he kissed it gently.

'I really do want you to come and stay with me, but I want to make sure that's what you want too.'

'It is.' She bit into her smile. 'It really, *really* is.'

Whatever was in her heart would wait. It would have to wait. Right now what mattered was the heat in his eyes…a heat that felt like a caress against her skin.

Heart hammering, she leaned forward and kissed him. It was a long, slow, deepening kiss, and hunger was zig-zagging through her body as he slid his hand around her waist. She arched against him restlessly, her fingers sliding through his hair.

'Mimi…' He groaned her name and then pulled his mouth from hers, breathing out unsteadily. 'We need to stop now.'

'Why?' she whispered against his mouth. 'Or is that your way of saying you won't be held responsible for what happens next?'

His glittering gaze locked with hers. 'Right now I'd say I'm definitely suffering from diminished responsibility.'

'Really?' She pressed her hand against his trousers. 'It doesn't feel very diminished to me.'

His eyes were trained on hers. 'We'll be home in five minutes.'

From somewhere inside his jacket his phone began to buzz, and after kissing him lightly on the mouth she slipped free of his arms. 'Don't worry,' she said softly. 'I can wait.'

Gritting his teeth, he yanked the phone from his pocket. 'This had better be important, Rebecca.'

The car slowed, then stopped, and with her head still spinning from Basa's kiss Mimi opened the door.

As she stepped out onto the pavement a group of maybe thirty *paparazzi* surged forward, seemingly from nowhere, pinning her against the car. She blinked, blinded briefly by the camera flashes, her hand fumbling for something to grab on to as they called her name.

'Mimi, over here!'

One of the men pushed his microphone into her face, his nostrils flaring with excitement.

'Mimi, what's happening with you and Basa? Are you two an item?'

She turned away, trying to cover her face with her hand. But, sensing her paralysis, they were hemming her in, all of them pushing closer, so close she could smell their collective aftershave.

'How long's it been going on? Are you living together, Mimi?'

'What do you think those pensioners will say when they find out about your affair?'

Her head was reeling, her skin crawling with panic, and she was finding it hard to breathe, much less move.

'What the—?'

She heard Basa swear violently under his breath, and then he was beside her, shielding her with his body, his size and the unforgiving expression on his face creating a space around them. He pulled her against him as he and his driver shoved their way through the clamouring pack and up the stairs into his house.

Her legs felt as though they were made of feathers. 'It's okay… I'm okay,' she mumbled.

'Of course you're not okay.' Basa's voice was taut, like a sail snapping in high wind. 'Here, sit down.'

They were in a living room, and gratefully Mimi sat down on a dark green velvet sofa as their driver followed them into the room.

'I'm so sorry, Mr Caine.'

'It's fine, Paul. Just get the car parked and then get someone to drop off another one. Nothing too eye-catching.'

Mimi was shivering. Her teeth were chattering and she felt sick. It had all happened so fast. One minute she had been in the car, kissing Basa, and the next it had been as if time had gone into reverse, and she was back outside the home she had once shared with her mum and Charlie.

Basa was holding out a glass of tawny liquid. 'Drink this.'

It was brandy. She didn't like brandy. But she drank it anyway, and after a moment breathed out unsteadily.

'I don't understand,' she said slowly. 'How did they know we would be here?'

Basa's face was like stone, and there was a roughness to his voice when he spoke.

'Somebody saw us in that street in Buenos Aires. They took photos of us. I guess from a distance it must have looked like a lovers' tiff.'

He held up his phone and she stared at the screen, wondering how something so small could cause so much damage. Her heart quivered. It felt strange, looking at herself and Basa together. The photo was nearly a week old, and in that week they had gone from enemies to lovers. But the camera didn't lie, and even though they were clearly arguing, she could almost see the pulse of attraction between them, in the angle of their bodies and the tilt of her heads.

And someone else had noticed it too.

She felt a flare of panic and her hands balled into fists, but Basa didn't notice. He was staring past her into the distance, as though he was watching something unfold that was visible only to him.

'My PA got a call ten minutes ago, asking her to confirm that you and I are a couple. That was her on the phone. She was trying to warn me, but she was too late.'

'I'm sorry,' she whispered.

She saw that his muscles were straining against his suit jacket, but even if they hadn't been she could feel his frustration, his anger vibrating off his skin like radio waves. And she couldn't blame him for being angry. He had warned her back in Buenos Aires about this happening and she had ignored him. And now they were all going to pay for her recklessness in leaving his home.

All of them—including Alicia.

Her best friend. Who was getting married in just a few months' time.

Her heart stopped beating.

She felt a sharp stab of realisation as the air in her lungs seemed to thin. How was this going to affect the wedding? And how must Alicia be feeling now she had heard about Mimi and Basa allegedly having some kind of relationship? Of course she wanted to believe that Alicia would be happy, but even if she was the timing was so bad. Mimi felt as though the room was tilting, as though she was drunk, but it wasn't the brandy making the world spin off its axis. It was *her*. She'd messed everything up.

His next words—or rather the distance in his voice as he spoke them—confirmed her fears.

'It's my fault. I should have made it clearer to you what was at stake if you left the house.'

But she had known what was at stake.

Her lungs seemed to shrivel, along with any hopes she might have had of making things work with Basa. Those hopes were gone now, thrown away by her in that smoke-filled street in Buenos Aires.

'You did tell me,' she said quietly. 'I just didn't believe you.'

It was a fitting conclusion to a relationship that had been destined not to happen. How could it when neither one of them had ever known when the other was telling the truth.

'This isn't about what I told you or what you believed. This is about you and me sleeping together—and that's on me as much as it is on you. More so,' he added. 'I'm in the public eye twenty-four-seven, so I knew the risks. I ignored them because you were worth it. So don't blame yourself.'

There was a beat of silence, and she felt a slow trickle of despair work its way down her spine as he pulled out his phone. He was being so reasonable, so nice, but whatever he said she knew he was just being kind out of guilt or concern.

She watched miserably as his expression hardened at the sight of something on his screen.

'What matters now is damage limitation,' he said. 'But you don't need to worry. I'm going to take care of this.'

Mimi stared at him, her heartbeat slowing. He was a good man. A good brother. A good son. He would work day and night to protect his family, to protect her, and she loved him for that. But she wasn't his responsibility and she didn't want to *be* his responsibility. Nor was she going to throw her best friend under a bus for the sake of a few passion-filled days in Patagonia.

So there were two ways of doing this.

She could sit it out and wait for Basa to grow tired of her—because he *would* grow tired of her. And he might even end up hating her again once the media got stuck in. Or she could make it easy for both of them. Make it so that her best friend's wedding wasn't overshadowed by the scandal that had so nearly ruined the Caine family two years ago.

'Would it be okay if I used your bathroom?' Her hair had come loose as they'd pushed their way into the house, and she touched it now by way of explanation.

'Of course. You aren't hurt, are you?'

His eyes widened suddenly, his pupils merging with his irises, and she felt as if she was falling into two dark pools, her body weighted with rocks.

She shook her head. She wasn't hurt. Not in the way he meant.

He showed her to the bathroom, and after closing the door she sat down on the side of the bath. It was all over before it had even begun. Just like every other part of her life, she had ruined it. Driving her father away, wrecking her career, and now sabotaging her relationship with the only man she had ever wanted.

Last time *he* had walked away. Now it was her turn. She didn't want to do it, but she couldn't blight the lives of the two people she loved most in the world. Nor could she bear this flame between her and Basa to be slowly extinguished by the mistakes of the past.

She reached into her bag and pulled out her phone.

When she came back into the living room, Basa was on his own phone.

'Look, I have to go, but I'll call you back later,' he said to the caller, then paused, his dark gaze resting on Mimi's face. 'Yeah, I'll tell her.'

He hung up and tossed his phone onto the sofa. 'That was Alicia.'

'I know.' There had been a softness in his voice, a protectiveness she'd recognised and loved, that had told her he was speaking to someone he loved. And this was her chance to protect him.

'Is she okay? Is your dad okay?'

His face tensed, and although she hadn't moved she could almost feel the space between them widen.

'They will be. They're holed up at Alicia's flat, but Philip's there, and my security team is going to move them once it gets dark.'

She winced inwardly. He must be so worried about Alicia, and even more so about his father, and yet he was playing it down. The matter-of-fact way he was talking about his life imploding made everything a thousand times worse.

'You're a good man.' Mimi tried to smile, but who could smile when their heart was breaking?

Basa frowned, and she knew that something of what she was feeling must show in her face.

'What is it?' he asked.

She took a deep breath, forcing herself to speak past the lump in her throat. 'I can't stay here—not now. Not with—'

He cut her off. 'This isn't how it's going be for ever.'

'Maybe not,' she said quietly. 'But we don't have for ever, Basa. Alicia is getting married in less than three months. And that's what's important here, isn't it? Making sure her wedding isn't ruined by a lot of messy headlines.'

She waited, the lump in her throat swelling. Part of her—the wretched, hopelessly in love with him part—was hoping that he would pull her against him like he had on the jet, and then in the car, and tell her that he loved her, that she was what was important to him, now and for ever. But of course she knew he wouldn't say that.

So before he had a chance to reply she said quickly, 'If Paul could give me a lift I have somewhere I can stay.'

It was his opportunity to stop her, and there was a part of her heart that trembled with the hope that he would. But he didn't say anything, and she felt something split apart inside her as he nodded slowly.

Five minutes later Basa led her through the house and out through the garden.

'You won't have any trouble leaving this way.' He glanced at the modest, nondescript saloon idling by the kerb. 'Especially not in this car. Just tell Paul where you want to go.'

His smile was taut, the muscles in his jaw tense like piano wire.

'Thank you.' It hurt her to smile—more so to look at his face.

'Mimi.'

Her heart leapt against her ribs as he pulled her into his arms.

'It'll be fine. I promise.'

She inhaled his scent, wishing she could hold it inside of her for ever, so that she would always have a part of him, but as his grip loosened she let go of her breath.

In the car, she tried to stare straight ahead, but as Paul started the engine she couldn't stop herself from turning back to look at Basa. For a few half-seconds his dark eyes rested on her face, and then the car was moving, and she sat there, her stomach clenched with hope, waiting for him to come after her, willing him to yank open the door and tell her that he loved her.

But as the car turned into the road and they joined the mid-morning traffic she realised that, far from wanting her to stay, he had been willing her to leave.

Three hours later she was curled up on the sofa in her friend Emma's tiny flat, the curtains drawn, a mug of un-drunk tea on the table in front of her. Normally she loved a cup of tea, but this one had grown cold as she'd stared blankly at the book in her lap.

She had showered and changed out of what she'd been wearing, hoping the hot water and clean clothes would help shift the lethargy that had overtaken her as Paul drove her to Emma's address. But it hadn't helped. Sitting here alone, with damp hair and an oversized sweater, made it all feel much more real and final.

Glancing over at her phone, she resisted the urge to pick it up and check for messages or missed calls. She had left a message for Alicia, apologising, and then called her mum, who hadn't picked up, so she'd left a message for her too. From Basa there had been nothing.

Her throat tightened, and she felt the heat of tears. But why would there be?

He was probably under siege from reporters and law-yers, and even if he wasn't, why would he want to talk to *her*? He might have said he didn't blame her, but that would change over time. And then there was Alicia...

Her stomach clenched. There would be no wedding film now. In fact, she wasn't going to go to the wedding at all. She felt her breathing slow, for she knew how upset Lissy would be. It might even be the end of their friendship.

The dread in her stomach was hot and stinging, and slippery like a jellyfish. Not to go would be cruel, but to go would be worse in the long run, for it would be wilfully negligent of the consequences. It had to be this way. Like amputating a limb with frostbite. You had to lose the leg to save the life, and Lissy and Philip were worth saving a hundred times over.

Basa too.

His whole life had been spent looking after other people—looking after his father, parenting his sister, taking over the family business. Not only to protect his family, but also to protect the livelihoods of all those people who worked for him. And he wasn't even thirty. He'd already sacrificed so much. She wasn't going to make him sacrifice anything else.

Someone was ringing the doorbell.

Her whole body tensed.

The bones in her legs had locked tight and for a moment she couldn't move. It couldn't be a reporter—they didn't bother waiting for you to answer. They lifted open the letterbox and shouted their questions through the door.

Her heart slid sideways. Only three people knew she was here. Emma, Paul and Basa.

Sliding the chain of the latch, she opened the door with a rush of anticipation.

But it wasn't Basa.

It was her mother.

'I got your message. I'm sorry I didn't get here sooner. I went away for a couple of days with a friend and the signal was terrible.'

Mimi swallowed. 'You didn't have to come back, Mum.'

Her mother frowned. 'Of course I came back—you're my daughter. I'm not going to leave you to fight off those wolves on your own.'

Stepping into the flat, she closed the door and pulled Mimi into a hug. For a moment Mimi stiffened, trying to pull away, but her mum wouldn't let her and finally she gave in to what she had been wanting to do since leaving Basa's house. She burst into tears.

'It will be all right.' Leaning forward, her mother smoothed Mimi's hair away from her face. 'It's just a photo, not a court case.'

'A photo of me and Basa. And people hold grudges, Mum. They hold on to things—to feelings—for years.'

'I know,' her mum said quietly. 'I held on to my past for far too long. But you've just spent a week with Basa—alone on an island. Everybody should let go of the past, and if you two can then so can everyone else.'

Mimi blew her nose. She'd expected her mum to be crying, or at least panicking, but she was calm—relaxed, even.

'I don't think Basa will ever really let go of it. Not if he wants to protect his family.'

'Did he say that?'

'No, not in so many words,' Mimi said slowly. 'But he didn't try to stop me leaving.'

'Maybe letting you go was his way of trying to protect you?'

She stared at her mother helplessly. 'I can't think like that, Mum. I just want it to be over. I don't want to feel like this any more. I don't want to feel anything. That's why I walked away.'

Her mother leaned over and wiped a tear from Mimi's cheek. 'But you can't walk away from love, Mimi. And you *do* love him, don't you?'

Hearing her mum say it out loud broke her open.

'But I messed it up—like I always mess everything up.' Tears were streaming down her face now, too many to wipe away.

Her mum frowned. 'Such as what?'

'Like you and Dad. You were so much in love, and then

I came along and ruined it. And then I pushed you into marrying Charlie so you wouldn't be on your own.'

More tears escaped and she brushed them away with her sleeve.

'Is that what I made you think?'

Glancing up into her mother's face, Mimi saw that she looked shocked and horrified.

'Mimi, that's not what happened. I know I used to talk a lot about how much me and your dad were in love, but that was only because I wanted to give you something positive about our relationship. I wanted you to know that you came out of real passion. It wasn't your fault your dad left me. We just weren't right together.'

She frowned.

'And as for Charlie—you didn't push me into anything. I was a grown woman and I liked Charlie. I didn't love him, but I wanted you to have a dad, and nice things, so I ignored all his little lies. If anyone messed up, it was me.'

Mimi shook her head, her hands balling into fists. 'But I've made a mess of my film too, and it was my fault that the photo was taken in Buenos Aires. Everything I touch, I ruin.'

'That's not true. You put yourself out there and sometimes things go wrong. But I am so proud of you. You are brave and talented and loyal, and any man—including Bautista Caine—would be lucky to have you.'

Her mother was crying now too.

'And, frankly, I will tell him so myself.'

She reached for Mimi's phone.

'No, Mum.' Mimi tried to grab it. 'It's too late.'

Shaking her head, her mum smiled weakly. 'Love doesn't come with a deadline, or hide away in the shadows.' She handed Mimi the phone. 'And neither should you, darling.'

CHAPTER TEN

PICKING UP THE top newspaper from the pile beside him, Basa scanned the front page before expertly flipping through the rest of the paper. His PA had been sending the papers over each morning since the story broke, ringing any relevant sections with a marker pen, but his dark gaze found nothing to interest him today.

The tabloids had a couple of stories each—nothing new, just the Buenos Aires photo padded out with some additional paragraphs about the trial.

He let out a breath and scooped the papers onto the floor. Overall, was not too bad. Probably tomorrow, the day after at the latest, the genie would be back in the lamp and by the time Alicia exchanged her vows with Philip the whole episode would be nothing but a footnote.

The worst was over. He had moved fast and effectively and, having been through it once before—twice if you included his mother's accident—he had known what needed to be done to kill the story. He'd done it, and now his sister's wedding would no longer have the spectre of scandal hanging over it.

Everything was under control. He should be happy. He was, of course. And yet his happiness felt staged, as if he was an actor playing himself. None of it felt real. And he wasn't sure it ever would…without Mimi.

He stared down at his phone. Alicia had called and left several messages, saying it was nothing urgent, to call her back, but from Mimi there had been nothing.

Unsurprisingly.

His paralysed silence when she had announced she was leaving had not exactly given her any incentive to stay in touch, and now it was nearly a week since she had got into that car with Paul.

Watching her leave, he'd wanted to chase after her, to ask her to stay. But he hadn't been able to ask or expect her to do that—not knowing what he did.

Two years ago she and her mother had been chased, snapped and vilified just for the crime of being related to Charlie and Raymond. It hadn't mattered to anyone, himself included, that they were innocent, unknowing by-standers. They had been judged fair game and treated accordingly.

His shoulders tensed and he felt his heart contracting with rage and regret. Mimi and her mother had had nobody to protect them—no security team to hold back the photographers, no lawyers fighting to defend their reputation, their name. They had been helpless and scared. And after watching her face as the *paparazzi* had penned her against his car the other day, he knew that fear hadn't dissipated over time.

And that was why he hadn't stopped her from leaving.

He hadn't been able to ask her to stay for him—not after everything else he had demanded she do. He hadn't been able to make her go through all that again, so he had let her go.

But he missed her.

From the moment he woke up in the morning and all through his restless nights she was there. No matter what he was doing she was in his head. He could hear her voice, her laughter, and sometimes when he closed his eyes he could feel her hair sliding over his skin, the soft whisper of her breath against his mouth.

He stood up, loneliness lapping like waves against his heart, and made his way to the window, as if by moving he could shift the feeling of fullness in his chest. Running a hand over his face, he stared at his reflection. He hadn't shaved for the last three days, and instead of his usual suit and tie he was wearing joggers and a T-shirt. It was slack of him, but the effort of dressing seemed to be beyond him right now.

As did eating.

Unless whisky counted as a food.

He glanced over at the half-empty decanter. He wasn't a big drinker, but he needed something in the evenings to blot out the ache, something to fill the hollowed-out space inside his chest.

He heard the sound of approaching footsteps. He took a breath and composed his face before he turned, fully expecting to see his housekeeper, Annie, her mouth set in a conciliatory smile as she offered the tray of food she would be carrying, for it wouldn't have escaped her notice that he had skipped breakfast again.

But it wasn't Annie. It was his sister Alicia and she didn't look the least bit conciliatory.

'I've been calling you all morning,' she said accusingly. 'Why didn't you pick up?'

'Sorry, I was just going to call back. I got caught up in something,' he lied. Crossing the room, he pulled her into a hug. 'We can talk now…catch up properly. Would you like a drink?'

Her eyes darted to the decanter. 'It's a bit early for whisky.'

He released her. 'I meant tea or coffee.'

Her face softened. 'Coffee, please. And a talk would be lovely.'

'So, what do you want me for?' he asked.

They were sitting on the sofa and, glancing over at his sister, he thought how well she looked. Her dark hair was shining and her skin looked almost luminous.

Being in love suited her, and it also seemed to be acting as a protective shield, so that although initially she had been upset by the news story she had quickly recovered her equilibrium. Equally surprisingly, his father had too. In fact, out of the three of them, he was the one who was struggling to deal with it. Not the practicalities, of course, but emotionally.

'I wanted to invite you to lunch.'

He stared at her blankly. Lunch? The thought made his stomach clench like a fist. He knew it was selfish, but the last thing he felt like doing was sitting down with Alicia and Philip and watching them gaze into each other's eyes.

'I'm not sure, Lissy…' He glanced down at the pile of papers on the floor, seeking and finding an excuse. 'I need to be here in case something kicks off.'

'What could possibly kick off?' Alicia frowned. 'You haven't left the house in days and Mimi's gone AWOL. All the photographers have cleared off.'

His chest tightened. It was the first time in a week that he'd heard anyone say Mimi's name out loud, and it felt like a kick to the stomach.

'Basa?'

His sister tilted her head and he realised she was still waiting for a reply.

He hesitated a moment longer, and then, flexing his hands, he said. 'Have you talked to her?'

There was a pause. 'We've texted,' she said after a moment. 'She's with her mum. They're doing okay.' Alicia hesitated. 'She was worried about all of us—about every-thing being dragged up again—but I told her it was fine.'

Basa nodded. It seemed crazy that only a couple of weeks ago he'd been desperate to break up their friend-ship. Crazy that he'd thought he could. Or should.

Alicia cleared her throat. 'I told her that she and I would be fine whatever happened—even if what the papers are saying is true.'

He stared at her, the ramifications of her words bump-ing off the walls as she put down her coffee cup.

'Why are you asking me? Why don't you just talk to her yourself?'

Something was loosening inside him. He could feel it slipping sideways, but it was just out of reach, so he turned his attention back to his sister.

'That's not a good idea.'

Alicia's soft brown eyes narrowed. 'I don't see why,' she protested. 'You wouldn't be asking me if I'd talked to her if you didn't care.'

'I care about you and Dad,' he said. 'You are my pri-ority.'

'Well, maybe it's time we weren't!'

His head jerked up at the frustration in her voice.

'Look, I love you. You're the best brother anyone could have and you've always been there for me—and I know Daddy feels the same. I know—' He tried to interrupt but she held up her hand to silence him 'I know he feels the same because I've talked to him about it. We are fine and you need to stop putting your life on hold for us.'

'I'm not doing that, Lissy.'

'Yes, you are. You're using the past as a shield, so you don't have to face your feelings.'

'That's not what I'm doing.'

He tried to keep his voice even, but it was hard with

her staring at him with that disbelieving expression on her face. For a moment neither of them spoke, and then she sighed.

'So why don't you call her?'

He felt his muscles tighten beneath his skin.

It was the same question he'd been asking himself for days. Asking, but never answering.

'You know why.'

Meeting his gaze, she cleared her throat. 'I do. I'm just wondering when you're going to stop pretending you don't.'

The air was hot and thin in his lungs, and he made himself take a breath. 'I'm not pretending anything.'

Her eyes filled with tears, and suddenly her lip was trembling.

'Yes, you *are*. You're pretending that this news story still needs you to manage it. You're pretending that I'm still fifteen and Daddy's still ill. But mostly you're pretending you don't love Mimi when you so obviously do.'

His shoulders tensed. Her words were scraping at the graze around his heart and he was conscious of his breath filling his chest. His heart shifted, growing lighter, as if something heavy had been lifted from it.

Of course he loved her!

That was why he'd been so devastated by her behaviour that night at Fairbourne and why he'd insisted she come to Argentina and Patagonia.

Why watching her drive off in that car and go out of his life had made him feel undone.

'I don't... I don't—'

For a moment the power of speech abandoned him. He couldn't finish the sentence. And he couldn't lie to his sister or to himself any more.

But he couldn't tell the truth either.

Back on the island Mimi had said that Alicia thought love was the solution to everything, and she was right. His sister was a fully paid-up believer in the power of love. How was he supposed to explain to her that on this occasion love wasn't enough?

By nature Alicia had always been sweetly optimistic, and her optimism often tipped over into naivety. It was what he loved about her, and why he'd been so protective of her all his life. But no matter how right she was now, how much he wanted to follow his heart, he knew that the world wasn't ready for a relationship between Bautista Caine and Mimi Miller. He only had to look at the aftershocks of one blurred photo to know that.

Going public with their relationship would magnify those problems tenfold, and he couldn't do that to Mimi. He'd seen how shaken she was by those few minutes with the *paparazzi*, knew how terrified she was of the past being resurrected—for hadn't she told him that was why she had given up the fight to get her embargoed film released? She had learnt the hard way that not all publicity was good publicity.

Alicia pulled him into a hug. He could feel her heart beating and the dampness of her cheek against his.

'I'm not going to try and change your mind,' she said. 'I just want you to remember that you have a life of your own to live.'

She released him. 'Look, I have to go, but promise me you'll come to lunch? About one.' Her brown eyes flickered over his joggers. 'And get dressed. Otherwise I'll be forced to put on my unicorn onesie.'

Nodding, he managed to smile. He could see she wouldn't take no for an answer, and what else was he going to do today?

His heart felt suddenly heavy against his ribs. Without Mimi, what was he going to do with the rest of his life?

Two hours later he let himself into Alicia's flat, holding a bottle of wine. He had showered, and changed into khakis and a polo shirt, but left the stubble. Right now his face felt a little treacherous, and having it there was somehow reassuring—like having a mask.

He liked Alicia's flat. In a word, it was charming. Big enough to feel comfortable, but small enough to feel cosy, and decorated with an easy elegance that she'd inherited from his mother. Today, though, it felt oddly quiet.

'You didn't say what we were having,' he called out, walking into the kitchen, 'but I went with white.'

'White sounds lovely.'

He froze, his whole body pushing back against his thousand and one involuntary reactions to that familiar, soft voice while his gaze was pulled to where Mimi was standing in the doorway, wearing faded jeans and a soft blue jumper, her long blonde hair loose over her shoulders, her eyes fixed on his face.

There was a good two minutes of silence. Mimi could feel her heart in her throat. She could hardly believe it was only a week since she had last seen him. It felt as if a whole decade had passed. And after the wild grandeur of Patagonia being with him here in Alicia's homely kitchen felt almost surreal.

He stood up, his chair scraping against the wooden floor. 'You two set this up.'

It wasn't a question, but she nodded. 'I'm not really equipped for roadside abductions.'

She tried to smile, but her lips wouldn't co-operate. Her whole body felt stiff and unwieldy. She was nervous, but she was also having to push back against the urge to cross the room and kiss him. It hurt to be so close and not be able to touch him, like having to hold her breath too long underwater.

'Mimi—'

'Basa—'

They both spoke at once.

He stared at her for a moment, and then he cleared his throat. 'After you.'

It was her chance to talk, to say what she needed to say, only now she was here she was paralysed, mute with fear that she would say the wrong thing.

But even she couldn't mess up three little words.

'I love you.'

She took a step forward, her limbs loosening as she spoke.

'I should have said it before, but I was scared. And I know you probably don't feel the same way, and I know the world doesn't want us to be together—'

'It doesn't matter what the world wants.'

Her heart jolted against her ribs as he began walking towards her, his dark eyes locked on hers.

'It's what *we* want—you and me. And I don't want— I don't—' Breaking off, he breathed out unsteadily. 'I don't ever want to be apart from you again.'

She couldn't breathe. Tears were filling her eyes and she could see that his face was pale and taut with the effort of holding back tears of his own.

'Why did you leave?'

He spoke shakily and she knew that it mattered. She knew that the shake in his voice meant he cared, and that gave her strength.

'I was scared. It was my fault they had that photo and I thought I'd messed up again.'

His hands caught her shoulders.

'It was just a mistake, Mimi. I get papped all the time—even when I'm on my own,' he said fiercely.

'I know, and I can see that now, but all my life things have gone wrong—my dad leaving, Charlie and Raymond stealing from all those poor pensioners, my film getting embargoed, you and me that night…'

'None of that was your fault.'

'I want to believe that, but it's hard to trust yourself when nobody else trusts you.'

'*I* trust you.'

His hands tightened against her shoulders and she felt as if her heart was going to burst as he pulled her into his arms, holding her tightly against him so she could feel his heartbeat merge with hers.

'And I need you.'

He pulled her closer, burying his face in her hair.

'I've been so miserable without you.'

'Why?' Her voice faltered. 'Why were you miserable, Basa?'

His eyes were dark and soft and unguarded. 'Because I love you.'

He leaned in and kissed her, his hands sliding up to capture her face as her heart slipped its moorings.

'I think I might even have loved you before we met.' He frowned. 'You know that night at Fairbourne…it felt so right—as though we'd been fighting our way to one another across time and space. The other day when you left I should have stopped you, but I was scared. For so long I've focused on other people's lives and not on my own. I've used the past as a reason not to think about my present, and when you said you couldn't stay…that was the first time in my life I've had to think about what *I* really wanted. And I panicked.'

He kissed the tears from her face.

'But I'm not panicking now.'

Mimi swallowed. 'And what *do* you want?'

'I want you,' he said softly. 'Because I love you. Totally and immeasurably.'

Reaching up, she stroked his face. 'And I love you.'

He stared at her in silence, his beautiful face showing everything he was feeling, and then he lowered his mouth and kissed her again, hungrily, kissed her until the past was forgotten and all that mattered was the two of them.

From inside her jeans pocket her phone vibrated twice. Loosening her grip, Mimi looked up into Basa's eyes, a blush creeping across her cheeks.

'That'll be Alicia. I made her promise to text in case it all went wrong.' She pulled out her phone. 'I'll have to text her back or she'll think the worst.'

She frowned.

'What is it?' Basa looked down at her.

'I don't understand,' Mimi said slowly. 'It's my lawyer. Apparently my film has been released for distribution.'

'Is that right?'

The teasing note in his voice made her look up from her phone. 'Did you have something to do with this?'

His dark eyes rested on her face. 'I might have applied a little pressure in the right places.' He pulled her closer, his gaze drifting slowly over her stunned face. 'I wanted to surprise you when we got back to England, but it's a little late now.'

Her pulse accelerated as he smiled slowly.

'So maybe it could be an early engagement present instead.'

She drew in a deep breath, trying to absorb his words. 'Are you asking me to marry you?'

He nodded, his face so serious and sweet she wanted to cry.

'I am—if you'll have me.'

She was both laughing and crying now.

'Hang on—is that a yes? Only, I don't want there to be any more misunderstandings between us,' he said softly.

'There's no misunderstanding.' Blinking back tears of happiness, she lifted her face to his and kissed him. It's definitely a yes.'

EPILOGUE

GLANCING UP AT the towering cobalt-blue sky, Mimi breathed in the smell of the sage that had been disturbed by the wheels of the SUV and instantly felt all tension leave her body.

For the last few days she and Basa had been staying with Alicia and Philip at the *palacio* in Buenos Aires, but yesterday they had travelled across the country to Patagonia. And it felt incredible to be here again in this beautiful epic landscape.

Basa and Philip had gone straight to the island, but she and Alicia had spent the night at the newly opened Guanaco eco-lodge, for some last-minute pampering before joining them.

And now they were stepping off the jetty into the boat.

It would be her third visit to the island, but her reverence and sense of wonder at its beauty and solitude was still the same and, taking a calming breath, she gazed across the unbroken surface of the lake, a pulse of happiness beating down her spine.

The ducks and swans were squabbling in the shallows, but their splashing and the rhythmic slap of the water against the shore were the only sounds to break the silence. Up above her the sun was almost white, but the lightest of breezes took the edge of the midday heat so that it felt exactly like the perfect spring day.

And it was, she thought, her heart beginning to beat a little faster. It was perfect—and in so many ways other than the weather.

'Penny for them? Or are they priceless?'

She'd been so deep in thought that Alicia's voice seemed to come out of nowhere and, turning, she found her friend smiling at her. It had been a pattern over the last few days and, meeting Alicia's gentle gaze, she grimaced apologetically. 'Sorry.'

Taking her hand, Alicia shook her head. 'Don't be. I think it's lovely.' Her face softened. 'Basa's just the same.' She giggled. 'Philip told me, but don't tell Basa I told you.'

Mimi laughed. 'I won't.' She gave her friend's hand a squeeze. 'I haven't been too bad, have I?'

'No, of course not.' Alicia frowned. 'Obviously you were nervous about making your engagement public, but we all were a little bit.'

She *had* been nervous. Actually, make that terrified. But, despite her fears that people would condemn her or, worse, condemn Basa, both the media and the public had seen their engagement as a positive footnote to the pension scandal—a kind of 'love conquers all' story.

'There's your mum,' Alicia said quietly.

Mimi felt her eyes start to burn. Her mum had been so fantastic these last six months. She could see that over time her mother had been slowly emerging from the hibernation of despair and regret, and seeing her daughter so happy seemed to have given her the final nudge she needed to take back control of her life.

Now, not only did she have a new hobby—wild swimming—but a new haircut and a new man.

'Hi, Mum,' she said warmly as they disembarked.

'Oh, darling.' Her mother's eyes were bright with tears, and her smile was trembling as they hugged.

They linked arms and, with Alicia following, they walked along the jetty across to the house, where four men were standing in a semi-circle, waiting for them.

Philip. Robert. Basa. And Emiliano, the celebrant who was going to conduct their wedding ceremony.

Something was dislodged inside her as her gaze rested on the man who was already her husband.

They had married at the Civil Registry Office in Buenos Aires, with only Alicia and Philip for witnesses. Neither of them had wanted a fuss, but both of them had known that they wanted to repeat the ceremony out in Patagonia, on the island where their love had finally overcome the scandal of their past.

And they were no longer alone in putting the past behind them. Both Robert Caine and her mother had accepted their relationship—accepted and encouraged it. She glanced affectionately back at her friend. For Alicia, of course, the past had never been an obstacle.

Her mother gave her arm a squeeze, and as they stopped in front of Basa her heart began to pound. He looked so incredibly handsome in a dark suit and pale blue shirt and, in a gesture towards the new openness they shared, the top button of his shirt was undone.

'Hi,' he said softly.

Gazing into his eyes, she saw tears that mirrored her own and felt her chest swell with absolute unconditional love as he took her hand in his.

The ceremony seemed to pass in seconds. But then from the moment Mimi had stepped off the boat, her veil fluttering in the breeze, time had ceased to matter, Basa thought, his chest tightening as she looked up into his eyes.

Her pale blonde hair was caught loosely at the nape of her neck and she was wearing a simple blue *ombré* slip dress the same colour as the sapphire engagement ring he had given her, for the mix of gold and blue reminded him of the sky that day they had spent in the hot air balloon.

He didn't think he had ever seen her look more beautiful.

Speaking his vows, watching Mimi speak hers, he felt his heart would burst—and not just with love, but with the knowledge of how close they had come to losing each other.

They hadn't been apart at all since that day in Alicia's kitchen, and last night he'd missed her unbearably. Now, despite the emotional intensity of the words they were saying to one another, he almost wished the ceremony was over, so he could pull her into his arms and hold her close.

Of course she was already his wife, but the ceremony in Buenos Aires had felt like a simple legal formality. He glanced past her at the clusters of evergreens, at the high cloud-capped peaks in the distance. For him, *this* was what their marriage was about. Standing here with the epic majesty of nature as their witness, with everyone they loved beside them.

But not quite everyone, he thought sadly. Although he could sense his mother in Alicia's soft eyes and gentle smile.

After the ceremony was over they ate a late lunch— lamb, straight from the hot yellow blaze of Lionel's willow-framed *asado*. Then there were speeches, and everyone toasted the marriage with a Merlot from Robert's estate. Seeing both their families talking and smiling in the sunshine made their marriage feel doubly blessed.

Much, much later, when the fire was a dull orange core, everyone retreated inside the house. But Basa led Mimi down to where Claudia had lit the deck with hundreds of tiny night lights.

Pulling her down onto the lounger beside him, he kissed her softly. 'I missed you yesterday.'

'I missed you too,' she whispered. 'But it was worth it. For today.'

He buried his face in her hair, breathing in her scent. 'Are you sure? I mean, I know we decided not to go for a big wedding...'

His sister's wedding had been vast. A three-day affair, with hundreds of guests, starting with a tango-themed party at the house in Buenos Aires and ending with the ceremony here in Patagonia. It had been the perfect society event, but he'd spent the whole time feeling grateful that he wasn't going to have to go through all that with his own wedding. Now he wanted to be certain that Mimi felt the same way too.

Her blue eyes flickered in the candlelight. 'I'm sure. I mean, look at this...' She waved up at the star-pierced darkening sky. 'We have our very own cathedral, all to ourselves—and, besides, I have everything and everyone that matters right here.'

Her cheeks were flushed with happiness, her eyes alive with warmth and love.

He tilted her face up to his and said softly, 'I do too. Now and for ever.'

And, lowering his mouth, he kissed her until their heads were filled with stars that were brighter than the ones in the sky above...

* * * * *

MILLS & BOON

Coming next month

THE SCANDAL BEHIND THE ITALIAN'S WEDDING
Millie Adams

"Why did you do it, Minerva?"

"I am sorry. I really didn't do it to cause you trouble. But I'm being threatened, and so is Isabella, and in order to protect us both I needed to come up with an alternative paternity story."

"An alternative paternity story?"

She winced. "Yes. Her father is after her."

He eyed her with great skepticism. "I didn't think you knew who her father was."

She didn't know whether to be shocked, offended or pleased that he thought her capable of having an anonymous interlude.

For heaven's sake, she'd only ever been kissed one time in her life. A regrettable evening out with Katie in Rome where she'd tried to enjoy the pulsing music in the club, but had instead felt overheated and on the verge of a seizure.

She'd danced with a man in a shiny shirt—and she even knew his name because she wouldn't even dance with a man without an introduction—and he'd kissed her on the dance floor. It had been wet and he'd tasted of liquor and she'd feigned a headache after and taken a cab back to the hostel they'd been staying in.

The idea of hooking up with someone, in a circumstance like that, made her want to peel her own skin off.

"Of course I know who he is. Unfortunately… The full implications of who he is did not become clear until later."

"What does that mean?"

She could tell him the truth now, but something stopped her. Maybe it was admitting Isabella wasn't her daughter, which always caught her in the chest and made her feel small. Like she'd stolen her and like what they had was potentially fragile, temporary and shaky.

Or maybe it was trust. Dante was a good man. Going off the fact he had rescued her from a fall, and helped her up when her knee was skinned, and bailed her out after her terrible humiliation in high school.

But to trust him with the truth was something she simply wasn't brave enough to do.

Her life, Isabella's life, was at risk, and she'd lied on live stream in front of the world.

Her bravery was tapped out.

"Her father is part of an organized crime family. Obviously something unknown to me at the time of her...you know. And he's after her. He's after us."

"Are you telling me that you're in actual danger?"

"Yes. And really, the only hope I have is convincing him that he isn't actually the father."

"And you think that will work?"

"It's the only choice I have. I need your protection."

He regarded her with dark, fathomless eyes, and yet again, she felt like he was peering at her as though she were a girl, and not a woman at all. A naughty child, in point of fact. Then something in his expression shifted.

It shamed her a little that this was so like when he'd come to her rescue at the party. That she was manipulating his pity for her. Her own pathetic nature being what called to him, yet again.

But she would lay down any and all pride for Isabella and she'd do it willingly.

"If she were, in fact my child, then we would be family."

"I... I suppose," she said.

"There will need to be photographs of us together, as I would not be a neglectful father."

"No indeed."

"Of course, you know that if Isabella were really my child there would be only one thing for us to do."

"Do I?"

"Yes." He began to pace, like a caged tiger trying to find a weak spot in his cage. And suddenly he stopped, and she had the terrible feeling that the tiger had found what he'd been looking for. "Yes. Of course, there is only one option."

"And that is?"

"You have to marry me."

Continue reading
THE SCANDAL BEHIND THE ITALIAN'S WEDDING
Millie Adams

Available next month
www.millsandboon.co.uk

COMING SOON!

We really hope you enjoyed reading this book. If you're looking for more romance, be sure to head to the shops when new books are available on

Thursday 6th March

To see which titles are coming soon, please visit

millsandboon.co.uk/nextmonth